## "I'm sorry about last night."

She glanced at Jesse, and knew instantly he was talking about the kiss. Her pulse quickened and her mouth felt dry.

"It's me who should be apologizing," June said. "For locking you up. But I had to be sure that you weren't the mole who'd brought the henchmen so close last night."

June looked up at him and her heart kicked.

"You're the reason they came looking, Jesse. Samuel is after your blood. I'm really sorry I locked you up."

Jesse's gaze went to the door.

"It's not locked. You're free to go."

He took a step toward her. June's knees felt weak.

"June, I am sorry, about the kiss."

"I'm not," she said, very quietly, her cheeks warming.

Dear Reader,

I love stories about second chances. We all make mistakes. Sometimes the results of those mistakes can be devastating, leaving us trapped by feelings of guilt that dog us through the remainder of our lives.

But what if, as in a fairy tale, a wand could be waved and a wish granted that enabled us to forget, just for a while, the guilt and pain that traps us in the past and stops us from truly living and moving forward into the future?

In romance, amnesia is often the magic wand that grants our characters that second chance. This is what happens to my hero in *The Perfect Outsider* when an accident temporarily steals his memory. But when my heroine, a rescuer at heart, tries to save him, it's he who saves her instead. By being forced to live solely in the present, he shows her how to forgive herself, and how to live again.

I hope you enjoy June and Jesse's journey toward their second chance at love.

*Loreth Anne White*

# THE PERFECT OUTSIDER

## BY
## LORETH ANNE WHITE

16-0812

[Har]lequin (UK) policy is to use papers that are natural, renewable
[and] recyclable products and made from wood grown in sustainable for[ests.]
[The log]ging and manufacturing processes conform to the legal enviro[nmental]
[reg]ulations of the country of origin.

[P]rinted and bound in Spain
[b]y Blackprint CPI, Barcelona

First published in Great Britain 2012
by Mills & Boon, an imprint of Harlequin (UK) Limited,
Eton House, 18-24 Paradise Road, Richmond, Surrey TW9 1SR

© Harlequin Books S.A. 2012

Special thanks and acknowledgement to Loreth Anne White for her contribution to the Perfect, Wyoming miniseries.

ISBN: 978 0 263 89549 0
ebook ISBN: 978 1 408 97242 7

**Loreth Anne White** was born and raised in southern Africa, but now lives in Whistler, a ski resort in the moody British Columbian Coast Mountain range. It's a place of vast wilderness, larger-than-life characters, epic adventure and romance—the perfect place to escape reality. It's no wonder she was inspired to abandon a sixteen-year career as a journalist to escape into a world of romantic fiction filled with dangerous men and adventurous women.

When she's not writing you will find her long-distance running, biking or skiing on the trails and generally trying to avoid the bears—albeit not very successfully. She calls this work, because it's when the best ideas come.

For a peek into her world visit her website, www.lorethannewhite.com. She'd love to hear from you.

To editors Patience Bloom, Keyren Gerlach and Shana Smith. And to fellow authors Marie Ferrarella, Linda Conrad, Kim Van Meter, Jennifer Morey and Carla Cassidy—for making this series happen. It's been a pleasure to work with you all.

# Chapter 1

Eager was trained to alert on human scent.

And that's exactly what his handler, June Farrow, was hoping to find as she worked her four-year-old black Lab in a zigzag pattern across the wind, the glow from her headlamp casting a pale beam into blackness. It was 4:00 a.m. Cold. The cloud cover was low, and rain lashed down through trees.

As June and her K9 worked their way up the thickly forested slope, the terrain grew treacherous, with steep gullies and hidden caves. June prayed that Lacy Matthews and her three-year-old twins, Bekka and Abby, were holed up in one of those caves, dry and safe from the storm.

Safe from Samuel Grayson's men.

Because if Samuel's men had found them, they were as good as dead.

Swaths of mist rolled down from the peaks and June's hiking boots began to lose traction. More than once she had to grab onto brambles to stop from slipping down into one of the ravines hidden by the darkness and bush. Sweat prickled under her rain jacket and moisture misted her safety glasses. Water ran in a stream from the bill of her hat and it trickled uncomfortably down her neck.

While Eager was able to barrel like a tank through the increasingly dense scrub, the twigs began to tear at June's clothes, hooking into her hair, clawing at her backpack, slowing her progress. This, she thought, as she stilled a moment to catch her breath, was why search-and-rescue teams used dogs—they could access places with ease that humans could not, especially a dog like Eager, who, with his stocky, deep-chested frame and thick coat, was impervious to the claw of brambles. And, having been bred from gundog stock, he was able to remain calm in the presence of loud rescue choppers and the big excavation machines often present in urban rescue.

June listened carefully to her surroundings, hoping to catch the faint sound of a woman's cry on the wind. But a forest was never quiet, and in a storm like this, trees talked and groaned and squeaked as their trunks and branches rubbed together in the wind. Pine cones and broken branches bombed to the ground, and rain plopped from leaves. The pine needles in the canopy above swished with the sound of a river.

She could detect no cry for help amid the other sounds of the stormy night.

Tension coiled tight in her stomach.

Working solo was foolish, particularly for an experienced SAR tracker who knew better. But a desperation to find those three-year-old twins and their mother burned like fire in June's chest, outweighing all caution.

Her own son had been three when he'd died.

If June had managed to dig deeper into her own reserves, search harder, faster, sooner, all those years ago, she might have arrived in time to save Aiden. Now she *had* to save Bekka and Abby. The reason they were lost in the woods was partly June's fault, and they'd been missing for two nights now. The clock was ticking and guilt weighed heavy.

"Eager!" she yelled over the wind. "Go that way, boy!"

Eager more sensed than saw his handler's directional signal, and he veered in an easterly direction, moving across the base of glistening-wet rock. All June could see of him was the pale green glow of his LED collar, and every now and then the wet reflection of his coat as he cut across the beam of her headlamp.

The moisture was actually working in Eager's favor—it enhanced his scenting abilities, but the wind was confounding. It punched down through holes in the canopy and swirled in eddies around the forest floor, carrying any scent that might have been pooling on the ground or in gullies with it.

June saw her dog hesitate a moment, then suddenly the green collar bobbed as Eager went crashing off in a new direction across the flank of a cliff.

He had scent.

June rushed after him, heart pounding as she shouldered through bushes and skidded over wet deadfall. Then she lost sight of the fluorescent light. She stilled, catching her breath as she wiped rainwater from her face. Her hand was shaking, and June realized she was exhausted.

She was going to make a fatal error like this.

She willed herself to calm. Life depended on it, and not just hers.

But as she dug deep for self-control an image hit her hard and suddenly of a search gone wrong five years ago. A search that resulted in the dramatic deaths of her husband and son. She closed her eyes for a moment, trying to shake the accompanying and familiar sense of sheer and utter desperation.

It had happened because of a cult.

Her husband, Matt, had been sucked in by a religious organization, and when June had pressured Matt to leave, he'd kidnapped Aiden from day care, planning to take him to live on the cult compound.

Thunder crashed and grumbled in the mountains and another gust of wind swished through the trees. June's nerves jumped. She braced her hand against the trunk of a tree.

*Focus. You're doing this for them. Everything you do now is because you messed up that time.*

That devastating incident was why she now worked for EXIT, a national organization quietly dedicated to aiding victims of cults. June's life mission had become running halfway houses for cult members who wanted to "escape." If she could rescue others, if she could get them into safe houses where they could access exit-counseling, it might give meaning, somehow, to the gaping maw of loss in her own life.

It might help assuage her guilt for not having understood how to help Matt back then.

And it was because of Samuel Grayson and his dangerous cult of Devotees that June was in Cold Plains, Wyoming, now. She'd arrived on behalf of EXIT three months ago. Right now she had five Devotees in the safe house. Lacy and her children were supposed to make the number eight.

But something had gone wrong—Lacy and her girls had failed to meet June at a designated meeting place in the woods on Monday evening, from where June was to have escorted them to the secret safe house.

June had searched the area, tracking Lacy and her twins back along the trail that led down the mountain toward the town. Around 11:00 p.m. that night, Eager had alerted on a small, sparkly red shoe belonging to one of the twins. The shoe had been lying just off the trail. From that point the footprints had gone into the forest. June and Eager had followed Lacy's trail deeper into the woods where more footprints appeared, and it looked as though two men had started following Lacy and the twins. June put Eager on the tracks, but the storm had broken and they'd lost the scent.

Before heading back to the safe house to grab an hour or two of rest that night, June had first hiked over to the southeastern flank of the mountain where she dropped the red shoe as a decoy. She knew Cold Plains Police Chief Bo Fargo would be mounting a search party and calling for SAR volunteers as soon as Lacy was reported missing, and she didn't want the official SAR party anywhere near the safe house or the area where Lacy had actually vanished.

Chief Fargo was bad news. He was a Devotee and one of Samuel's main men. June needed to find Lacy and the girls before the cops did, or they'd end up right back in Samuel's clutches.

On Tuesday morning when Lacy had failed to open up her coffee shop, she and her children were reported missing. By Tuesday afternoon, Chief Fargo had called in SAR volunteers and a search had been mounted. Fargo had asked June to see if she and her K9 could track any scent from Lacy's house.

By Tuesday evening, June and Eager had led the search crew to the decoy shoe on the east flank. A command center had been immediately set up on the flank of the mountain and the area divided into grids. Teams had searched until dark, volunteers agreeing to regroup at first light Wednesday.

Instead of grabbing a few hours' rest like the others, June and Eager had hiked straight back to the west flank, where they were now in the dark predawn hours of a stormy Wednesday morning. And, as the hours ticked by, June was beginning to fear the worst.

Suddenly, Eager started barking excitedly somewhere in the dark. Energy punched through June.

He'd found something!

She clambered up the slope into blackness, making for

the sound of his barking. Rain beat down on her, branches snapped back against her glasses. She felt pain as something cut across her face, but she kept moving, faster. Then she heard her dog come crashing back through the woods in her direction.

He leaped up against her, his breath warm against her face, and he barked again before spinning around and bounding back to his find.

"Where is it, Eager? *Show me, boy!*"

June reached him standing over something in tight scrub under the cliff face. She crouched down, and with the back of her hand she edged aside dripping leaves. And there, in the halo of her headlamp, was a handgun in black loam.

Tension rippled through June.

"Good boy, Eager!" She tried to pump enthusiasm into her praise as she pulled out his bite toy and began a rough game of tug, rewarding him for his success before anything else. Eager lived for his tug game and June's praise. It was what kept him focused for hours at a time on a search.

She let him yank his toy out of her grip. "You win, boy. You got it!"

He clamped his jaws over the bite toy and shook it wildly, mock-killing it, then he gamboled around like a puppy, as goofy in his big Labrador heart as he'd always be. While he played, June turned her attention to the weapon.

In her line of work articles found on a search could become evidence in a crime, so she was careful to preserve any prints as best she could in an environment like this, with no equipment. At the same time she knew that handing this weapon over to Chief Fargo would be as effective as throwing it into a black hole. The FBI, however, might want to see this. Special Agent Hawk Bledsoe had been watching this town for some time, and his noose was slowly closing around Samuel.

June shrugged out of her backpack and located her digital camera. She snapped several pictures of the gun—a Beretta—then recorded the location of her find on her GPS.

Using her bandanna to pick the weapon up, she aimed the muzzle to the ground, released the clip. Three rounds remained inside the eleven-round magazine. She racked back the slide, popping another round out of the gun chamber. Once she was certain it was unloaded, she wrapped it in her bandanna and secured it at the bottom of her backpack.

June carried her own handgun in a holster on her hip tonight.

Anxiety whispered through her as Eager brought his toy back, snuffling like a happy pig. June took it from him, told him to be quiet. She listened intently to the forest, and an eerie sense of a presence nearby rolled over June. With it came a sharp stab of vulnerability.

She and her dog were in the dark, surrounded by miles of Wyoming wilderness, and even if she wanted to call for help, there was no cell reception on this side of the mountain. June's sole backup was a two-way radio connection to the safe house in the next valley. Even so, the current occupants of the safe house were ill-equipped to help her out of a pickle. And the radios were for serious emergency calls only—there remained the possibility that Samuel's henchmen could be in the area and pick up a broadcast should they manage to tune in to the same frequency.

Inhaling deeply, June got up from her haunches. She took hold of her dog's collar, which made him look up into the glow of her headlamp, his eyes reflecting the light like a zombie beast.

"Eager, are you *ready?*" she whispered. "You want *work,* boy?"

His muscles quivered as he waited for the release.

She let go of his collar, swinging her arm out in the direction she wanted him to work. *"Search!"*

And off he went sniffing the air, left to right. She followed, fighting down fatigue and despair as the first gray light of dawn fingered through the leaves and rain.

Eager suddenly got wind of fresh human scent, and his head popped sharply in a ninety-degree angle to the left. His tail wagged loosely as he zeroed in on the scent cone.

"Not too far, Eager!" June yelled, trying to keep up, but suddenly he vanished.

She stopped in her tracks, breathing hard, heart hammering. Then she heard the crash of breaking brush, followed by wild barking. Quickly, she scrambled in the direction of the barking, but as she pushed through low scrub, the ground suddenly gave out under her and she realized too late that she'd overshot the lip of a ravine hidden by a tangle of brambles. Groping wildly for purchase, June tumbled down a steep bank.

Her fall was halted as her shoulder *whumped* into a log. She gasped in pain and lay still for a moment, mentally regrouping as sweat and rain dribbled into her eyes. Tentatively she edged onto her side and with relief she realized she wasn't badly hurt, just bruised. She kicked the toes of her boots into the loam on the steep slope to find purchase, and she began to inch down to the ravine floor. Eager came gamboling and crashing back up the slope, oblivious to the precariousness of her situation, and he hit her body with his front paws, as if to say, *"Come, come, I found it, Mom, I found it!"*

"Good boy—take it easy," she said a little shakily. "I'm right behind you, buddy."

It was dark at the base of the bramble-choked gulley as June pushed branches aside and saw what Eager had found.

A man lay on his side. Big. Maybe six foot two. His face was hidden from view and his dark hair glistened with rain. His denim jacket and jeans were soaked through. June noted

he wore serious hiking boots, and the bottom of his left pant leg was soaked in what looked like blood.

"Good boy, Eager," she whispered, tossing his toy to the side for him to play with as she crouched down beside the man.

June carefully rolled him over. His head flopped back, exposing a mean gash across his temple. She felt his carotid. He was alive, but unconscious, his skin cold.

Her peripheral thought was that he was devastatingly good-looking, in a rough, tanned, mountain-man kind of way, and maybe in his early thirties. She hadn't seen him around Cold Plains before—a guy like this would be hard to miss.

Then she caught sight of the leather holster at his hip—empty. And for a nanosecond June froze. It must have been his Beretta she'd found.

*Had he fired at Lacy and her children?*

Sweat broke out over her body and her paramedic training warred with a need for safety. Because if this man was carrying, he could very likely be one of Samuel's henchmen.

Samuel eschewed weapons in the hands of his Devotees, but his personal murderous militia were the exception.

Bitterness filled her mouth as she reached quickly for his leather belt, first removing a GPS handheld device so she could undo his buckle, which was engraved with the name *Jesse*. It sounded like a brand of Western wear. June quickly undid the buckle and the zipper of his jeans. She edged his pants down over his hip. And there it was—a small *D* tattoo—the branding mark Samuel Grayson personally gave each one of his true Devotees. And if this Devotee was carrying—he was most certainly a henchman.

*Bastard.*

But before she could think through her next move, the man's eyes flared open and he grabbed her wrists. A hatchet of panic struck into her heart. She tried to jerk free, but his grip was like iron.

He blinked into the glow of her headlamp, and June saw his eyes were a deep and unusual shade of indigo-blue. In them she could read confusion.

"What are doing with my pants?" His voice came out hoarse, rough. Eager growled, hackles rising.

"Quiet, Eager," June whispered, fighting to tamp down the fear swelling inside her. "I'm here to help you," she said as calmly as she could. "I…needed to see if you had the Devotee tattoo on your hip—to see if you were a local, one of us, from Cold Plains."

Confusion filtered deeper into his eyes. "Devotee?" he said.

"You have a *D* tattooed on your hip, the one Samuel Grayson personally gives his true followers," she said.

He stared at her, features blank. Then he tried to move his head, wincing as he did. The movement caused fresh blood to flow from the gash down the side of his face. His jaw was dark with stubble. She wondered how long he'd been lying here.

"Where am I?"

"Looks like you took a tumble into the ravine," she said. "You've got a pretty nasty cut on your head and your leg is bleeding. Let me go so I can look at it."

He stared at her, refusing to relinquish his viselike grip on her wrists. His hands were big, calloused. He was impossibly strong, even in his injured state.

June's mouth went dry. She could easily disappear down here with her dog, and no one would find her until it was too late.

"I haven't seen you around Cold Plains," she said as calmly as she could. "My name is June Farrow. I'm a part-time paramedic with the Cold Plains Urgent Care Center, and a SAR volunteer. This is Eager, my K9. He's pretty friendly, but if he thinks you're going to hurt me, he'll attack. I'd hate for that to happen, so why don't you let go of me and maybe I can help you?"

His gaze shifted to her dog. Slowly he let go of her hands.

June lurched up to her feet, jumped back and pulled out her gun. She aimed it at his head.

*Careful, don't blow your cover, June.*

To the best of her knowledge, no one in town knew she worked against Samuel. Like most of the two thousand residents of Cold Plains, June attended his motivational seminars on Being the Best You. She pretended to hang on to his every word, painting herself as a potential Devotee on the cusp of conversion. Samuel had even suggested she come to one of his private counseling sessions, which were where he did most of his mind control. He was a master at preying on any insecurity, exposing a person's deepest fears and then promising to make them feel safe. His message was that as long as you were a Devotee, you were safe—in turn he wanted obedience, time and money. But if you tried to escape, as Lacy just had, he wanted you dead.

"What's your name?" she demanded. "What are you doing out here in the woods?"

His hand went to the holster at his hip.

"I have your weapon. It's missing rounds. Did you shoot at them?"

He frowned.

"Shoot at who?"

"There's a young mother and her two children lost in these woods. I'm looking for them. Are you chasing them? Did you hurt them?"

He tried to sit up, groaning in pain. And as he moved June caught sight of something lying in the soil behind his shoulder—*a little, sparkly red shoe.*

Rage arrowed through her body, obliterating any trace of fear.

"Don't move! Or I will shoot you dead. Where did you find that shoe?"

"I don't know what you're talking about… I can't seem to remember…anything." His voice faded and he touched the wound on his brow, his fingertips coming away bloody. He stared at the blood, a look of disorientation on his rugged features.

"What's your name?" she repeated.

His gaze lifted slowly and met hers, and in his eyes June saw the beginnings of fear. "I… Jesus—I don't know my name," he whispered.

June swallowed.

Was he playing her?

What was she going to do with him now? Leave him out here to die—which he might if he was disoriented and lost more blood. And if hypothermia kicked in, he was finished.

June glanced at his GPS device lying near her feet.

"Where were you going when you fell down here?"

"I told you, I don't know."

"Which way is Cold Plains?" she said.

"Cold Plains?"

"You've never heard of Cold Plains?"

"I…" He cursed softly.

June swore to herself. She was not capable of leaving him to die out here. She was programmed to rescue, had been ever since she was a kid. June was the child who saved bugs from puddles. It was why she became a paramedic. It was why she worked for SAR—she was wired to help those in despair.

But she had not been able to help her husband. The sudden memory stab, the sharp reminder of her inadequacies, hurt.

Holding her gun on him with one hand, she reached down and picked up his GPS with the other. She pressed the menu button, saw that he'd been saving his route—and he appeared to have hiked in not from Cold Plains, but from over the mountains.

"You've come a long way," she said. "You've saved a route into these mountains from forty miles north—where were you before that?"

He groaned, lay back. "I wish I knew."

He needed help—he was still losing blood. He might have been lying here for hours. She had no idea how bad his leg wound was. And daylight was beginning to filter down into the ravine. She had maybe an hour to hike all the way down into Cold Plains and to head around to the search base camp on the other side of the mountain, and she'd still found no sign of Lacy and the twins.

Her only solution—if one could even call it that—was to take this stranger back to the safe house and hold him there until she could fetch FBI Agent Hawk Bledsoe. It was risky, but she didn't have time to think further.

"I'm going to help you, okay?"

He nodded.

"I'm putting this gun away." *Please don't let this be a mistake...* "And if you hurt me, you're going to die out here, alone, understand?"

His eyes remained locked onto hers. "I don't hurt people."

She holstered her Glock. "How would you know?" She shrugged out of her backpack as she spoke. "You don't even know your name."

Crouching down next to him, she opened her pack and removed her first-aid kit. His pulse was within range, and he was breathing okay—she'd seen that much.

"Can you move your limbs? Any numbness in your extremities?"

He grunted. "No. Just...weak."

Blood loss was her priority now.

"I'm going to cut open the bottom of your jeans. I want to take a look at that injury on your leg," she said as she reached for her scissors and began splitting open the base of his pants. The gash on his head was bad, but the one on his leg could be worse—she needed to see what she was dealing with.

He groaned in pain as she peeled the bloodied and rain-soaked denim off a deep gash on his calf.

He was going to need sutures.

She worked quickly to clean and dry the wound as best she could, shielding him from the rain with her body. There was no arterial damage or obvious fracture—just a big surface gash probably caused by sharp rock during his fall.

Pulling the edges of the cut together, she applied butterfly sutures from her kit. Then she wound a bandage tightly around his calf, urgency powering her movements.

"This should work as a temporary stopgap," she said as she began to clean the cut on his temple.

His gaze caught hers and she stilled for a second—the intensity in his eyes was disturbing. He smelled faintly of wood smoke.

"You been camping?" she said.

He inhaled sharply as disinfectant touched his cut. "I—I really don't know." Then, as he thought deeper: "Do I have a backpack with me?"

"I can't see one."

He closed his eyes, clearly straining to remember. Then he swore softly again. "I feel as if I might have had a pack or something. That I was going somewhere…important."

The cut on his head, if ugly, was also superficial. However, given his apparent memory loss, he could be suffering from some sort of intracranial hemorrhaging due to blunt-force trauma, which could become dangerous.

"I'm going to give you three words," she said. "*Radio, belt,*

*Jesse.* Can you memorize them for me? I'm going to ask you to repeat them to me in a little while, okay?"

*"Radio, belt, Jesse,"* he repeated. "Got it."

His voice was beautiful, she thought, deep and husky like Matt's used to be. Matt had been fair, but similar in stature to this man—an ace helicopter pilot she'd met on one of her very first recue missions. She'd loved going camping with Matt—loved the way fire smoke lingered in his checked lumberjack shirt, how the stubble on his cheeks grew rough in the wilderness. Emotion pricked into her eyes. June pushed it away, startled at the freshness of it all. It had been five years. She'd dealt with it.

"You sure you don't recall firing your weapon?" she said, trying another angle as she taped more butterfly sutures to the cut on his temple. Eager was watching obediently from the side, waiting for new directions.

"No."

"But you knew you had a gun—you went for it at your hip."

"I…guess."

"And you're sure you didn't see a young mother and her children in the woods?"

"No!" Frustration bit into his tone "I'm not the hell sure of *anything.*"

He was scared of what was happening to him, thought June.

"Why do you have that little red shoe?"

He was quiet a moment, then his eyes flickered as if a memory suddenly crossed before them. "I told you, I have no idea what you're talking about."

June wondered if he was lying.

"That shoe—" she jerked her chin to where it lay "—belongs to a three-year-old twin. She and her sister call them their Dorothy shoes. They like to take them everywhere so they can put them on and click their heels like Dorothy in *The Wizard of Oz* and be home safe whenever they need to be. Their names are Rebecca and Abigail. Their mother is Lacy Matthews. Lacy runs the coffee shop in town. They've been missing in these woods for two nights, and I'm thinking the girls will be wanting their magic shoes to take them home about now."

His gaze went to the shoe and he stared at it as if he'd never seen it before in his life.

"There, that should tide you over," she said as she applied a bandage over the sutures.

He pulled up his jeans zipper, buckled his belt and immediately tried to get to his feet, but he swayed and slumped heavily back to the ground.

"Easy, big guy," she said, helping him back up by the arm. "You lost a fair bit of blood. Move too fast and you're going down like a rock."

"I need to go—" He started to stumble through the brush, then swayed and leaned heavily on her. "I've got to get to…" His voice faded, and his features twisted in frustration.

"Get to where?" she said.

"I… Jesus, *I don't know.* I was going somewhere. Urgent—had to do something…important, for someone. Something… dangerous."

A chill trickled down her spine.

"Do something for whom? Samuel Grayson?"

"I… The name feels familiar."

"Yeah," she said bitterly. "He'd be the one who tattooed your hip. Can you walk, if you lean on me like this?" She hooked his big arm around her neck, taking the brunt of his weight across her shoulders.

June began to help him up the bank. He was solid muscle and their progress was slow. When the bank got too steep, she let him climb in front of her while she supported him from behind. She also wanted to be in a position where she could draw her gun again if she had to.

June's immediate goal was to get this injured stranger into the safe house, further assess his condition and administer whatever additional medical aid she could. Then she was going to press him hard on the whereabouts of Lacy and the twins—he was her *only* clue right now.

She'd also ask the others in the house if they'd seen him around Cold Plains. If they did recognize the stranger as one of Samuel's cult enforcers, she'd keep him under lock and key, fetch Hawk Bledsoe and hand him over to the FBI.

Hawk was one of the few people June could totally trust in this surreal, picture-perfect and sick little town. Four months ago Hawk's sister-in-law, Mia, had been brought to an EXIT psychologist for "deprogramming," which is how EXIT had got wind of the cult in Cold Plains.

Mia had told EXIT there were other members who wanted to get out, but they had no resources and were afraid for their lives if they spoke out against Samuel. Mia had passed on the name of Hannah Mendes, a widow in her seventies with a ranch on the outskirts of Cold Plains. Hannah had been trying to set up a safe halfway house with the aid of her sister-in-law from Little Gulch over in the next valley. EXIT had contacted June and asked if she'd run the house and help Hannah with an evacuation program. They presently had five people in the safe house waiting to move into an EXIT program, and June had done the early stages of counseling with them. Lacy and her twins would have brought the number of occupants to eight.

As they edged up over the ravine lip, rain was coming down hard again and the wind soughed, swirling mist like wraiths through the trees. Dawn had done little to dissipate the gloomy eeriness of the forest. June paused and gave the stranger some water. His face had a pallor that worried her, and he was weakening.

"Where are we going?" he said, handing her water bottle back to her.

"Shelter. A safe place." Hooking his arm over her neck again, supporting his weight with her shoulders, June led him through the trees toward a hidden crevasse that would lead into caves and a tunnel to Hidden Valley on the other side of the mountain. That's where the safe house was.

As he began to lean more heavily on her, June prayed she wasn't taking a cult enforcer, her worst kind of enemy, into the very heart of their safe house.

# Chapter 2

As they neared the opening of the crevasse that led to the cave tunnel, the pager on June's hip sounded. Tension whipped through her. She leaned her shoulder against the rock face, the stranger heavy against her body as she checked the page.

*Chief Fargo.*

Her pulse quickened. The police chief was probably wondering why she and Eager hadn't shown up with the rest of the SAR team at first light this morning. June would never make it down there in time now, not if she had to take this injured man back to the safe house first. Sweat prickled over her lip.

With the FBI's noose tightening around Samuel, and with more and more of his Devotees disappearing into some rumored safe house, the entire town was on edge, looking for the traitor among them. The *last* thing June needed was to give Fargo, Samuel or anyone else in Cold Plains cause to suspect her.

As part of her of her cover, June rented an outbuilding on Hannah Mendes's ranch as her "official" residence in Cold Plains while she worked two days a week as a paramedic for the urgent-care ambulance service.

Hannah covered for June on all the other nights and days she spent working at the cave house in the mountains. The ranch was likely the first place Fargo might go looking for June when she didn't show up for the search party or answer this page. Fargo might see June's truck still in the driveway, start asking questions. Hannah could come under scrutiny, as well.

June cursed to herself—she was going to need a damn fine explanation to satisfy Fargo.

This community with its seemingly picture-perfect facade was like a ticking time bomb. June just wished the FBI would hurry up and get something they could actually use to take Samuel down and prosecute him before the whole place blew sky-high, Waco-style.

She hooked her pager back onto her belt and tried to get her patient moving again, but his legs were buckling under him and he appeared to be fading in and out of consciousness. Worry speared through June—he might need a hospital. But it was too late even to consider trying to make it all the way back into town with him in this condition. And then there'd be questions.

The cave house was closer, safer.

"Hey, you," she whispered, lightly slapping the side of his rugged cheek with her palm. "Can you hear me?"

He moaned. His complexion was deathly pale and blood was seeping into the white bandage on his head. The sutures must be pulling loose.

"Listen to me—I'm going call you Jesse, okay? *Jesse,* can you hear me?"

His eyes flickered, as if with sudden recognition.

"Good. Now, stay with me, Jesse. We're almost there."

June's muscles burned as she maneuvered Jesse through the narrow rock crevasse. At the end of the crevasse there was an apparent dead end hidden by a tangle of creepers. June moved the curtain of vegetation aside, exposing the opening to a large cave. These mountains were riddled with them. She clicked on her headlamp, and helping Jesse bend over, they entered the gloom.

"Where are we?" he said.

"A cave. At the back is a tunnel that leads to a valley on the other side. We're going to a shelter built into more caves on that side."

The tunnel was wide, but the roof was low, which meant Jesse leaned even more heavily on June as he was forced to bend double. June's energy began to sag under the weight of well over six feet of Marlboro Man. In close proximity, his stubble rubbed against her cheeks, and June realized peripherally that she had not had a man like this in her arms since Matt had died.

Her pilot had been all rugged brawn and macho power, as well, an A-type personality in total command of his life. Until the one rescue mission that had burned him.

There was always the one mission, thought June. Posttraumatic stress disorder was a little-acknowledged aspect of rescue work, and it often went undiagnosed, as it had in Matt's case. She should have seen it.

She should have given Matt the benefit of the doubt—she should have realized he was incapable of leaving the cult on his own and she should never have given him the ultimatum that had sent him over the edge.

June braced her hand against the cold cave wall as she struggled to catch her breath. She thought she'd managed to put the guilt from the past in perspective, but now it was haunting, so very real again, in the shadows of this cave. It was this stranger—he was doing this to her. Something about his physical presence reminded her too much of the only man she'd ever truly loved. And now the ghosts were coming back.

She glanced at Jesse—when his memory returned, if it returned, would he be friend or foe?

He slumped suddenly to the floor of the cave, trying to grab onto the wall as he went down. June dropped to her knees besides him. His breathing was shallow, his skin cold, clammy. Urgency bit into her.

"Jesse, hang in just a little while longer. We're almost there."

She struggled to help him up, and as they shuffled along, the tunnel grew narrower, darker. Her headlamp started to flicker, the battery dying. Shadows leaped and lunged and the air grew dank, musky. A bat fluttered past her face, making a soft wind.

The journey through the crevasse and tunnel combined was less than a mile, but tonight it felt endless. June's breath was ragged and she was perspiring with the effort. Then suddenly she saw faint light ahead. Relief washed through her body.

They were almost through into Hidden Valley, a narrow delta on the other side of this mountain range. It was inaccessible by road—the only way in was via this secret tunnel or by foot over the mountains, or to fly in by chopper. It was where an eccentric architect-turned-survivalist had chosen to build a large house into a deep warren of caves, and it was in this house the architect had lived, quietly and off-grid, until his death. He'd left everything he owned to his sister, who'd helped turn it into a safe haven for escapees from Samuel Grayson's lethal cult.

The front of the cave house had been walled in with locally sourced rock. Large tinted windows looked out over Hidden Valley, and a stone porch, partially shaded by a rock overhang, ran the length of the house. A narrow boardwalk led from the tunnel entrance and hugged the rock face all the way to the porch and front door. A creek cascaded from a fissure in the rock face and ran under the boardwalk before meandering out into the valley.

The rooms deeper inside the caves had no windows but were vented via stone flues to the ground on top, and the chill inside, even during summer, was eased by a great stone hearth in the central living area and by smaller cast-iron wood-burning stoves in the rooms. When the architect had left the house to his sister, she'd had no idea what to do with it and had let it stand empty; the place had faded from the memory of those who had known about it. When she found out that Hannah Mendes, a relative by marriage, needed a safe house to help cult victims escape, she had offered the cave house as a perfect solution because of the hidden-tunnel access to the valley on the other side.

As June and her injured stranger reached the boardwalk, Jesse passed out. She struggled to hold him, but he slid from her grasp and slumped with a dull thud onto the wooden slats of the walkway. Adrenaline thrummed through her as she checked his pulse. It was steady, and he was still breathing. She worried now about intracranial swelling pressuring his brain.

Laying him in a prone position on the boardwalk, she ran to the house and banged on the door.

"I need help! Can someone come out here and help me!"

The door swung open. Molly, an eighteen-year-old whom June had brought to the safe house last week, stood in the doorway, pulling on her sweater, eyes wide circles of consternation. "What's going on! Did they find us!"

*God, I hope not.*

"I found a man down a ravine while I was searching for Lacy. He's got a Devotee tattoo, and he's hurt—"

"Is he a henchman?" Molly peered nervously down the boardwalk. "Why did you bring him here! Does he know what happened to Lacy?"

"I don't know who he is. He doesn't remember anything—"

"You shouldn't have brought him here!"

"Molly, calm down and help me carry him. We'll lock him in my room until we stitch him up and learn more."

Molly refused to budge.

"*Molly,* we can't leave him to die out here. Go get Davis and Brad—now!"

The two men came running out into the rain and helped carry Jesse inside.

"Take him to my room!" June yelled as she rushed behind them. "Molly, get me some towels, hot water, the big medical kit from the main bathroom."

June shucked her wet jacket. "Lay him on my bed. Brad, ask your mom to come light the fire in the stove in my room."

She checked Jesse's breathing again—still steady. His pulse was okay, too. June palmed off her wet peaked cap, and Molly pulled a side table alongside the bed atop which she put the medical kit.

June shone a small flashlight into the stranger's eyes. His pupils responded normally, then, as if irritated by the light, he blinked fast, moaning as he came around again.

Relief washed through June. Maybe the guy was just exhausted. She wondered how long he'd actually been in the mountains, how many hours he'd lain, wet and cold, in the ravine, and when he'd last gotten some calories into him. She had to remove his wet clothes, warm him up.

"Molly, please go heat up some of that soup Sonya made the other day—I'm beginning to think our stranger has been walking through the wilderness for some time."

"Why do you want to help him—you said he's a Devotee,

and look, he's got a holster. Only henchmen carry sidearms. He's got to be a henchman."

June shot her a glance. "Do you recognize him? Has anyone in this house seen him before?"

"No."

"Then let's give him the benefit of the doubt, okay?"

The one thing she had not given Matt.

"Just because I don't recognize him from Cold Plains doesn't mean he's not a henchman."

"Molly, just get the soup. And on your way to the kitchen, ask Davis to fetch a change of men's clothing from the closet in the big room. There should be sweatpants and a T-shirt in there large enough to fit him."

June made sure there was always extra clothing in the safe house—she never knew who might arrive in an emergency with only the clothes on their back.

Molly trudged to the kitchen, shoulders set in a sullen slouch. The kid was acting out of fear, thought June as she propped Jesse up on several pillows. Molly was terrified Samuel's reach would extend into the safe house and June couldn't blame her.

"I'm going to get you into some dry clothing, Jesse," she said calmly, maneuvering his wet denim jacket off his shoulders. "Then I'll clean those wounds properly and stitch you up."

He cleared his throat. "You're calling me Jesse—why? Is it my name?" His voice was hoarse.

"That's what your belt buckle says—probably a clothing brand. But I had to call you something." June helped him lift his damp T-shirt over his head.

"Great." His lips almost curved, then he sighed heavily, closing his eyes as he leaned back into the pillows.

His torso was sun-browned, as if he made a habit of working outdoors without a shirt. And his large hands were calloused—a man of physical labor, or a rancher perhaps? June didn't peg this guy as the poolside- or beach-tanning type.

A thick scar curved down one side of his waist, as if he'd been gored by something. Another scar snaked up the inside of his arm.

June frowned. A violent life, or a bad accident of some kind?

But apart from the old scars there were no fresh swellings or lacerations that she could ascertain.

His chest hair was dark. June's gaze followed the whorl of hair that ran down his washboard abs and disappeared seductively into his low-slung jeans. She needed to get him out of those wet pants, and the idea suddenly made her think of sex, which was ludicrous. She was a trained paramedic. The human body was part of her job. She never reacted like this.

Nevertheless, this rugged mountain man was doing it for her, and it made her uneasy.

She glanced up at his face. His eyes were closed, and he was breathing deeply, rhythmically, his bare chest rising and falling. He had a fine scar across his chin, too, and crinkles fanned out from his eyes—smile lines and sad lines. Deep brackets framed his mouth…a beautifully shaped, wide mouth. She couldn't help noticing. Or imagining what it might feel like to have those lips brush hers.

She cleared her throat. "I'm going to get you out of your boots and jeans. Is that okay, Jesse?"

No response. Worry washed softly through her again, and inside her heart compassion blossomed.

She shook his shoulder. *"Jesse?"*

He nodded, eyes still closed.

"Are you just exhausted, or do you have pain anywhere else?"

"Tired," he whispered. "Just…really tired."

June removed his boots and wet socks and quickly unbuckled his belt once more. She edged his pants down over his hips and swallowed.

His thighs were large, all muscle, his legs in stunning shape apart from a massive scar across his left knee—looked as if he'd had some kind of surgery there.

She covered him with a soft blanket, pointedly ignoring the dark flare of hair between his thighs and trying not to think about how well-endowed he was. She put his wet boots in front of the cast-iron stove and hung his jeans over the back of a chair to dry. Flames glowed in the little stove window, and June realized she was perspiring, pulse racing.

She ran her hand over her damp hair, feeling edgy, perturbed. She hadn't wanted sex since she'd lost Matt and had thrown herself wholly into cult and rescue work. And she preferred it that way. It helped her stay focused. She needed every ounce of her focus right now because that dark and rugged stranger lying naked on her bed *could* represent everything she'd devoted her life to fighting—he could be a cult enforcer, violent and potentially deadly to everyone she was trying to protect in this safe house.

June returned to his bedside and looked at him. He wore no wedding band, no jewelery, nothing that could clue her in to his identity. Apart from his watch. She removed it and studied it. It was high-tech, complete with altimeter, barometer and compass, the kind of equipment a serious outdoor enthusiast would wear. Her thoughts turned to his GPS and the route he'd save on it. She made a mental note to get it out of her pack and go through it thoroughly later.

"Do you need anything else?"

June spun round, startled by the male voice.

It was Davis. The middle-aged man had entered the room, placed a pile of clean clothes on the chair next to the bed.

June's face felt hot. "Thanks, Davis. I think we should get someone out to stand guard at the canyon entrance for a while—I'm worried Samuel's men might come looking for this guy, if he is actually one of them, and stumble upon our passageway. Can you do it?"

Davis looked at her oddly. "Are you okay, June?"

"I'm fine," she said a little too crisply. Then she rubbed her brow. "I'm just really worried about Lacy and the twins. I should have found them by now. I—"

"You *will* find them, June. If anyone can, it's you and Eager."

Emotion surged into her eyes, and the burden of responsibility she'd undertaken, the amount of trust these people put in her, was suddenly overwhelming.

"Thanks, Davis."

"I'll take the first watch. Brad can replace me."

"Don't forget to take a radio. And one of the shotguns."

He paused at the door. "You really think they'll come?"

She glanced at Jesse. "I hope not."

*I hope I haven't made the biggest mistake in my life by bringing him here.*

"Make sure Molly has a receiving radio tuned in to the right frequency. Tell her to keep it with her at all times and to pass it on to someone else if she wants to sleep."

Davis closed the door behind him as he left.

June busied herself cleaning and disinfecting the wounds on Jesse's head and leg. She administered local anesthetic, stitched him up and applied dressing. He remained conscious but in a state of exhausted half sleep, which both puzzled and worried her.

She put dry track pants on him and took a moment to study the tattoo on his hip again.

With surprise she realized the *D* was fresh—maybe only seven to ten days old, the skin around the ink still pink and slightly inflamed.

She frowned. This didn't fit the picture for one of Samuel's henchmen. The enforcers Samuel used tended to be solidly entrenched Devotees who'd proved themselves to him and demonstrated they were able and prepared to defend Samuel's empire violently. Or, at least, those were the henchmen she knew of.

June's chest tightened with conflict as she covered the stranger with more blankets. She packed up her first-aid kit, and suddenly a wave of fatigue hit hard. She told herself it was just the adrenaline wearing off. She still had to go out and look for Lacy and the twins—she'd start along the west flank where she and Eager had found Jesse and his gun. There was no way she'd be able to put in even a cursory appearance with Fargo's search party at this late stage of the morning, so she'd spend her time searching solo with her K9.

Molly entered the room carrying a tray with a bowl of steaming vegetable soup. She eyed Jesse with hostility as she set the tray on the table next to the bed.

June shook his shoulder, gently rousing him. "Jesse— Molly brought you some soup. I think you should get some warmth into you."

His thick lashes fluttered and he turned his head from side to side.

He could hear her voice—soft, sexy, feminine—as if it were coming from a faraway place with warm light. He felt her hand on his bare shoulder—her skin soft, cool. So feminine. He struggled to swim up to full consciousness—to her—and his eyes fluttered open. But everything was a hazy blur, bright. Then slowly, the room came into focus. And he saw her, sitting beside his bed.

An angel. With flaming-red hair. Beautiful, fine-boned features. Porcelain-pale skin brushed by freckles, eyes the color of a pale summer sky that reminded him of the sound of bees and lawn mowers and watermelon by the pool. Her mouth was full, wide. Kissable.

He frowned, trying to place her face, his memories of summers past.

And, as he pulled things into focus, he realized her red hair was damp, tendrils drying in soft spirals around her face. The rest was pulled back in a braid, and there were bits of leaves stuck in it.

He remembered now—it had been pouring. She'd had a peaked cap on when she'd found him, and a headlamp, shining down into his face. Where was he?

He tried to get up. But she gently placed her hand on his shoulder, her willowy body belying a resilient strength he could sense in her touch, see in her clear eyes. He sagged back into the pillows, feeling as though he'd been hit by a ten-ton truck. His head throbbed. His leg hurt—his whole body felt stiff.

"Christ, what happened to me?"

"You fell down a ravine, hit your head and gashed your leg. I've sewn you up and the injuries look fine, but you need to take it easy, Jesse. You've lost blood."

*Jesse.* That's right—she'd named him Jesse because he couldn't the hell remember who he was, where he was going or where he'd come from. Despair sank into him, along with a bite of frustration.

She was watching him intently. So was the young woman with straight mousey-blond hair she'd referred to as Molly. The kid looked hostile.

What did the redheaded angel with the porcelain skin say her name was…*June.* She'd said she worked as a part-time paramedic in a town called Cold Plains. Thank God—he wasn't completely brain-dead. And he could recall hiking with her assistance through a narrowing rock canyon, into a cave and a tunnel. After that his memory was black again.

*Cold Plains.* Why did the name of that town seem so familiar, yet not? Another name came to him. *Samuel Grayson.* Tension reared up inside Jesse along with a gnawing urgency. He struggled to sit up—he had to go somewhere, but he couldn't recall where, and it had something to do with a man named Samuel Grayson.

June pressed him gently back against the pillows. "Do you recall those three words I gave you earlier, Jesse?"

*What words?* Oh, wait…he did remember. He cleared his throat "*Radio, belt* and—" he gave a wry smile "—*Jesse.*"

"Your short-term memory is intact. That's a good sign."

"Yep. Great." *Too bad about the rest.*

"Do you remember anything else, like where you were coming from?"

Frustration heated his body. He tried to dig deeper into his memory, but all he got was a thick sense of fuzzy confusion.

"No, I—I think I was… No, I can't recall a damn thing."

"I checked your GPS. It appears you were traveling into Cold Plains over the north mountains. Do you remember how long you've been in the wilderness? Where you were going? Can you tell me why you have a *D* tattooed on your hip?"

"I have a tattoo?" Had June told him that already—or did the familiarity stem from a buried memory?

"He has the *D* because he's one of Samuel's enforcers," Molly spat at him. "He knows *exactly* what you're talking about, June—he's lying that he doesn't remember anything. Don't fall for it."

June said, quietly, without looking at the young woman, "Molly, can you please go to the kitchen and man the radio. Let me know if Davis reports in."

Molly stomped out of the room and banged the door shut behind her.

"She's afraid," said June.

"Of *me?*"

"Of Samuel Grayson and whoever works for him, and if you're one of his, that includes you."

*Samuel.* Why did that name strike such a strident cord in him? "Did you tell me about him already, in the ravine?"

"Samuel is the leader of a cult in Cold Plains," June said, assessing him carefully as she spoke. Jesse got the sense she was watching for some kind of reaction to her words, something that would show he was lying. Anxiety curled through him.

"He calls his followers Devotees," she said. "And, as Molly pointed out, he personally tattoos a small *D* on the hip of each one of his true followers." She paused. "None of this sounds familiar?"

The trouble was, it did. But he couldn't figure out why.

"No," he said.

Her mouth flattened and something in her eyes changed. "Earlier you were muttering about Samuel and something urgent you had to do."

Jesse's heart began to race. His mouth felt dry. He did recall that now. But he didn't know what it meant. And he didn't like what was happening here. He glanced at the pistol holstered on her hip, then his gaze went to the door. It struck him there were no windows in this room. Claustrophobia crawled around the edges of his mind.

"I don't remember saying those things." He was lying now, and he knew it. He felt in his gut he had to, but didn't understand why.

"You pulled a gun on me," he said.

Her gaze was steady, cool. "You grabbed me."

He frowned. The action hurt his head. His hand went to his forehead.

"Don't touch." She got to her feet, went over to a dresser that had framed photographs on top. She brought him a hand-held mirror.

"You can take a look."

He took the mirror from her, his hand brushing against her cool, slender fingers as he did. Jesse saw a wedding band on her left hand, and felt a sharp and sudden stab of remorse, guilt. Shame.

He glanced at his own hand. No wedding band—not even a tan line. But he felt as if something *should* be there. A deep uneasiness bored down into him. Slowly, he looked into the small mirror.

The face that looked back was familiar. His. But he could attach nothing more to it. She'd done a neat job of the stitches along his brow. A memory hit him. A woman, brunette, running through the dark forest. Rain. She had two young children in her arms. She was screaming hysterically.

*Bastard! No henchman is going to get my children!*

She had hit him with a branch across his brow.

Gunfire. He could recall shooting. There were men—running through the forest. Then he was falling, falling. Pain in his leg.

Then nothing. Swirling mist, blackness.

Sweat broke out over his torso.

Slowly he lowered the mirror.

Those clear, summer-sky eyes were staring intently at him. She was waiting.

But he said nothing. He was afraid he might have done something—he felt bad about it and he didn't understand why.

She sat on the chair next to the bed and leaned forward, her elbows on her knees, her hands clasped in front of her. A quiet urgency buzzed about her.

"If you remember *anything,* Jesse, you need to tell me—it could help the lives of a mother and her small children."

He looked away. Her black Lab was lying in a basket by the stove, watching him, too. The bed he was lying on was queen-size. There was a closet at the far end of the room. The walls of this room were uneven, and he realized suddenly that they were rock.

"Where am I?"

"A safe place. Look, Jesse, before anything else, I need you to try harder. A young mother in her thirties, brunette, went missing with her three-year-old twin girls in these woods two nights ago." She paused, her intensity sharpening. "Her name is Lacy Matthews and she runs the coffee shop on Main Street in Cold Plains. Her twins are in the local day care. Lacy was a Devotee. Like you, she has a *D* tattooed on her hip. But she wanted to get out of the cult. I was supposed to meet her to bring her to this safe house, but she never showed up."

"You help people escape the cult?"

Her eyes narrowed, and he thought he detected a sliver of fear.

"Yes," she said coolly. "This is a halfway house, a place from where escapees can access exit-counseling, and then go on to start new lives somewhere else."

"*You* do deprogramming?"

"I'm trained to offer early-stage exit-counseling."

The words *cult, Devotee, henchman* circled around and around in Jesse's brain, as if they were important to him. But he couldn't slot them into any bigger picture.

The image of the brunette screaming, fleeing from him, sliced across his brain again, sharp, like pieces of broken mirror.

Jesse swallowed, met her gaze. Was he a bad guy—did he work for Samuel Grayson?

"Did you see Lacy and her daughters, Jesse?"

He cursed, suddenly agitated, angry. "I wish you'd stop asking me the same questions—I don't remember a goddamn thing!"

She watched him in silence for several beats, as if weighing his words for truth.

"If you did see them," she said very quietly, an anger now flickering deep in her eyes, "and if you told me where, I might be able save their lives, if they are even still alive."

His heart hammered and his head pounded. She was repeating herself, pressing him as if she didn't believe him. "Maybe if you searched where you said you found my Beretta," he said quietly.

Her mouth flattened. "I never told you what kind of gun I found."

He said nothing.

She lurched to her feet, hostility, determination in her movements.

"Well, that's *exactly* where I'm going to start searching, Jesse. And believe me, if you've hurt them, I'm going to make you pay. I'm going to make damn sure you go down for it."

He didn't doubt her for a second.

She stalked toward the door, her black Lab surging instantly to follow at her heels, his claws clicking on the polished stone floor. She opened the door. Outside was a passageway, warm light. One hand on the door handle, she turned to face him.

"Someone will be armed with a shotgun and standing right outside. Try anything stupid and they'll shoot you right through the door."

"I'm a prisoner?"

"You're tattooed with the *D* of a Devotee and you were carrying concealed, which implies you could be a cult enforcer. I don't know if you're playing me, or whether you actually have lost your memory, and I don't know what you were doing in the woods where an innocent mother and her children went missing. Until I do know, you're staying where you can't hurt anyone."

"You have no right to keep me locked in this…cave room, or whatever it is."

"Until I can get the FBI, yeah, I figure I've got that right."

June stepped out of the room. She shut the door with a snick. And Jesse heard a key turn in the lock.

Outside the door June leaned back against the cool rock wall and closed her eyes for a moment, trying to gather herself. She'd been rattled by her sharp and instant physical reaction to this rugged stranger she'd found in the woods—a man who could easily turn out to be an archenemy, someone who symbolized everything she detested, everything she'd devoted her life toward fighting.

"Everything okay?"

June blushed and cursed her redhead's complexion. "I didn't hear you coming, Molly. Listen, don't go back into that room, not until I return. He's got what he needs in there and he can use the en suite. Just make sure someone is outside here 24/7 with a loaded shotgun. If he causes trouble, threaten to shoot him through the door."

Molly's lips curved slightly. "I knew you'd see him for what he was. You shouldn't have brought him here, June."

"I couldn't let him die. That's not who I am."

"Then what are you going to do with him?"

"Hand him over to FBI Agent Hawk Bledsoe, but my priority right now is Lacy and the twins. I'll call Hawk when I'm closer to town and within cell-tower range."

"Has Agent Bledsoe actually been to the cave house?"

"He knows it exists, but I haven't brought him or any of the other agents in yet. It hasn't been easy knowing who to trust, Molly—the fewer people who know where the house is the better."

"But you do trust Agent Bledsoe?"

"He's one of the only people out there I can trust. His

sister-in-law is the reason I came to Cold Plains. I don't know about the other agents, though. I haven't wanted to take the risk."

June left Molly standing outside the door as she went to get some dry clothes from the supply closet. She changed into jeans that were too large and cursed herself for not having the foresight to gather clothes from her own room before locking Jesse in—but she wasn't going back in there now.

She checked her gear, fed Eager, grabbed an apple and headed back out into the rain with her dog. But as they reached the entrance to the tunnel, her pager beeped again.

It was Fargo. He was still looking for her. Tension strapped across June's chest. It was just a matter of time before he went looking for her at the ranch, and when he saw her truck there, but no sign of her or her dog, he was going to get suspicious.

The clock was ticking on her cover.

June clicked on her headlamp and ducked into the black tunnel, hoping that rescuing a perfect stranger wasn't going to be her downfall.

Or death.

# *Chapter 3*

Jesse paced in his prison.

He appeared to be in some sort of cave room.

He felt the walls with the palm of his hand—they were definitely natural rock, cold, uneven. But the wall with the door had been constructed of concrete and was smooth and whitewashed, as if perhaps a dwelling had been constructed inside a giant cave and various rooms walled off. The air felt chilled in spite of the fact a fire burned in a black cast-iron stove in the corner. His gaze followed the stove flue up to the roof. It had been vented through a hole hewn into the rock ceiling. There were two more vents in the ceiling at different intervals—possibly to circulate air from the outside.

A small bathroom adjoined the bedroom. Jesse entered. It contained the bare basics—towels, a toothbrush, toothpaste, shampoo, body lotion, a comb and brush with some long red hairs.

No windows anywhere.

Claustrophobia tightened around him. He didn't like the feeling of being underground and his was a prison not only of physical space, but of his own mind. He—the real Jesse, whoever he was—had been locked down somewhere deep inside his brain.

He exited the bathroom and paced the length of the room, then back again, working stiffness from his legs. The wound on his calf hurt, but better to keep it mobile, he thought, or that would stiffen up, too. And as he paced he had to ward off the stifling waves of anxiety induced by being confined in a small space.

Jesse needed wide-open spaces, wilderness, jagged snow-capped peaks...*horses*.

He froze.

Horses, snowcapped mountains—they felt like a part of him. Closing his eyes, he strained to unearth more around the images. But nothing more would come. He tried visualizing himself on a horse. He could almost feel the movement of the saddle, hear the creak of worn leather, the chink of a bridle. He saw a sandy trail unfolding in front of him. He could scent pine and he sensed at his side—within easy reach—a 270 *Winchester*.

Sweat prickled over his body.

That was a very specific piece of information on the rifle, just as he'd known his official sidearm was a newly issued .40 Beretta. He stilled, heart kicking.

*Issued.*

*Official.*

He tried to dig even deeper but the clues scurried away from his consciousness into the shadowed crevices of his brain. It frustrated the hell out of him.

The words *cult, Devotee, Samuel, henchman* began to circle through his mind again, and again, and they came with a crushing, devastating sense of loss, guilt. Abandonment. Deception.

Sharp images sliced like shards through his head…the woman running, children screaming. Him raising his gun, anger pumping through his blood. Remorse. Something terrible…*his fault*.

Jesse braced his hands on the dresser, head down, brain spinning, and he closed his eyes, trying to force the memories into his head.

But nothing more would come to him

He slammed his fist onto the dresser.

The photos atop the dresser jumped and one of the frames toppled over. Startled at the force of his own simmering aggression, he picked up the frame to set it back on its stand and realized it was a photo of June. In it, she was crouching next to a man in a flight suit. A child stood between them with his little arms around the neck of a yellow Labrador. The photo had been shot in front of a small helicopter behind which there was dense forest and mountains. *Pacific Northwest, maybe,* thought Jesse.

The man in the photograph with June was tall, athletic build, sandy-blond hair in a buzz cut. His features were angular, his gray eyes sharp. He had his arm around June's shoulders—possessive, protective, yet somehow intimate and loving. Jesse examined the photo more closely. The boy, maybe three years old, looked like the man's son—same eye shape, same color. But the boy's hair was more strawberry blond than sandy.

Jesse's attention shifted to June and her red hair.

She was smiling, her eyes bright, her cheeks pink. Jesse imagined the air must have been cold that day.

She really was beautiful, in a way that he liked—tall, slender, yet possessing a strength and confidence that showed in her athletic body, in her intense gaze, in the way she held her head. Not cutesy-pretty, but sexy as all hell to him. Her hair in this photo was loose and hung in thick, soft waves around her shoulders. He liked redheads.

Jesse swore. How did he know what he liked in a woman?

How could he remember some things about himself without having a full sense of his own identity or where he came from or where he was going? He plunked the photo down and swiveled around, suddenly desperate to get out of here.

He strode over to the door, rattled the handle.

A young female voice sounded from the other side. "Touch that freaking door again and I'll shoot a hole right through it and you!"

It sounded like that kid Molly. She'd probably do it, too.

He spun around and stared at the bed with its functional bedding, the plain rug on the floor, the dog basket near the fire. Given the photo on the dresser, the red hairs in the bathroom, he figured this must be June's bedroom, yet it didn't feel lived-in. Maybe she was just minimalist.

He strode over to the wardrobe standing against the far wall and yanked open the doors. There was a full-length mirror inside. Jesse stared at himself—his bare chest, the scars on his torso and arm. He leaned closer and examined the thin scar across his chin, then he rubbed his jaw. He needed a shave. A good haircut, too.

He angled his body and lowered the gray sweatpants down his hip to examine the small *D* tattoo in the mirror. The skin around it was still pink.

June's soft, sexy voice curled through his mind: *You're a Devotee, Jesse, carrying concealed, a member of the Cold Plains cult...henchman...did you shoot at them, hurt the mother and her children?*

A wave of sickening guilt washed over him.

He glanced up into his own eyes.

*Are you hiding from yourself, Jesse? Running from something you don't want to remember?*

He flicked the wardrobe door shut and slumped onto the bed, dropping his face into his hands, feeling dizzy, strange.

Did he even want his memory to return?

Was he bad? Had he hurt those twins and their mother?

Was it his fault they were missing?

He honestly didn't know.


Using her GPS, June had tracked back to where she and Eager had found the .40 Beretta.

She now stood in the spot. The light in this dense part of the forest remained dim and mist still fingered through the trees, but the rain had finally abated. It wouldn't be long, though, before the next—and bigger—storm front rolled in. She needed to find Lacy before it did.

June had brought a sealed plastic bag with her. In it was the red shoe and some other belongings she'd taken earlier from Lacy's home. She removed the bag from her backpack now and began to open it. Eager watched attentively. But June stilled when she heard the noise of a twig breaking and then a rustle in leaves. Eager's ears went alert.

June's pulse quickened. She could hear water plopping onto leaves and trickling through cracks in rock. A wind soughed through the treetops, and the trunks of two trees creaked and groaned as bark rubbed together. A squirrel chirped a high-pitched warning at something.

It could have been wildlife breaking the twig, thought June. Or it could be henchmen come to look for their missing comrade. Anxiety torqued through her. She had to work faster.

She held the bag open and let Eager sniff the articles inside.

"This, Eager, find *this*," she said softly.

He nuzzled the articles then started snuffling the ground, living up to his name, eager to find, eager to please. He alerted on something almost instantly, his body wiggling as he pawed at moss.

June crouched down, saw spent shell casings. Her chest tightened. These were 9 mm, not from the .40 Beretta—which meant they hadn't been fired from Jesse's gun, *if* it was truly his. She was beginning to doubt everything now.

She photographed and bagged the casings, this time in paper bags she'd brought from the safe house. If there were fingerprints or DNA on these casings, plastic would compromise the evidence. She put the bags in her pack and began to work Eager up the mountain, through the trees, toward the base of the cliff from where the wind was coming. Eager indicated again, this time on a log about the thickness of an arm.

Around the log June found broken leaves, scuffed loam, crushed ferns. Using a stick, she rolled the log over. On its underside was something dark, sticky, looked like blood. Beside it, another shell casing glinted in the loam—a .40 caliber. This one could have come from the Beretta. And there was more blood on the underside of the leaves.

Had Jesse shot and injured Lacy here? She didn't even want to contemplate the little twins being hurt. She inhaled deeply, trying to temper her adrenaline.

"Good boy, Eager," she whispered, ruffling the fur on his chest. She took hold of his collar and she said, "Do you want to find more? Are you *ready?* Are you ready, boy? *Search!*"

She let him go and he was off like a rocket again. June ran after him, feeling the weight of her backpack, her hiking boots like lead on her feet—she was more tired than she'd realized. Her pager went off again. She stopped, catching her breath as she quickly checked it.

Bo Fargo, yet again.

Had he been to the ranch yet? Seen her truck? Questioned Hannah? But before she could think further, June saw something change in Eager's posture—a slight pop of his head in a new direction, fresh tension in his body, his tail wagging loosely. He was onto human scent, and he was making a beeline for a tangle of thick vegetation along the base of the cliff wall.

He started barking excitedly.

June caught up to him and grabbed his collar. "Lacy?" she whispered into the bushes.

A harsh whisper sounded from inside the brush. "*June? Is that you!*"

Eager started to bark louder.

"Good boy, Eager! Where's Lacy? Show me!"

Panting with excitement, he wiggled his muscular body through the tight brush. June followed. Twigs pulled at her hair, dislodging her peaked hood as she pushed through.

And there they were, Lacy and the twins, huddled together in a small cave hidden by the scrub.

"June! Oh, thank God, it is you!" Lacy threw her arms around June and began to sob with relief as Eager wiggled about them, tail thumping in pride. The twins—Abby and Bekka—sat dead-silent, watching wide-eyed.

"Thank you for coming," Lacy whispered, finally pulling herself away, wiping her eyes with shaking hands. Her face was as pale as a ghost's, her eyes dark holes, her hair and clothes bedraggled. Her little bundle of gear rested next to her children.

June moved quickly toward the kids.

"Are you guys okay?" she said, noting that at least their shelter was dry, and they'd had some food, judging by the granola wrappers and a juice bottle on the dirt next to them. June took the Dorothy slipper out of her pack.

"Look what I brought, girls. One of your Dorothy shoes.

And I know where the other one is, too." June smiled shakily, her own eyes pricking with moisture as she offered the shoe to Abby. "I can get the other one for you, then we can click the heels together and you'll all be in a safe and warm place, okay?"

The child stared with huge brown eyes. Then suddenly she lunged forward, her little arms wrapping as tightly as a limpet around June's neck.

Tears flowed down June's cheeks, emotion racking through her body. She hugged the child as tightly as she dared, closing her eyes, thanking the universe that this time, she hadn't lost a child, but saved two.

It made losing her own little Aiden just a bit more bearable. It gave his short life just a little more value—because of him, because of what had happened to Matt, June was here right now, in this cave, helping this mother and her children. And she knew what she was doing was right.

June pulled back, wiping her face with the back of her hand. She needed to stay strong. She needed to get this little family all the way back through the dark tunnel and into the safe house. Before anyone else arrived.

"What happened, Lacy? Why didn't you show up at the meeting place? Are you *sure* you're all okay?"

"We're just cold, tired, scared. We had some granola bars and juice." She stared to cry again. "I always carry juice and stuff for the twins."

Placing her hand on Lacy's shoulder, June said, "That's what mothers do. It's okay, Lacy. I'm going to get you all somewhere safe, but you need to tell me everything that happened so I know what we're dealing with."

"I—I tried to go to the big black rock sentinel where Hannah said you'd come meet us. We were a bit early, and as we were coming up the trail, we heard voices. I ducked down, told the twins to stay put, and I crept forward. I saw two henchmen through the branches, patrolling the area. They had rifles and handguns."

"They were waiting at the rock sentinel?"

Lacy nodded.

Anxiety punched through June. "How did they know about the rock?"

"I don't know!"

"It's okay, Lacy. I'm not blaming you...I just need to know."

*It could mean we have a mole, or that Hannah's security has been compromised.*

"And you're sure they were henchmen?" said June

"*Yes!* I've seen them before, going into Samuel's underground room at the community center. They both used to work for Charlie Rhodes, before he was shot. The one's name is Jason Barnes—he's good friends with a girl named Monica Pearl—and the other guy they call Lumpy because of how beaten up he's gotten in the past."

June thought of Jesse and his scars.

"And what happened when you saw them?"

Lacy moistened her lips. "We started to sneak away, deeper into the forest. After a while I didn't know where we were. Then it got dark. We hid in the forest for the night, and in the morning we started moving again, but I realized we'd gotten turned around somehow and were lost. That's when the rain started. I wasn't sure what to do. I thought maybe the whole safe house and everything had been compromised, and I knew we'd be in trouble if I tried to find our way back to the village." Tears ran afresh down her cheeks. "I was so scared for my babies."

June comforted her. The twins were holding on to Eager. He was doing his job as a good Labrador: Loving people. Licking their faces. Lacy reached out to touch him, and June noticed that her usually perfectly manicured nails were chipped and broken. Her hair, always so impeccably styled, was in disarray. She looked so vulnerable, and in that moment June hated Samuel and his followers with such raw passion it frightened her.

"Then last night," Lacy was saying, "while we were looking for somewhere dry and warm to hide, they must've heard us, and they started running toward us in the dark. I picked up the twins—that's when we dropped the other shoe—and I tried to run, carrying them. But I fell, and by the time I got up, one of them, another man, was coming from the opposite direction." Her jaw tightened and her eyes glittered. "He... he tried to tell me to stop, asked me where I thought I was going in the dark." She sucked in a huge breath.

"I didn't even give him a chance. I wasn't going to let them take my babies. I picked up a huge log and, I swear, superhuman strength filled my body as I swung that sucker right at his face. I screamed at him that no henchman of Samuel's was going to hurt me or my children. He went down like a rock, but then I heard the other two coming up behind him. The henchman on the ground went for his sidearm, but I just picked up my twins and ran for our lives. I could hear him shooting at us as we went."

"So there were *three* men?"

She nodded.

"And no one came after you once you'd hit one of them with a log?"

"No. I—I guess maybe they stopped to help the hurt guy."

"What did he look like, the guy you hit?"

"I—" She exhaled heavily. "I don't really know. I was in a panic. It was dark. But he was big, tall. Denim jacket."

"Dark or fair, can you remember?"

"Dark hair, definitely dark."

June bit her lip. "Would you recognize him, do you think, if you saw him again?"

"I don't know. Maybe. But I hope I never see him again. I hope he's dead."

"Lacy, we need to move quickly, before Samuel's men come back." June picked Bekka up as she spoke. The child was petite, light as a feather, and June's heart ached as memories of her own child swelled inside her. She sucked air in deeply. She had to keep sharp focus if she was to get these two precious little bundles and their mother out of trouble and into the safe house.

Lacy gathered up Abby.

"Let's click heels to go someplace safe, shall we?" said June to the twins.

Abby smiled and nodded, and Bekka chuckled. It warmed June's heart and it steeled her resolve.

With Bekka on June's hip and Lacy carrying Abby, they edged cautiously out the cave and through the undergrowth. Eager panted happily, taking up the rear. June checked her GPS bearings, and figured they could hug a route along the cliff base and cut back across the forest to where they could access the tunnel.

They reached the cave house by noon. An hour later, the twins had been fed, bathed and were sound asleep in the room that functioned as a nursery. There was a bed in the nursery that Lacy would use, too. But she was still wound up on adrenaline and was now sitting with June and Sonya and Tiffany at the big wooden table in the kitchen, a large mug of herbal tea cradled in her hands.

Molly was back on her guard shift outside Jesse's door, and Davis was doing another round of sentinel duty at the canyon entrance. Brad was sleeping so he could take up a night shift if necessary. A two-way radio rested on the table within June's reach.

Lacy knew Sonya—a soft and rounded woman in her

forties who'd "disappeared" from the Cold Plains hardware store—fairly well. She also knew Tiffany, Brad's mother. Tiffy was a secretary at the school. Molly and Davis she'd seen around town. Cold Plains was a small and intimate community, and every good Devotee attended Samuel's seminars.

"I can't believe you got them all out, that they're all *here,*" Lacy said in wonderment, her gaze scanning the room.

Above the kitchen table hung a huge chandelier made of antlers. Other lamps had hide shades. June was a vegetarian. She'd have preferred the decor to be, as well, but it was the least of her concerns right now.

"How do you get electricity in here?" said Lacy, looking up at the chandelier.

"Solar panels, up on the cliff," answered June

"This place is so awesome—it's kind of artsy, yet rugged. I really love it."

"Lacy, I need you to—"

But suddenly Lacy began to cry. "I just don't know what's going to happen to my coffee shop now, the staff…it had all seemed so perfect, the town, the people. I so *badly* wanted to believe in it all. I feel so cheated, so deceived. So damn angry that I let myself get sucked up like that."

"Lacy." June placed her hand on the young woman's arm. "Your reaction is normal. I'm going to start you on some exit-counseling and then we'll get you into a program where you can talk to people who understand exactly what you're going through right now. They'll help you work through everything you're feeling, and you're going to be fine. Abby and Bekka are going to be fine. The FBI is finally going to get something to nail Samuel. They *know* he's bad, they *know* what he's doing—it's just a matter of finding evidence they can use in court to effectively prosecute him. He's smart, but the noose is tightening. In the meantime, I need you to do something for me. I need you to be strong, okay?"

Lacy glanced up, wiped her eyes. And June could see the resolve in her face. This young woman, a social butterfly who loved material things, had chucked it all to save her kids and herself. She'd made a bold move, braver than many in town were capable of. June's heart went out to her, and it bolstered her own resolve.

"What you've done, Lacy, gives me faith in what we're trying to do. It makes me believe we're going to see Samuel and his sick empire taken down."

Lacy bit her lip and nodded.

June leaned forward. "But there is just one more thing I need you to do, Lacy. Eager and I found an injured man in the forest last night. He'd fallen down a ravine and had a bad gash across his forehead. He can't recall what happened and he doesn't know who he is."

Lacy's face went sheet-white. *"Henchman?"*

"I can't be sure. He does have a tattoo—"

"And you brought him in here! Where my twins are!"

"Lacy, easy. There are some things about him that don't add up. I need you to see if you recognize him."

Her eyes, unwavering, huge, glared at June.

"Will you come take a look at him, Lacy?"

"I can't!" Her hands pressed flat on the table. "I just can't."

"You can, Lacy. He's hurt, he's lost his memory and he's unarmed. You're safe here. I'll have my weapon with me. Molly will be right outside the door with the shotgun. And I swear, Eager will take him down if he so much as even tries to lift a finger against us."

Doubt flickered through Lacy's features. "June, please, don't make me do—"

"I'll bring Brad and Tiffany and Sonya in with us. I want you all to take a real hard look at this guy and tell me if you might have seen him in Cold Plains before. There'll be safety in our numbers."

June wanted to watch Jesse's face, too, when she brought Lacy and the others in to see him. She'd be looking for a flicker of recognition in his eyes, anything that might indicate he was lying about his memory loss.

The group waited outside June's locked bedroom. Lacy fidgeted nervously. June took a deep breath and rapped on the door.

"Jesse—I'm going to come in," she yelled. "Can you go sit on the bed, please, and stay there while we enter? I have some people I want you to meet."

Silence.

*"Jesse?"*

"Yeah, yeah, I hear you," he yelled back, and June could hear the irritation in his voice. "I'm on the bed, sitting nice and still. You can come in now."

"I am armed," she warned, nerves skittering through her stomach suddenly. "And so is the guard who will remain right outside your door. Try anything and you're dead, understand? Because I *will* kill you rather than let you hurt these people here."

"I said I hear you," he growled from inside.

She drew her Glock and unlocked the door. Gun leading, Eager in a tight heel at her left side, June stepped inside.

But she stalled at the sight of him sitting on her bed.

He'd put on the white T-shirt Davis had left for him, and it was stretched taut across his honed pecs. His hair had dried into a roguish tumble and his indigo-blue eyes crackled with anger. His whole body seemed to vibrate with a quiet electricity.

June swallowed and met his gaze as she motioned for Lacy to step inside.

His eyes narrowed slightly at the sight of Lacy, but his features betrayed nothing else.

*"It's him!"* hissed Lacy, grabbing June's arm. "He's the one who tried to stop me. He shot at us."

"Are you sure?"

"Damn right, I'm sure. You bastard!"

"You can leave now, Lacy. Tell the others to come in."

Brad and Tiffany entered the room, followed by Sonya. Both Molly and Davis had already told June they didn't recognize Jesse.

"Have you seen him before?" June asked, her attention fixed on Jesse's face.

There were murmurs of denial.

"Thanks, guys, you can go. Tell Molly to stay outside with the gun."

"Are you sure, June?" Brad whispered, casting a leery glance at Jesse, who sat totally motionless, muscles taut.

"I'm sure."

Once she was alone with him, she said, "That was Lacy. I found her and the twins—"

"Congratulations." His voice was bitter.

"She told me that you tried to block her escape. She hit you across the face with a log, then you shot at her while she fled. I found a log with blood on it, and spent casings, .40 caliber, likely from your Beretta."

He glowered at her.

She felt hot.

"Why did you try to kill Lacy and her children, Jesse?"

"I didn't."

"How can you say that with such unequivocal assertion, yet you can't recall anything about what happened preceding the blow to your head?"

He lurched up, neck wire-tense. "Because I know, dammit! I just *know*…I don't kill people!" He pointed at the door. "Especially not a woman and her children." His hand went suddenly to his brow.

"*What,* Jesse, *what* are you remembering?"

He inhaled deeply. "Look, maybe I have some recall of a brunette and her kids running through the dark, but I feel no urge inside me, no whisper, not one damn thing that tells me I wanted to, or needed to, or did anything to hurt that woman. Nothing. Just…just…" He turned away.

"Just what?" June said.

"I can't place it." There was dejection in his voice now. "But I feel guilt. I feel responsible for something awful that involves a woman, maybe not her, maybe some other woman."

He turned back and his eyes met June's. The raw honesty in them took her aback and her heart clenched. She'd seen a similar look of need, anguish, desperation, in Matt's eyes when she'd told him to choose between her or his religious cult. It was the night before he'd kidnapped Aiden from day care and fled with him into the wilderness.

June had never seen either alive again.

If she'd understood the desperation in Matt's eyes, if she'd been kinder, if she'd sought proper therapy for him, he and Aiden might still be alive. She tried to swallow the sudden sharp surge of emotion swelling inside her, but couldn't.

"There you have it," Jesse said. "I'm opening up, being as honest as I can. What in hell else can I do?" He sank back down onto the bed.

Empathy swelled through June. She sheathed her Glock, and tentatively sat on the edge of the bed beside him.

"Jesse?" she said gently.

He didn't look at her.

She reached out, placed her hand over his.

He stared at her hand, her pale skin against his dark tan, then he looked slowly into her eyes, and she imagined the warmth of his lips against hers. June's stomach swooped and heat pooled low in her belly.

Her raw, physical response to him shocked her. What on earth was going on with her?

A wry smile twisted his lips. "You know what? When I woke up in your bed I thought I was drowning, but then I saw your face and I thought I was seeing an angel. You were surrounded by warmth, light. It made we want to come back up."

Her cheeks went hot. She wanted to remove her hand from over his, but couldn't.

He glanced around the room. "Now I'm in some prison."

"Just until we know who you—"

"I'm not talking about these walls, I'm imprisoned in my own head. What if I never find out who I am? What if this has more to do with a psychological block than an injury to my brain? What if I'm running from something inside myself?"

Silence filled the space between them, loaded, simmering. His skin was hot under her fingertips. He leaned closer, too close. "What does that tell you about me, June?" he whispered.

She got up quickly, heart racing. "I'm just a paramedic, not a doctor. Or a psychologist."

He stared at her for several beats, and June knew he'd seen the unbidden flare of lust in her eyes. She felt naked. Afraid, suddenly, at what was happening inside her.

"I need to talk to Lacy again," she said, making for the door.

"You can't hold me here."

June paused, hand on the doorknob. "I won't, not for long. I'm going to bring in the FBI."

"I don't want to see the feds."

"If you're innocent you won't have anything to worry about, right?"

"I told you, June, I don't know why I feel guilt. Maybe I have done something bad. Maybe I've broken the law in some small way. But I'd like to know who I am, and what I did, before you turn me in."

"You need to see a proper doctor, Jesse. The FBI can help with your ID and with getting you medical care."

"June, help me figure it out before turning me over to the feds."

She scrubbed her hand over her brow. He could be a con artist, playing her. Her gaze flickered to the photo on mantel. Jesse followed her eyes.

"Where is he—your husband?" he said.

She tightened her mouth. She shouldn't answer. That's how they did it—con artists. Little by little, they found your weak points, zeroed in. Then they had you. It's how Samuel had done it with every one of his Devotees.

"He died," she said quietly. "Five years ago."

"You still wear a wedding band."

"To remember why I do what I do."

"What exactly is it that you do, June?"

Without answering, she stepped out the door, locking it behind her.

And June realized her hands were shaking.

Jesse stared at the closed door, heart banging hard against his ribs.

She was a widow—why did it mean so much to him?

His thumb worried his own naked ring finger and desperation swelled in his chest, followed by an indescribable sense of loss and loneliness.

He needed to find the reasons for his feelings of guilt and remorse, and he had to do it before June brought in law enforcement. And he sure wasn't going to find them holed up in here. If he was going to find answers anyplace, it would be in Cold Plains. Jesse needed to go there, and he had to find Samuel. Everything was tied to Samuel.

He lurched to his feet, banged on door. "June!"

No response.

He banged again, then jiggled the lock.

"I'll shoot your ass off!" came Molly's voice.

Jesse didn't doubt it.

He was trapped. At June's mercy. In some cave room. Inside his head.

# *Chapter 4*

June heard him banging as she went down the passage and her jaw tightened, hands fisting at her sides. She wasn't going to be able to contain him in there much longer. She could even face legal implications down the road. Her pager sounded again.

Tension strapped tighter across her chest.

Now that she'd found Lacy, she needed to head down the mountain, back to Cold Plains, to her job. What in hell excuse was she going to give Bo Fargo?

She couldn't tell him she was out of pager range. Although there were dead cell-phone zones in these mountains, the pager system had greater reach.

She entered the living room, which opened out onto the kitchen. Gray light streamed down from skylights and a fire crackled in the stone hearth to ward off the underground coolness that permeated the cave house. It was safe to burn wood now, with the cloud socked low over the mountains—

no telltale smoke would be seen from afar. Otherwise, they burned only at night.

June found Lacy pacing in front of the fire, rubbing her arms in a nervous gesture.

"I need sleep, June—but I can't rest with that man in the same house as my twins. I just can't." Accusation, bitterness filled her eyes. "I don't know why you brought him here. Maybe I should have stayed in Cold Plains. At least if I'd stuck it out with Samuel my children would be safe."

June took hold of Lacy's shoulders. "Look at me, Lacy. That's exactly where Samuel gets his power—by subtly threatening violence or death for disobeying him. He's a sociopath. He's sick—evil. And his is the worst kind of mental abuse. It's no way to live, and you know it. You did the right thing, for your children, for yourself, for your future. I'm going to get you into an exit-counseling program real quick, okay? Which will mean moving you out of the house as soon as we can."

"I thought you did the counseling yourself."

"I do some of the initial work, yes, but I want you to get out of here and into a good program as soon as is feasible."

She sniffed, wiping her nose. "Why? Because I'm more vulnerable than the others?"

"No, Lacy, it's because you've been through an incredibly stressful experience in those woods, and you have your children to think of. You *all* need critical-incident stress counseling as much as you need deprogramming work. Your fear right now is your worst enemy."

Tears filled Lacy's eyes and June hesitated over what she was going to say next, but decided she had to press forward. "Lacy, I need you to walk me through what happened in the woods just one more time. Can you do that?"

Lacy's mouth thinned.

"Please," June said. "Come sit here by the fire. I know you're tired, but this is important."

Lacy lowered herself into a chair next to the hearth, her hands clutching the armrests. June drew up an ottoman, sat in front of Lacy and took her hands. They were ice-cold. Her face was ghost-white.

"Close your eyes," June said gently. "Try to go back to when you first saw the two men near the rock sentinel. What did the air feel like on your face?"

Lacy was silent for a few minutes, then she inhaled deeply.

"It felt damp, full of moisture."

"What could you smell?"

"Soil. Pine needles…" She hesitated, then smiled. "And cherry. Bekka was eating a candy. She smelled like sugar and artificial cherry flavor."

"This is good, Lacy, really good." June was careful to keep her voice calm, soothing. "Now you see the two men—tell me what you're seeing."

"I'm looking at them through bushes—berry bushes, I think. The boughs from the conifers are hanging low. I'm peering through them."

"What's the ground underfoot like?"

"Squishy. Quiet. No noise giving us away."

"Are you holding the twins now?"

She shook her head. "I told them to wait a few yards back. They were so quiet in the forest, the two of them. They must've read my fear." A tear slipped out from under her lashes. "I guess that's where Abby dropped the first shoe."

"And that's where I found it, Lacy. I took it and planted it on the east flank of the hill so they'd think you went in that direction. That's where Bo Fargo, his men and the other SAR volunteers are searching right now. They don't know you're here. You're safe."

Another tear slipped out from under Lacy's lashes and

tracked slowly down her pale cheek. "I saw Jason Barnes and that guy Lumpy."

"Monica Pearl's friend?"

She nodded. "They were standing near the tall black rock sentinel where Hannah told us to wait for you. From there you were supposedly going to lead us to the safe house. But we were early."

June swallowed. "And Jason and Lumpy had guns?"

"Rifles and pistols in their holsters. They were pacing in front of the rock, as if waiting for someone—me—to arrive."

"And you never told a soul you were coming here?"

"Not even Gemma Johnson, and she's the one who helped me see the Devotees for what they really are."

A sinister sense unfurled in June. She had to check on Hannah, see that nothing had happened, or that her cover hadn't been blown. Glancing at the clock on the mantel above the fireplace, she said to Lacy, "And that's when you backed away, sneaked off into the woods."

"Yes."

A banging resounded from down the corridor—Jesse trying to get out. Molly could be heard yelling back at him. Tension wound tighter.

"Let's go right to where you encountered the man in the denim jacket. What was the scent in the forest like there?" June said, trying to get her to go deeper in a form of cognitive interview.

"Still wet, loamy. It was raining heavily, and it was dark, misty. He…the man, just appeared, looming out of the forest, blocking my way. I—I guess his backpack made him seem even bigger than he was."

June's heart kicked. "Backpack?"

"A large one. Like one of those backcountry camping things you take when you go out for a couple of days, with a tent and sleeping roll."

June frowned. There had been no backpack near Jesse. Eager would have found it. Could Jason and Lumpy have taken it? Did it have identification in it?

Blowing out a deep breath, June asked calmly, "What was the first thing Jesse said to you when he appeared in the dark?"

"He…held up the palms of his hands, like this," Lacy said, lifting her hands. "And he said, 'Whoa, where are you off to in such a hurry?' Then he looked at my twins, and he—" Lacy paused, surprised. "He appeared startled, concerned."

"As if he didn't expect to see you and your kids in the dark, rainy woods?"

"God, maybe." She opened her eyes and put her hands to her face. "I…didn't notice that at the time. I just dropped Bekka and Abby on the ground, lifted the first thing I could find, a log, and swung it at him."

"And what did he do then, exactly?"

Lacy made a motion, arms defensively going up to her face, ducking back.

"He ducked from you?"

"I guess. I was in panic, not thinking clearly."

"Close your eyes again, Lacy. Tell me what happened next."

She inhaled deeply. "I yelled at him, saying, 'No henchman of Samuel's is going to hurt my babies.'"

"You said all those words?"

Lacy nodded. "He reeled from the blow and then went down like a rock. I heard the others coming from behind him, crashing through the woods. I dropped the log and picked up Bekka and Abby, one on each hip, my bag over my shoulder, and I just ran. He started shooting at me."

"Did any bullets hit near you?"

"I was too busy running to notice. It was dark. I didn't

want to fall. My only instinct was to get away as fast as I could."

June thought of the .40 caliber shell casings she'd found near the log with blood on it, not far from where Jesse appeared to have fallen down into the ravine. The 9 mm casings were a distance away from that spot.

She bent forward. "Lacy, was there *any* chance Jesse could have been shooting at the other two men and not you? *Could* he have been trying to protect you instead of hurt you? And they fired on him because of it?"

Tears ran fast down Lacy's face now. "I—I suppose…"

"Lacy, listen to me, you did a great thing. And thank you for doing this. Now go try and get some sleep."

Lacy's gaze darted nervously to the passage that led to June's room.

"I can't sleep with him in here."

"He might not be a bad guy, Lacy. You just told me that yourself. We have to give him the benefit of the doubt. He might be lost and in trouble, too."

"We don't know for sure."

*We sure as hell don't.*

"That's why we're going to keep him locked up with a guard outside that door until the FBI takes him away. I'll call Agent Hawk Bledsoe when I go into town."

"You're *leaving?*" Panic showed in her face.

"I need to put in an appearance, cover my bases. It might take some hours, but you'll be safe with everyone else here."

Lacy got up from her chair. "Are you sure?"

"Hundred percent." June forced a smile. "Trust me, everything is going to work out fine."

June watched the young woman walk out of the living room. She wished she believed her own words.

A white polo shirt enhanced Samuel Grayson's tan, which in turn brought out the vivid green of his eyes. His dark hair was impeccably cut—he was movie-star handsome, and he knew it as he stood in front of his office window waiting for Mayor Rufus Kittridge to arrive. He'd positioned himself so the sun coming through the window would backlight him. It gave him an edge and sent a subliminal message of superiority, godliness. He used lighting to similar effect when he gave his seminars.

A bottle of his Cold Plains Creek "tonic" water had been carefully positioned on his desk beside a clean glass. The creek was the reason Samuel had chosen Cold Plains to establish his business five years ago. Legend dating back centuries claimed water from the creek possessed rejuvenating and healing properties. It was this legend that Samuel sold.

His Devotees bottled the creek water for him out of a sense of duty to their community. And he sold the bottles back to them at $25 a pop, usually at his seminars where peer pressure helped them fork over the dollars. Samuel personally pocketed a hundred percent of the profits. He was now shipping a set quota of bottled water to other towns, too. It was a nicely growing concern.

A rap sounded at his oak door.

"Come in!"

Mayor Rufus Kittridge, in his fifties, limped into the room. His face was round, friendly, and the touch of gray at his temples bespoke experience. The limp was all that remained from injuries sustained in a car-bomb attempt on his life three months ago. Jonathan Miller, the demolitions expert responsible for the bomb, had since been taken into custody in Cheyenne.

"Rufus!" Samuel said warmly as he stepped forward and clasped the man's hand.

The mayor had a firm grip and easy smile. Everyone in town knew him to be a keen Devotee, but few knew their congenial mayor also oversaw two groups of Samuel's militia-style enforcers. One of the groups was headed by Lumpy Smithers, who'd taken over from Charlie Rhodes after Charlie was shot during an FBI raid on the community center. The other group was headed by the deceptively sweet Monica Pearl. Compartmentalization was key to keeping the unsavory—but necessary—deeds committed by the groups at a legal arm's length from Samuel. If the FBI ever got evidence on any of the murders, it would be Rufus, Monica and Lumpy who went down—nothing would stick to Samuel. He was incredibly careful about that.

But he *was* worried right now.

Special Agent Hawk Bledsoe and his FBI team were closing in. On top of this, a total of eleven Devotees had disappeared without a trace in the past three months. And these were *not* "disappearances" sanctioned by him.

Samuel had begun to fear that he had a mole—possibly even a network—working on the inside to get vulnerable Devotees out of Cold Plains, and he'd heard rumors of a safe house.

Under Samuel's orders, Rufus had engaged eighteen-year-old Molly Rigg to pose as a Devotee desperate to get out, and it seemed to have worked—Molly had vanished. But she'd made no contact with Rufus or his men, and Samuel was beginning to fear she'd been deprogrammed. The idea enraged him.

And now Lacy Matthews and her kids had gone missing. The whole town was abuzz with talk of her disappearance from the coffee shop, which was a gathering place, and Samuel needed to quell the fire, make an example of Lacy and her twins, fast.

This was why he'd summoned Rufus to his office.

Before she'd vanished, Lacy had written some words on a notepad in the coffee shop and then ripped off the page.

However, the imprint of her words had remained on the pad. They'd read: "Black rock sentinel, west flank @ 7:00 p.m."

Police Chief Bo Fargo's men had found the notepad, and Fargo had reported the find to Samuel.

He cut right to the point. "Are you sure your men were waiting at the right location?"

The smile on Rufus's face faded.

"It's the only big black rock on the west flank that could be called a sentinel. Lacy never arrived. My men found her around 1:00 a.m. She was screaming at a stranger in the woods but fled as my guys approached. The stranger fired on my guys. One of his bullets hit Jason Barnes in the neck. Lumpy Smithers returned fire. He thinks he hit him because he fell down into a ravine."

"*Thinks* he hit him?"

Rufus remained silent.

Samuel smiled benignly. "Did they look for him?"

"Lumpy made the decision to bring Jason into the hospital right away—he was hurt bad."

Samuel inhaled, slowly. "I presume they got a good look at this stranger's face?"

"No, they did not—"

"What do you mean?"

Rufus moistened his lips.

"It was dark, raining," he said. "The situation was fluid. Lumpy returned to the site where the man had gone down the ravine, but there was no one there."

"So the Matthews woman escaped, and so did this unidentified stranger?"

Rufus cleared his throat. "We do have his backpack—he dropped it."

"Any ID in it?"

"No." Rufus eyed the water on Samuel's desk. "The pack contained food, maps, survival blanket, tent, sleeping bag—

he appears to have been on an extended hike through the wilderness. But no ID."

Samuel opened the bottle of water on his desk as he spoke, poured a glass, then sipped without offering any to Rufus. "The priority was to get the woman and her twins, not Jason Barnes," he said calmly.

Rufus met his gaze. "Jason's condition was critical."

"Damn!" Samuel slammed his glass down. "Jason's not likely going to make it out of ICU, anyway. He's going to die, *and* the woman got away! Get back out there, find her!"

"We're looking. One of the kids' shoes was found on the east flank of the mountain," said Rufus. "We have police and SAR crews combing that area."

"The rock sentinel is on the west flank, and you said your men saw her on that west flank at 1:00 a.m. How do you explain the kid's shoe on the east side?"

"Maybe she fled in that direction."

"Get back out onto the west side with a search party of your own. I want that woman, and I want that stranger. Dead or alive. And keep it quiet that you're looking on that side, understand?"

"Yes, sir." Mayor Rufus Kittridge did not look a happy man.

"And what about Molly Rigg? What happened to our damn mole!"

Rufus smoothed his hand over his hair. "We're still waiting for contact."

Samuel abruptly turned his back on Rufus and stared out the window. It was the mayor's cue to leave.

But as Rufus reached the thick oak door, Samuel said suddenly, "Who found the red shoe on the east flank?"

"June Farrow and her K9."

He did not turn around to face the mayor. "Is she there with the search party now?"

"I would assume so."

Rufus Kittridge exited and closed the door quietly behind him.

Samuel stared into the street. Smiling people walked the sidewalk, greeting each other with respectability. They were his people, it was his town, and it was a clean one—nothing like it had been five years ago before he'd run the drunks and cowboys out.

These people had a lot to thank him for, and he was not going to see a group of renegades taking him down. He made a mental note to ask Fargo about June Farrow and the red shoe.

June attended most of his motivational seminars, but she was not yet a full Devotee. It was time she came to a personal consultation. He wanted to get inside Ms. Farrow's pretty red head—she was a dark horse, newish in town. Samuel didn't feel he knew her well enough.

He glanced at his gold designer watch. It was time for his specially scheduled seminar entitled How to Identify the Enemy Within and Stop It from Sabotaging Efforts to Be the Best You.

June raced up the bank to where Bo Fargo and the SAR team had set up command. Fargo was talking to one of the volunteers under a temporary awning where maps, a coffee urn and radios littered a portable table. It was spitting rain again, more big black clouds rolling in over the mountains.

Fargo caught sight of June and turned to face her as she approached.

He was a big and imposing man in his fifties who'd been widowed mysteriously some years ago.

"I've been trying to reach you," he said, his watery blue gaze running over her.

"I'm sorry, Bo," she said, breathless. "Eager was bitten by

something yesterday and I had to take him to the vet over in the next town."

*"Bitten?"*

"I don't know what got him. He swelled right up. He couldn't breathe. I administered antihistamine but he just got worse—"

"Your truck was still at Hannah's place."

So he'd been to look. This was not good.

"I was too stressed to drive. I got a ride from Hannah."

"What's wrong with the vet in Cold Plains?"

"The local vet and I have had—" She inhaled, her brain racing. "Look, it's personal, Bo."

"How so?"

June reminded herself Fargo was a Devotee, one of Samuel Grayson's main men. Everyone was supposed to get along happy-happy in this smiling facade of a town, and it was making her so damn tired and angry.

"The vet and I have different perspectives on treatment," she said quietly. "But it's not something we can't work out as we move forward. In fact, I'm going to go around and see him again later, because it's so much easier keeping all our business in town." June forced a smile. "I learned that the hard way last night. The vet in the town over is not all he's cracked up to be, either."

"Who is he? Which town?"

She glanced at her watch. "Look, Bo, I really need to get to this special seminar Samuel is putting on." She met his gaze. "I got a serious shock with Eager and I could do with some motivational bolstering right now. Since I don't have my dog with me, can you manage today's search without us, while I go sit in on the seminar?"

Bo Fargo studied her. She knew she looked like a wreck.

"I've been in a state," she said for emphasis.

"How's the dog now?"

"He's going to be okay. Vet is keeping him overnight to be sure."

His watery eyes narrowed—he wasn't totally buying her story. She was on thin ice here.

"I'm beat, Bo. I just—"

"Go," he said. "Leave things to us."

She took the gap and rushed off, feeling his eyes burning into her back as she went. He was going to put her under a microscope for sure now. It was just a matter of time before he found something.

"Samuel will be pleased to see you!" Fargo yelled behind her.

June hesitated at something in his tone, then decided not to look back as she hurried toward her truck.

June slipped quietly into the back of the community-center auditorium. She was a few minutes late, and the audience was already being held rapt by the charismatic man striding across the stage as he spoke—no one even glanced her way as she quietly opened the back door. But Samuel noticed her entrance. He stopped on the stage and smiled, as if right at her.

June felt a little punch to the chest.

She nodded her head and smiled back, hatred filling her body. But she needed to put in an emergency appearance to shore up her cover with Samuel. Her facade had started to slip—the stakes were death.

This was Jesse's fault, she thought as she edged along the crowded back row of the auditorium and took a vacant seat, her heart racing.

"When you become the best you that you can be—" Samuel was saying into his mike "—it can arouse feelings of envy and inadequacy in others who have not yet attained this change for themselves."

He stilled, faced the audience. Silence hung. The audience, almost imperceptibly, leaned forward.

The lights dimmed slightly, while a single spot simultaneously brightened on Samuel. His hair seemed to shine, his shirt turn whiter. His eyes appeared to dance.

He was a true master of subliminal effect, thought June—the bastard.

"We're reformers, all of us here," he said with a wide sweep of his tanned and muscled arm. "We have found a new way of seeing the world. But—" He paused, seeming to meet each Devotee's gaze individually.

"Reformers by their very nature are defined by their adversaries, who feel threatened by the change in status quo—they want to tear down the very houses we build!" His voice rose, and he himself seemed to grow in stature. "They want to break down our community!"

Heads in the audience nodded and there were murmurs of assent.

"And it's appropriate that these adversaries be identified, and the truth of them be told! Our foes are many and they include corrupt and abusive federal officials."

He was referring to the FBI, thought June, Hawk in particular.

Samuel strode smoothly, deliberately, to the other end of the stage, as if pondering something very grave and heavy indeed. "Our foes include corporations, and they include groups who disguise themselves by offering to help Devotees 'escape' the perfection we have created here."

June felt her face warm. She focused intensely on not showing any further outward reaction, but she feared that somehow Samuel had already seen something change in her, even from where he stood.

*Don't be ridiculous, June. You're giving him the same power these Devotees have given him.*

"These incompetent organizations are filled with even more incompetent individuals who want to tear each and every one of you away from the wonderful thing we have built right here, in Cold Plains, Wyoming! Our home!"

Samuel reached for a bottle of Cold Plains water on the podium. The water seemed to sparkle in the spotlight. He poured a glass, set the bottle down.

"These enemies," he said somberly, "also hide among us, I'm afraid. They could be our neighbors." He watched the audience carefully. "They could wear the guise of friends. They could even be members of our own families. And the closer they are to us—" he held up his hand "—the more dangerous they are to our well-being. We must oust them, each and every one, and they must be cast from our souls and our town!"

June's hands tightened in her lap—he was starting a bloody witch hunt! McCarthyism was going to have nothing on this guy, and she was in his crosshairs.

It was dark and still raining by the time June returned to the cave house in the mountains. She was beat, her emotions simmering far too close to the surface. She hugged Eager tightly and put her face in his fur. His doggie scent, his soft Labrador ears, his delight in seeing her always grounded June.

After she'd showered quickly and changed, she went to the kitchen to feed Eager and prepare a meal for her captive. Guilt gnawed at her.

Before returning to the cave house, June had checked in on Hannah, who seemed to think their cover was still intact. But they were all on edge now. June had also tried to call Hawk Bledsoe, but the FBI agent's voice mail said he was out of town.

June had then driven out to the ranch where Hawk stayed

with his new wife, Carly, and Carly's sister Mia. Carly had
informed her that Hawk had flown back to the D.C. field
office and would be gone for a few days. She suggested June
go to the other FBI agents at their cabin in the woods. But it
was Hawk June trusted, and it was his input she wanted. June
decided she'd think on it until morning. Until then, Jesse was
her responsibility, and it weighed heavily upon her.

She'd heard no rumors in town about a missing male, and
after what Lacy had described, and what June had seen on
Jesse's GPS, plus the freshness of his tattoo, she was becoming increasingly convinced that he was *not* one of Samuel's
men.

Then again, after hearing Samuel's seminar today, June
wouldn't put it past him to try to get a mole into their safe-
house system. With eleven of his Devotees suddenly missing now, Samuel knew *something* was going down. And June
couldn't rule out the possibility Jesse could be Samuel's mole,
and that he'd been sent in over the north mountains with a
fresh tattoo as some kind of ruse.

Carrying the tray of food and some clean clothes, June
took a deep breath as Brad, who'd taken over the guard position from Molly, unlocked the bedroom door for her.

She entered and he locked the door behind her.

Jesse was reclined on the bed, shirt off, and he was reading a book. He glanced up. Nerves bit at her.

He made her room seem small, intimate, warm. He made
her feel ridiculously feminine. And the partial nakedness
of his body, the casualness with which he relaxed in her
space, made her ache suddenly for a once-familiar feeling
of having a lover, a partner. Someone, just sometimes, she
could lean on. A team. As she'd once, so long ago now, been
with Matt.

This vignette, irrespective of who he was or where he'd come from, just drove home how lonely June really was.

"It got a bit hot in here." He closed the book, sat up and swung his legs over the side of the bed. "Some fresh air would be nice."

She cleared her throat and approached the bed. "I brought you some clean clothes and some supper," she said, setting the tray on the table. The neatly folded jeans, socks, shirt and underwear she placed in a pile on the bed beside him. His belt lay atop the pile.

He stared at the buckle—the bronze letters: *Jesse.* A strange look crossed his face.

June dug into her jeans pocket and handed him his watch. "I took it off when I stitched you up."

He looked up into her eyes, and she felt a jolt of electrical energy.

"So now I'm allowed to know what day it is, even if I can't see daylight?"

June swallowed, still holding the watch out to him. "I'm sorry, Jesse. It's only…for a short while."

"What're you waiting for? The feds to arrive?"

"You really that afraid of law enforcement?"

Slowly, he reached up, took his watch from her hands. His skin brushed hers as he did. His hand was warm, rough, and the touch sent a wave of goose bumps chasing up her arm. Then suddenly, he grabbed her wrist.

And before she could even think, he had her Glock out of her holster with his other hand.

June cursed her stupidity as panic licked through her stomach.

"June," he said quietly as clicked off the safety, his eyes intense, "I don't want to hurt you, but I *need* to get out of here."

# Chapter 5

Jesse could see the fear and anger in her eyes—fear he'd put there.

"I should have known better than to trust you." Her voice was hoarse.

He could smell her shampoo—she'd just had a shower, and her hair was drying in loose waves over her shoulders; it looked like it did in the photograph on the dresser. She was wearing a soft blue-and-white-checked flannel shirt over a white T-shirt and her narrow jeans were tucked into Ugg boots. Not an ounce of makeup adorned her finely boned features. Apart from the angry flush in her cheeks now, she looked tired.

Compassion mushroomed softly in his chest.

"I need to go to Cold Plains," he said quietly. "I need to find Samuel Grayson."

She swallowed, her gaze flicking to the gun. "Why?"

"Because it might help me figure out why I came here."

"Maybe you're his mole," she said.

"Why would I be wanting to leave, then?"

She was silent for several beats. "I don't know. Samuel is a sociopathic con artist, a master at mental games. Perhaps he sent you in over the mountains to play one of those mental games with me."

"I don't think so, June."

"Maybe you don't *know* so." Her features were tight. "Maybe your amnesia is genuine—you did get a knock on the head. And you could regain your memory, recall why you're here and then hurt the people I'm trying to save."

Jesse got up suddenly and she tensed. He went to the dresser and put the loaded gun on top, then he put on his watch. He walked over to the chair where she'd set the pile of clothes and pulled a fresh white T-shirt over his head.

"I see you found some jeans my size," he said, taking off his track pants.

Her gaze darted between him and the gun on the dresser as he pulled on the jeans and put on his belt. The anger spots high on her cheekbones darkened and confusion crept into her eyes. Be damned if it didn't make her sexier.

"What're you doing?" she said.

"Getting dressed."

She hesitated, then edged toward the dresser, picked up the gun, turned to face him. "Why'd you do that?"

She was shaking slightly.

"Because I can, June. I wanted to show you that I can overpower you if I want to. I *can* hurt people if I choose to." He faced her squarely. "I wanted to prove to you that even when the situation is in my control, I won't hurt you, or anyone else in this house."

She moistened her lips. He could see conflict in her features, and Jesse had an absurd desire to hold her, comfort her, tell her she should get some rest from saving the world.

"Maybe it's just part of your mind game," she said coolly, holstering her weapon.

"Not going to keep the gun pointed at me?"

"There's a loaded twelve-gauge outside that door." She jerked her chin toward the door. "I just have to scream."

He smiled. "You trust me now, even just a little."

"I don't trust you as far as I could throw you."

"But you'll let me out."

She said nothing.

Jesse inhaled deeply. He had to try another tack.

"How far is it into town?" he said

"A few hours on foot."

"You said you were a part-time paramedic. You spoke about a cult of Devotees and this being a safe house. Did you bring the occupants in here—did you rescue them all from Samuel Grayson's cult?"

"Jesse, I—"

"Please," he said. "*Help* me. The more I know, the more it might jog my memory."

She raked her hands over that gorgeous red hair. She was unsure about him, yet she cared, too. She was a good, strong and fascinating person, clearly with a keen sense of duty that kept a fire burning in her.

"June, you said earlier that you do what you do because of your husband—that's why you wear his ring, as a symbol. Can you tell me about him? What happened?"

She glanced toward the photo on the dresser.

"Is that him in that photo? Is that your son?"

Her eyes flashed to him with such a sudden fierce and crackling energy it took him aback.

"If you need anything else," she said coolly, "just call out to the guard outside." She turned to leave, her shoulders tight, and Jesse saw that her hands were fisted at her sides.

"June, please, talking to me might help me figure out who I am. I—I *need* you to talk to me."

She stilled, her back to him. And she stayed like that for several beats.

Jesse came up behind her and he placed his hand on her shoulder. It was slender, her muscles tight.

"June," he said very softly, turning her around, and he saw tears pooled in her eyes.

"Come," he said, sliding his hand down her arm and taking her hand. "Come sit down." He tried to lead her to the bed.

But she shrugged him off and swiped the tears from her face.

"I'm tired," she said crisply. "That's all."

"Tired of doing what you do?"

"Look, it's been a long day." She reached for the door. "Please, just stay in here tonight. I'll have something worked out by tomorrow."

"What were their names—your husband's and son's?"

She seemed suddenly frozen.

"At least you have your memories, June," he said quietly. "I have nothing but the present."

"That's how *he* does it, you know. Samuel finds the chink, then he pries it open, makes you talk, and then he's got you."

"That's not what I'm doing, June."

"And how would I know?"

He hesitated a beat. "You wouldn't."

She studied him, and he could see the intelligence in her features. He also wanted to kiss her mouth. Damn, he wanted to take her in his arms, do a lot more.

But as the thought occurred to him, he was slammed by an image of a dark-haired woman, screaming, in pain. And in his mind he heard a child crying—terrible cries. And he felt desperate, helpless. Responsible. Then there was just blackness—an awful, aching void of nothing.

The blood drained from his head. He reached up, touched his stitches.

"Are you all right?"

Her gaze shot to her. "I don't know."

She hesitated. "I'll talk to you, Jesse, but only if you eat while I do. You need to eat something. Is that a deal?"

He snorted softly at the power shift. "Deal."

June moved to a chair near the stove and sat. Light from the flames inside flickered like soft copper fire over her hair. She released a big breath of air. "I feel bad enough as it is about locking that door—I suppose I owe you. I just wish I could trust you, that I had some kind of proof you don't belong to Samuel."

"Believe me, I'd like to know, too."

"Case rested for locking you up." But a smile curved her lips when she said it, and Jesse's heart stalled for a nano-second.

"You should do that more often," he said quietly.

"What?"

"Smile."

She flushed, and his blood heated. Jesse seated himself at the small table where she'd placed his food. He picked up the knife and fork. "See? Eating."

"My husband's name was Matt," she said quietly. "Matt Farrow."

"He was a pilot?"

She nodded, hands tight in her lap.

"It's difficult to talk about?"

She nodded again, eyes glimmering, her nose going slightly pink. Then she lurched to her feet.

"It shouldn't be," she snapped and began to pace the room, her long legs sexy as all hell in those jeans. An image of getting those sheepskin boots off her flashed through his mind.

On the back of it came the faceless image of the dark-haired woman. His pulse quickened.

"Why shouldn't it be difficult?"

She spun to face him.

"It's been *five* years, Jesse. Matt and Aiden have been gone that long now. I—I've been fine—dealt with it."

"You're still wearing his ring, June."

"I don't mean that I want to forget him. I mean I thought I'd put the grief into perspective, that I'd gone through the stages. But…I don't know. It's just hurting at the moment. I don't know why."

Jesse set his knife and fork down slowly, a sense of loss filling him, as if June was reminding him of something. He heard the baby screaming again in his memory somewhere. Then he saw an image of a hospital. He felt the guilt again. The name Samuel Grayson began to circle in his head.

"Is the food not good?"

He stared at it—vegetable lasagna and salad. "No, it's great, I…thought I was remembering something, that's all." He glanced up at her.

She assessed him for a beat, then reseated herself beside the stove. "My son's name was Aiden," she said.

"How old was he?" Jesse asked quietly

She inhaled deeply. "Jesse, I really don't want to do this, not with you. I'm beat. This whole thing…this day…no sleep…it's just left everything a little raw. I'm not usually like this."

"*What* whole thing?" he said, a kind of desperation rising in him.

She turned her face away from him, stared at the flames in the little window of the stove.

"Finding you," she said finally. "Finding you has messed everything up. I… Jesus, I'm sorry, Jesse, but my actions, the fact I brought you here instead of going on an official search—it's made my cover thin. It could cost lives. And I don't know what the hell to do with you."

"Cost lives?"

She looked at him. "Samuel is dangerous. He's a murderer. The feds know it but they haven't managed to get enough on him to lay charges and prosecute."

He took a bite of his vegetable lasagna, chewed as he digested what she'd said. And in part of his brain he wondered if she was vegetarian. He liked his meat—venison. He stilled. It was another small snippet of revelation. He had a sudden image of blood, warm on his hands. And then it was gone.

"So you work as a paramedic and a SAR volunteer in Cold Plains," he said. "This is your cover. Meanwhile, in the dark of night, you bring people to this…cave place, whatever it is."

"That pretty much sums it up."

"And you were searching for Lacy and her kids when you stumbled upon me."

She nodded. "I should have been on an official search for Lacy on the other side of the mountain—it's a long story. But I couldn't just leave you down that ravine." She swore. "Now a crooked cop is going to look deeper into me and my background and people I care for are going to get hurt or killed."

"June?"

"What?"

"Thank you. For saving my life."

She raised her arms as if in defeat. "And where does that get me—us—now?"

"Maybe I can help you."

Surprise darted through her eyes. Then she said, very quietly, "Jesse, you could still be a mole."

He scooped up the last mouthful of lasagna and chewed, watching her.

"Tell me about Matt," he said.

She slumped back in her chair.

"He was a helicopter pilot who flew SAR missions. It's how I met him, on a search. We married young. Well, I was young. He was quite a bit older than me, and we had Aiden. We were good together." She sat silent awhile. "PTSD is a little-acknowledged fact of SAR life, and there always comes one mission that gets to you for some reason. That day came for Matt, a seasoned veteran, when he was called out to look for another chopper that had gone down in the Cascades. The search turned into a recovery mission. The craft had crashed into the side of a mountain in heavy weather. No survivors. The pilot was a close friend of Matt's—brothers-in-arms kind of thing. And it was a pretty gruesome recovery effort. It cut Matt up big-time."

She sighed deeply. "And it left him questioning the meaning of it all, life. One of his friends suggested Matt go with him to a church meeting. That meeting led to another, and then another, and pretty soon, he was sucked in by a religious cult." Her eyes narrowed and Jesse could see she was struggling.

"It wasn't like Matt was weak," she said. "But what I just didn't get at the time is that you don't have to be somehow weak or stupid to be sucked in by a cult. And there was my guy—an über A-type personality, a total daredevil who was so in control and command of his own environment—being sucked in by the ministerings of some cult leader."

"What did you do?"

She snorted. "I tried to talk sense into him. Then we argued. The arguments got worse. Then I went to some meetings in an effort to see what in hell he was talking about. And—" she shook her head. "I still didn't get why my intelligent guy couldn't just snap out of it. But that's not how it works, I've learned. And then the church wanted money. Matt was starting to dig into our savings, giving everything we'd worked for together to the cult. I'd lost him, Jesse. He spent more and more time away from home. And I began to worry about Aiden. He was only three years old at the time, and Matt started taking him to the church meetings. And when Matt started talking about us all moving onto the church's rural compound in the mountains, I drew my line in the sand. I told him he had to choose between our marriage and the cult, because he was bleeding us dry."

June rubbed her face. "I thought—I honestly believed, at the time—that it was a matter of making a decision, that Matt was strong, and that he would make the right choice. But that evening I was called out on a missing Alzheimer's case. I took Aiden to my mom's house and she promised to get him to day care in the morning.

"When I went to pick him up the following evening, they told me Matt had come earlier in the day and taken him. I knew right away he was taking him to the cult compound. I called the cops. It turned into a huge manhunt. Matt went into the woods. I used the dog I had at the time, tried to track them." Her eyes began to gleam with emotion.

"I tracked the whole night."

She sat silent awhile.

Jesse pushed his plate aside.

"What happened?" he said, his voice hoarse.

She snorted softly. "Matt reached a helicopter base in the next town and he took Aiden with him in one of their choppers. The police took a helicopter up, followed him. I—I knew he wouldn't have taken Aiden up with him unless he was totally desperate, not thinking. Otherwise he'd have known there was a finite amount of fuel, that he'd have to set down, that the police would pick him up when he did."

"He crashed?"

She nodded.

Wood popped in the fire.

"I'm so sorry," he said. He felt lame.

"I learned a lesson that day, Jesse. A brutal lesson about the psychological power of cults. I learned that you can't just snap out of it, that you need professional help to do so. If I'd gone about it a different way, found counseling, helped Matt deal with the real reasons he'd gone to the church in the first place... Because, in retrospect, he was suffering from critical-incident stress. I didn't see it, and he certainly was too macho to talk to me about what was going on deep in his head. I loved him, and I should have found a way to help him. Instead, I gave him an ultimatum that pushed him over the edge. I killed him and my son."

"June—"

She raised her palm and shook her head. "It *is* my fault. I don't care what people say."

"So now you help others out of cults, and you do it in memory of Matt and Aiden." *Or do you do it to try and assuage your own feelings of guilt—is it the only thing you* can *do now, June?*

She nodded. "I learned everything I could after that. And I started working for EXIT, an international network of like-minded professionals and volunteers who help families get loved ones out of cults and into halfway houses, safe places, where they can access deprogramming or exit-counseling. I move around the country, operating safe houses where necessary."

"And that's how you came to Cold Plains?"

"Yes."

"Who brought you here—I mean, which family?"

"In this case the existence of the Devotees came to EXIT's attention via one of the escapees, Mia Finn, who was brought in for deprogramming. She's now the sister-in-law of the FBI agent investigating Samuel. Samuel's believed to be responsible for orchestrating the murders of at least five women and possibly others."

"This is dangerous."

"That's an understatement."

Jesse's respect, his attraction to June, mushroomed.

"I can't believe I'd be working for a guy like Samuel," he said.

"Yet you mentioned his name. You said you had something urgent to do. You have a tattoo."

He inhaled deeply. "I'm obviously here in connection with Samuel, or the town. That's why you need to unlock that door for me, June, let me go and find out why I'm here."

"Let me sleep on it, Jesse. You need sleep, too." She got up and made for the door.

He got up and grasped her wrist. "June—"

She turned. She was so close. And he could see the rawness of the emotion glimmering in her eyes, in the slight pinkness of her nose. Her eyes darkened and he could see physical attraction. The notion hung suddenly, tangible between them.

Fire crackled and popped softly in the stove.

"What?" she whispered, her voice thick, and Jesse was suddenly unable to tear his attention from her lips, the way her breathing was making her chest rise and fall. And before he could even think to finish his sentence, he leaned in and he kissed her mouth.

She jerked back, eyes wide in shock.

But before she could say a word, a loud banging sounded on the bedroom door.

June spun around just as the door was flung open by Brad, shotgun in his hand, his face white.

Sonya was right behind him, her eyes bright with fear, a radio in her hand. Molly was at her side. She pointed straight at Jesse, arm outstretched.

"It's his fault!" yelled Molly. "He brought them here!"

"*What's* his fault?" said June. "What's going on?"

"Davis just called in," Sonya said. "A posse of five henchmen is approaching the rock crevasse that leads to the tunnel. He could hear them talking. He thinks they said something about a mole in the safe house."

"See?" yelled Molly, borderline hysterical. "You shouldn't have brought him here. He's leading them in somehow."

June shot a glance at Jesse

He was tense, eyes narrowed and hard as he stared at Molly.

"It's not possible," June said. "Jesse has no way of contacting—"

Davis's voice crackled suddenly through the radio in Sonya's hand. June took it from her, stepping out into the passageway. Brad started to close the bedroom door.

Jesse placed his hand on the door, stopping it from closing. "June, let me help," he said.

"Are you crazy? It's your fault they're here!" Molly kicked the bedroom door closed in his face, and he heard the key turning in the lock.

His muscles strapped tight in a band across his chest. He jiggled the handle. Locked.

Cursing, he swung around, glared at the windowless rock walls, listening to the sound of urgent talking fade down the passage. He raked his hand angrily over his hair, frustration burning through his blood, and he swore again. He felt as though he'd entered some kind of surreal universe, being trapped in a cave room by a woman and a motley assortment of kids and adults with guns.

He could break down the door, do something rash, which was what he was pumping to do right now, but he had little doubt that that trigger-happy Molly kid would blow him apart with that twelve-gauge before he was out.

Maybe henchmen arriving would be a good thing.

*  *  *

There was better reception in the kitchen where the radio could pick up waves through the windows from the portable repeater June had rigged up outside.

"June to Davis. Can you repeat? What's going on?" June released the key, tension winding tight in the kitchen. She glanced at the others gathered around her.

The radio crackled to life. "Davis to safe house. Five armed henchmen combing the woods." He spoke quietly, as if he wasn't far from the men.

"They came close to the crevasse entrance but veered south before discovering it. I followed them for about two miles. They're actively searching for something with hunting spots—all are armed. Are you getting this, June?"

"Loud and clear. Go on, Davis," June said, releasing the key again.

"I heard one say something about a mole on the inside and that they were waiting for the mole to make contact."

Ice shot down June's spine. She keyed the radio.

"Are you sure?"

"That's what it sounded like. Over."

"Are they still moving south, away from the tunnel entrance?"

"Yes."

"Go back and guard the tunnel entrance, Davis. I'll send someone to relieve you in an hour. Copy?"

"Copy."

Molly's eyes were huge. "Do you want me to go relieve him? I'll go now."

"You need sleep," June said crisply.

"*Sleep*—are you crazy? With them out there?" She flung her arm out in the direction of the hill.

"It's Brad's turn next." June's tone brooked no argument. Molly scowled and stomped out of the kitchen.

June slumped onto a stool at the kitchen counter, heart pounding.

*Maybe Jesse really is a mole.*

The memory of his kiss filled her mind. She thought of the compassion she'd seen in his eyes and sensed in his touch. He *felt* like a good man. Or was she being completely blinded by her physical attraction to him? Was seducing her a part of his game?

June scrubbed her hands over her face, wondering when this job had gotten so damn complicated. She wished Hawk Bledsoe would return. She wanted him to nail Samuel and for this whole thing to be over, because she was wearing dangerously thin.

# Chapter 6

It was morning, early. The rain had stopped and the sun was painting the world that beautiful gold that comes when the angle of the sun is still low. June put on a pot of coffee, feeling exhausted. She'd taken one of the beds in the nursery where Lacy and the twins were sleeping, but she'd lain wide-awake listening to the others breathe, thinking how different the rhythm of a child's breathing was from an adult's, how close this mother and her babies had come to losing their lives.

Were they alive now because of Jesse?

June had also mulled over what Davis had told her when he'd returned to the cave house later in the night. Instead of going back to guard the canyon entrance as June had instructed, Davis had taken it upon himself to follow the posse of henchmen deeper into the woods as they'd beat the bush and panned hunting lights through the trees.

"I definitely heard them say the word *mole*," he'd told June.

"But it wasn't clear that this mole was inside our safe house?" she'd asked.

"No. At first I assumed they meant the mole was in the safe house, and I figured immediately that the mole was Jesse, but as I followed them farther it became blatantly clear that they're no friends of our stranger—they were hunting him. I heard one say Samuel wanted him dead or alive."

"They referred to him by name?" June said.

"No—they don't know who he is."

*So he isn't working for Samuel.*

Adrenaline trilled through June.

"One of them said the stranger shot Jason Barnes. And, June, I heard them say Barnes died from his wound earlier today."

*Jesse had killed him.* June cursed softly. Samuel was not going to let this slide. This whole town was going to blow. "Did you recognize the guys in the posse?" she said quietly.

"Rufus Kittridge was leading the group."

"The *mayor?* Are you serious?"

"Lumpy Smithers was there, too. And Monica Pearl. I saw both their faces when they were momentarily illuminated by the hunting spots, but I didn't get a good look at the others." Davis shook his head as if in disbelief. "Who'd have thought Monica Pearl was one of Samuel's enforcers. She's so…sweet."

And pretty, thought June. That was the danger of Samuel Grayson and his cult. The more clean, friendly, benign the facade—the more sinister what lurked beneath.

"Just before I left them, I heard Mayor Kittridge yelling at Lumpy that he should've gotten a better look at the stranger's face. Lumpy argued it was dark, raining and that Jason was badly injured. Rufus hit back that Samuel maintained Lumpy should have gone after the Matthews woman and her kids instead of trying to save Jason. I swear, June, they were wire-tense, really going at each other. Lumpy sounded real choked about Jason dying."

Davis had also returned with a small, muddy pacifier that he'd found while following the men.

"Maybe it belongs to Dr. Black's baby?" he said.

Dr. Rafe Black's infant son had been kidnapped last month and so far there'd been no leads, no ransom notes, nothing— Rafe was devastated. June made a mental note to go search the area around where the pacifier had been found. Rafe Black was a good man, and he was not a Devotee.

Once the coffee was ready, June poured a mug and set it on a tray along with a toasted bagel for Jesse. Outside the bedroom door she waited while Sonya unlocked it.

"Morning," he said as the door opened. "I take it we weren't invaded last night. Too bad. The enemy might have sprung me."

"They didn't find the tunnel," she said as she set the tray on the table. He'd just showered—his hair was damp. He was wearing jeans, his engraved belt and a button-down denim shirt over a white T-shirt—he looked all Wyoming cowboy, and it was a look that really did it for June.

"I'm sorry about last night," he said quietly.

She glanced at him and knew instantly he was talking about the kiss. Her pulse quickened and her mouth felt dry. All she could think about suddenly was how she'd wanted to kiss him back. Instead, she looked away and fiddled unnecessarily with the napkin on the tray. "It's me who should be apologizing," she said quietly. "For locking you up. But I had to be sure that you weren't the mole who'd brought the henchmen so close last night."

She looked up at him and her heart kicked. He exuded a new kind of energy this morning. Sleep had restored him.

And his eyes crackled with an intensity of focus that made her feel hot inside.

"Either way, you are the reason they came looking, Jesse," she said. "When Davis returned he told me the men were armed and actively hunting you. But it seems no one saw your face the other night and they don't know who you are."

A quiet electricity seemed to ripple through his body. "I'm not sure whether I should be pleased or disappointed," he said.

"It appears you killed one of them, Jesse. A man named Jason Barnes died of a gunshot wound to the neck."

Silence filled the room.

"Jesus," he said softly.

"Samuel is after your blood." She inhaled deeply. "Obviously you don't work for him. I'm really sorry I locked you up. I—I've never done anything like this in my life. It's just—things got desperate."

His gaze went to the door.

"It's not locked. You're free to go."

His attention shifted back to her, eyes intense. He stood slowly and took a step toward her. June's knees felt weak.

"Don't go into Cold Plains, Jesse, please—they'll kill you."

"You said they hadn't seen my face."

"You can't just show up in a town like Cold Plains with stitches on your head and no belongings. They'll instantly peg you for the man they were hunting."

"June, I—"

"*Please,* it could endanger us all."

He studied her intently. "Show me around the house," he said, something dark entering his voice.

A whisper of trepidation feathered over her. "You don't want your breakfast?"

"Not in here. But after a tour of the house I'd love a cup of coffee, if you'll share one with me."

She smiled. "You make it sound like a date."

His eyes held hers for several beats. "June, I am sorry—about the kiss."

"I'm not," she said very quietly, her cheeks warming.

But even as she said the words, she realized the stupidity of them—she was physically attracted to, and quite possibly falling for, a man she didn't know at all. He could have loved ones waiting for him to return, worrying about him. There might be no room in his life for someone like her.

June turned and walked to the door, telling herself she didn't want there to be room for her, anyway—she had a life mission. Falling for a stranger who might wake up and realize he belonged to someone else would break her heart. It was ridiculous even to be thinking like this.

She opened the door and strode briskly down the passage. "Kitchen and main living area are this way," she said coolly.

Jesse entered the living space behind June. A fire burned in a big stone hearth, next to which sat a gaunt, hook-nosed, middle-aged man with wary eyes. He was drinking from a pottery mug. Eager was curled at his feet. The man nodded at Jesse. Eager's tale gave a small thump.

"Morning," the man said.

"This is Davis," June said. "He's the one who followed the hunting party last night."

Davis got up, and Jesse stepped forward to shake his hand. Davis had a firm, wiry grasp. Jesse put him in his fifties, and his eyes were not friendly.

"Those guys want your head, mate, whoever you are," he said to Jesse.

Jesse snorted. "Thanks for bringing back the information. Got me out of the bedroom."

Davis, however, wasn't going to let Jesse off that easy.

"No one knows we have a safe house out in this valley," he

said coolly. "Those henchmen were not looking for a secret crevasse or a tunnel or a cave house. They were looking for you—*you* brought them out onto the west flank. We're just lucky they didn't stumble onto the tunnel. Because if they find it—people are going to die."

"I'm sorry." Jesse didn't know what else to say, and he judged it imprudent to point out that henchmen had already, apparently, been on the west flank searching for Lacy Matthews and her daughters.

Davis reached for his gun. "I'm going to relieve Tiffany, who's out there with a radio right now, watching. But we're not militia. We're not trained for this. We're just ordinary folk who want to get safely the hell out of Cold Plains now."

"We'll have you all moved out of here within the next few days," June told Davis. "That hunting posse didn't find any sign of Jesse. I don't think they're going to come back this way in a hurry."

Davis grunted and left.

"Do you believe that, June?" Jesse said, watching Davis go.

"That they won't be back for a while?" She sighed deeply. "I hope they won't. Because Davis is right. We're not equipped for this.

"This is the kitchen." June stepped into a beam of sunlight streaming down from skylights above and sun flamed like fire on her hair, stalling Jesse's thoughts entirely. And in that instant he wondered if he'd ever come across a more enigmatic or beautiful woman. He liked everything about her— her grace of movement, her strength. Her surety of vision. Her courage. He loved the way she looked. And when she turned to face him in the kitchen—dear God—those clear, summer-sky eyes.

His chest clutched and desire welled sharp and sudden in him, along with a raw urge to make her smile. He wanted to hear her laugh, see the light dance in those eyes. Bottom line, Jesse had an urge to protect her, to help her with this burden she'd undertaken.

Was that the kind of person he was? Or was it his lust speaking?

"Everything in here is run off solar power," she said.

Jesse turned to study the kitchen—the wood cabinetry was high-end, the countertops granite. The windows at the far end of the room were tinted and large and looked out onto a valley of low scrub and pockets of trees. Light fittings were crafted from wrought iron or bone—shades made from what looked like hide. In fact, everything about the place seemed rustic high-end, artistic and wilderness-inspired.

"What is this place?" he said. "It's incredible."

"It was built into the caves by a manic-depressive architect who decided to go survivalist and live off the grid, but in style. There are more rooms this way," she said, holding out her arm.

June led him down another stone passageway into a room that had been equipped as a nursery.

Lacy and her twins were sitting on one of the beds. Lacy had a book in her hands and was reading her girls a story. She glanced up sharply as they entered. The twins seemed to sense tension in their mother and instinctively cuddled closer.

Jesse stilled in the doorway, struck by the vignette. The children were brunettes, like their mother, and identical. And he knew one thing about himself with abrupt certainty: if someone tried to kill this young mother and her children again—he'd shoot the bastard dead.

What did that say about him?

"Hello," he said to the girls, his voice coming out too deep. "My name is—" He glanced at June. "They call me Jesse."

"You're the bad man," said one of the twins

"I...don't think so."

The kids stared at him.

Jesse suddenly felt hot, and a dark cesspool of guilt swirled inside him. With it came twinges of rage, remorse, hurt. A cool sense of betrayal.

He shook himself, wanting to bury the uncomfortable sensations but knowing on some level they were parts of his memory coming closer to the surface of his consciousness, like tiny agitating bubbles in a pot of water ready to break into a boil and release steam. And it scared him to think what lurked down there.

June touched his arm, jolting him back to the present.

"The other rooms are this way."

"It's a big place," he said as she showed him a series of bedrooms, bathrooms and a games room complete with billiard table.

She nodded. "When the architect died, he left everything to his sister, who lives in the town over. She didn't know what to do with the place. It's not legal, no building permits, and there is no road access. Then her sister-in-law, Hannah Mendes, needed a safe house. It was the perfect solution. We heard about Hannah from Mia Finn during her deprogramming sessions. That's where I came in. Hannah is in her seventies, works at the Cold Plains water-bottling warehouse, and she identifies vulnerable cultees and gets them out. They come here, then go into an exit-counseling program." June showed him into a hallway that led to what appeared to be the front door.

Jesse noted a gun rack mounted near the door. A shotgun rested on the wood slats. Beside the rack was a cabinet that held ammunition. The key to the cabinet was in the lock. He saw there were boxes of both shells and slugs in the cabinet.

His gaze shifted down to June's hips, to the Glock in her holster.

She opened a heavy oak door and he followed her out onto

a stone patio covered partially by a rock overhang. The morning sun was warming the valley and the vegetation smelled like summer. A sense of familiarity washed over him, and he was gripped by a powerful notion that he belonged outdoors, that he slept often under the stars. That he needed to roam the mountains. On the back of that thought rode the dark, cold feelings of guilt again. Jesse began to itch with irritability, impatient to get deeper inside his head, find the answers.

"This is Hidden Valley," June said. She was standing next to him, and he could smell her shampoo again. Eager was at her feet, sunlight glinting off his black fur. Jesse walked to the end of the patio where a small creek burbled, the sun warm on his shoulders. It was a calm place, a healing place, he thought.

"How did this architect bring in the building materials for the house?" he said.

"Chopper. He had a pilot friend. He also had wealth."

Jesse whistled softly. "It's a perfect place to hide." He turned to June. "You said you move people from here into exit-counseling. How do the safe-house occupants get out of the valley from here?"

"We have to hike out that way, to the next town." She nodded to the mountains. "It's a fair trek, takes several hours. I've learned exit-counseling myself, so I start that right away. There's a town called Little Gulch on the other side of that mountain. EXIT has stationed a psychologist there who handles counseling and helps with transitions."

Jesse put his hand to his temple and felt the line of stitches. His head was beginning to hurt.

"You okay?"

"I… The idea of needing to get someone into deprogramming feels familiar somehow."

He saw a flicker of nervousness in her eyes. "Maybe you came here trying to get someone out, Jesse. Could you have been thinking of faking your way in with a false Devotee tattoo?"

He frowned, the image of a slight, dark-haired woman curling into his mind again. He felt himself fiddling with his ring finger and a wave of nausea hit him.

"I have no idea," he said quietly. The woman in his mind began to scream again. And this time he saw flames. He felt the heat of fire, heard it crackling, consuming, swallowing her. His mouth felt dry. He wanted June to shut up.

June saw a haunted look creeping into Jesse's eyes and the despair in his features made her chest tighten. She couldn't help it—she reached out, placed her hand on his arm.

"Hey," she said. "It's going to be okay. It'll come back to you."

"Maybe I don't want it to," he whispered. "Maybe I am some kind of bad guy, June. Maybe I've done something terrible."

And again that little whisper of doubt curled through her. "Jesse—"

But before the next word could come out of her mouth, screaming came from the bushes.

They both spun around to see Brad crashing out from the brush, his eyes wide with fear. Eager began to bark excitedly as Brad ran toward the patio yelling. "Help! Molly's in trouble!"

Adrenaline punched through June. *The henchmen—they must be here!*

She rushed indoors, grabbed the shotgun from the rack and hurriedly unlocked the cabinet, reaching for a box of shells.

Brad reached the patio and bent over, bracing his hands on his knees as he tried to catch his breath. "Bears!" he said. "Molly's trapped by a mother bear and her cubs."

June froze, gun in hand. *"Bears?"*

Brad stood up. His face glistened with sweat. "They have Molly cornered at that end of the valley." He pointed toward the mountains.

"She said she was going to pick some berries. I followed her—I wanted to see where the berries were. But there's a big bear and her cubs stalking her."

June began to load the gun. Jesse placed his hand on her arm, stopping her.

She shot him a glance.

His eyes were narrowed. "Give it to me," he said, grabbing the gun from her with force.

Shock licked through June. "No, Jesse! What the—"

He turned away from her and went back inside. She rushed after him, anger spearing into her.

"What do you think you're doing? Give that back to me—Molly's in trouble."

He reached into the cabinet and took out a box of slugs. He reloaded the gun.

"Buckshot is useless against a charging bear," he said, quickly loading the gun. He clicked it in place. "You need slugs. Even so, you have to hit just right or you're dead."

She stared, dumbfounded.

"Come," he said. Then he nodded at Brad. "You, too. We stick together in a group—it'll make us look big to the bears. Follow my lead, and whatever you do, don't run. Which way is she? Show me," he said to Brad.

Brad led them to a narrow trail through the low scrub.

Jesse began to hike into the bush.

"Wait!" June quickly grabbed Eager's collar and took him back to the house. "I'm taking him back. I don't want him to get hurt," she said.

"Catch up to us, then," Jesse called over his shoulder.

June ran back to the cave house with Eager and yelled for Sonya to look after him.

"How do you know this stuff about bears?" June said, breathless, when she caught up to Jesse and Brad.

"I don't know. I just do."

June struggled to keep up with Jesse. He moved with ease and stealth through the wilderness, like a great big mountain lion, all powerful muscle. Brad was panting heavily behind her, crashing through brush clumsily.

They crested a ridge. The sun was warm on their backs.

Jesse pointed. "There they are."

There was a reverence in his voice that made June look up at him. He was squinting into the sunlight and crinkles fanned out from his eyes. He looked rugged—a real Marlboro mountain man, as if he belonged out here, and June felt safe with him.

She'd always been confident on her own in the wilderness. She knew how to navigate, she'd done her survival courses, she knew her firearms, but this sense of security she felt standing beside Jesse was something different. It was like having someone at your side, someone you could lean on if the going got rough, someone who'd take a few knocks and fight off the bad guys for you—as he'd done for Lacy and her daughters.

And June realized again how deeply she missed Matt and being part of a team.

The bears—a sow and her two cubs, their coats reddish-brown—were grazing along a flat part of the valley. They were beautiful, majestic.

"They're healthy," June whispered. "It's not common to see them here. She must've brought her cubs down along the spine of the mountain range."

"This way," said Jesse as he began to walk along the crest of the ridge.

"We're going to approach them head-on?" asked Brad, clearly terrified.

"I want them to see us, to pick up our scent in the wind," Jesse said. "That way they'll most likely just move away."

As he spoke, the mother lifted her nose and tasted the wind.

"There." Jesse smiled. "She got us."

The sow stared in their direction for a while.

"Definitely black bear," June said.

"But they're brown," said Brad

"Black bear can be anything from a soft cinnamon color to pitch-black," Jesse said. "You can tell they're not grizzlies from the shape of their heads and the sow's shoulders. She has no hump."

"So they're not as dangerous?" said Brad.

"Black bears are responsible for more predatory attacks on humans than grizzlies are. You need to respect their space just the same."

"Jesse," June said softly. "Have you seen grizzlies in the wild?"

He nodded. Then turned suddenly to her. Sunlight danced in his eyes, and a smile curved his lips. "I recall being on a horse, in mountains, and seeing bears—brown bears. Not just once. I...feel like it's a part of me."

"You don't get brown bears in this part of Wyoming," she said. "If you've seen them in this state, it's in the northwest. Maybe the Wind River range, Yellowstone, Grand Tetons."

He closed his eyes a moment.

"And I can feel forest, snowcapped peaks, shale slopes. Being out for days at a time."

As he spoke, June saw relief in his features. He liked what he was seeing.

"See?" She grinned, infected by his sudden good energy. "I told you it would start coming back."

"I see Molly!" Brad interrupted. "Over there—look. She's trapped behind the bears and can't get back on the trail."

June saw a figure moving through the scrub a distance behind the bruins.

"She's downwind of them. They don't know she's there," Jesse said. "Come, we need to crowd them a bit, get them to move eastward, away from her."

He began to hike down the ridge, toward the bears, June and Brad following quietly behind. The sow reared up on her hind legs, waving her head back and forth, mouth open.

"She's going to attack," whispered Brad.

"She's just getting a better look, tasting the air," Jesse said.

The bear dropped back onto all fours and began to lumber, slowly, out of the valley, making her way east. The cubs followed.

Molly hugged June, breathless with relief to see them, but Jesse noted she had no basket, no berries.

He walked behind the three of them on the return to the cave house and more memories washed over him. This time he felt himself riding a horse again, with a packhorse tethered to his saddle. He had everything he needed for an extended stay in the mountains—his 270 Winchester rifle at his side and his twelve-gauge Remington WingMaster shotgun. His Beretta was holstered at his hip.

And in his memory he was looking for something… *poachers*. Jesse stopped dead in his tracks, pulse racing, perspiration breaking out over his body. He tried to dig deeper, but the images were gone.

Slowly he began to walk behind June, Brad and Molly again. Molly dropped something—it looked like a cell phone. She quickly scooped it up and glanced behind her to see if Jesse had seen. He looked away, pretending he hadn't.

When they reached the house, Molly and Brad went inside,

but June lingered outside in the sunshine. Jesse was pleased. He liked to watch the way the sun burned fire into her red hair. Her cheeks were pink from the walk and he realized how tired and pale she'd been looking—she still looked tired, but the color in her face stirred something deep in Jesse. He wanted to help her rest, find peace. He wanted to see her smile again.

He held out the shotgun to her.

"Keep it," she said. "I trust you."

Her words sent a warm rush through his chest. June made him feel good. She chased away the darker sensations lingering just under his consciousness, and Jesse realized he was falling, hard, for this woman. It worried him.

Would he be falling for June in the same way if he knew who he was?

She placed her hands on the banister that ran around the edge of the patio overlooking the creek. "Those bears were beautiful, Jesse. It was like a gift seeing them." She paused, looked up at him. "Thank you," she said quietly. "For a moment back there I thought you were going to take the twelve-gauge and split. You didn't have to help Molly." She laughed. "She hasn't exactly been endearing herself to you."

He came up to her, stood closer than he needed to.

"June, do you get cell reception out here?"

"Why?" she said, her features instantly guarded again.

"Just curious."

"We're out of cell-tower range in this valley. There's no reception on the west flank of the mountain on the Cold Plains side, either."

"What about over there?" He nodded in the direction they'd found Molly.

"I don't know," June said. "I haven't tried out there."

"You said there's a town over that far ridge?"

"Yes, Little Gulch. That's where we have an EXIT counselor who handles the transitions from the safe house."

"So, conceivably there might be some cell reception from a tower on the Little Gulch side."

"Like I said, I haven't tried to use a cell phone out there, but I suppose it's feasible."

"How do you get radio reception in the house?"

"Why all the questions?" He heard the suspicion in her tone.

He smiled. "I'm just interested. Radio reception is sketchy even in a parking garage. A cave can't be any better."

Her shoulders relaxed a little. "I rigged up some portable repeaters, same kind as we use for SAR work in remote areas. But there's always a worry one of the Devotee henchmen will stumble upon our radio frequency, so we limit communication to emergencies. Parking garages, huh?"

"Don't ask me how I know."

Her smile deepened.

And Jesse didn't even think about what he did next. He put his arm around June and drew her close. She stiffened for a moment and looked up at him in surprise. Then she looked out over the sunny valley and allowed herself to lean into him. Jesse could feel the tension draining from her muscles as she did. He rested his cheek against her hair. It was warm from the sun, and soft. An ache began in his chest.

"You fit me," he said quietly. "As if you belong."

She said nothing, and when he glanced down at her face her saw the glisten of tears on her cheeks.

"June—"

She shook her head. "It's nothing. I—I've just missed being held."

They stood like that in silence for a while, and more than anything Jesse wanted his memory back, to know who he was. Because he wanted June in his life—he *needed* to know it was possible.

"I have to go to Cold Plains, June," he said. "I need to lay my eyes on this Samuel Grayson, see if it jogs my memory free."

"They'll kill you. We've had this discussion."

"I can't just do nothing."

She pulled out of his embrace.

"Wait for the FBI, Jesse. I trust Agent Hawk Bledsoe. He's away right now, but—"

"No feds."

She swallowed, and concern filtered into her eyes. "Are you really so worried the FBI is going to find something on you, lock you up?"

He didn't answer for a few beats. Worry deepened in her features.

"I told you, I believe there *is* something dark in my past." He paused, trying to figure out how best to articulate his feelings. "Thing is, June, if I've done something illegal, I'll buck up and take the knocks, but I want to know what I've done and why I did it. I want to understand my guilt, my motivations. I don't want to be locked up and just told I've committed some act. I'd prefer to atone for my deeds by choice, in my heart. Does that make any sense at all?"

She was staring at him, a strange look on her face. "Jesse, going to Cold Plains and getting killed is not going to help whatever is haunting you."

He inhaled deeply. "The reason I came here, I believe, is *because* of what is haunting me, June. I've got nothing to lose—"

"Apart from your life!" she snapped.

"But," he said quietly, his gaze holding hers, "I could have everything to gain."

Her heart was thudding hard—he could see it in the pulse at her neck.

"Don't do it, Jesse—don't go."

He grasped her shoulders. "If anything, my leaving will take the heat off you guys here," he said. "If I stay in the house, those men might come back looking for me. You heard Davis. Next time they might find that tunnel."

"Hawk Bledsoe will be back in two days—"

He shook his head. "I'm leaving, June. I won't be here when he arrives."

She stared at him in silence. He became conscious of the chuckling creek, a soft breeze rustling the reeds that grew nearby, the sound of birds.

"I have an idea," she said very quietly. "A plan."

"What kind of plan?"

"It could work, on more than one level—but if it doesn't, we're both dead."

# *Chapter 7*

"It'll be risky," June said as she outlined her plan.

They were sharing breakfast at a small stone table outside, near the water and partially shaded by the rock overhang. From their vantage point they had a full view of the valley and would be able to see anyone approaching. Even as they enjoyed each other's company, they remained watchful.

Eager was lying at June's feet, a warning system himself as he listened to their environment.

"But if you hike out of Hidden Valley that way—" she pointed in the direction Molly had gone earlier "—you reach Little Gulch in about four hours. It's a slightly bigger town than Cold Plains, maybe three thousand residents, and it has a small airstrip. I'll give you a pack and supplies, and you've got GPS." She hesitated. "And I'm going to let you take Eager."

He set his coffee mug down. "Why?"

"Because it will bolster the story I gave the Cold Plains

police chief, Bo Fargo." She rubbed her brow. "I told him the reason for my absence was that Eager got bitten by something, and that I'd taken him to stay overnight at the vet's in Little Gulch because I've had clashes of opinion with the Cold Plains vet—something I need to mend now. So, if I hike back into Cold Plains and pick up my truck, I can—"

"Truck?"

"I live a double life, Jesse. It's complicated. I rent a place on Hannah Mendes's ranch on the outskirts of town. Hannah covers for me all the nights and some days that I am here at the safe house. And I work two days a week for the Cold Plains Urgent Care Center's ambulance service as a paramedic, so I need to put in appearances for that. The job is what allegedly brought me to Cold Plains."

"Plus there's your volunteer SAR work."

She nodded. "And there've been a fair number of searches these days for which they called me because I'm the only volunteer with a validated K9."

"You can't keep this up, June. You've got to find a way to slow down."

"There's no way out now, Jesse. Only one way to go and that's to the end." She took a sip of her coffee. "Once I've got my truck, I'll drive around the mountains to Little Gulch, allegedly to fetch Eager from the vet. I'll make sure someone sees me heading out of town without Eager, and I'll make it known that I'm going to pick him up. Meanwhile, when you get to Little Gulch, go wait for me at a place called Dixon's Pub and Beer Garden. It's a bit of a dive, but it's dog-friendly and it's right on the outskirts of town—it'll be one of the first places you see, big pink neon sign, can't miss it. I'll meet you there later this afternoon."

She took another sip from her mug, and Jesse noticed her hands were shaking slightly.

"June, you really need to rest. You'll—"

"I'm fine," she said briskly. "Tonight is the annual Cold Plains corn-roast festival. We'll drive back into Cold Plains, right down Main Street, while everyone is gathering outside the community center for the festivities. If they see us coming in from the outside, with Eager this time, and if no one recognizes you, I'll tell them that I picked you up from the airstrip when I went to fetch Eager from the vet. You're Hannah's new help for her ranch."

He smiled. "Hope there's a cowboy hat in it for me."

Her eyes remained serious. "Davis has one. You'll need to hide that cut on your head, anyway. Remind me to give you back the cash Sonya found in your jeans pocket before she tossed them."

"She tossed my jeans?"

"I cut the leg open, remember, to see where you were bleeding?"

"And there was nothing else in the pockets?"

"Just a hundred bucks in notes."

He frowned, wondering why he'd had absolutely no identification on him at all.

"If all goes smoothly, we'll mingle awhile at the corn roast. I'll tell everyone we used to date way back, and that I recommended you for the job on Hannah's ranch because you're out of work." Her cheeks pinked a little, and Jesse loved the way her complexion revealed her moods. She probably hated it.

"You better look after Eager—that dog is everything to me."

June was giving him her complete trust, and the scope of what she was trying to achieve struck him square in the chest.

God, he could love this woman, and the thought just fueled his desperation to get out there and find out who he was.

"If we can pull it off tonight, then you can use the work on Hannah's ranch as a cover while you figure things out.

Hannah will pay you for anything you do on the ranch, of course."

"I don't want her money."

"You have a hundred bucks to your name, Jesse. That's it."

"Maybe I'm rich." He grinned. "But I just don't remember."

This time she did smile.

"Yeah, and maybe I'm the Queen of Sheba."

He laughed. Then sobered almost as quickly. "You're right, June, it is risky. Because if someone does recognize me, *you* go down with me. I don't want to take that chance."

"If it works, Jesse, it shores up my story about my absence. It gives Hannah added protection, and you can help us, hiding in plain sight."

"I don't know, June."

She leaned forward. "It's the *only* way you're going to get into Cold Plains alive, Jesse, and God knows Hannah and I could use someone on our team. Besides, if I don't do something to bolster my story with Bo Fargo, stat, he's going to look into it, and I'm going down, anyway. So, do we have a deal?"

Her gaze was direct. Adrenaline rippled through him.

"Deal," he said quietly. "With one caveat. If I think you're going to get hurt, I pull the plug." As Jesse spoke, he caught sight of Molly watching them from behind the window.

"And one more thing—we don't tell anyone in the safe house what we're about to do," he said, his eye on Molly.

"Because?"

"Because they're safe in what they don't know."

June trusted that kid—but he didn't.

Before he got his gear together, Jesse went to find Molly.

"So, were the berries good out there, Molly?"

Her eyes narrowed in suspicion. "I dropped my basket of berries when I saw the bears. What's it to you?"

"There were no berry bushes there," he said.

"I ran to that area to get away from the bears. The berries were in another place."

He studied her for a beat. "Do you have a cell phone, Molly?"

"Of course. What of it?"

"Is there reception out in that end of the valley?"

"I wouldn't know—I didn't try to call anyone."

"Not even for help when you saw the bears?"

"Who would I call—Samuel? Yeah, right, wiseass. And I couldn't call anyone in the house, because, *duh,* no reception."

With one hundred bucks in his pocket, cowboy hat tilted low over his brow and a backpack on his shoulder, Jesse threw June a broad grin. It made his blue eyes twinkle against his tan, and it made June's stomach heat.

"You look like you're actually champing at the bit to get out into those mountains with my dog."

"I am," he said. "I'm going to find myself. Maybe the search dog at my side will help."

In spite of his upbeat mood, June felt anxious. She hoped the answers he did find were the ones he wanted. Crouching down, she hugged Eager, burying her face in his fur for a moment. And the idea of possibly losing her dog with a stranger suddenly filled her eyes with emotion.

"I won't lose him," he said.

"You managed to lose yourself, big guy—I'm not sure I can take your word for it." She ruffled Eager's fur. "Look after the cowboy, Eager." She got to her feet, pushed a fall of hair back from her face and her gaze met Jesse's.

"Take care. And don't forget to give Eager water."

Jesse leaned forward suddenly, grasped her wrist and pulled her toward him. Tilting her chin up, he kissed her softly on the mouth.

June's world spiraled as her lips opened under his. She kissed him back, suddenly hungry, desperate, her tongue seeking his, her hands going up his muscled arms, hooking behind his neck, drawing him down, kissing him deeper.

He pulled away suddenly, a strange and dangerous look in his eyes, the pulse at his neck throbbing.

"Be careful, June." His voice was thick, hoarse.

June stepped back, aching inside for something she wasn't sure she could have.

"See you at Dixon's," she said.

He nodded.

She hesitated a moment, then with a quick glance at Eager, she swung her own pack onto her back and headed toward the boardwalk that led to the tunnel entrance. She didn't look back. But she knew he was watching.

Even when she reached the tunnel, she wouldn't look back. She told herself it was a dangerous game, to fall for a perfect stranger, a man who had another, as yet, secret life. She was going to get burned. And June couldn't afford to get burned by a relationship again.

June hiked along the ridge where Davis said he'd found the baby's pacifier. This route would bring her down to Hannah's farm via a trail on the eastern flank. The day was clear and hot, the sun bright. She could see Cold Plains in the valley below; such a pretty storybook town on the surface, such dark secrets it harbored.

She shaded her eyes and glanced up at the steep slope of giant black boulders on her left. It was almost as sheer as a cliff, and she knew it to be riddled with small caves—this whole area was pocked with caves. She'd helped search this boulder slope when Rafe's baby had been taken, and it had come up clean. But given the pacifier that Davis had found here, June wondered if the kidnapper might have backtracked and be holed up with the baby somewhere in there now. A sinister chill unfurled inside her, and an eerie sense of being watched prickled over her skin. With it came a whisper of fear. She didn't want to go up there and face a kidnapper alone. She'd return with Jesse and Eager. June marked the location on her GPS, and as she continued along the trail she realized she was thinking of Jesse as an ally, and it felt damn good to have one.

*Be careful, June.*

By the time she reached the ribbon of paved road that led to Hannah's ranch, the August sun was high and burning down hot on her head. A black SUV approached from the distance. As it neared, it slowed.

It was Mayor Kittridge. He pulled off onto the shoulder and rolled down the window, sticking his elbow out.

June cursed under her breath.

"Mr. Mayor!" she said with an exaggerated smile as she came up to the side of his vehicle.

"Hello, June." He looked tired, most likely from his night-time search for Jesse. She spied a rifle on the backseat. Caution skittered through her.

He was eyeing her pack. "Where've you been? Where's Eager today?"

Thank God she'd taken the effort to come down via the eastern flank. "Eager's at the vet," she said. "He was bitten by something. I'm going to get him this afternoon." And before he could press for specifics, she glanced at her watch.

"I must be off to fetch him now. I'd like to be back in time for the corn roast. Hopefully Hannah and her new help will join me."

Interest, sharp and sudden, crossed Kittridge's features.

He tried to hide it with his easy smile, but his eyes lied. A newcomer in Cold Plains was going to be of interest to the mayor, especially so if said mayor was also one of Samuel's militia leaders.

June still couldn't see anything in Rufus Kittridge's face that would indicate he was a coldhearted killer. How did one ever know they were looking into the eyes of a murderer? This place was so damned creepy, it made her sick.

"What help?" said Kittridge.

"She's hiring an old friend of mine—old boyfriend, actually—for some heavy-duty lifting on the ranch. Hannah's feeling her age and I think it's a good thing she's finally admitting she needs more help. My friend is flying into Little Gulch. I'm going to pick him up when I go get Eager."

Anxious he'd ask for specifics, and that he and Chief Fargo might team up and go investigating in Little Gulch, June quickly changed the subject.

"Will you be there?"

"Where?" he said, suddenly distracted.

"At the corn roast."

"Of course. I—"

"Well, see you there." She turned to go. "I must leave to fetch Eager or I won't make it back in time," she called cheerily, giving a jaunty wave. Her heart hammered in her chest.

He drove off, slowly.

June's mouth was dry as she crossed the field to the outbuilding she rented from Hannah. She moved quickly. Hannah needed to be apprised of the details of the plan June had cooked up before anyone else spoke to her.

When June drove out of town twenty minutes later, she glanced uneasily into the rearview mirror. It was one thing to be seen driving out of town without her dog, quite another to be followed. To her relief the road was empty as she left Cold Plains.

She put her foot on the gas, wound down the window, and the wind blew warm through her hair as the fields of rural southeastern Wyoming rolled by. Gradually, as she clocked the miles between herself and Cold Plains, she began to relax, and June realized suddenly what a deep and negative toll the perfectly evil town and its Devotees were taking on her. Jesse's words crept into her mind.

*You can't keep this up, June. You've got to find a way to slow down.*

Jesse was at Dixon's Pub, sitting at a wooden picnic table in the shade of a trellis in the beer garden out back. Eager snoozed at his feet, a water bowl near his head. June's heart clutched at the sight of them—man and dog, good and tired from their trek over the mountain.

Eager sensed her presence instantly, lifting his head then surging to his feet, body wiggling as he came toward her. June felt surprise at her sudden surge of emotions again. Everything was riding just a little too close to the surface. She had to tamp this down.

She dropped down to her haunches and ruffled her dog's coat. "Good boy, Eager. You made it. You showed him how to get over the mountains, did you?"

She avoided looking up, but she had to eventually. Jesse had gotten to his feet and was standing near the table, giving her space. He smiled, teeth bright white, stubble shadowing his strong jaw.

His tan had deepened during the hours of hiking. He'd shucked the denim shirt and his white T-shirt was taut over his pecs. His jeans were dusty. His jacket hung over the bench next to the pack she'd loaned him, but he'd kept his hat on.

Damn, he looked good. She thought of their last kiss and

a nervousness, excitement, raced quietly through her blood. For a moment she wished he could be just Jesse. No hidden past. And that she could be just June.

She got to her feet, brushing back strands of hair from her face.

"You made it," she said.

"So did you. It's good to see you." His grin deepened. "I got to thinking, as long as I have your dog you're not going to abandon me."

Something sobered inside June, and she knew by those words he was feeling vulnerable, too.

"Can I get you a beer?" he said.

"A cold one would be excellent." The August afternoon was sweltering. Country music floated softy through the open doors into the beer garden. No one else was sitting outside. A few hard-time drinkers and ranch hands lingered inside, playing pool, minding their drinks.

Jesse motioned to a young server who brought two ice-cold beers, the bottles sweating with condensation.

"It's on me," June said, reaching for her wallet in her back pocket.

He placed his hand on her arm. "No."

"Jesse," she whispered, "that's all the money you have to your name right now. You might need it."

"I still think I have a big bank account that I can't remember."

"Yeah, dream on, buddy."

He paid the server and June took a deep swig right from the bottle, relishing the soft, cold explosion of bubbles in her mouth, the scent of hay being cut a distance away, the warmth of the afternoon. And, slowly, a decompressing sensation filled her body.

"I haven't done anything like this in ages." She stretched

her legs out and scratched Eager's neck with the toe of her boot.

"When we get back to the cave house," Jesse said over his bottle, "after we're through with the dog-and-pony show at the corn roast, what can I help you guys with?"

She liked his positivity. It bolstered her.

"Hannah hasn't got anyone who needs to be evacuated right now. But I could do with your help on another front." She hesitated, taking another swig of her beer, deciding how best to tell the story.

"There's a doctor in town, Rafe Black, whose baby boy was kidnapped last month. Rafe is not a Devotee, but some time ago he had a relationship with one of the five victims believed to have been murdered by Samuel or his men. Her name was Abby Michaels. She had a baby boy and when the child was three months old, she contacted Rafe and told him the boy was his. Rafe believed her. He sent her money and then came to town to find her. But Abby and the alleged infant had disappeared."

"Alleged?"

June nodded. "No one in Cold Plains would attest to Abby actually having a baby, but she'd sent Rafe a photo, and he believed her. Then, two months ago a baby boy—a dead ringer for the photo Abby had sent Rafe—was left on Bo Fargo's desk at the police detachment. He was strapped into a car seat with a note pinned to him saying he was Devin Black. Rafe was overjoyed."

"Jesus, that's weird. Where'd the kid suddenly appear from?"

"No one knows. The note was anonymous. The person who wrote it said they'd found Devin abandoned, and they'd taken him and fallen in love with him. But when they heard Dr. Black was looking for his son, they felt duty-bound to give him back."

Jesse sipped his beer. "How did this anonymous person get all the way into a police detachment and leave a child in a car seat on the chief's desk without being seen?"

"Again, no one seems to know, or if they do, they're not saying. Rafe was nevertheless thrilled to have found his son. Then last month, while Devin was sleeping in Rafe's house, he was taken."

Jesse whistled. "It must've killed the doc."

"He's distraught. There's been no ransom note, and the police have no leads. Teams searched the mountains, but Bo Fargo called off the search pretty quickly, as if he didn't actually want this kidnapper found."

"What about the feds?"

"They've got no leads, either."

"So how do you need my help?"

June checked her watch. It was getting late—they needed to leave if they wanted to be back for the corn roast. "Last night when Davis was tracking the henchmen he found a baby's pacifier under a slope riddled with caves. The caves were searched after the kidnapping, but I think there's a chance the kidnapper could have returned and holed up in one of those caves. I'd like to take Eager up there, but I didn't want to go alone."

"So you want me to come?"

"You can be my armed backup." She smiled.

But his eyes narrowed. "This is for the police, June."

"Are you kidding me? Bo Fargo *is* the police in Cold Plains, and Fargo is Samuel's puppet. If Samuel doesn't want that kidnapper found, Fargo's not going to find him."

"Is that what you think happened?"

"I don't know—like you said, it's weird how a baby in a car seat can suddenly appear on the police chief's desk with no one seeing a thing. And then the search was called off pre-

maturely. I haven't seen Fargo or his men doing a thing more
to investigate the case since then."

"The FBI should be on it."

"You're right. But the agents Hawk Bledsoe brought with
him to Cold Plains are suits, not SAR technicians. They'd
still need to bring in dogs, trained searchers. By the time they
get those kinds of resources together the kidnapper could be
long gone. His scent trail will be cold. Eager is right here.
He could track from the location the pacifier was found. If
we come across something, we notify the feds."

Jesse was silent for several beats. "We'll talk about it,
okay? But we should probably head out now."

June sighed heavily.

He placed his hand over hers. "Hey, I just don't want you
to get hurt."

He fingered her wedding band.

June swallowed, feeling suddenly uncomfortable.

"Matt was a lucky man, you know that?"

"If he was lucky, I would have saved him."

"June?"

She looked up into his indigo eyes.

"You can't keep carrying guilt."

"What of it? I'm doing good work because of what happened."

"It'll crush you eventually. You're afraid to let it go, aren't
you? You're scared you'll have nothing left then."

Irritation flared in her. "I don't need a shrink, Jesse.
Maybe you should sort out your own demons before you
cast stones." June got up abruptly, but he grasped her arm.

"June, I care for you."

"Please, don't touch me. I—I can't do this. It's not going
to work. I have no idea who you are. You might have a family
or something waiting for you."

*I couldn't bear to lose someone again.*

"Fine," he said, letting her go. "Let's go get this over with." His voice was brusque, and his movements were angry as he led her and Eager out through the dim pub interior and into the parking lot at the front of the establishment.

Big trucks and a Harley were parked outside. Heat waves oscillated off the paving. Above the building the *D* in the pink neon sign that read Dixon's Pub and Beer Garden flickered like a Devotee omen.

June felt a swish of nerves return as she climbed into her truck cab. She fired the ignition, and, as she pulled out of the lot, Eager sitting between her and a heavily silent Jesse, she told herself it was going to be fine. He'd find out who he was, go home. And Hawk would get something on Samuel, arrest him, and then she could go on to a new job in another state.

The late-evening sun lingered gold over the picture-perfect town as June drove into Cold Plains. Smoke curled from the barbecues on the lawn outside the community centre and crowds gathered around the food tents. A band played on a stand at the far end where tiny colored lights had been strung up. Already, some of the townsfolk were dancing.

Laughing kids gamboled on the grass, and mothers with smiling faces pushed strollers, husbands at their sides, offering greetings to neighbors as they passed. A bitter taste filled June's mouth.

She glanced at Jesse, felt his tension

"Remember, it's all in the attitude," he said as he tilted his cowboy hat a tad lower over his eyes. "If you believe the story, so will they."

She nodded, slowed and waved at Chief Bo Fargo, who was over by the main tent, talking to Mayor Kittridge. Both turned to look. Fargo began to walk over the lawn toward the truck.

"Oh, Jesus," she whispered. "Party time."

She stopped the truck, wound down the window. Eager gave a soft growl. He didn't like Fargo any more than she did. The man had a bad vibe, even for dogs.

"Hey, Bo," June said cheerily. "I just wanted to say thanks for letting me off the SAR hook the other day. I really needed that seminar. It's always good to hear Samuel speak. Gives one a real boost."

Fargo's watery blue gaze darted over her truck, then he peered into the cab, his attention on Jesse.

"So Eager's better?" he said.

"One hundred percent. I just went to fetch him. In fact, I got two for one." June forced a grin. "This here is Jesse… Marlboro. He's an old friend of mine from back West. Hannah needed some help on the ranch and—" she shot Jesse a look "—I volunteered him." She forced a big smile.

Jesse placed his hand on her knee and June tensed inside. But it was a good call, because Fargo noted the gesture.

Behind him Mayor Rufus Kittridge was hurrying over the grass toward them now.

"Well, we should find some parking." As she spoke, June could see Samuel watching them from under another tent. Her chest tightened.

*It's all in the attitude.*

Kittridge was coming closer.

"You guys going to stay for the dance?" Fargo addressed Jesse.

"You betcha," Jesse said with an easy grin.

June pulled off, found parking and turned off the ignition. She sat silent awhile, gathering herself, her heart hammering.

Jesse said, "Marlboro?"

"Just came to me." Then she snapped, "We should have worked this out in more detail. We should have had a surname ready." She turned in the seat to face him. "So, does being here jog your memory—do you recall *anything?*"

"Not a damn thing," he said. "I've never been to this place in my life. I'm sure of it. Nothing at all feels familiar about it."

"But you came here sporting a *D* tattoo," she said, exasperation creeping into her voice. "You *knew* about this place, about Samuel."

"Let's go eat and dance, June," he said quietly. "Then tomorrow morning we go to the caves, early."

She inhaled deeply, staring at him. Then nodded. "Thank you."


"Samuel, that was an excellent seminar," June said, putting her cob of corn down onto her paper plate as Samuel Grayson approached her and Jesse's table. They were eating under the colored lights that had been strung up near the dancing area where the band cranked out a feisty country tune.

Samuel's eyes, however, were fixed solely on Jesse, and June knew he *had* to be wondering if Jesse was the mystery man from the woods.

Jesse got to his feet and warmly held out his hand. "Jesse Marlboro—pleased to finally meet you. I've heard so much about you from June."

Samuel shook Jesse's hand firmly and smiled. "Samuel Grayson."

"This is a great event," Jesse said, hooking his thumbs into his belt. Inwardly June smiled.

"It's a celebration of being the best town we can be," Samuel said. "And it's a nod to the approaching end of summer, hence the berry desserts, the corn on the cob, the burgers."

"Please, take a seat." Jesse gestured to the table, his demeanor assertive, confident, but warm. June was amazed.

He was totally engaging, friendly, yet always alpha, and so very far removed from an image of an injured man in the dark woods that she began to believe he was actually going to pull this off.

"Don't mind if I do, but just for a few," Samuel said, swinging his leg over the picnic bench and seating himself. He gave his trademark Pierce Brosnan–style smile, his twinkling green sociopath's eyes belying whatever was going on in his mind.

"June has been telling me about your seminars and explaining the philosophy behind Cold Plains, and when I hit a rough patch workwise, and she mentioned Hannah was looking for a hand on the ranch, I thought it would be perfect to try and start fresh." He threw June a glance then smiled conspiratorially at Samuel. "And then there's June."

She felt her cheeks flush in spite of the situation.

"Mayor Kittridge tells me that you two used to date."

*So he'd already spread the word about the stranger's imminent arrival.*

"Off and on," she said. "Before Jesse found work on the rig."

"Oh, really, which rig?"

"Off the coast of Nigeria," Jesse said quickly. "I know, it was far, foreign, but I—I needed cash." He snorted. "And there were no casinos out there. I thought I'd be able to square some savings away." He placed his hand over June's. "Then the job fizzled—labor unrest, political upheaval. Nigeria is not an easy place to do business. I went on a bit of a downer." He inhaled, squaring his shoulders. "But hey, now I'm here. *And* there are no casinos."

Samuel was watching him closely. Then he smiled, cautiously, thought June, like a shark.

"Sounds like you'll be a very good match for our community, Jesse." He stood up, holding out his hand again. "And a good match for June. Pleased to have met you, Jesse. Hope to see you at my next seminar."

"You betcha."

They sat in silence watching Samuel stride over to the next table, doing his rounds.

The band had switched to a slow, sad tune. Couples were swaying quietly to the music, holding each other close. The air was warm.

"Christ," muttered Jesse. "That's the second time I've used 'you betcha' tonight." He repositioned his hat, scrubbed his brow. "Like some cowpoke."

*"Nigeria?"* she asked.

Then they both laughed.

"Hey," June said, giving him a mock punch, "I think you pulled that off great."

"And you look beautiful tonight, you know that?"

"Jesse," she warned.

"Just stating a fact. Come, dance with me."

"I don't think that's a good idea. I—"

He got up, took her hand. "Samuel's watching," he murmured. "It's a *very* good idea."

Swaying to the music with June in his arms couldn't have felt more right to Jesse. Her curves fitted perfectly against his body, and her hair smelled of lavender. He liked the way it felt against his cheeks. He enjoyed the sensation of her breasts pressing firmly against his torso, the way she moved against him.

He glanced down and saw that her eyes were closed. Heat speared to his groin.

"Would be nice to have a beer," he murmured against her hair.

"I'm afraid you're looking at a choice between a $25 bottle

of water. Or a $25 bottle of water. There's no overt consumption of alcohol in Cold Plains."

"So the food at the festival is free, but the water is not?"

"It never is, even though it comes straight from a creek. Samuel's people bottle it for him without being paid. He sells it back to them and pockets one hundred percent of the profits."

"You're kidding me?"

"'Fraid not."

Jesse whistled softly. "It's like a freaking Stepford town. Reminds me of that movie *The Truman Show*. You feel like someone is watching you from a control tower."

"You *are* being watched," she said quietly, nestling against his arm as she moved. Jesse stirred, his jeans going tight.

"Samuel is the control tower. That was good, by the way, what you said about hitting a rough patch and the gambling. He's going to home right in on it, perceive it as your weakness."

The music changed, another slow tune.

June pulled back. She looked tired.

"I think we can make an exit now," she said. "We still need to drive back to Hannah's ranch and then hike in to the cave house."

Eager, who'd been sleeping in the truck, thumped his tail with excitement to see them. But as June was about to climb up into the driver's seat, Jesse placed his hand on her arm.

"Let me drive," he said. "You look beat."

She hesitated, then handed him her keys. "Gee, thanks."

"Beat but still beautiful."

"Flattery will get you everywhere," she said as she climbed into the passenger seat. She didn't want to admit it to herself, but she was beyond exhaustion now. She gave him directions to Hannah's ranch, and as they drove, she felt herself nodding in and out of sleep.

"He's powerful, got big charisma," Jesse said as he wheeled the truck onto the dirt road that led to Hannah's house. "I can see why Samuel has pull over people."

"But seeing Samuel doesn't bring anything back? You still have no idea why you wanted to come here, why his name was familiar to you?"

"Nothing," he said. "Not a goddamn thing. I don't know any of those people from a bar of soap."

"Maybe it'll come still."

"Yeah, maybe."

About half an hour after introducing Hannah to Jesse, he and June were hiking up the trail into the mountains again, small headlamps lighting their way through the darkness. Before they headed out of cell-tower range, June once again tried to contact Agent Hawk Bledsoe but the call went straight to voice mail, which said he'd be back day after tomorrow.

The cave tunnel was dark, spooky. Jesse had only vague recollections of coming through here with June the first time. She was brave, he decided as he felt a bat flutter past his face. Braver than any woman he'd known.

He stilled in the darkness. How many women had he known?

Another image came to him. Making love to a slight, dark-haired woman with fiery blue eyes; a raw, shocking sadness ripped through him. Then there was nothing, just a feeling of depression and the now sickly familiar chill of guilt. Jesse was relieved to finally exit the tunnel, but the cold, dark sense of guilt lingered with him.

He paused outside the door of the cave house. June was right. He couldn't do this to her, to himself—or to whoever might be waiting somewhere in this world for him to come home. He had to know who that dark-haired woman was before he could even think of touching June again.

"You can take one of the spare rooms," June said as they entered the hallway.

He nodded as she closed and locked the front door behind him.

He watched while she went to her own room and he heard the door snick shut. A hollowness filled his heart.

# *Chapter 8*

By the time June, Jesse and Eager reached the base of the boulder slope, the morning sun was hot, the east-facing black rocks absorbing heat and radiating it back at them like an oven.

Eager was panting hard, his black coat soaking up heat, too. June stopped to give him water while Jesse scanned the horizon, hand shading his eyes. From this vantage point he could see for miles.

He carried a loaded shotgun in his hand and his Beretta in the holster at his hip—June had returned it to him. She carried her own weapon.

Once Eager was watered, June panned the rock wall above them with her binoculars, considering search strategy.

"We need to get up to that ridge on top of the boulder face," she said, pointing.

"Why?"

"The heat rising from these rocks is causing upward air currents. If there is human scent in the caves, it will rise with the currents to that ridge. I need to work Eager across the currents. If he picks something up, he can zero down onto the scent cone."

Tension rippled softly through Jesse as he squinted up at the boulder face. He tried to imagine a kidnapper with a baby up there in one of the dark holes, and he wondered how long an infant could possibly survive. An image sliced through his brain again—a baby screaming, and the dark-haired woman yelling for help. The same woman he'd slept with.

Flames crackled suddenly through his mind, devouring the image, and he felt searing heat. Jesse shook himself. The heat was from the rocks, the sun. But it unsettled him. He *had* to find out what those haunting images meant, or he would not be able to go forward. Seemed he couldn't go back, either. He was trapped in a web of present.

"Okay," he said quietly. "We go up, but we go around that way." He pointed to a talus slope to the left of the giant boulder wall.

"The ground inclines less sharply over there, and we won't be visible to anyone who might be hiding in one of the caves above. You go first," he said, eyeing caves, unable to shake an eerie sensation of being watched. "I've got your back." He clicked the safety off the shotgun.

June began to clamber up the shale slope, small stones skittering out from under her boots. Eager bounded easily ahead of her, unleashing his own shower of tiny rocks. Jesse waited until there was a bit of distance between June and the small avalanche of shale she and her dog were creating.

And as he waited, he watched June climb.

Her red hair hung in a neat braid down the middle of her back. She was wearing a lightweight khaki shirt, rugged cargo pants and hiking boots with gaiters. Her SAR pack, he knew, contained a first-aid kit, water and other survival essentials. She carried her radio in a vest pouch at her front for easy access.

The sun made her hair shine and exertion made her skin gleam, and she climbed with athletic grace. He suddenly wondered what she was like in bed. The idea made him hard.

Abruptly, she raised her hand, pointed. With her other hand she was restraining Eager by his harness. The dog's tail was wagging and his vision was totally focused on something he'd detected in the rocks to their right.

Jesse scrambled quickly up the shale behind her.

"What is it?" he whispered when he reached her side.

"Eager scented something," she said very quietly as she pointed. "It has to be something in that cave over there."

"Good boy," she whispered, hooking a leash into Eager's harness. "Leave it for now.

"I don't want to let him go," she explained to Jesse. "It could be dangerous for him if the kidnapper is holed up in there."

"There's no way for us to approach at all without being seen," he said softly.

They watched quietly, in silence, trying to detect movement. The sun bore down on them. Jesse could hear the soft sound of bees somewhere, the sharp cry of a bird up high, Eager's panting.

June's gaze went to the bird of prey circling high above them. There was a second bird wheeling on air currents even higher.

"Not a good sign," she whispered. "Those birds are often the first indication a search has turned into a recovery mission. Once when—" She froze suddenly and then gripped Jesse's arm.

"Did you hear that?" she whispered

Jesse angled his head. "What?"

Then suddenly he caught the sound—a mewl. His heart slammed into his rib cage. *Baby!*

Crying.

Oh, Jesus. He lunged blindly forward, images slamming into him. He could hear the fire coming. Crackling. Roaring. The baby's screams growing louder and louder and louder in his head. His baby. Going to die! Got to save him!

Jesse scrambled wildly across the boulders toward the cave, toward the sound, toward his son. Perspiration drenched his shirt, trickled down his brow. Small stones clattered loudly down the slope.

"Jesse!" June hissed. "Stop! What…in hell are you doing!"

She began to clamber after him, panic lacing through her. It was as though some switch had triggered in him, and he'd gone stark, raving mad. She reached him as he struggled to ascend a large slab of rock to the cave above, and she grabbed his ankle.

"Jesse!' Her heart was racing.

He spun around, eyes wild. He was wire-tense, muscles amped, sweat soaking his T-shirt, gleaming on his face. He looked totally unfocused, dazed.

"What's going on, Jesse? *Talk* to me."

His hand went to his brow. His eyes seemed to come back into focus. Then shock rippled through his features as he realized what he'd just done.

"Come down here," she said softly. "Come under this overhang before someone tries to fire on us or throw rocks from above."

He allowed himself to slide down and he slumped back against the rock under the slab he'd been trying to mount. He was breathing hard.

"What happened, Jesse?" she whispered, gathering Eager to her side, thinking they might have put themselves in a real bad spot. If they tried to move now, they'd be sitting ducks.

At the same time, June could still hear the baby crying above them somewhere. Tension coiled through her stomach.

*Rafe's son?*

And someone had to be with the infant—it could not have survived up here by itself. A mix of urgency, thrill, fear, cocktailed through her.

"I thought I was…in another time, another place," Jesse was saying. He raked his hand through his hair, which was damp with perspiration.

June offered him water, and he drank deeply. Head injuries were strange things, she thought as she watched him. Perhaps she should take him to the hospital in Little Gulch.

"I thought it was another baby," he said finally, his voice hoarse.

"Whose baby, Jesse?"

His features twisted with some inner anguish. "I…" His gaze met her eyes square, held for a moment.

"I don't know."

She held his gaze, wondering if it was a lie. And something slipped inside her chest.

"I thought there was fire."

"What happened in the fire?"

He shook his head, pain in his eyes. "I don't know."

"Jesse—" But she stilled at the sound of a male voice coming from above them.

"Hello! Who's there?"

They both froze.

"Can anyone hear me?"

"Go that way, Jesse," she whispered, pointing to the far side of the overhang. "I'll create a distraction by stepping out from under the overhang on the opposite side. You keep me covered from the rocks on the far side."

He inhaled, collecting himself, and nodded.

"Eager, you park here. Park, boy." Her dog sat, his body tense as he watched her intently with his trusting brown eyes.

June tossed a rock out from under the overhang. It clattered loudly, starting a diversion. Jesse began to move.

She called out loudly, "I'm coming out. I'm unarmed."

June stepped out from under the rock overhang. Out of the corner of her eye she saw Jesse with his gun ready. He nodded.

June edged out into full view, hands to her side, palms open.

A man stood on a rock slab above her, tousled dark hair blowing in the hot breeze. He was slender, young. Pale face. No weapon in his hands.

His T-shirt was stained with dirt.

"My name is June Farrow," she called up to him. In her peripheral vision, June saw Jesse creeping higher up the side of the ridge. He placed shotgun stock to shoulder, drawing a bead on the young man.

"I thought I heard a baby crying," she called.

"Where's the guy you were with? I saw two of you coming up."

"He's still under the ledge below me," June lied. "He twisted his ankle when he tried to climb too fast. He's resting it."

"I know you," the young man said. "You're from Cold Plains. You're the K9 search-and-rescue handler. I recognize your red hair and the dog. Where's the dog now?"

"With my friend."

She racked her brain. He was vaguely familiar, but she couldn't place him.

"What's your name?"

"Tyler."

"Tyler who?"

He hesitated, and June saw him glancing over his shoulder. A small hatchet of panic struck her chest.

"Did you take Dr. Black's baby, Tyler? Is that who we can hear crying?"

"No," he said. "I took my baby."

*Go easy, June—he could be delusional, thinking Rafe's child is his.*

"Do you know where Dr. Black's baby is, Tyler?"

"It *wasn't* his baby!" She saw he was shaking. And she thought she could see the glimmer of tears running down his face. "It never *was* his baby! Samuel Grayson's men made me leave my own son at the police station so Chief Fargo could pretend it was Dr. Black's boy."

*Jesus.*

"Okay, Tyler, listen to me. I'm coming up."

"No! You're *not* going to take my baby."

"I'm not going to take your son, Tyler." June climbed up as she called out to the young man. "I want to help you both. I have a first-aid kit in my pack. I have water, food. Are you hungry, Tyler?"

He nodded. As she got closer, June deduced Tyler was maybe in his early twenties—a very young father, if he was telling the truth.

Where was the mother?

June reached the slab of rock that jutted out in front of the cave and climbed up. Tyler shot a nervous glance into the dark space behind him.

"Is the baby in there, Tyler? Do you mind if I call my friend and dog up? They can help."

Uncertainty crossed his face. His eyes were huge with fear, his skin bloodless. His shirt hung loose over a gaunt frame. He'd been trying to live in the wilderness for some time, thought June. She hoped the baby was okay.

June signaled to Jesse and whistled for Eager, then she

ducked quickly into the darkness of the cave. It was hot inside, the air still.

The baby was lying on a wad of clothing. Silent now.

Too silent. Her heart dropped

"He's fine," Tyler said. "We just ran out of formula this morning. I go into town after dark and steal it from the day care—there's a window that doesn't lock."

The infant indeed had a good pulse. It wasn't emaciated. And it was sleeping now, having cried itself out. June shot Tyler a glance.

"Do you leave the baby here when you go thieving?" She shrugged out of her pack as she spoke.

He hesitated. "I—I don't know what else to do."

June cursed under her breath. "You're lucky as the blazes. There are wild animals in these mountains. You—" June stopped. Tears were rolling down the young man's face and he was shaking hard.

She examined the infant in silence. There were no bruises, cuts. Its little limbs seemed fine. Emotion, relief burned into her own eyes as her adrenaline began to ebb.

She gathered the baby boy into her arms and sat with him out in the sun on the plateau, just holding him for a while, Tyler watching.

Jesse had come up onto the ledge with Eager. He stared at the baby boy, his features tightening. He shot a fierce look at Tyler.

"I was scared," Tyler said softly.

"What's the baby's name, Tyler?" June said.

"Aiden."

She felt blood drain from her head. Speech eluded her for several moments. When she spoke, her voice came out hoarse. "It's a good name."

Jesse was watching her intently now. She knew he understood the significance—it was the name of her own dead son.

"Where's Aiden's mother?" June asked, her voice thick.

"She's dead." Tyler suddenly sank down onto the rock and clutched his arms around his knees, rocking slightly.

Compassion mushroomed in June's chest, along with a cool whisper of suspicion.

"Tyler," she said, "I'm going to ask you a question, and you need to trust me with the answer. You need to be honest. Are you a Devotee?"

Fear, almost sheer terror, whitened his face.

"I can help you if you are, Tyler. You won't ever have to go back to Cold Plains."

"No police?"

"Not the Cold Plains police."

"I'm not a Devotee, but my wife was."

"Aiden's mother?"

He nodded.

"Tell us about her. Tell us what happened with Chief Fargo, and why you left Aiden on his desk."

He began to rock again.

"Aiden's mother's name was Sally. We got married against Samuel's will. We did it in Cheyenne. But we came back—we should never have come back."

"Why did you?"

Tyler sniffed, rubbed his nose. "Work. I'm a mechanic, and I could get work in Cold Plains. We needed money. Sally still believed in Samuel. She was confused. He promised her things she didn't have, that I couldn't give. Samuel had wanted her to marry an older guy. He was furious when he learned she'd married me instead and was carrying my baby. But even though he was mad as hell, Samuel still wanted to do private counseling sessions with Sally. I—I don't know why she listened to him, why she went." Emotion surged and his voice cracked.

June's heart cracked. She thought of Matt, of how illogical his behavior had seemed to her toward the end.

"He took her for several counseling sessions after she had the baby, then when she told Samuel she was going to move back to Cheyenne with me, she had the accident."

"What kind of accident?" Jesse interjected.

Tyler glanced nervously at him, then June. "She drowned in the lake. I think he killed her. I'm *convinced* he killed her. I—I think he was sleeping with her, too." Tears sheened down his cheeks.

Rage arrowed through June's heart. If Tyler was telling the truth, it could make Sally murder victim number six. And June believed more of Samuel's victims would yet surface.

"I asked for an investigation," Tyler said. "But Chief Fargo claimed it was obvious that her death was an accident. I *know* it wasn't. Sally never went near the lake. She couldn't swim. She was afraid of water."

"And you've been caring for Aiden since she died?"

He nodded. Tears welling again. "One of the people from the Urgent Care Center came to take him away. They said they looked after babies like Aiden. But I refused to let him go. I began to make secret plans to leave, and I started saving money. But then a guy called Jason Barnes and his friend Lumpy Smithers came to talk to me. I knew they were henchmen. They said I must leave Aiden with Bo Fargo and write a note saying my son was Devin Black."

June's throat went dry.

"They said they were going to give Aiden to Dr. Black to keep the community whole. I was given two days to make up my mind. Then, when I went to work the next morning, I discovered I'd been fired. I came home and my landlord said I owed him two months rent, which was a lie. He gave me notice at the same time. My truck was stolen, and my bank account was frozen." He swallowed. "Then Jason Barnes returned and said maybe I better do as he asked—they had contacts, and things would get worse for me if I didn't obey them."

"Did Jason say Samuel sent him?" Jesse said.

"No, but I know Jason Barnes works for Samuel."

So, no evidence to pin on Samuel himself, thought June. That bastard was like Teflon.

"I had no place to stay. No money, no work, no transport. I was afraid for my life, and they promised Aiden would be well cared for by Dr. Black. So I did as they said. Then...I—I just couldn't handle it. I kidnapped my own son back, and we had nowhere to go so we hid in the mountains."

"You have a safe place now, Tyler. We're going to take you and Aiden there. This is my friend Jesse. He—" she met his eyes "—helps me. And this is Eager." She smiled. "Eager helps just about anyone who lets him. If he doesn't first love them to death."

Tyler gave a tremulous smile and tears pooled again in his eyes. "Thank you, June," he whispered.

"Hey, it's what I do. And you know what, Tyler?" She glanced down at the baby sleeping in her arms. "It's worth every moment."

She felt Jesse's large hand on her shoulder. He squeezed. And June had to struggle to tamp down her own emotions.

Later that day, back in the safe house, Jesse sat near the hearth feeding Aiden from a baby bottle. Tyler was sleeping and June was busy in the kitchen making sandwiches. He could feel her watching him, though, and when he glanced up and met her gaze, there was a strange look on her face.

"What is it?" he said.

She inhaled deeply, turned away.

"You're thinking about your Aiden, aren't you?"

She stilled, her nose going slightly pink and her eyes

watery. "I was thinking how good you look holding that baby," she said quietly. She picked up a knife and dug it into a pot of mayo. "You look experienced," she said.

There was an odd tone in her voice, almost accusatory.

She spread the mayonnaise over a slice of bread, her movements jerky, a little angry.

"Back at the cave, when you thought it was another baby crying, when you thought there was a fire—are you *sure* you don't remember whose baby was in your mind?"

So that was it, thought Jesse. She hadn't believed him when he'd told her he didn't know.

He glanced down at the dark-haired infant in his arms. The baby in his memory was dark-haired, too. And he'd believed in that blinding instant that it *had* been his child. But on the back of that feeling rode another, harder sensation, one that told him while the baby in his memory *was* somehow connected to him, it also wasn't. It was the same mixed-up conflict he had over the hazy memory of the slight, dark-haired woman—the woman he remembered making love to at some point; the woman who brought on emotions of guilt, rage, hurt, sorrow. The woman who made him finger an absent ring.

"I don't know what baby I saw," he said quietly, and Jesse didn't feel he was lying to June. He couldn't honestly say one way or the other whose baby he was remembering, and he also didn't want to express his doubts about it to June because he didn't want to chase her away.

"I need to go tell Rafe Black about Tyler and his son. Rafe's going to be devastated." She bagged the sandwiches and reached into the fridge for a bottle of water. She put it all into her pack.

"*We* need to go tell Rafe," he said, getting up, the baby still in his arms.

June braced both hands on the counter and dropped her

head. She was silent for several beats. Then she looked up, a strange determination in her eyes. "I need to go alone, Jesse."

"June—"

She spun around and marched out of the kitchen, leaving her pack on the counter.

Jesse quickly went to find Lacy and he handed baby Aiden into her care.

When he came back into the living area, June was near the front door lacing up her hiking boots. Her face had been washed and her eyes were red-rimmed. Her mouth was set in a tight line.

"So you believe Tyler's story, June?" he said.

"Yeah, I do. Rafe will want a DNA test for proof, of course, but I believe the baby is Tyler's."

"Do you think Rafe's baby even exists?"

"He believes his son is out there somewhere." She got up, swung her pack onto her shoulders.

"We had a deal, June."

She stilled, hand on the door. "What deal was that?"

"I help you—you help me. We work as a team. I'm coming with you."

"It hurts to be with you, Jesse."

"Why?"

"You know why," she said quietly. "And I think you're lying to me. I think you have a baby, and that means a woman in your life."

"It *doesn't* mean a woman in my life. And, June, I'm not lying. I won't do anything to hurt you. I promise you that."

"How can you promise me anything?" she said crisply. "You don't even know who you are."

She stomped out of the house.

Jesse grabbed his gear and followed. The fact she didn't try to stop him gave Jesse a small flare of hope.

\* \* \*

It was late afternoon by the time Jesse and June were sitting with Dr. Rafe Black at his kitchen table watching his fiancée, Darcy, making coffee. The doctor was a dark-haired man with serious brown eyes and a kind demeanor. Darcy was a lot younger than him, blue eyes, thick dark hair. And the way she looked at her fiancé… What he'd give to have a woman look at him like that again.

*Again?*

His heart kicked.

He shot a glance at June, worried that something might have been revealed in his features, but her attention was on Darcy, who was setting mugs of coffee on the table. Jesse returned his attention to Darcy—there was something about her looks that made him uncomfortable.

Rafe cursed after hearing June out. He surged to his feet and began pacing the kitchen, anger, desperation powering his movements. Darcy watched him, concern growing in her eyes.

"To convince someone to give up their own child?" Rafe shook his head. "I can't believe even Samuel and Fargo would stoop *so* low." He spun round. "And to think I actually *thanked* Fargo and Samuel for their help!" He raked a hand through his thick black hair.

"That baby boy looked so much like the picture I had of Devin. Same hair color, same eyes—I believed in my heart it was my son. Why would they do this?"

"Maybe to shut you up, Rafe," June said. "Maybe they felt you were getting too close to the truth, and whatever the truth is, it must be detrimental to them. Perhaps they figured if you believed Aiden was Devin, then you'd be quiet, leave town."

"*If* what Tyler says is true," Jesse cautioned.

Rafe nodded. "DNA will either prove or disprove his story." He turned to June. "Have you informed the FBI?

They've been involved in the kidnapping investigation from the get-go."

"I'll be speaking to Agent Hawk Bledsoe when he returns to Cold Plains tomorrow. I'm going to invite him to the safe house to speak to the occupants. I've sheltered them from law enforcement until now, but Tyler's story is just unreal. This whole thing is getting way too dangerous."

Both Darcy and Rafe stared at June in silence.

She rubbed her face. "I'm not giving up, if that's what you're thinking."

Darcy reached out and took June's hand. "Hey, it's okay. Samuel and his flock are getting real edgy." She glanced at her fiancé. "Rafe and I are worried this place could turn into a Waco any day now."

Rafe nodded, drew up a chair, reseated himself at the table. "You okay, June? You look tired."

"Fine." She said it a little too crisply.

"You should take a break, get some rest."

"Listen to the doctor, June," Darcy said with a kind smile.

Concern wormed into Jesse. June *did* look more drawn and pale than usual, and her hands were still shaking slightly, although she tried to hide it, as she was doing now, by clutching them both tightly around her mug as she sipped her coffee.

She ignored the concern, changing the subject. "Now we know why Bo Fargo called off his search for the kidnapper," she said. "Without Tyler, there's no one to prove Aiden was not your son."

"Then where *is* my son?"

"All we can do is keep looking, Rafe," Darcy said. "We can't give up. Just like I'm never going to give up the search for my real mother."

Rafe smiled, his affection tangible as he looked at his fiancée.

At least they had each other, thought Jesse as a pang of

loneliness speared into his chest. And the sudden ache, the sense of aloneness was so sharp, so real, that Jesse thought he couldn't possibly have a child or a wife in his life—or else he wouldn't feel like this, would he?

"Have you found anything new in the search for your birth mother, Darcy?" June was saying.

"I took the digitally enhanced image of Jane Doe, murder victim number two, back to my adoptive mother's town of Horn's Gulf. I showed it to anyone who'd look, but no one could verify Jane Doe was Catherine George. I just wish I could confront Samuel, and ask if he is my father, and if Catherine is my mother, which of course is out of the question." Darcy sipped her coffee. "I can't help thinking that if I go and look at the area where they found Jane Doe's body, I might learn something."

"Her body was found four years ago, Darcy," Rafe said. "There won't be anything there now."

"Maybe the killer goes back," she said. "Maybe a dog like Eager could find evidence of him visiting the site."

"I tell you what," said June. "As soon as I can find some time, we'll take my truck out there and search the site with Eager, look for human scent, any articles that might have been dropped by someone."

"Are you serious?" said Darcy.

"Sure I am." June glanced at Jesse. "Jesse will help."

"Thank you so much. I can't thank you enough."

"You shouldn't have promised Darcy you'd search the old crime scene with her—you're just going to let her down," Jesse said as he drove back to Hannah's farm. The afternoon was segueing into evening, the sun lowering in the sky, the light growing balmy and gold. June was relieved to have Jesse behind the wheel. She'd developed a mother of a headache and it was making her vision blur.

"I don't feel like discussing it," she said quietly, drawing tactile comfort from the way Eager was pressed against her.

Jesse's jaw tightened. The silence in the cab grew heavy.

"They have a good relationship. They make a nice couple," he said abruptly.

June massaged her temples with her fingertips, trying to make the pain go away. "Yeah, they do. Why does it upset you?"

"It doesn't."

"Sounds like it does."

He said nothing. She glanced at him—his profile was strong, his hands tight on the wheel, his neck muscles tense. Then because it was irking her, she said, "Does *none* of this bring back anything, Jesse?"

"No."

Jesse turned onto Hannah's ranch road. Dust boiled behind the truck, red in the evening sun.

By the time they reached the cave house it was dark.

June shrugged out of her pack and dumped it in the hall. She bent down to untie her hiking boots.

"I still think it was ridiculous to offer your help in searching a four-year-old murder scene," Jesse said, kicking off his own boots.

"What's it to you, Jesse?" June snapped. "Why are you so damn uptight about me helping Darcy out? I felt bad for her, okay? That's all."

Jesse dropped his voice to a harsh whisper as he realized the house was quiet, its occupants likely sleeping already. "You volunteered *my* help, June."

"Don't help me, then." June locked the front door and started down the hall for her bedroom. "I don't need your help," she called over her shoulder.

"You're a bleeding heart, June," he said, following her.

"You can't help every single person out there, you know. You're going to het—"

"Oh, don't start with me again." She spun around in front of her bedroom door. "Why are you so angry with me all of a sudden?"

"I'm not angry at *you*." He kept his voice low, but couldn't keep the edge out of it.

"Well, you're doing a damn fine job pretending—" And it hit her suddenly. "Oh, wait, I get it. You're mad because I said I'm bringing in Agent Hawk Bledsoe tomorrow."

"You could have mentioned it to me."

"Why? So you can run away quickly?"

"Maybe I'm not ready to meet him."

She glared at him. "Yeah, maybe you'll never be *ready*, Jesse."

She turned her back on him and entered her room. But he blocked her from closing the door.

"June—"

Anger fired inside her. "Jesse, please, leave me alone. Leave the safe house. I don't care where you go. Just—"

He grabbed her shoulders suddenly and yanked her hard up against his body, crushing his mouth down onto hers. Desperation, pent-up frustration, everything that had been simmering in June unleashed in his arms with explosive and blinding passion.

She opened her lips under his, moving her mouth against his, feeling his rough stubble against her cheek, and suddenly nothing but the present mattered—no past, no future, just this moment. She fumbled urgently to pull his shirt out from his jeans.

Edging her into the room, kissing her deeply, his tongue tangling with hers, slick, hot, wet, urgent, Jesse kicked the door shut behind them and backed her toward the bed. She could feel the rapid beat of his heart against her chest, and she felt the bulge in his jeans pressing against her pelvis. Her world tilted, began to spin. Liquid heat speared between her thighs, and she wanted him, all of him, deep inside, as she'd never wanted a man before. She began to breathe so fast she thought she might faint. Buttons pinged and bounced on the stone floor as she ripped his shirt open. She angled her mouth, kissing him deeper, moaning softly as her hands explored the hard, muscled lines of his torso.

His skin was hot, smooth, supple. She felt the ridges of his scars under her fingertips, and June was unable to articulate a single thought as a wild and furious urgency mounted inside her. She needed to grasp onto what she could before the past intruded on the present, before it shattered the future. Before Jesse knew who he was.

He slid her shirt back over her shoulders, exposing her bra, her belly, and she quickly began to unbuckle his belt. She felt the backs of her knees bump against the side of the bed as he lowered her down onto it.

# Chapter 9

June peeled Jesse's jeans off his hips, her world narrowed to nothing but this moment. The light from the fire in the cast-iron stove danced copper over Jesse's naked, bronzed body. He stilled as he stood above her, his chest rising and falling, his eyes dark with passion and just a little wild, his hair mussed from her hands. And in that moment June knew with her whole being she could love this man. A raw ache swelled in her to have him, hold him, know him. Keep him.

His gaze holding hers, he reached out and removed the hair tie from the end of her braid. He loosened her curls around her bare shoulders.

"I thought you were an angel when I came around in your bed, you know that?" he whispered. She undid her bra as he spoke, and her breasts swelled free, nipples tight.

He placed his large, calloused hands on her shoulders and guided her onto her back as he lowered himself over her. He cupped her breast, rasped a rough thumb over her nipple. Something tightened low in her belly.

She reached up and placed a finger on his lips. "Don't talk," she said. She didn't want to think, and talk made caution whisper darkly around the edges of her consciousness. She wanted to stay only in the present.

He undid her jeans, slid them down her hips. Then he kissed her mouth and June felt his hand exploring the curves of her breasts, sliding down her stomach, cupping her hard between her legs as his kiss deepened.

June's vision spiraled as he slid a finger up inside her. Then another. He massaged parts of her that made every nerve in her body scream. It made her shake. Her vision turned red, then black as a low moan built in her throat. He moved his fingers deeper into her. She couldn't go slow like this. She wanted him fast, wild, furious. Hard. She hooked her hand around the back of his neck, yanked him down, and she kissed him almost angrily, moving her tongue inside his mouth, arching her back, opening her legs wider, rotating her hips, needing to deepen the sensation. She could feel the roughness of fingers inside her, the pad of his thumb rubbing on her swollen, sensitive nub, and she grew searing-hot, wet, delirious with physical pleasure.

Jesse groaned with pleasure at her urgency, thrusting his hand deeper, as his hips moved against her body and his erection pressed hot and hard against her thigh. It drove her wild, past a point of no return, and June could not hold back a moment longer.

She dug her nails into his back, trying to grasp onto the pleasure, to make it last, but every muscle in her body went tight and still for a moment, and then she shattered with a soft cry as wave after wave of contractions rocked through her body.

Jesse's control cracked. As she was shattering under him, he forced her legs open wider with his thighs and entered her with a hard, long thrust to the hilt. She was hot as molten metal inside, and he could feel the aftershocks of her contractions rippling over the length of his erection as he moved inside her.

She arched up her hips, gasping as he sank deeper and her fingernails dug into his neck. He moved wildly, bucking, grinding into her, deep as he could. She groaned in pleasure, rotating her hips, meeting him for every hard thrust he made.

Heat began to build. His vision turned scarlet. He could barely breathe. Every nerve in his body felt exposed, tingling, singing, right down to the hot tip of his erection. Every frustration that had been building in him quivered to the surface of his skin until Jesse felt he was going to explode. His muscles tensed as his vision darkened and his eyes rolled back in his head, and with one final thrust he released into her.

Breathing hard, body slick with perspiration, Jesse slumped down beside June, holding her close as she kept her legs wrapped around him. And as he gradually softened inside her, a memory began to return, like fire, crackling softly at the edges of his mind. The flames grew louder, bigger, hotter, coming closer. He began to panic as the sound became a roar of cracking and popping and spitting wood as his house burned.

Jesse froze inside.

His heart began to thud all over again.

*Not now,* he thought. *Not right now.* But more images came fast, furious, slicing like a hot knife through his brain. He saw the woman again. This time he saw her face. She reminded him of Darcy. That's why being with Rafe and Darcy had made him so edgy, angry, earlier.

But why the burning rage?

The dark-haired woman smiled at him. Her eyes were large and sparkling blue. In the next sharp image she was wearing white. A bride. He was sliding a smooth gold wedding band onto her finger.

Oh, dear God. Sweat beaded along Jesse's brow.

He closed his eyes tight, holding on to June, not wanting to let her go, terrified of what these images might mean to him. To her.

He saw a gold band on his own finger and another image flashed through his head—the dark-haired woman, very pregnant. Jesse's hand was on her stomach.

She was smiling. Anna…no, Annie. His throat turned dry. Her name was Annie.

But then she was crying. He was looking at the dark-haired baby in his own arms…or was it Tyler's baby? No, not Tyler's—Annie's. His. Jesse tried to calm his breathing. It was all coming back—finally coming back. And he didn't like it. Not one bit. The memory pieces felt like bad snap-shots, harsh colors, from a family album that didn't really belong to him, yet it did. And like a series of random snap-shots they were confusing, still not a smooth, continuous picture.

Jesse saw himself on a horse, going away. Far away. There were mountains, snowcapped peaks all around. His horse was negotiating rocky trails and he was going into higher, wilder places in search of…peace, of…something he couldn't put his finger on. The woman—Annie—his wife's screams suddenly shattered the peace. Jesse could see fire again. The baby was crying, stuck somewhere in the dark, and the flames were coming. He felt terror grip his heart.

Then nothing. Just silence. Mountains. And guilt. Sicken-ing black guilt. Fear rippled through Jesse. He'd done some-thing to Annie, to the baby. He felt it in the core of his bones. Something bad had happened.

He fingered his naked ring finger and slowly he opened his eyes.

June was propped up on her elbow, watching his face. A fall of red hair curtained her cheek and firelight was soft on her alabaster features. Her eyes glimmered, and she smiled, a little tentatively at first, then it deepened. With surprise Jesse registered she had a dimple.

She could light up a room with that smile. His gaze drifted down to her breasts. The way she was propped up on her side deepened her cleavage and her nipples were dark rose.

He allowed his gaze to go lower. Her stomach was flat, muscles firm. The hair between her legs was the same color as the waves hanging soft over her slender shoulders. He began to stir somewhere deep and carnal all over again.

Her words sifted softly into his mind.

*Jesse, please, don't touch me. I can't do this. It's not going to work. I have no idea who you are. You might have a family or something waiting for you.*

He swallowed. He'd made a mistake, he'd overstepped the line. And now he had to end it, because Jesse knew with sharp and sudden clarity he could not continue this with June—he was married. And he could not do this to June until he fully understood his relationship with Annie and the baby boy in his memory. Or until he knew where they were now.

A sick wave of nausea crawled up his chest and into his throat. And he didn't like the bitter taste that came with it.

"What are you thinking, Jesse?" Her voice was soft, sexy. She trailed her fingertips along his waist, feathering the line of a scar.

"About you."

"They're like a map, your scars," she whispered. "A map to your past, carved with blood into flesh. If only I had the key."

As she fingered the scar on his waist, another image slammed through him: his face hitting dirt, the taste of sand in his mouth. He heard hooves thundering, saw the horns of a steer flash past his eye. Then it was gone. But the taste of dirt and blood in his mouth seemed to linger.

"I think I could love you, Jesse Marlboro." Her eyes gleamed with sudden emotion. "I wish you could be just him. Just Jesse."

Her words cut. He felt pain in his chest, so raw. And with sudden clarity he knew it *was* his name—Jesse. The engraved belt buckle had been a Christmas present from Annie. He could see himself opening it by the tree, her smiling as he did.

He felt sick.

Self-hatred twisted into him.

He got up, went into the bathroom and closed the door carefully behind him.

He stood in the darkness for a moment, feeling his heart pound, listening to the rush of blood in his ears. Another image of Annie came to him. She was on a horse, riding behind him with other people. They were single file on a rocky trail in the mountains. Her short hair gleamed almost blue-black in the sunshine. She wore a Western vest and boots. Her laugh was like a wild brook. Sunlight, happiness, sparkled in her eyes. Another image bisected the first. He and Annie making love in a tent. In the mountains, *his* mountains. As abruptly as the vision had come, it was gone, like another night critter scurrying into the dark alleys of his brain.

Jesse flicked on the bathroom light and went to stand over the basin. He stared at his naked body in the mirror. There was no doubt about it, he'd been beaten up in the past, and the history of violence was written in a map of scars all over him, as June had said. His skin gleamed with perspiration and sweat beaded his lip. His eyes looked crazed. He turned on the tap and splashed ice-cold water over his face.

As he did, another memory washed over him. Adrenaline

was pounding through his blood, it was hot, a cowboy hat was on his head, a rope swinging in his hand. Muscles burned and hooves thundered on hard-packed dirt.

*Steer wrestling.*

It hit him with the weight of a hammer—he used to wrestle steers. He'd been gored, stomped on by his horse. But…it felt distant, further away than the memories of the dark-haired woman, the baby. This memory came from a more distant and youthful past. A wilder past.

Jesse peered intensely into the eyes that stared back at him from the mirror.

*My Jesse with the blue eyes.* He recognized the voice as his mother's, from way, way back. He glared harder at his own image, trying to dig further, unearth the secrets still buried in his head.

Jesse swore viciously to himself.

*Think, dammit, think!*

What did he know about himself? He liked physical action, adrenaline. He abhorred confined spaces, needed the great outdoors. He'd hunted poachers.

He rode horses and had wrestled steers. He slept often under stars.

He'd married a woman named Annie, with laughing blue eyes, and there'd been a child.

Suddenly another image hit him. He was fighting with Annie—they were yelling at each other, really going for it. Jesse felt the rage of the memory in the muscles at his neck, in the clench of his fists on the basin. Annie was crying. Then suddenly they were having sex again—wild, hot, angry. Guilt hammered down on the image, black and ugly.

*Jesse! Jesse! Help!*

She was screaming suddenly, locked somewhere in his head, the fire raging around her. His fault. But instead of helping her and the screaming baby, he was riding away, on a horse. Far away from her, from the baby.

His mind went blank. He was breathing so hard he felt he might hyperventilate

He slammed his hands down on the edge of the basin, hung his head down, trying to slot the disparate pieces together.

But all he could think of was June, lying naked in the bed on the other side of this door, and how much he wanted *her*.

His eyes burned.

He was falling in love with her. Absolutely no doubt about it. But he had another life and in it was a woman named Annie.

So why was he here in Cold Plains, with no ID, just a pack on his back and the name Samuel Grayson in his mind?

Was Annie in Cold Plains somewhere? With their child? Was she trapped by Samuel and his cult?

He had to find out.

And he had to do it without June.

Jesse needed to know how Annie fitted into his life before he could even begin to think again of June. He had to walk away, now, and it cut him to the core. Because he knew it was going to hurt her. And it was going to hurt him.

He'd hike out of Hidden Valley into Little Gulch before dawn broke. From Little Gulch he'd find an FBI field office. He'd ask the feds to help trace his identity.

If he'd done something terrible to Annie, he *had* to have done it for a reason, because Jesse couldn't believe he was an evil guy, a bad guy. Sometimes, he thought, a good person could be forced into an act the law might not deem justifiable. And sometimes the legal system itself was morally indefensible.

With a heavy and painful heart, Jesse took a quick shower.

He stepped out of the bathroom with a white towel around his waist.

June was lying on her back on the bed, a sheet covering her body. Her hair was splayed out in a soft halo of waves on the white pillow. She'd fed more logs onto the fire and the room glowed orange. Her eyes were wide, skin pale, and a nervous tension tightened her features as she watched him exit the bathroom.

"Are you okay?" she said quietly.

He raked his hand over his damp hair. "June...I..."

*Christ, I don't know how to say this.*

She sat up, gathering the sheet tightly around her chest, and he hated what he was about to do to her. He told himself he was not running away. He was doing this with the faint hope he could find his way back to being with her—if she'd still have him by then.

Taking a deep breath, he jumped.

"June, I need you to understand—" He swallowed. "I need to go away, leave the safe house. Now."

"Why?" Her eyes crackled suddenly, hands tense on the sheet, her face tight.

His heart hammered. Jesse came up to the bed and sat on the edge.

"I've decided to leave before sunup and hike over the mountains to Little Gulch. From there I'll find an FBI field office and ask them for help in tracing my ID."

She was silent for what seemed an eternity. Her eyes began to water.

"I...don't understand, Jesse. I thought you said you didn't want to involve the feds until—" It hit June suddenly and she sat up, stiff.

"You've remembered."

It wasn't a question.

"Not all of it. Just slices. But I need to fill in the rest. I have to find out why I am here. I…think someone I know, from my past, might be in danger in Cold Plains."

"Who?"

He reached out to touch her and she pulled away, got out of bed, wrapping the sheet tightly around her.

"June—"

"Who, Jesse!"

"I'm not sure."

"It's a woman, isn't it? Someone you're involved with."

He swallowed. Then nodded.

Her face went white as the sheet.

"What's her name?" Her voice came out hoarse.

"Annie," he said, bitterness filling his mouth, his eyes burning. "I…married her."

An almost imperceptible shock rippled through her body.

"June—"

She pulled back from his touch.

"I don't *feel* married. I have no ring." He hesitated. "We had a baby. I can remember a baby in the house."

Her eyes filled with moisture. A single tear shimmered down her pale cheek.

"Did you know any of this before…before—"

"Before I slept with you? No. I had snippets, but they made no sense. They suddenly seem to be slotting together."

"Do you know who you are, your name?"

"It is Jesse—the name on my belt. My surname still eludes me. I—I know things that I've done, June, not good things. They're just disjointed pieces, sensations, floating around my brain, and I still can't put them together in a whole picture. Which is why I'm going to ask the feds to help me."

"You were afraid of the FBI before. So why now?"

"Now there's you."

"I don't understand."

"Now I will take whatever knocks are coming, because I want to see if I can clear the way to be with you, June."

He reached for her hand, but June pulled away. She stared at him.

The hurt on his face was visceral. It cut like a knife through her stomach. She felt herself starting to shake inside. "Wait for Agent Bledsoe, please. He'll be here tomorrow. You can talk to him. You don't have to go."

"I can't be here with you. Not until I sort this out. I don't want to hurt you, June. So I'm going to get help."

June's world tilted on its axis. Maybe he was telling the truth—maybe he didn't know he had a wife and child before sleeping with her.

*You need to give him the benefit of the doubt.*

Which she hadn't given Matt. And it had killed him.

But it didn't change what had happened, or the way she felt. Or how wretchedly she hurt. But this was her fault—she'd let it happen. She'd allowed him to open the cracks in her heart. She made the decision to sleep with him, too.

*You didn't know him, and he didn't know himself, yet you took the risk, anyway...*

She struggled to breathe, and it took a few more beats before she could speak again.

"So you're just going to cut yourself off from me? From Cold Plains? What if there is someone in Cold Plains you came to save?" She heard the plea in her own voice, and she hated it.

"June, it's not like that."

"What's it like, then?"

"I can't save anyone until I know who it is I might have come here for."

A darker thought struck her.

"You do remember, don't you?" She stepped closer to him. "You recall exactly what terrible thing you did, and now you're fleeing from the law, before Hawk gets here." She inhaled shakily, going hot. "Is that what you were doing here in the first place, Jesse? Coming to hide from the law inside a cult? Is that why you had the *D* tattooed on your hip and carried no ID?"

"No!" He ground the word out through clenched teeth, and anger, dark and hard, twisted into his features.

A thin, cold fear trilled through her.

*Be careful, June. He really could be dangerous. To you and to everyone in here. Especially if he's just remembered who he is and what he's done.*

"Fine," she said guardedly, trying to sound vaguely calm while her insides were jelly, while her chest was bursting with anxiety and pain.

"I acknowledge this is my own fault, Jesse. I knew all along you might have a life that couldn't include me. I knew you might need to leave the minute you remembered what was waiting for you. I rolled the dice." Her voice quavered. "And I lost. I'm a big girl—I can handle it."

The anger on Jesse's face dissipated. Raw concern filled his eyes. And he almost imperceptibly leaned toward her, as if reaching out to her, as if every part of him wanted to touch, comfort. Hold on to her.

Tears pricked into her eyes and her throat ached with the effort of trying to keep it all bottled in. "Go," she said, very quietly.

He gathered his clothes, then stalled near the door. "I'll be gone before dawn."

She said nothing.

He opened the door, started to leave.

"Jesse?"

He spun around, anticipation—*need*—in his eyes.

"If you do anything that will hurt these people, jeopardize the safety of this house—"

"That's not who I am, June. You've got that wrong."

He waited, as if there might be some answer, something she could say to him, or do, that would change his mind, change everything.

She began to shiver.

"Go," she said again.

He stepped into the passage and the door snicked shut behind him.

Tears, silent, slid down her face.

June sank onto the bed and buried her face in her hands, and she allowed herself to sob like a small child. Every emotion she'd pent up for five years seemed to come out now in great big body-jerking spasms. She had not sobbed like this since she'd watched her little Aiden's casket being lowered next to his daddy's bigger one, since she'd heard the dark, damp sods of Washington earth thudding onto the lids, taking them away from her forever.

And when June stopped crying, she had no fuel left in the tank, nothing to shore her up, to keep going with the fight. Jesse had been the last, soft straw that had broken the back of her resolve and dropped her to utter rock bottom. She curled up in a tight fetal ball on top of the bed, and felt empty. Nothing. Just blackness.

Jesse opened the door to one of the spare bedrooms, planning to change in there. He was surprised to feel Eager's wet snout nuzzling against his leg as he did so. Flicking on the light he saw Eager was all body-wiggle excited to see him.

Jesse ruffled the dog's fur wondering why he'd been locked in here. To the best of his recollection Eager had come into the hallway after he and June had hiked back to the safe house. The dog had then headed straight for the kitchen, in search of his water bowl and food, while Jesse had followed June to her bedroom.

Once he'd changed, Jesse checked his weapon and sheathed it back in his holster. He smoothed his hand over Eager's square head. "You'd better stay in here, bud. I don't want to be letting you out if this is where your handler wants you, big guy."

He closed Eager into the room, then went into the kitchen. It would be another long hike and he'd need to take water, some food. He should probably eat something now, too, although he had no appetite for anything. *Focus,* he told himself. He was on a mission for the whole truth of his life. It was an obstacle he needed to conquer if he wanted any chance in hell of finding his way back to June. But his heart grew even heavier at the thought.

If he did have a wife and child, he had responsibility, and Jesse knew in his gut he was not a man to shirk that.

Nor was June a woman who would take a man into her life under those circumstances, even if she loved him.

The kitchen was dark, but light from a waning moon outside painted the valley silver through the big living-room windows. Small clouds scudded across the moon, and a wind was making the trees sway. It looked like another storm front brewing—not an ideal time to set out into the backcountry.

As Jesse reached for the light switch in the kitchen, a movement outside caught his eye. His hand stilled. The shadow moved again and his pulse quickened.

Leaving the switch, he moved quietly across the dark kitchen and crossed the living room to the big window, staying carefully to the side. Outside, partially hidden by the shadows of a pine tree, was a human figure. Jesse's blood began to thrum with adrenaline.

The figure stepped out from the shadows and into a puddle of moonlight. Jesse saw pale hair.

*Molly.*

She was talking into a radio.

Quickly, he moved to the front door and opened it quietly. He heard a voice, male, deep, crackling over the radio: "How long is this tunnel? Over."

Molly keyed her radio. "If you've got radio reception again, you're almost at the end," she said quietly. "Once you exit the tunnel, you need to cross a wooden boardwalk and—" Molly froze like a deer in headlights as she caught sight of Jesse.

He barreled out of the front door, and she screamed as he grabbed her arm.

He snatched the radio from her hand, his fingers digging into her upper arm.

"What in hell do you think you're doing?" Jesse growled.

The male voice crackled over the radio now in Jesse's hand. "Okay, we're out of the tunnel now—can see the boardwalk ahead. Take cover, we're coming in."

Jesse heard a click.

Both he and Molly spun around.

June stood at the safe-house door, shotgun stock to her shoulder. In this pale lunar light she looked ghostly, eyes dark holes.

"Let her go, Jesse." Her voice was strange.

"June—this is—"

Her finger curled around the trigger. "Give that radio to Molly and let her go."

He released Molly, but kept the radio.

Molly ran to June's side.

"You bastard." June spat the words at him. "You played me. You, Samuel, Fargo, Kittridge—you set me up and I fell for your stranger story, your charisma, just like they all fall for Samuel's stories. Your amnesia was a ploy to get me to bring you to the safe house, wasn't it? So you could figure out what we were doing. You absolute sick bastard." Her voice caught. "What's worse, I slept with you. Was sex a good bonus?"

Jesse knew *exactly* what June was feeling right now—he could taste the bitterness of betrayal in his own mouth. An overwhelming remorse filled his body...and it hit him, square between the eyes.

Annie had betrayed him. She'd slept with another man.

"It's not what it looks like, June. I saw—"

Molly grabbed June's arm. "He was telling two henchmen on the radio how to find the safe house! You heard it yourself, June. You saw the radio in his hand," Molly said urgently. "They're almost here! It's his fault. *He's a mole.*"

Jesse set the radio down on the ground and held his hands out to his sides, tension thrumming through him.

"Molly's lying. She's the traitor. You've got to get inside, get to safety. Now."

Her mouth flattened. "I'm not going to fall for you again. Once a mistake—twice makes me a fool."

But as she spoke, a thudding of boots sounded along the boardwalk.

"June—get inside!" Jesse yelled. "They're here!"

Molly darted off into the dark bushes.

June swung her weapon to the source of the sound. Gunfire cracked through the air. Then everything seemed to continue in slow, sick motion. Jesse saw June stumble backward against the doorjamb. The shotgun fell to her feet. Her hand went to her chest. She seemed frozen in time for a moment, then slowly she slid down the doorjamb and crumpled into a heap on the threshold.

# *Chapter 10*

Jesse raced toward June just as the two henchmen emerged from the shadows. One of the men fired and a bullet buzzed like a hot hornet past his ear.

He flung himself to the ground, rolling off the edge of the patio into the creek bed as another bullet *thwocked* into the trunk of a tree beside him, shooting out shards of wood.

Jesse reached for his sidearm. His heart was hammering, every sense and reflex heightened by adrenaline. He could scent moss, loam. Creek water was cold on his leg. He inched carefully up and peered over the edge of the patio.

A bullet zinged off rock and an image burst sharply into his mind; of another time when he'd been cornered and shot at. In an instant Jesse knew what that time was—he'd come across signs of poachers in the Wind River Mountains. They'd killed and field-dressed an elk and packed out the meat, leaving flies buzzing around the carcass in a field of wildflowers. He'd tracked them for two days, finally coming upon their camp near evening. But the father and son had ambushed him.

They'd killed his horses, taken his weapons. He'd escaped, badly injured. But he'd survived in the Wind River Mountains for three weeks before hiking his way out.

And with that memory came a whole tumbling series of others—and Jesse knew what he was. A warden for the Wyoming Department of Fish and Game—a wilderness cop who owned a ranch in the Wind River foothills. The knowledge fired his resolve. It fed a sense of righteousness and dogged determination, of *duty* into his blood.

As he edged up to see over the patio again, more images, fueled by intense adrenaline, burned into his brain.

He'd taken the warden job after Annie had cheated on him and become pregnant. After she'd given birth to a son, Jesse had left her and the infant on his ranch and gone into the mountains, searching for a way to deal with the possibility that Annie's baby belonged to another man, searching for a way to handle the pain of betrayal, a way to move forward with his wife.

Another bullet zinged past him and he saw the two men running in a crouch toward the safe-house door.

*What are they going to do? Kill all the sleeping occupants of the safe house, including the children?*

Jesse took careful aim, fired on the first henchman.

The man stalled, stumbled sideways, then hit the ground hard. The second man made it to the door. Jesse fired on him, hitting the doorjamb and splintering wood as the man clambered over June's body and ducked inside.

Jesse scrambled onto the patio and raced in a crouch to June's side, gun in hand. Relief punched through him when he saw her eyes flicker.

*She's alive.*

But terror climbed onto the back of his relief as he saw a

pool of blood, black in the silver moonlight, glistening on the floor beside her shoulder.

"June!"

*"Go..."* she whispered hoarsely, grabbing his shirt. "Please, Jesse, *go save them!*"

He hooked his hands under her arms, pulling her to cover.

"Leave me, dammit! It's a flesh wound. I—I'll apply pressure. Just don't let me lose them, Jesse. *Please.*" Tears gleamed on her cheeks. "Get the children first, Jesse."

Conflict warred inside him. In his memory he heard Annie's baby screaming, and he heard the fire coming.

"Don't make it all worth nothing, Jesse."

He removed her handgun, placed it in her hand. She clutched her other hand over the wound in her shoulder.

"Hang in," he whispered. "I'm coming right back for you."

He ran along the outside of the cave house to a window on the far side. He broke it, kicked glass free, climbed through and rushed first to the nursery where Lacy, the twins and Tyler's baby were still sleeping. Tyler was in another room with Brad. Davis was in yet another. Sonya, he knew, shared a room with Molly and Brad's mom, Tiffany. Jesse couldn't reach them all in time.

*Get the children first, Jesse.*

As he entered the nursery, Jesse could hear Eager barking madly. Then he heard a woman's scream.

Panic stabbed into his heart.

Lacy was sitting up in bed, roused by the noise.

"What's happening?" she said.

"Henchmen."

"They *found* us?"

"Get your kids and Tyler's baby, Lacy. Take them and go out the window in the games room. It's broken. Keep the children quiet. Stay hidden in the woods until I come find you."

He raced down the passageway. Davis was coming out of

his room. He was carrying a shotgun and he'd already met up with Brad and Tyler, who had freed Eager. Brad was holding him by the collar.

"Henchman got inside," Jesse whispered.

"My baby—"

"It's okay, Tyler. Lacy has him. She's hiding with him in the woods. You've got to stay here and help me get this guy, understand?"

The sound of a woman's scream reached them again.

"That way," he whispered. "Sonya's room."

Brad pressed himself against the wall on one side of Sonya's door. Tyler stood on the other.

"Davis, you stay right behind me."

Jesse kicked the door open.

Sonya screamed again. She was trying to fight off the henchman with a baseball bat. The henchman swung around as he heard Jesse enter, and Sonya took the gap, crashing the bat down hard across his shoulders. The man grunted, stumbled, then buckled to the ground in pain. Eager burst past Jesse and attacked the man, biting into his leg.

The man tried to kick Eager off. Jesse grabbed the man as Davis got hold of Eager's collar and pulled him off.

The man's pant leg was torn and there was blood. His face was white with pain.

"I know him," said Tyler, staring at the fallen henchman. "He's Lumpy, Jason's friend, who came to make me give up my son. You bastard!" Tyler lunged for the man.

"Hold him back, Brad. This guy is not going anywhere."

Lumpy glowered at Jesse. "You're him, aren't you?" His voice was hoarse with pain. "You're the guy from the woods who killed Jason Barnes."

"Tyler, Brad, get him up," Jesse said, holstering his Beretta. "Lock him in the utility room, watch him until I get back. Davis, you take the shotgun, go look for Molly outside."

Lumpy swore and then groaned in pain as they tried to lift him.

"I think she broke my ribs with the bat, man. I—I can't breathe."

Jesse raced back to where he'd left June.

He found her passed out against the wall, gathered her up into his arms and carried her quickly into her bedroom, which was warm from the fire. He lay her on the bed and flicked on the light. Memories, everything he knew about himself and his past, rushed like a wild stream through his head. The life-and-death situation, the kick of adrenaline, must have shocked it all back, and Jesse now knew exactly who he was—Jesse Grainger.

He knew what had happened to Annie and the baby. He also knew why he no longer wore a wedding band. And it was a promise he'd made to Annie on her deathbed that had brought him here to Cold Plains. Above all, Jesse was now certain there was room for June in his life, and here she was, slipping away from him.

He could *not* lose her now.

He could not let her die thinking he was evil, a traitor.

"June," he whispered, emotion burning in his eyes, panic licking through his stomach.

"Wake up, June. Stay with me."

She moaned, and her eyes flickered open. Relief punched through his chest. Jesse worked quickly to take off her shirt. There was an ugly gouge through the outside of the flesh on her upper arm. God, she was lucky—the bullet had only ripped through flesh.

"Sonya!" he yelled. "Tiffany!"

The two women came running. "Get me June's first-aid stuff! Get me a bowl of hot water, cloths. Hurry!"

June was delirious, moaning.

"Stay with me, girl, hang in. I love you, you know that? You're not going to get away from me now."

Jesse cleaned and disinfected her wound, his own basic first-aid training kicking in. He pulled the edges of skin tightly together with adhesive butterfly sutures from June's kit, and he bound her arm firmly with a bandage.

With a cool, damp cloth he wiped her face.

She opened her eyes.

"Hey," he said, his chest cramping with relief. "You're going to be okay. You got lucky—it's a flesh wound."

"The children—"

"Everyone is safe, June. We got the bad guys." He smiled.

But she was not looking right. He needed to get her medical attention. Sonya brought him a fresh shirt for June.

"Is she going to be okay?" said Sonya.

He nodded. "But I want to get her to the hospital."

*"No."* June's voice was hoarse as she grabbed his arm. "Not the hospital in Cold Plains. I can't go there, not after this attack. None of us can go into Cold Plains right now."

"June, your pulse is weak, something's going on with you—"

She shook her head. "It's just a flesh wound. I'll be fine." Confusion crossed her face suddenly. "Jesse—the radio in your hand. You were guiding those men in."

"No," he said gently. "It was Molly. I was in the kitchen when I saw her outside talking on the radio. I'd just grabbed it from her when you came out the door."

"She…can't be. Not Molly."

"I'm afraid so, June."

She frowned, a confused look entering her eyes.

"She must have infiltrated via your rescue system," he said. "My guess is that she didn't expect to arrive at a house outside of cell-phone range, and that the plan was for her to call in her location. But once here, she had no way of letting the men on the outside know where she was without blowing her cover. I believe that's why she hiked out to the end of the valley the other day, when she encountered the bears. She might have gotten enough of a signal to let them know the safe-house radio frequency, or they got lucky and tuned in."

"That means there could be more men coming, Jesse," she whispered.

He took her hand in his.

"Perhaps," he said. "But there's also a chance those two henchmen didn't have a chance to pass on information about the safe house."

Her eyelids fluttered closed and she sighed deeply.

"So...tired," she whispered. "So...very tired."

Jesse glanced at Sonya, who was standing to the side. She looked as worried as he felt.

"June?" he said, turning back to her.

Silence.

"I think she's fallen asleep," said Sonya.

"I'm going to fetch Dr. Black," Jesse said, standing up. "And then I'm going to get the FBI. Watch her, Sonya." Emotion choked his voice. "Don't let anything happened to her, and stay off the radios, okay? I'll tell the others to stand guard."

He took June's shotgun and several boxes of shells from the cabinet. Thrusting them into a pack, he hurried to the utility room where Molly Rigg and Lumpy Smithers were now being held.

He knocked on the door.

Tyler opened it. Jesse stepped in. The utility room was tiny, rock walls, stone floors, no windows, vented from above. Using June's climbing rope, the men had managed to tie both Lumpy and Molly—whom Davis had found not far from the safe house—to the heavy plumbing that ran along the bottom of one wall.

"Lumpy said he wants to talk to the feds," Davis said quietly in Jesse's ear. "He's broken up about Samuel wanting him to leave Jason to die. I think he's done being a Devotee. Agent Hawk Bledsoe might actually get something concrete out of him he can use against Samuel."

Jesse glanced at Molly. Her face was tight with rage. He doubted she was going to break in a hurry.

"I'm going to fetch Rafe Black and Agent Bledsoe," he told them. "Once Dr. Black has looked at June, he can take a look at Lumpy here. Have you got a cell phone I can use to contact Bledsoe?"

"Take mine." Davis handed Jesse his phone.

"Thanks. I'll call ahead for Black to be ready to roll as soon as I get there. I'll call Bledsoe on my way down."

"Both their numbers are in my contact list," Davis said. "If you go into town via the south trail you'll actually hit Bledsoe and Carly's ranch before you hit town."

As Jesse left the room Molly yelled at him: "You sick SOB—Samuel will find us! His men will find us! This place, June, they're the evil among us. She and this house go against everything the Devotees are trying to build. She's like a cancer!"

Her voice faded as Jesse made his way down the stone passage, urgency mounting in him.

But, as he went, Jesse tried to temper his anger at the kid. She'd been indoctrinated by a sick sociopath. Yes, she was dangerous, but she needed help, too. She was also a victim of Samuel's.

Just as his young brother-in-law, Michael, was a victim.

And Jessie knew now that he'd promised Annie on her deathbed to come to Cold Plains and get Michael out.

When he stepped out the door with his twelve-gauge and his pack, the sky was already black and low with clouds, and rain was beginning to spit. Thunder rumbled in the hills.

By the time Jesse was out of the tunnel and the canyon on the other side, the rain was coming down hard and the wind was whipping debris down from the treetops. He moved fast along the south trail with the aid of a headlamp and his GPS. He was now certain of who he was. He trusted his law-enforcement training and his experience in the wilderness, and his sense of purpose was clear and fierce, as was his sense of justice.

He had a brother-in-law somewhere down in that town—he could see lights through the rain and trees now. His duty was to keep a vow to his deceased wife—a woman he'd always cared for but had struggled to love since her infidelity. And now there was June, a woman he *did* love, her well-being hanging by a thread.

Thunder crashed and a bolt of lightning forked across the black dawn over Cold Plains; like an omen, thought Jesse, because the wrath of justice was going to strike down Samuel Grayson and his perfectly evil little community. Thunder growled again and echoed into the mountains. Jesse could now make out lights from what must be Hawk and Carly Bledsoe's ranch house. He bent into the wind, face wet, muscles burning as he began to jog down the last stretch of meadow trail that led to the ranch. Rain was pelting horizontally at him as he banged on the door.

More lights went on inside the house.

The door swung open.

A tall, muscular man with sandy-blond hair and brown eyes stood in the doorway. The man's hand went to his hip where he had a pistol holstered.

"Agent Hawk Bledsoe?" said Jesse.

Hawk identified himself, eyes narrowing.

"My name is Jesse Grainger." And it felt damn good to say it. "I've just come from the safe house run by June Farrow—she's been shot. They've been attacked by henchmen."

Hawk motioned him inside.

Quickly, Jesse explained who he was, why he'd come and how the two men had attacked the cave house. "One man went down when I returned fire. The other is being held captive in a utility room along with the Devotee mole."

As Jesse explained that he was on his way to fetch Dr. Rafe Black, two men and two women appeared behind Hawk. He introduced one of the women as Carly, his wife, and the others as his team of FBI agents assigned to the Samuel Grayson investigation.

"I mapped my route from the cave house," Jesse said, handing Hawk his GPS. "All you have to do is follow the waypoints. When you go into the rock crevasse, it narrows to what appears to be a dead end. Move the creepers aside, and you'll expose the opening to the cave with a tunnel leading off the back. Go through the tunnel until it pops out into Hidden Valley on the other side. The cave house is at the end of a boardwalk that leads from the tunnel."

Carly was pulling on a rain jacket as Jesse spoke. "I'll take you to Dr. Black's in my SUV," she said. "Telephone lines and the cell tower are down because of lightning strikes."

She flung open the door and, pulling up her hood, began to run through the pelting rain to a vehicle. Jesse followed her.

Thunder clapped as she opened the driver's door, her face white in the simultaneous flash of lightning. The lights inside the house dimmed and flickered. Urgency kicked through Jesse.

By the time they pulled up outside Rafe and Darcy's place,

water was running in rivers over the roads. Jesse banged on the doctor's door.

Rafe flung open the door, eyes sharp with adrenaline. "Did you find Devin?"

"No, Rafe, not yet. It's June—she's been shot. It's a flesh wound but I'm worried about her. Something else is going on—can you come to the safe house?"

The disappointment in the doctor's eyes was keen, but he barely blinked as he hurried to pull on some gear and grab his kit. Darcy stood in the lit doorway watching them pull off.

Tires skidded on mud as Carly struggled to get the SUV as far up a logging track as the vehicle could go in order to make the hike shorter.

"That's one good thing about this weather," said Jesse as they climbed out of her vehicle, pulling up their hoods. "There's no one around to see us."

"Good luck," Carly called behind them as they started up the trail. "Be careful!"

The concern in her voice was sharp, and Jesse felt a sense of kinship, of being part of a greater team, something he'd been missing for a long, long time.

Carly left her headlights on, lighting their way until they disappeared into the trees.

Rafe, Jesse noted, was fit, and although remaining cautious in wilderness terrain in the dark storm, the two of them moved quickly.

It was not long before they were at the cave entrance.

Jesse watched as Rafe finished suturing June's wound. Hawk and his team had arrived ahead of Jesse and Rafe, and were now busy with the captives in the utility room.

"Does she need to go to the hospital?" Jesse asked the

doctor, still worried about June's sheet-white complexion and the deeply bruised look under her eyes.

"I'm fine," June murmured.

"I'm asking the doc, not you," Jesse said with a big, forced smile, thinking that even her voice seemed flat, listless. And he didn't like the way she was avoiding eye contact with him.

He had to tell her, now, about who he was. She still didn't know.

Rafe packed up his medical kit. "I'll be back in a while to check on you, June," he said as he worked with practiced calm, "after I take a look at Lumpy Smithers. Sounds like he might have broken a few ribs. And I'm going to check in on Tyler's baby while I'm here."

Lacy, the twins and the baby were safely back in the house, and Jesse heard the ache in Rafe's voice and knew he was thinking of his own son. He followed Rafe out of the room and took him aside in the kitchen.

"Rafe, what's really going on with her?"

Rafe set his bag on the counter. "June has been putting herself under extreme mental and physical stress, day in and day out for over three months now. I think her system is just giving in under the strain. I wouldn't rule out critical-incident stress, either. She might need counseling herself, Jesse. More than anything, June needs to rest."

"I don't think she knows *how* to stop."

Rafe nodded. "She needs help, Jesse. She needs someone to take over for her for a while, and insist she put her feet up."

Jesse snorted. "Like June is going to allow anyone to take over and give orders."

"Someone has to." Rafe shook his head and picked up his bag. "I've told June to take it easy, but she's dogged in her drive to help others. Sometimes I think she's just as trapped by it all as the Devotees are by Samuel."

"It's because of her husband and child."

"I know," Rafe said. "And I get it. I'm just as driven to find my own son as she is to set right the perceived wrongs of her past."

Emotion burned in Jesse's chest as he watched the doctor go down the passage toward the utility room. Rafe had summed it up. He was a good man and an astute doctor. There were a lot of good people mixed up in this net of Samuel Grayson's.

Jesse opened the door to June's room.

"Hey," he said gently.

She turned her head on the pillow away from him, and something dropped like a stone in his stomach.

He came up to the bed, sat down on the edge and tried to take her hand. She moved it away, still not looking at him. Eager, however, nuzzled against Jesse's leg, clearly worried about his mistress. Jesse stroked his soft fur instead.

"Hawk Bledsoe has things under control," he told her. "He's hopeful he can get Lumpy to give him something on Samuel."

She said nothing.

Exasperation, worry, whispered through him.

"June, we're going to win this."

She turned her head, looked at him. His heart sank at the pallor in her face, the vacancy in her eyes.

"We?" she said quietly.

"Yes, June. You and me."

"You're wet," she said, looking a little confused again.

He snorted. "It's raining cats and dogs out there, worse than the night you found me. June, listen—"

"Lacy and the twins, the baby?"

"They're all fine. We saved *everyone*."

Her eyes moistened and she bit her lip.

"June, I have something to tell—"

Hawk gave a knock and entered the room. Jesse cursed silently.

"You doing okay, June?" said the agent.

She nodded. "Thanks for coming, Hawk. I've been trying to reach you."

He smiled as he came forward, his brown eyes guarded but friendly. The man exuded a cop's air of authority and confidence.

"You can thank Jesse," said Hawk. "Landlines and the cell tower went down in the storm. Jesse hiked down the south trail and came banging on our door at the ranch in the thick of it all. Carly drove him down to get Doc Black while we headed straight here using his GPS mapping."

June frowned, glanced at Jesse. "*You* fetched Hawk?"

"Looks as though we might get Lumpy Smithers to turn on Mayor Rufus Kittridge and Monica Pearl in a plea bargain," Hawk interjected. "Lumpy was close to Jason Barnes and he feels betrayed by Samuel wanting him to let Barnes die. If we can charge Kittridge and Pearl, Samuel's two militia leaders, we might finally get something from them to pin on Samuel. It would help if we could locate Samuel's twin, Micah. He was the one who started this ball rolling, saying he could help us take his brother down."

"What happened to him?" asked Jesse.

Hawk gave a half shrug. "He vanished into thin air. No leads on him at all. Perhaps Samuel got to him first."

"What about Molly Rigg?" June said, trying to edge herself higher up to sit back against the pillows.

"As tough-talking as that kid is, once we start interrogating her, I have a feeling she's going to give."

"Promise me you'll allow Molly access to counseling, deprogramming, legal advice, before you interrogate her," June said, and Jesse's heart hurt for her—even in her weakened state she was still worried for others.

"Of course," said Hawk. "I've seen firsthand with Mia what a cult can do to a loved one, and how deprogramming can work like a switch—I believe in what you do, June, can't thank you enough, none of us can."

"Did Sonya show you around the safe house?" said June.

"She did—I'm impressed. And from what Lumpy and Molly are saying, no one beyond the two of them now knows the location of the cave house—it's still secure to the best of my knowledge." He turned to Jesse, paused, a grave and businesslike look entering his already-serious features.

"When you're ready, Jesse, we've got some procedural stuff to go through with you."

Jesse nodded.

He'd shot and killed two men in self-defense since his arrival in Cold Plains. One of them was lying dead outside right now. There would be consequences that would need to be legally addressed, statements made and taken.

He waited for Hawk to exit, then he got up and closed the door, desperate for a moment of privacy with June.

"Jesse," June said quietly, turning her head away from him as if she couldn't bear even to look at his face. "I need to be alone."

He came and sat back down on the bed beside her.

"Please," she said.

"I'm not going anywhere, June. Not anymore. I remembered. Everything."

She turned her head, met his gaze.

"Everything?" she whispered.

"I know who I am, June."

A nervousness crept into her eyes.

Emotion suddenly crackled hard and fierce into his chest, and he took her hand in his. "And I *know* there is a place in my life for you."

# Chapter 11

June met his gaze. His energy was palpable, his eyes fierce with a kind of fervor she'd not seen in him before, and she was suddenly afraid of what he was going to say. She'd wanted so desperately to allow herself to love him, but in taking the risk she'd seen just how raw she still was about loss, and how much she could still be hurt. June wasn't sure she could ever give herself wholly over to someone again, or if she even wanted to try. The cost of losing again was too high for her.

"What do you mean, 'a place in your life'?" Her voice came out hoarse. She felt shaky. Her shoulder throbbed. Part of her suddenly wanted to flee.

"June—" His hand tightened around hers—large, calloused, capable, protective. And threatening. Her pulse quickened and her skin felt hot.

"My name *is* Jesse—Jesse Grainger. I know weapons, wildlife, bears, because I work as a game warden in north-western Wyoming. I came to Cold Plains because of a promise I made to my wife—"

"So you *are* married," she said flatly, not wanting to hear more.

A muscle pulsed at his temple. Time seemed thick, slow. And June could see pain in his eyes. As exhilarated as he was in rediscovering who he really was, June could see the memories were not easy for him.

"I'm a widower, June."

She stared at him, heart beginning to hammer.

"My wife, Annie, died from injuries sustained in a fire."

"How?" she whispered.

He glanced away for a moment, and swallowed. June's heart squeezed and she slid her hand along the bed, tentatively touching her fingertips to his thigh, just making the barest of physical connections, yet afraid, still, of what he was about to say, afraid to dare to believe. And hating herself for the whisperings of exhilaration she was beginning to feel in the face of his loss.

"I'd been doing some renos to our ranch house. I'd put in the wiring myself and there was a problem with the electrics. The wiring caught fire and the blaze spread very quickly through the house. Our son was sleeping in a room at the back of the house." Jesse hesitated. "He…died in the fire."

Her heart began to pound, loudly, in her ears, images of her own son drumming through her mind.

"Annie tried to save him, but couldn't reach the room in time. Firefighters managed to pull her out of the house alive, but she succumbed to her injuries and died in the hospital two days later."

"What was your son's name?"

"Cameron. I was in the mountains when it happened. I was contacted via radio, and managed to make it back in time to be at Annie's bedside when she passed."

Silence trembled thickly in the air.

"I'm so sorry, Jesse." June placed her hand on his thigh.

He sat still for a while, his pulse throbbing at his neck.

"When did this happen?"

"Four months ago." He inhaled deeply. "The worst thing, June, is the guilt I feel for not having been there. That's the guilt that has been dogging me even though I couldn't recall why. I feel bad because of it. If I hadn't been out in those mountains, I might've been able to save them. And I'm weighed down by the fact it was my wiring that started the fire. I killed them, June."

"Jesse, you can't blame yourself. You were doing your job—"

"I *can* blame myself. June, listen to me—" He put his head back and stared at the ceiling, as if gravity might hold back some of the emotion suddenly gleaming in his eyes.

"I had unresolved issues with Annie," he said quietly. "I hadn't found a way to love Cameron yet. I wasn't even supposed to be in those mountains for so many days, weeks, months at a time. But I'd taken the warden job expressly to be away from Annie and the baby, from the ranch, to figure it all out. To find a way to deal with Annie's infidelity and the fact that Cameron was probably not my child."

"Oh, Jesse." June pushed herself higher onto her pillows.

He leveled his gaze at her.

"I needed the time to decide whether I wanted to go the DNA–paternity test route, or just to accept and love Cameron as my own. It wasn't his fault, and he was a beautiful child. But this idea of never knowing haunted me. And I couldn't help thinking of what Annie had done to our marriage every time I looked at 'our' baby boy—he was fair with green eyes. Annie had blue eyes, like I do, and almost blue-black hair." He swallowed. "In fact, I realize now that Darcy reminded me of Annie. I couldn't figure out why it bothered me looking at her, why her affection for Rafe seemed to cut at me so badly. Why I envied their obvious love."

"Tell me about Annie," June said softly. "How did you meet her?"

He rubbed the dark stubble on his jaw. "Some years back, before I ever considered the game-warden position, I used to guide hunting trips on horseback. I'd take time out from my cattle ranch in the Wind River foothills—leave the place in the hands of a manager—and guide a few high-end trips each season. Annie came with her father from New York one year, and she fell in love with the mountains, with me. I think it was more the whole Wyoming-cowboy image that got her, the romance of the open sky, the big ranch, which has been in my family for four generations… Whatever it was, her attention was intoxicating… We married a year later and settled on the ranch. She kept up her freelance editing business, flying back to New York for business once or twice each year, in addition to other travel." He paused.

"It worked well for a time, June—things were looking good. But then Annie met up with an old flame on a social-media site, someone she'd known from school who'd always had a thing for her. This guy flew down to see her, and they met at a town over, in a hotel bar. I learned from another rancher that she'd been seen there with a guy, and that they'd stayed overnight at the hotel together. I confronted her about it—it led to a terrible argument. Apparently they had hot monkey sex… She said it was a mistake, said she was sorry, wanted me to forgive her. She claimed it was a last-fling kind of thing, something she'd needed to get out of her system."

Jesse cleared his throat. "I took it hard, June. It wasn't so much a blow to my ego as the fact I'm a one-woman kinda guy. Commitment is huge to me. We battled along for some months, sidestepping each other. She grew unhappy. I was unhappy." He stared at June's hand on his jeans and the brackets around his mouth seemed to deepen, as did the lines around his eyes. June's heart broke for him.

"I fell out of love," he said quietly. "It was that simple, and that complicated. All the affection, the passion, just fizzled to nothing. It was a heavy time, and then came the news of her pregnancy. I figured the timing was such that it could've been from her night with her old flame. Annie said it wasn't, but only a paternity test would prove either way. That's when the job of game warden came up. It's what I had trained for when I left school, back in the days when I was young and wild, and when I used to do things like steer-wrestling." He smiled sadly, and June suddenly loved him, so wholly that it scared the crap out of her. She cleared her throat.

"So you took the warden's job?"

He nodded. "Mostly because it took me away, out into the wilderness, alone, sometimes for weeks at a time. I wanted to think—just me, the horses, the mountains, the big skies. I wanted to find a way to forgive her, June. I *wanted* to love the baby as our own. But you know what really cut? I'd wanted kids, and every time I'd broached the issue, Annie had stalled, saying she wasn't ready. And there she was, giving birth, caring for what was possibly another man's son." He swore softly. "It messed with my head."

"Are you sure he wasn't yours, Jesse?"

"Deep down, yeah, I was convinced Cameron wasn't mine. I think I was just afraid to do a test because it would just prove it with finality, drive it home, and I'd have to deal with it. We'd both have to make decisions. If I didn't do the test, I could still believe. There was still a chance. And that's what I was trying to work through when news of the fire reached me."

There was pain in his face, in the way he held his shoulders, in the corded muscles in his neck. And June understood—it was lack of closure. Because he hadn't done the test, there would forever remain the chance his own son had perished in the fire. Closure was a tough nut to crack, and the need for it sometimes difficult to understand.

"You didn't want to do a test…after?" she said.

He snorted softly. "Why? To make my grief worse? To mourn less for little Cameron because he wasn't my blood? Knowing doesn't diminish the fact a baby died."

She placed her hand on his forearm where he'd rolled up his shirt. His skin was warm, his dark hair coarse, masculine.

"Why'd you come to Cold Plains, Jesse? What was the promise you said you made to Annie?"

He scrubbed his brow, then winced slightly as he connected with the stitches along his temple.

"I sat with Annie at her hospital bed, until the end. She was in a lot of pain, badly burned. She pleaded again for my forgiveness, and I told her she had it, that I understood."

"Do you…understand?"

"I'm old-school, June. I try to get it, to see myself in her shoes if the situation had been reversed—I can't."

"So you lied. You can't feel bad about that, Jesse. You told her what she needed to hear so she could pass peacefully."

He lurched to his feet, began to pace the room. He reminded June of a caged mountain lion. At first he had been caged by his amnesia. Now that he remembered, the bars were his guilt. She understood guilt. She knew how it could pervade and darken one's life—even if logic told you it was irrational. You might try to push the guilt down into the basement of your subconscious, but it was always there, lurking, coloring everything else, no matter what you did in an effort to assuage it…no matter how many people you rescued from cults. And June realized with a start she was thinking of her own guilt, of Matt and Aiden. And her own relentless drive to set right the wrongs of her past.

"On her deathbed," Jesse said, "Annie told me her younger

brother, Michael, had been sucked in by a cult in Cold Plains. She said the cult was run by a man named Samuel Grayson and that his followers were called Devotees. I didn't know until that day that it existed, or that Michael was even in Wyoming. Annie hadn't mentioned it to me, or asked for my help up until then, because we were dealing with the problems between us, and she hadn't wanted to impose her own family issues on me. But as she was dying, she begged me to try and get Michael out. Annie explained it would be difficult, and she was the one who told me about the *D* tattoos."

June frowned. "What's Michael's surname?"

"Millwood."

Her pulse kicked. "Mickey Millwood? Early twenties, sweet, gentle guy, dark hair, big blue eyes?"

*"You know him?"*

"It's a small town, Jesse, and I've made it my business to try and know the Devotees. Michael works at Samuel's water warehouse where Hannah does the bookkeeping three times a week."

He stared at her, neck muscles, jaw, tight.

"So Hannah has access to him?"

"Yes, she does. She's been looking out for Michael—she calls him Mickey. Hannah feels he's...vulnerable."

"He's dyslexic. And a little slow, yeah, I know. Annie told me he'd come to Wyoming because she was here, but before he could make it up to Wind River he came through Cold Plains, and he got sucked in by Samuel. Then he stopped all communication. She was worried sick about him, especially because of his disabilities."

Hatred for Samuel washed afresh through June and her blood began to pound hard, her old energy, her fire, returning, burning into her veins. "Samuel takes advantage of whatever he can," she said bitterly. "A kid like Michael is especially defenseless—it makes me sick to the gut what Samuel's doing."

"I came to get him out, June. I vowed to Annie I would, if it's the last thing I did. That's why I had such a sense of mission and a feeling that my presence here was somehow connected to the name Samuel Grayson. That's why the words *Devotee* and *cult* felt somehow familiar to me. My plan was to hike in with nothing but my backpack, posing as a down-and-out ranch hand looking for work. I figured I'd let drop that I had a bit of a gambling problem, which I hoped might provide an opening for Samuel, make him sympathetic to me. I thought I'd attend his seminars, make it look like I was a potential Devotee. I had the *D* tattoo done, like Annie had described, in case I needed it as a way to get in—I wasn't sure what to expect when I arrived."

He slumped back down onto the bed beside June and rubbed his hands over his face.

"It took me three months after I buried Annie and Cameron to get my act together to come here. I had to hire someone to take care of the ranch and I had to sort out my finances. I packed up everything and resigned my warden's position—I didn't know how long it might take to get Michael out, or how long I'd have to be here. It didn't matter. I had nothing else."

He paused.

"And I didn't expect to find you."

"Hey, it was *me* who found *you* down that ravine, remember?"

A sad smile toyed with the corners of his beautiful mouth. "Good thing I picked the side of the mountain with a search-and-rescue expert and her K9, huh?"

She laughed. It felt good, and it hurt, too—both emotionally and physically. Her hand went to the bandage on her arm.

"You okay?"

"Yeah, I'm fine. Really."

*I'm a widower, June.*

Those few words had tipped her world onto a different axis. But caution whispered through her. His loss was fresh. And she felt as though she was balanced precariously at the edge of a precipice—both exhilarating and terrifying.

"The last thing I ever wanted was to hurt you, June," he said, his deep indigo gaze holding her. "And I never expected to fall so hard for you."

She wanted to tell him she'd fallen for him, too. Much too hard and much too fast, but the words wouldn't come.

"It's why I tried to step away from what was happening between us when I recalled marrying Annie. But at the same time I didn't *feel* married—I needed to figure out what it all meant, and I couldn't do it here. I couldn't hurt you. And I couldn't be here without wanting to be with you."

He paused, took her hands. "Can you understand that?"

She nodded. "I can," she whispered. "It was my fault, Jesse—"

He touched his fingers to her lips and shook his head. "I shouldn't have allowed myself to feel for you, June. But now I'm glad I did. And when I've got Michael out, I want you to come with me, back to the Wind River, where you can rest awhile." His eyes were serious, sharp, his rugged features, resolute.

"Eager would love it there," he said very quietly.

June swallowed. He was telling her that he was free to love her, possibly even make a life with her in the foothills of the Wind River Mountains, on his ranch, if she'd come home with him.

Suddenly it all felt too fast. June began to panic at the thought of leaving what she knew—her mission. She was compelled to keep working for EXIT, saving victims from cults like Samuel's.

"How about it, June? Come back with me."

He was asking her to jump off the edge of that mental precipice upon which she so precariously balanced, and she honestly didn't know if she could risk loving so deeply and wholly again, and losing again. A second time would kill her—she knew this in her heart. A raw and irrational kind of terror swelled inside June's chest. Her mouth turned dry and the walls of the cave room suddenly seemed to press in on her.

Worry crawled into Jesse's eyes.

"It's beautiful country up there, June. Rolling hills. And in the distance, the jagged range of snowcapped peaks. It's free, wild, open. I have land, horses." He paused, concern deepening in his features. "Do you ride?"

She fiddled with her wedding band, forcing herself not to glance toward the photo of Matt, Aiden and her on the dresser—to not think of the two ghosts that walked quietly and constantly at her side. But their presence was strong. They'd come to define who she was. They were the parameters of her life and she didn't know how to separate herself from them, or how to live without the specter of them.

Abruptly, June swung her legs over the side of the bed. She waited for a nauseating wave of dizziness and pain to pass, then got to her feet, a little wobbly.

"What're you doing, June?" Jesse said, standing up beside her, steadying her with a hand on her elbow. She moved out of his reach, walking over to the dresser where her firearm lay in its holster beside the framed photo—she stared at the image, the past swirling into the present and blurring the future.

"We need to go and get your brother-in-law out," she said, reaching for the holster and strapping her weapon to her hips. "It's time to pull Hannah out, too. It's getting too dangerous for her—I'm worried that as soon as Samuel learns his henchmen aren't coming back, and if Hawk arrests the mayor, this whole place is going to blow. Hannah is going to get hurt, or worse."

"You're not going anywhere." His tone was brusque. "I promised Rafe I'd make you rest."

She turned to face him, could see the pain in his features, and her chest hurt. "Jesse, you can't make me do anything. You're not in charge here."

"You're running, June. You're running from yourself and you know it."

"I am not! This is triage. This is urgent. This is what I do!"

"You're afraid to let it go, aren't you? You want to hold on to your past like a shield."

"Jesus, Jesse—Hannah's and Michael's lives could be in danger."

"So is yours. You're going to kill yourself like this, June."

"Oh, please." She grabbed a rain jacket from her closet and realized her hands were shaking. He was right, and she didn't want to—*couldn't*—admit it. Her arm hurt like hell as she pulled on her jacket.

"June, I'm not asking you to give up your work for EXIT. Do you understand that?"

She hesitated, then zipped up her jacket.

"All I want is for you to rest, heal, and for us to spend some time together, get to know each other better. I thought you'd love it out there. It's who you are—that wilderness. It's who I am. We could make it work."

"It can't work, Jesse—I don't see how it can. My work keeps me mobile. And I won't give it up."

"June." His voice softened. "You can do this. You do live somewhere now, right?"

June stilled. Perspiration beaded on her lip in spite of the chill she felt in her bones.

"I have a small apartment in Portland," she said quietly. "It's my base at the moment, but I'm never there, Jesse—"

"Let my ranch be your base, temporarily. Baby steps."

She felt blood draining from her head. She felt hot. Anxiety, she thought. She was having a panic attack.

"I need to go."

"Sit down, June," he said firmly, taking her hands and leading her back to the bed. He seated himself beside her.

"Listen to me, and don't take this the wrong way. Don't say anything, either. I just want you to think about what I'm going to say." He inhaled deeply.

"You're trapped, June, not so much by your fight against cults, but by your notion that fighting them can change something about the past—that it can make right what happened to your husband and son."

"They're part of me," she said quietly. "Fighting the evil of cults is part of me, too, now."

"And it always will be. All of us are composites of our past experience. Our pasts shape us, make us who we are. But you can't change the past."

"I can give it meaning."

"You have."

"And where I wasn't able to save Matt and Aiden, I'm saving others. They didn't die in vain."

"I know. But you're not living, either, June. You're like an addict, obsessed with this fight, needing more and more, and if you don't stop, it's going to kill you. Even Rafe said so."

Anger mushroomed in her chest. "This is ridiculous," she said, trying to get up, but he held her back.

"Let me go, Jesse," she warned.

"You need balance," he countered, features stern, eyes unyielding. "And you need rest. Now."

"Who in hell are you to talk, anyway! Look at *you*—

haunted by your own demons for something you never even did, for closure you can't have."

Hurt flashed through his face and she hated herself even as the words came out of her mouth, but she was unable to stop.

"You couldn't even get that DNA test because then you'd have to face the truth."

His eyes narrowed.

"I learned something from losing my memory, June," he said very quietly, his voice thick. "For a short while I was forced to live entirely in the moment, and in that moment, I allowed myself to fall in love with you." He paused, his gaze tunneling into hers, intense. "I think you allowed yourself to drop into that moment with me. I think you do care. And I'm not going to let you throw this away now."

Her throat closed in on itself. Panic flared afresh. With it came a kind of pounding thrill, an undertow of exhilaration. He'd said he loved her.

Could she do it?

She glanced at the clock on the bedside table and tensed.

"Time is running out, Jesse. I can't think about the future now. I need to think about how to get Hannah and Michael out. I'm also due for a paramedic shift this afternoon. If I don't show, Samuel and Fargo are going to tie me with the missing henchmen. They're going to take a deeper look at Hannah. Something's going to give."

He swore softly. "You're like a pit bull on adrenaline, June. You *can't* even think anymore, can you? This is going to kill you, and you don't care, do you?"

June sucked in a chestful of air, and it hit her—Jesse was right, she hadn't cared. She knew she was on a one-way track until the end, and deep down in her subconscious maybe she wanted it to kill her. Because she had nothing else.

Now there was Jesse.

Now she *did* care.

She glanced slowly up into his eyes, and her heart wrenched at what she saw there. June bit her lip, struggling to hold down the huge painful and sudden surge of emotion burning in her chest. She reached down, felt Eager's velvet head, thought of wilderness and mountains and endless land. Tears pooled in her eyes. It was all she and Matt had ever dreamed of.

And now Jesse was offering it to her. He was offering her a second chance. He was trying to pull her back from the brink. And she was too scared to let him. He was right there, too. Because she was afraid to stop.

She was holding on to her guilt and her past as a way of escaping pain, as a way of fending off emotion, love. It was fear that was trapping her, not cults. Fear to feel—*really feel*—again. And she could see it now, through his eyes. Fear was at the root of it all—June Farrow, SAR worker, paramedic, so brave in the woods, so capable, so independent…and all she was, truly, deep down, was weak, alone. Afraid.

Jesse had cracked something in her open. And it was bleeding out.

"I promise," she said, very softly, "that I will rest after I've got Hannah out. Let me tie this job off, Jesse. If something happens to Hannah now, if I don't do something to help her now, I'll never be able to live with myself. I can get Michael out, too—he works with Hannah. She has a shift with him at the warehouse today." She paused. "*We* can get them both, Jesse. Help me do this one last thing, and I will help you honor your promise to Annie."

Emotion pooled in his eyes and twisted raw through his rugged features. He cupped her face, firmly, in his hands.

"Then will you at least just think about my proposal?"

"Yes," she whispered.

"I love you, June," he said, voice thick. And he kissed her, so tenderly, caringly, that she felt she was melting from the inside out, becoming fluid, one with him. And for a moment June wanted time to stand still, for him to hold her forever. She wanted, just for a while, to be cared for. To lean on him. And to be a team. It struck her then—she could have this. Possibly forever. If she was brave enough to reach out and take the hand he was offering to her.

While Jesse went to find some dry gear, June braided her hair in front of the mirror. Her arm was stiffening, and the pain was uncomfortable, but she knew her medicine and the wound wasn't going to kill her. She noted the deep black circles under her eyes, the contrasting pallor of her complexion. She'd lost weight, too—how had she not noticed that?

June realized with a start that she actually looked fragile, ill. Had she been so blind to herself as not to see? Had she been similarly blind to what was driving her into the ground?

She glanced down at the family photo of her, Matt, Aiden and their old yellow Lab, and a warmth filled June, an acceptance. She studied Matt's features, and Aiden's; the way they seemed so close, yet so independent; the way Matt had his arm over her shoulders. And June allowed all the good memories to come, to wash over her until she felt Eager nudge against her leg. Then she slipped off her wedding band, opened a small box on the dresser and removed a chain.

June slid the ring onto the chain and fastened it around her neck. The metal was warm on her skin. She clasped her hand over it.

Matt would want her to have a life. Maybe it really was time to move on—to let go of the bad memories, hold on to the good. To live in the present and dream of a future.

Samuel put down the phone after speaking to Mayor Rufus Kittridge. He leaned slowly back into his leather chair, trying to hold on to a measure of calm as he mulled over what Rufus had just told him.

Two of his henchmen, Lumpy Smithers and Harvey Daniels, had not returned after making apparent radio contact with Molly Rigg on the west flank where Lacy Matthews had vanished, and where the mystery mountain man had shot Jason Barnes.

Samuel chewed on several possible scenarios. The one that concerned him most was that Smithers and Daniels had fallen into the hands of Agent Hawk Bledsoe. Samuel knew how choked Lumpy was over the death of Jason Barnes. Lumpy could become a problem if offered a plea bargain by the feds. But in that event it would be Rufus who went down, not Samuel.

Still, if the good citizens of Cold Plains—his flock— learned that their kindly mayor was possibly a violent and dangerous man who killed any Devotees who attempted to escape, it was going to make things very complicated for Samuel. It could even signal the beginning of the end. Rage surged suddenly through him and he lurched to his feet and paced his office.

The more he'd thought about it, the more he'd begun to realize that vulnerable Devotees among his flock had first begun to "disappear" shortly after Mia Finn—Agent Bledsoe's new sister-in-law—had "defected" and apparently undergone deprogramming.

Samuel's thoughts turned again to the stranger in the woods who had helped Lacy escape.

Who was he?

His mind went to how June Farrow and her dog had found Lacy's kid's shoe on the opposite side of the mountain, miles away from where Smithers and Barnes had seen her fleeing in the dark. The image of June with that newcomer—Jesse

Marlboro—sifted into Samuel's mind. A cold, sinister suspicion began to unfurl in him.

He grabbed the phone on his desk and dialed Police Chief Bo Fargo.

"Fargo, when did June Farrow first arrive in town?"

"Early April, I think."

"When did the first Devotee disappear into a rumored safe-house program?"

Samuel could hear the sound of flicking paper—presumably Fargo looking something up.

"Actually, they started disappearing shortly after June Farrow's arrival in Cold Plains."

Samuel picked up a pencil, held it tight in his hand, his vision darkening. "She saw that paramedic job in the new paper—that's what brought her here?"

"Correct."

His hand fisted around the pencil. The old-fashioned clock on his paneled wall ticked. It was almost 9:00 a.m. "And you didn't notice these parallels before?"

Fargo cleared his throat. "June Farrow helped on the searches for the missing Devotees. There was no reason for mistrust."

Several beats of silence hung between them. Then Fargo said, "But recently, she has been acting out of character. She's been going over to Little Gulch for things she should be able to access here, like a vet, and then to pick up that Jesse Marlboro character she apparently used to date."

Rage peaked inside Samuel—he was surrounded by imbeciles.

"Check her out," he said very calmly. "See if her background story ties up. And take a deeper look at her landlady, Hannah Mendes. Also, look into the story behind this Jesse Marlboro, find out where Mia Finn went for deprogramming."

"You think June Farrow is part of the underground evacuation program?"

"That, Fargo, is your goddamn job!"

Samuel put the phone down and swore. Then he took a slow, deep breath—showing anger implied weakness. He must not display weakness. He was God to these people.

But the more Samuel considered it, the more it made sense for June Farrow to be the insider. The mole. The traitor. Stealing away members of his flock. The woman trying to personally undermine *him*.

A bitter and murderous rage blossomed through his chest. June Farrow was his enemy and he wanted her gone. Now.

Concern showed in Hannah Mendes's keen gray eyes as she opened her door to Jesse and June. "What's going on—what's happened?"

Jesse saw that Hannah's silver hair was long and tied smoothly back from a tanned and angular face. Even in her seventies Hannah was clearly an attractive woman with strong features and a slender body.

"We need to kill the evacuation program, Hannah," June said as she and Jesse entered Hannah's hallway.

"What do you mean?" Hannah said, pulling her sweater closer around her body.

"Two henchmen attacked the safe house last night. We had a mole inside, Molly Rigg. She led the attackers in via radio."

"Oh, my goodness." Hannah paled as her veined hand went to her chest. "Is everyone all right?"

"We're all fine—but things are going to blow. We need to pull you out, now."

"Come into the kitchen," Hannah said, leading the way. "I'm going to put the coffee on while you tell me everything."

"Agent Hawk Bledsoe and his team have Lumpy and Molly in custody, and it looks as though Hawk will soon be arresting Rufus Kittridge. He's apparently one of Samuel's lead henchmen, along with Monica Pearl."

"Are you serious?" Hannah hesitated, coffeepot in hand.

"Dead serious," June said, seating herself at the big wooden table in the middle of the warm and generously sized kitchen.

"I never pegged Rufus or Monica for being killers," Hannah said quietly. She put the pot on and took mugs from the cupboard. She moved with a certain elegance and grace, thought Jesse. And for a startling moment he could imagine June looking like Hannah at that age. The unbidden thought fueled the fire burning in him to have her with him forever. He glanced at June.

She caught his eyes in return. A moment passed between them. Hannah saw, and stilled briefly before busying herself with teaspoons and cream and sugar.

While Hannah poured the coffee, June told her who Jesse really was, and how he'd come to Cold Plains to free his brother-in-law.

"I know Mickey," Hannah said, seating herself across from them. "He's a dear boy—too vulnerable, too easily manipulated. I've been wanting to get him out for a while."

"Do you think we'll have a problem convincing him to leave, Hannah?" Jesse said.

Hannah pursed her lips. "He's not inclined to violence, if that's what you mean—not an angry bone in that boy's body. But he might be fearful and raise the alarm."

"I'll be ready to use force as an intervention if I have to," Jesse said. "But I don't want to. If you can help smooth my way with him, I'd be eternally grateful, Hannah."

Hannah nodded, glanced at June. "And you want to do this *today?*"

June leaned forward. "We *have* to move today, Hannah.

And we have to get you out today, as well. The evacuation program has become far too dangerous now."

"Oh, June, I can't just leave. There will still be people who need me, who need to escape Samuel, *especially* if things start to go off the rails now that Hawk is closing in."

"Hannah, you're not going to help anyone dead."

She set her mug slowly onto the table. "I don't run, June." She shot Jesse a glance, a hint of reproach in her keen gray eyes, as if he was somehow responsible for the decision to kill the evacuation program. As if he'd swayed June in some way. "Nor do you run, June," she said.

"I do, Hannah," June said quietly. "I've been running a long time." June reached for Jesse's hand and covered it with her own as she caught his eyes. "It's time I stopped running now and faced my fears. Faced change."

His heart almost burst.

"Besides, Hawk and his FBI team *are* closing in. It's not going to be long now and this *will* be over."

Hannah shook her head, her eyes sad. "My heart is in these mountains, June, in this valley. I grew up on this ranch. I buried my husband here. I cannot just up and leave. Where would I go?"

"The cave house is still safe, for now," June said.

"And for how long, if what you say is true? And I'm not as confident as you that Samuel is going down without a very long fight, yet. Where would I go in the interim? I have no-where."

"My place." The words came out of Jesse's mouth before he even thought them through.

June and Hannah both looked at him.

He cleared his throat. "I have a ranch in the Wind River foothills, Hannah. You'll love it—all the mountains and space you could ever need. I've got guest cottages, horses. You could stay there for as long as it takes for the feds to wind things up with Samuel here."

Hannah stared at him. And June's eyes said it all—*thank you*. The affection he felt coming from her made his heart swell.

"Do it, Hannah," June said, leaning forward. "Go pack a bag with the essentials, now. Give it to Jesse. He'll keep it with him in my truck after he's dropped me off at the Urgent Care Center for my ambulance shift later today, then he'll immediately drive out and park near the warehouse. You go to work as normal. Then at about 3:30 p.m., shortly after I've started my shift, you get yourself near Michael and a telephone, and you develop serious chest pains."

"I don't know, June, that's like tempting the fates. I don't like to tempt the fates."

"It's about getting yourself and Michael to safety, Hannah. Samuel's deception must be fought with deception of its own. It's what we do, remember?"

Hannah inhaled deeply. "What then?"

"You ask Michael to call 9-1-1. Dispatch will send the call straight through to me. The dispatcher will keep Michael on the line, near you, which is what we want. I'll bring the ambulance around to the warehouse door at the back."

"Aren't there two of you in the ambulance?" Hannah said.

June nodded. "Ted is on call with me this afternoon. He'll be driving. The whole thing will seem very real to him, Hannah, given your age. No offense."

"None taken." Hannah smiled. "I think."

"Chest pains are funny things," June said. "Not to be taken lightly even if there is no other physical sign of distress, so I'll get out the gurney, insist you come to the hospital for a checkup. You hang on to Michael's hand, tell him you need him to come in the ambulance for moral support."

"That could work," said Hannah. "Mickey would bend

over backward to help anyone, and he does have a soft spot for me—we've built a bond."

"So he'll trust you. That's good. Meanwhile, Jesse will be waiting outside the building with my truck, parked right near the delivery entrance where we'll back the ambulance up. If anyone asks, he'll say he's come to pick up a check from you for ranch supplies."

Hannah nodded. "That would ring true, since he's my new hired help."

"Good. Then while Ted and I push you on the gurney back to the waiting ambulance, you start fretting about your purse and the money inside, or whatever. Make a scene. I'll tell Ted to go back and get your purse. While he does, Jesse grabs Michael, and I get you off that gurney, stat, and into the waiting truck. If all goes to plan, we'll be gone before Ted even returns, especially if you put your purse in a place difficult to find."

Hannah stared at them. Silence swelled, and the kitchen clock ticked.

"This is really it?" Hannah said quietly.

"It's down to the wire now, Hannah."

"We can never come back after we pull something like this off—not while Samuel is still around."

June nodded.

"Are you *sure* it's that dire?"

"Even Hawk Bledsoe said this whole place is set to blow," Jesse said. "No one wants another Waco, but Samuel is apparently getting desperate, and who knows how far he will go to protect what he has?"

Hannah sucked in a deep breath. "Okay...let's do it."

# *Chapter 12*

June's heart pounded as they burst out of the warehouse pushing Hannah on the gurney toward the waiting ambulance, Michael running at their side as he held on to Hannah's hand.

Jesse stepped out of the shadows behind the warehouse door. "Michael!" he whispered.

Michael froze dead in his tracks at the sudden sight of his brother-in-law, shock, confusion, then fear crossing his face.

"Quick, Michael, over here," Jesse said in a harsh whisper.

"Jesse? What…what are you doing here? Is Annie here?"

"I need to talk to you about Annie, Michael—"

"My purse!" Hannah suddenly screamed hysterically. "I left my purse inside. I need it. It has my money, medication, everything in it!"

Ted shot a glance at June.

"I—I've got to have my purse!"

"Ted, can you go back and get it for her?" June leaned

down and said calmly to Hannah, "Where is it? Can you tell him?"

"It's…by my desk in the accounting office at the back of the warehouse."

"Go," June said briskly to Ted. "I'll be fine getting her in by myself. We'll be ready to roll as soon as you're back."

He hesitated. "Go!" insisted June forcefully. "We might need whatever medication she has in there."

Relief washed through her as Ted turned and raced back into the building.

"Quick." She rapidly unstrapped Hannah and helped her off the stretcher. Taking her arm, they rushed toward the idling truck before Ted could return. To June's shock Michael was sitting passively in the backseat with Jesse behind the wheel.

June helped Hannah into the back so she could sit beside Michael and keep him calm. She flung herself into the passenger seat, slammed the door. "Go!"

Jesse hit the gas and wheeled out of the warehouse parking lot, tires spinning on loose gravel. He headed for the road that would take them to Little Gulch.

June turned around in her seat. Michael was crying softly in the back, murmuring Annie's name. Hannah's hand rested on his knee.

"I told him about Annie," Jesse said, eyes fixed on the road as they sped past the ranches, heading toward the mountains. The plan was to drive straight out to Little Gulch and leave Hannah there with her sister-in-law while a flight out to Wind River could be organized for her.

June, Jesse and Michael would meanwhile tackle the long hike back to the cave house from Little Gulch. The hike would be too much for Hannah, and there was no point in bringing her unnecessarily all the way back to the safe house.

Jesse had contacted his ranch manager, who would send a vehicle to welcome Hannah at the airstrip in Wind River.

"He didn't know about Annie and the fire?" June said.

"No. I told him briefly what happened, and that I'd promised Annie I'd come get him. It was all such a shock he came peaceably."

"It's going to be okay, Michael," June said softly, turning around in her seat to hand him some tissues.

Michael's face was still as open and innocent as a young boy's, his eyes large and filled with pain. Her heart went out to him. "I promise you it's going to be all right."

"I—I didn't know," Michael sobbed. "I would've come if I'd known about the fire, if Jesse could have gotten hold of me—"

"We didn't have a contact number, Michael," said Jesse.

"S-Samuel t-told me it would be better not to have any contact until…I got a solid grasp on being the best me I could be. S-Samuel said family often tries to stop you from im-provement. They're the gatekeepers, he said. They t-try to sabotage you." He blew his nose. "I feel so bad, Jesse. I wasn't even there for her memorial service."

"There's nothing you could have done, Michael," Jesse said, eyes still on the road, his shoulders tight. "I'll tell you more about what happened when we get somewhere safe, but Annie made me vow to come find you, and I did. She wanted you safe. She understood what was happening here. And she will now rest in peace because you're out of there."

"You did the right thing, Mickey," Hannah said gently, putting her arm around the young man. "You'll see. June's right—it's all going to be okay."

They drove in silence, the ribbon of road undulating behind them as they left Cold Plains in the distance. Up ahead, along the distant horizon, there was a break in the cloud and sun streamed through onto the mountains.

June reached out and placed her hand on Jesse's knee.

"Thank you," she said quietly. "We make a good team."

He shot her a glance, unable to temper the light in his eyes, and a ghost of a smile curved his lips. "That's what I kept trying to tell you," he said.

Jesse took one hand off the wheel, covered hers on his knee and realized the wedding band on her finger was gone.

He felt a lump form in his throat, and emotion pricked behind his eyes. And he knew he'd won. He was going to take her home.

*Five days later...*

News of Mayor Rufus Kittridge's arrest by the FBI spread like wildfire through town as Devotees flocked down to the municipal offices to watch in shock and horror as their avuncular mayor was handcuffed and frog-marched by agents in bulletproof vests toward a waiting federal vehicle.

Samuel watched the whole thing from his window—the feds taking *his* mayor, his key militia leaders. His ace in the hole. Rage pounded through his blood—the effrontery of it, right there in the street below his own office window.

He stilled suddenly as he saw another two federal agents marching Monica Pearl down the street toward the gleaming black SUVs. Monica wore a summer dress of modest length, patterned with small roses—Samuel knew the dress intimately. Her blond hair was tied back demurely and her pretty cheeks were flushed—he could see that even from here.

People were gathering on sidewalks to watch, many of them Devotees who'd arrived early for the nightly seminar. And right then, as the bumbling agents put the handcuffed

Monica into the black SUV and closed the door on her, the bells of the community center began to peal—calling his Devotees to the seminar.

Hawk Bledsoe had orchestrated the whole thing for maximum effect, to undermine Samuel in the eyes of his Devotees. Before Hawk got into his own vehicle, he glanced up at Samuel's window, catching his eyes.

It was like a punch to his gut.

The shameless, impudent boldness of it! The barefaced audacity—parading Rufus and Monica in front of the others like that, staging a production designed to undermine *him,* Samuel Grayson! It cut to the heart of his pride, his grasp on complete power. Now he was going to be forced to address this incident in his seminar tonight, and it was going to look as if he was covering something up.

A knock sounded on his oak door.

He swung around.

It was his assistant, Jenny Smith. "I started the bells ringing, Samuel. You will be at your seminar tonight, won't you?"

"Why the hell not!" he barked, his face feeling hot. He hated that. He never showed loss of control in front of a loyal Devotee.

He breathed in deep and then exhaled slowly, counting to three. He smiled warmly.

"I apologize, Jenny. The arrest of Mayor Kittridge has come as a big surprise to us all—I'm still personally reeling from the shock, but the seminar will go on as planned."

"They say he's going to be charged with murder, of our *own,*" she whispered. "I even heard rumors he could be involved in the Cold Plains Five murders, and Monica Pearl, too… I just can't believe—"

"And so you shouldn't," said Samuel. "The FBI needs to show something for their efforts here, and this is simply a witch hunt." Samuel placed his hand on Jenny's shoulder.

"In fact, it's a sign we're finally achieving our goals. Because the higher you go, Jenny," he said affectionately, "the better you become, the more it threatens people who have not managed to improve their own lives." His gaze held hers so she couldn't escape, couldn't think, couldn't do anything other than look at him, hear the authoritative but kind cadence of his voice, see the wisdom in his eyes.

"You *know* you are successful when people like Agent Hawk Bledsoe move in like parasites. They will try to tear down what we have built, and, more than ever now, we must rally together during this trial."

Jenny smiled, nodded. "Thank you, Samuel."

The adoration in her eyes bolstered him.

"Now go. And, Jenny," Samuel called out behind her, "make sure the bell rings extra loud and extra long tonight. I shall be holding a very special address."

Samuel listened as the peals designed to resemble an old church bell—sonorous and uplifting and goose-bump inducing—resounded down the streets of Cold Plains, Wyoming, through his cleaned-up cowboy town, across the ranches and into the hills and forests where somewhere there was rumored to be a safe house he had yet to find.

And outside, down in the streets, the doors of the black federal vehicles closed, and they drove off in a convoy with flashing lights as they took away Mayor Rufus Kittridge and Monica Pearl.

June came out of the room where she'd been counseling Michael.

"How's he doing?" Jesse said.

She smiled. "Great. He's a good kid, Jesse. He's totally guileless and so easily manipulated, but the shock of actually seeing you in Cold Plains, and hearing about his older sister's death at the same time, jolted him right out of whatever spell Samuel had him under. He's going to be fine."

He touched her arm. "Come outside. I've got sundowners out on the patio."

The cave house was empty at the moment, apart from her, Jesse, Michael and Eager. Over the past five days June and Jesse had moved the others out to where they could access further counseling from EXIT and go on to new lives.

"Michael needs a dog," June said as she followed Jesse out onto the stone patio. "He's thriving in the company of Eager—" She stilled suddenly at the sight before her.

The sky was streaked with cirrus clouds that had been painted hot-pink and orange by the sinking sun. The air was warm and filled with the soft sound of birds.

Jesse grinned. "See? I thought it might be nice to sit out here for a bit."

Her heart filled. She loved him more than she could imagine. But as she moved toward the stone table, she froze again, this time at a sound in the distance.

"Did you hear that?"

Jesse came up beside her and listened, the warm evening breeze ruffling his hair.

"It's Samuel's bells," he said.

She nodded. "Sometimes when the air currents are just right you can hear them ringing all the way over here, summoning his flock to the community center."

"You think he's worried?"

"He has to be," said June. "Hawk was going to do the arrests right before the seminar." She looked at her watch. "If all went to plan, Rufus Kittridge and Monica Pearl should be in federal custody about now, thanks to the quick plea-bargain acceptance from both Lumpy Smithers and Molly Rigg."

"You've done good here, June."

"I'm not done yet. Samuel still has to go down."

"It'll happen. Soon." He put his arm around her shoulders and drew her close as they stood watching the clouds change color and the sky deepen to indigo—the same color as Jesse's eyes, thought June. His eyes were the color of an early-evening sky. Up high above the forest, two eagles soared, watchful over the Wyoming hills and valleys.

"Mostly," he said, very quietly, "I want to thank you for saving my life, June, and for helping me honor my vow to Annie. I can move forward now."

"Did you love her, Jesse?"

He was silent for a long while.

"I stopped being able to love Annie some time ago," he said quietly. "Maybe we weren't even a good match to start with, but I like to believe we could have made a go of it, because when I make a promise, June, the commitment, it's everything to me."

"I know," she whispered as she leaned into him, enjoying the solid strength of his body, the fact she actually had someone to lean on after all these years.

"We could be good together, you know that?" he said.

She smiled. "Yeah," she said softly, "I think we could."

Jesse's heart kicked. *Easy, boy—don't rush it. You came on way too fast and strong the other night, asking her to move in with you so soon.*

He said cautiously, "June, once our work here—"

She glanced up at him. "*Our* work?"

"Which part did you miss about being a team?"

"Yes, but—"

"But what? I want to help you finish here. You helped me put my promise to Annie to bed, now I want to help you fulfill your promise to Matt and Aiden."

She stared at him. "It was never like that, Jesse—it wasn't a promise."

"Well," he said, a mischievous playfulness entering his rugged features, "I wasn't going to call it an obsession or anything."

She laughed, and, damn, it felt good to be able to laugh about something like that. Then she sobered as she saw lust darkening in his eyes.

"I'm not scared to let them go anymore." She smiled. "I'm not afraid to take a second chance." She leaned up, hooking her arms around his neck, drawing him down to her.

"I love you, Jesse Marlboro," she whispered against his lips.

He smiled against her mouth. "Grainger."

She shook her head. "I always wanted a mountain cowboy, just like in those old ads, so I'm going to keep my Marlboro Man." And she kissed him as the sun began to sink behind the hills, and the bells in Cold Plains grew silent.

*Three days later...*

The FBI had made further arrests and laid charges against Rufus Kittridge and Monica Pearl for their roles in three of the Cold Plains Five murders, specifically twenty-nine-year-old Shelby Jackson, thirty-four-year-old Laurel Pierce and twenty-five-year-old Abby Michaels.

Shelby Jackson was rumored to have been dating Samuel Grayson when she'd disappeared five years ago. Laurel Pierce was the estranged wife of local rancher Nathan Pierce. And Abby Michaels was the mother of Rafe Black's still-missing nine-month-old son, Devin.

Agent Hawk Bledsoe had informed June and Jesse that he expected to get more evidence soon, something to finally nail Samuel himself. But until then, everyone remained restless and nervous—things were coming to a head.

Meanwhile, June and Jesse had driven out from Little

Gulch to meet Darcy Craven two towns over. From there they'd hiked in to where the body of Jane Doe, murder victim number two, had been found.

Darcy now stood atop a rocky ridge, hands on her hips as she caught her breath. Her cheeks were pink from exertion and her hair damp from a soft summer rain. All around them the forest was shrouded in heavy layers of mist.

They'd been following Eager on an air-scent search all morning, and they'd found nothing apart from litter and the odd garment left by hikers.

While Darcy rested and June watered Eager, Jesse had gone down the opposite side of the ridge to check out a small trail they'd seen earlier.

"June, I want to thank you both for doing this," Darcy said. "I know you didn't believe we'd find anything. But I just had to come and look."

"Hey, it's the least we could do, Darcy. I just wish we *could* find something for you that would help with your mother's identity," June said as she screwed the cap back onto her water bottle.

"Isn't this near where Samuel once had a cabin?" Darcy asked, turning in a full circle.

"I had no idea he had a cabin in these parts," said June, checking her GPS.

Darcy frowned and bit the inside of her cheek. "I *think* the cabin was supposed to be in this area—I'm sure that's what I heard Officer Ford say some time ago, that Samuel and his brother used to camp out this way when they were young."

June reached for her radio and keyed it. "June for Jesse?" she released the key and the radio crackled.

"At your service, K9 team."

June grinned, and keyed again. "Any signs of an old cabin down your way?"

"Negative. Trail seems to go nowhere. I'm going to head back up."

But as June hooked the radio onto her belt, Eager's hackles rose and his tail suddenly went straight as an arrow. June stilled, feeling a sudden eeriness, as if they were being watched.

"Easy, boy," she whispered to Eager as she turned in a slow circle, carefully scanning the woods, her hand going instinctively for her weapon.

"What is it?" Darcy came up to her side, suddenly nervous.

"Are you sure you weren't followed out here, Darcy?"

"I—I'm pretty sure."

A branch cracked. June spun to face the trees from whence the noise had come. She waited.

Fingers of mist curled out from the trees, swirling around the bases like wraiths. Branches rustled suddenly. June's mouth went bone-dry.

Eager growled, baring fangs.

"Who's there?" June called as she drew her gun and clicked off the safety.

"Maybe it's an animal," whispered Darcy.

"It's human," June said, eyes fixed on the bushes. "Eager reacts differently for animals."

A dark shape moved suddenly behind the branches.

"Identify yourself or I'll shoot!" June yelled.

Silent as the swirling mist, a dark shape shifted forward. June's heart began to thud. It was a man. Tall, broad of shoulder. Wearing military-style camouflage gear. And as he emerged from the mist she saw he held a shotgun. It was aimed right at her face.

"It's *Samuel!*" Darcy hissed, grabbing June's arm.

Sweat broke out over June's body. He came closer, his eyes transfixed by Darcy. "My God," he said to Darcy. "You look just like Catherine."

Darcy slumped to the ground in a dead faint. And up close, June saw that while this man was almost the spitting image of Samuel Grayson, he was not the cult leader.

"My name is Micah," the man said, lowering his weapon and crouching down beside Darcy, feeling for her pulse. She came around as Micah touched her, and he helped her into a sitting position, staring hard at her.

"You really do look like Catherine George—we used to come out here to the cabin. Her, me, Samuel. Sometimes others."

June swallowed as it hit her square between the eyes—she was looking at Samuel Grayson's fraternal twin, the legendary mercenary. The man Hawk Bledsoe had been searching for to help him take Samuel down.

Micah turned his attention to June. His features were fiercely handsome, his hair dark, his eyes a vivid green, and he exuded the same palpable presence that his powerful brother did—except different.

"I'm June Farrow," she said, still a little unsure of whether to holster her Glock. To her relief she saw Jesse coming up the ridge. And before Micah could aim his twelve-gauge at Jesse, June said, "And that's Jesse Grainger."

Jesse froze for a nanosecond.

"It's not Samuel," June called out to him. "It's his twin, Micah Grayson."

They all stared at him, a little in awe. The Mercenary had returned.

* * * * *

# "You need to leave. Now."

"I can't just leave you..." he said.

"Why not?" she asked. "You didn't come here to protect me. You came here to force me to provide you with an alibi. I can't do that. I can't perjure myself and swear you never left me that night."

"I didn't want you to perjure yourself," he said. "I wanted you to tell the truth."

"I have," she said.

He wished he could be certain that he believed her.

"So why are you still here?" she asked.

He gestured toward her bedroom, to where their daughter lay sleeping. He couldn't put into words what he already felt for his daughter—the protectiveness, the affection, the devotion...

"Until a few hours ago you didn't even know she existed," she reminded him.

"Whose fault was that?" he asked, the question slipping out with his bitterness.

# BABY BREAKOUT

## BY
## LISA CHILDS

MILLS & BOON®

First published in Great Britain 2012
by Mills & Boon, an imprint of Harlequin (UK) Limited,
Eton House, 18-24 Paradise Road, Richmond, Surrey TW9 1SR

© Lisa Childs-Theeuwes 2012

ISBN: 978 0 263 89549 0
ebook ISBN: 978 1 408 97243 4

46-0812

Harlequin (UK) policy is to use papers that are natural, renewable and recyclable products and made from wood grown in sustainable forests. The logging and manufacturing processes conform to the legal environmental regulations of the country of origin.

Printed and bound in Spain
by Blackprint CPI, Barcelona

Bestselling, award-winning author **Lisa Childs** writes paranormal and contemporary romance for Mills & Boon. She lives on thirty acres in west Michigan with her husband, two daughters, a talkative Siamese and a long-haired Chihuahua who thinks she's a rottweiler. Lisa loves hearing from readers, who can contact her through her website, www.lisachilds.com, or snail mail address, PO Box 139, Marne, MI 49435, USA.

To my babies, who are now amazing young women. Ashley and Chloe, I am so proud and blessed to be your mother. There is nothing the two of you can't accomplish with your intelligence and determination.

# *Prologue*

The high-pitched beep of a breaking-news bulletin drew Erica Towsley's attention to the television screen. "During a prison riot tonight at Blackwoods Penitentiary in northern Michigan, cop killer Jedidiah Kleyn was among several prisoners to escape."

*Jedidiah Kleyn.*

Legs shaking, Erica dropped onto the edge of her sofa. She grabbed a pillow and clasped it against her chest as she struggled to breathe.

*No. No. No. Not Jedidiah...*

The report continued, "He is considered extremely dangerous."

Goose bumps lifted on her skin. *Dangerous* was an understatement for Jedidiah Kleyn's capacity for violence. Images flitted through her mind, as she recalled the graphic photographs she had been shown of the scene of the horrific crimes Jedidiah had been convicted of committing.

"If anyone believes they have seen this man or any of the other escaped..."

Ears buzzing with her pounding pulse, Erica could catch only snatches of what the serious-faced anchorwoman said.

"...contact authorities immediately. Do not approach these men..."

What if one of these men approached her? Would she have time to contact authorities before he killed her?

## Chapter One

"Jed, let me bring you in," DEA agent Rowe Cusack's voice crackled in the beat-up pay-phone receiver.

Because everyone had cell phones nowadays, Jed had been lucky to find a pay phone, let alone one that was still working. But then this small mid-Michigan town was a throwback to about fifty years ago. With bright-colored awnings on its storefronts that faced out onto cobblestone streets, Miller's Valley might as well have been called Mayberry.

"You're not safe out there," Rowe continued.

Even at night, with the antique street lamps barely burning holes into the darkness, it was hard to imagine any danger here. Despite the cold and blowing snow, in any other city, people would have still been out—selling or buying things or services that shouldn't be commodities. Jedidiah Kleyn would like to believe that there was actually a place where no crime happened, where no evil existed, but he'd learned the hard way that nothing and nobody were ever as innocent as they might appear. And at times, some things and some people weren't as guilty, either.

"Is that because I'm a cop killer?" Jed asked quietly with a quick glance around him to make sure nobody overheard. But the cobblestone street was really de-

serted. No one lurked in the shadows here, as they had
at Blackwoods.

This town, on the outskirts of Grand Rapids, Michigan, was so rural that everyone was early to bed, early
to rise. So hopefully no one, inside their little houses
behind their picket fences, was awake yet to notice the
stranger in the borrowed dark wool jacket with the knit
cap pulled low over his face, walking the snow-dusted
streets of their town.

"You're not a killer." The certainty in the lawman's
voice eased some of Jed's anxiety.

"That's not what a jury of my peers and a judge decided three years ago." He had been convicted of killing his business partner and a police officer who must
have happened upon the murder.

"I've been going through the case file and the court
transcripts," the agent said.

For the past three years he'd wanted to get his hands
on those files, but his lawyer hadn't been able to get
the records past the guards at Blackwoods Penitentiary.
The maximum security prison had had no law library,
no way for prisoners to learn about their legal rights.

The warden hadn't cared that even convicted killers had the right to aid in their own appeals. Jefferson
James hadn't been just the prison warden. He'd been
the judge, at least the appeals court judge, the jury and,
more often than not, the executioner.

But Jed was no longer in any danger from Warden
James. The warden was the one behind bars now. So
Jed focused on what was truly important—on what had
kept him going for the past three years.

"Did you find anything that will prove I was framed?"
And who the hell had done it?

A sigh rattled the already crackling connection. "Not yet. But I will."

Jed appreciated the agent's support but there was only so much the man could do. "You don't even know where to start."

"You do," Rowe surmised. "That's why you broke out of prison."

"The prison broke," Jed reminded him. From the gunfire and explosions, the brick, mortar and wood structure had nearly imploded. "It was more dangerous to stay than to leave."

"Not now. It's too dangerous for you on the outside," the DEA agent insisted, his voice deep with a life-and-death urgency. "You need to let me handle this."

Over the past three years, Jed had learned that his black-and-white code of integrity was something few people followed. Most people, even law-enforcement officers, lived life with shades of gray. Some darker shades than others.

"Is there a shoot-on-sight order out on me?"

Rowe's silence confirmed Jed's suspicion.

The prison guard who had stepped aside and let him escape the burning ruins of Blackwoods had warned him that his life would be more at risk on the outside. That there were lawmen who took it very personally when one of their own was killed. Cop killers rarely survived in jail or on the outside.

"Then it's not safe for me to go back into custody, either," Jed pointed out. "No doubt I'd wind up having a fatal *accident*."

"*I* will bring you in," the DEA agent said. "And I'll vouch for your innocence."

A smile tugged at Jed's lips. "Do you really think

anyone is going to take your word that I'm innocent just because your girlfriend says so?"

"She's not my girlfriend."

Jed's breath left his lungs in a whoosh of surprise. He had only seen Rowe Cusack once since helping the agent survive his undercover assignment at Blackwoods Penitentiary, but during that brief meeting in the midst of the riot, he had been able to tell that the guy had fallen hard for Jed's younger sister. "Is Macy all right?"

Because if Rowe had hurt her, the DEA agent would be seeing Jed again—but not to bring him back to prison.

"She's my fiancée now," Rowe said.

"You proposed?" The guy had fallen *really* hard.

"She's everything you told me she was," Rowe said, his voice gruff with emotion, "and so much more. I would have been a fool if I let her get away."

Jed had been a fool like that once. He'd fallen hard but had let the woman get away. In the end, it had cost him his freedom. And given that shoot-on-sight order, it could wind up costing him his life, too.

"I hope she wasn't a fool to accept," Jed said. As he'd learned, people weren't always what you thought they were or what your heart wanted them to be.

"Your sister is no fool," Rowe said, defending her, his voice sharp with anger now.

"No," Jed agreed. Macy was the only one who had believed in his innocence…until the DEA agent. But Jed suspected that Rowe just believed in Macy, which was fine with him. His younger sister deserved to have someone who supported her and who obviously loved her. "Congratulations."

"If I had my way, she would already be my wife,"

Rowe admitted, "but she won't set a date for our wedding until your name is cleared."

Jed choked on a laugh. "So Macy's given you some incentive to help me."

"You gave me the incentive—when you saved my life," Rowe reminded him. "Twice."

"I didn't do that to give you incentive," Jed said. "I did it because it was the right thing to do." And because he could never have lived with himself had he let an innocent man be murdered.

"I know," Rowe said. "That's why I believe you. That's why I want you to do the right thing now. Tell me where you are, so I can bring you in."

Jed blew out a breath that steamed up the cracked Plexiglas of the old pay-phone booth. He'd already talked to the agent too long, just hopefully not long enough for the man to have tracked Jed's location. "Tell my sister I love her."

"If you love her, you would—"

"Stay alive. That's what Mace wants most of all," Jed said with absolute certainty, "my safety." Macy would have broken him out of prison herself if he'd agreed to go along with her plan. But he hadn't wanted her to risk her freedom for his. And for years he had believed that justice would prevail and his innocence would be proven—the real killer finally caught.

He wasn't that idealistic and naïve anymore. He knew that he was the only one who could prove his innocence. "I won't be safe until I have irrefutable proof that I killed no one."

*Yet.* Because he couldn't trust the justice system to work, he might have to take his own justice.

"Jed, you have to come back, or it won't matter if you clear your name," Rowe said, trying to reason with him.

But no one really understood that *nothing* mattered to Jed but clearing his name. Not even his own life...

"I'll keep in touch, Rowe."

Jed hung up, hopefully before Rowe had had time to trace his call. The DEA agent would excuse his interference as help. But Jed didn't need anyone's help. He had broken out of prison because there were certain things—certain *people*—only *he* could handle.

Erica Towsley was one of those people. He wadded up the page he had ripped from the dangling phone book and shoved it into the pocket of his jeans. He had found her. For over three years he'd had his lawyer looking for her to no avail. In the three days since he had escaped from Blackwoods Penitentiary, Jed had tracked down his alibi.

He stepped out of the booth and sucked in a breath as the wind picked up, whipping icy chunks of snow at him. But then he thought of *her,* and his blood heated. Oblivious to the freak late-spring snowstorm, he trudged along the deserted street deeper into the heart of the small town. The businesses were closed, the storefronts dark. But above a few of those businesses, lights glowed in some of the apartments on the second and third stories.

Behind the blinds at one of those windows, a shadow moved. He couldn't see any more than a dark, curvy silhouette, but his pulse quickened and his breath shortened.

He knew it was her.

ERICA SHIVERED BUT NOT because of the cold air seeping through the worn frames of the front windows. She shivered at what she saw as she gazed through the slats of the blinds.

Despite it being spring for a few weeks now, winter had snuck back into Miller's Valley in the form of a blizzard. But the return of winter wasn't what chilled her blood even with the snow blowing outside, nearly obscuring the street below the third-floor apartment. Nearly.

Erica still caught a glimpse of someone standing on the sidewalk across the street. He was just a tall, broad-shouldered shadow. But she could feel his gaze as he stared up at her window. And it chilled her far more than the cold air.

"There is no way that he found you," she whispered, reassuring herself again, like she had been doing since that special report three nights ago. Nothing was in her name. Not the business. Not the building. Not even the car she drove. "It's safe here."

But despite all of her assurances, those doubts niggled at her, jangling her already frazzled nerves. That was why she was up so late, because every creak and clunk of the old building had her pulse jumping and heart racing.

Even though her eyes were gritty and lids heavy, sleep eluded her. So she paced and kept watch, making sure those creaks and clunks were nothing but weather testing the structure of the old building.

But what about the shadow watching her window? She stepped closer but caught no glimpse of him now. Had there really been someone there, or had her overwrought nerves conjured up the image? She studied the street for several more moments, but the wind picked up, swirling the snow around and obliterating whatever footprints might have been on the street or sidewalk.

The snowstorm was late in the spring even for Michigan's unpredictable April weather. The temperatures had dropped, and rain had turned to sleet and then snow. No one would be out walking in such a storm.

She must have just imagined someone watching her. She exhaled a shaky breath of relief. As her nerves settled, exhaustion overwhelmed her. Maybe she could finally sleep. She stepped back from the window and crossed the living room to shut off the light switch by the door before heading down the hall.

*Bam!*

Her heart slammed into her ribs. This was no creak or clunk.

*Bam! Bam! Bam!*

Midstep, she stopped in the hall and whirled back toward the door that rattled under a pounding fist. Her hand trembling, she reached out and flipped on the lights as if the light alone would banish the monsters that had crept out of the shadows.

"Who's there?" she called out, her voice quavering as her nerves rushed back and overwhelmed her. She couldn't move—couldn't even step close enough to the dead-bolted door to peer through the peephole—as if he might be able to grab her through the tiny window.

"Ms. Towsley," a gruff voice murmured through the door, "I'm an agent with the Drug Enforcement Administration."

How the hell did he know who she was? And what could he possibly want with her? She knew nothing about narcotics; she rarely even remembered to take her vitamins.

"Prove it," she challenged him.

She shook off the nerves, so that she had the courage to press her eye to the peephole. But the man was so tall that he blocked most of the light in the hall. And he stood so close to the door that Erica couldn't see his face, only his wide chest.

"What?" he asked with an impatient grunt.

"Prove that you are who you say you are." Because she had been fooled before; she had thought a man was something he wasn't, and the mistake could have cost her everything.

Now she had even more to lose…

"Open the door," he replied, "and I'll show you my credentials."

"Just hold your ID up to the peephole," she directed him.

She had once chuckled over Aunt Eleanor installing the tiny security window in the door—given that no one had ever committed a crime in Miller's Valley. But now she was grateful for her great aunt's paranoia; too bad it had actually been the first symptom of the Alzheimer's that had eventually taken the elderly woman's life.

The shadows shifted as he stepped back and finally she was able to see—but just the identification the man held up: Rowe Cusack, Special Agent with the Drug Enforcement Administration. He was the lawman the news hadn't stopped talking about since the prison break. He was the DEA agent who had gone undercover to expose the corruption at Blackwoods Penitentiary and had nearly lost his life.

"Why are you here?" she asked.

What possible business could a DEA agent have in Miller's Valley? Fear clutched her stomach, tying it into knots. Perhaps this wasn't about drugs at all but about whom he'd met on that last assignment of his at Blackwoods.

"I need to talk to you about Jedidiah Kleyn," he said. His voice was raspy and gruff—just as it had been when he'd made his brief replies to the reporters' incessant questions.

She fumbled with the dead-bolt lock and opened the door. "Do you think he's looking for me?"

The man stepped inside and shoved the door closed behind himself. "He's not looking for you."

His dark eyes narrowed, he stared down at her—his gaze as cold as the snow melting on his mammothly wide shoulders. Dark stubble clung to his square jaw. "Not anymore."

Her heart slammed against her ribs as she realized her mistake. Once again she had fallen for this man's lies.

"He's found you," Jedidiah Kleyn said.

Erica had let a killer into her home. And now she was probably going to become his next victim…

*Chapter Two*

Despite having sworn that she wouldn't watch the news anymore, Macy Kleyn couldn't look away from the television screen. But the reporters or, worse yet, the mug shot from when Jed had been arrested weren't on the TV. The man whose face filled the screen was devastatingly handsome with a strong jaw, icy blue eyes and golden-blond hair.

But she didn't have to watch the news to see him. All she had to do was glance over to where he sat at a desk in a corner of his open apartment. It was what he was saying to the reporters gathered for that prerecorded press conference that held her attention.

"Jedidiah Kleyn is not the dangerous convict that earlier reports are claiming," he said, his deep voice vibrating in the TV speakers. "If not for Mr. Kleyn, I would not have made it out of Blackwoods Penitentiary alive. He saved my life, not once, but twice."

Macy's breath caught, but she released it in a shuddery sigh of relief. She would never be able to thank her big brother enough for saving the man she loved. But proving Jed's innocence would be a great place to start. If she had ever been able to figure out where to start…

"Are you suggesting that three years in prison reformed him?" a disembodied voice asked from behind the camera.

Rowe snorted. "Blackwoods reforms no one. Three years incarcerated there would have broken a lesser man than Jedidiah Kleyn."

"You seem to have an awful lot of respect for a cop killer," another disembodied voice, this one full of derision, remarked.

"That's not a question," Rowe pointed out. "But I'll answer it anyway. I don't believe Jedidiah Kleyn is guilty of the crimes of which he was convicted. And I intend to prove his innocence."

"Is that because Kleyn saved your life or because you're dating his sister?"

The screen went black, the speakers silenced instead of vibrating with his sexy voice. So she turned toward the real man.

"Thank you," she said.

"I'm not doing it for you," he replied, as he tossed the remote onto the couch and turned back to his laptop.

She crossed the room to his desk and leaned over him. Pressing against his back, she rested her head on one of his broad shoulders. His soft hair tickled her cheek, making her tingle.

Everywhere.

She caught just a glimpse of his laptop screen before he snapped it shut. "GPS?" Hope quickened her pulse almost as much as being close to her fiancé had. "Did you find him?"

Rowe shook his head. "He terminated the call before I could pinpoint his location."

"But you found out something," she surmised.

He opened up the screen again and pointed to the number on it.

"There aren't enough digits," she said, her hope dashed.

"No," her fiancé admitted, but he didn't sound as defeated as she felt. "But the area code and first few digits indicate that he called from a pay phone."

"Pay phone?"

He turned his face slightly toward her, his lips curving into a slight grin. "Apparently they still exist."

"And you can track it down?"

"Yes. But that number—well, the digits we have of that number—is registered to several phones in rural areas surrounding Grand Rapids."

"Rural?" Pay phones in farm towns? Maybe it made sense given that there were fewer towers and poorer cell reception.

Rowe shrugged. "Maybe he's hiding somewhere in the countryside…"

The sick feeling in her stomach convinced her otherwise. "We both know Jed didn't break out of prison to hide," she said. "My brother isn't hiding."

She suspected that he actually wanted to be found. Not by authorities but by the person who had framed him.

After a slight hesitation, Rowe said, "He's trying to clear his name."

"You don't believe that's all he's doing."

"Do you?" Rowe asked. He spun his chair around and tugged her down so that she straddled his hard thighs. His hands cupped her face, tipping up her chin so that their gazes met.

"No," she admitted. "If I had been framed for something I didn't do, I'd want justice." Even if she had to dole it out herself…

But did her brother want justice or revenge?

JED COULD KILL HER—for everything she had cost him: his freedom, his reputation, his heart…

But despite her duplicity, she still looked beautiful to him. She had the pale golden hair of an angel; it shimmered even in the dim light of the antique chandelier dangling from the high ceiling of her apartment. And her eyes were a bright clear blue—wide now with fear. With her delicate features and flawless skin, she looked so young and innocent.

Where were the lines of guilt and stress? Where was the regret for what she had done to him? Was she so heartless that she had never given him another thought after she'd so callously destroyed his life?

"You're impersonating a government agent," she accused him, gesturing toward the badge Jed had lifted off Rowe Cusack when he had saved the DEA agent during the prison riot.

With a twinge of guilt, he slid it back into the pocket of his jeans. Rowe hadn't mentioned it, so he probably hadn't realized that Jed was the prisoner who had stolen it from him. The riot had been so chaotic and dangerous that the man had, no doubt, been more concerned about his life than his badge.

"That's the least of the charges I'm facing," Jed pointed out. "Thanks to you."

"Me?" Her voice cracked with emotion, and she stepped back, as if cowering from him in fear. "I had nothing to do with any of the things you've done."

"You had everything to do with it."

She shook her head. "No…"

He followed her, closing the distance between them. "Why did you do it?"

For three years that question had nagged at him. He could not figure out what her motivation had been.

Greed? Revenge? Once he had thought her too sweet and innocent for either emotion, but he'd had three years to realize how wrong he'd been about her.

"Wh-what did I do?" she asked, as if she really didn't know.

He chuckled at her attempt to feign innocence. But then those looks of an angel had probably always let her get away with her misdeeds. No one would ever suspect how devious she really was. "You set me up, sweetheart."

He had once called her sweetheart and meant it; he had been such a fool. "What did you get out of it? Money?"

If she had, she hadn't spent it on this place. There were cracks in the plaster ceiling and walls, and the hardwood floors were worn. The curtains even fluttered at the windows, as if the cold air blew right through the thin panes of glass.

He moved closer, trapping her between his body and the wall she had backed up against. "Revenge?"

He'd thought that she had understood why he'd had to break up with her before he left for Afghanistan. It wouldn't have been fair to expect her to wait for him, especially when there had been a strong possibility that he might not even return.

But he shouldn't have worried about her; she definitely hadn't waited for him. When he had come back home after his year-long deployment, she had already been wearing another man's ring.

"Revenge?" She echoed his question. "What are you talking about?"

"I don't know," he admitted. She hadn't seemed to care enough about his dumping her to want revenge on him. But then they hadn't been going out long when he'd received his deployment orders, calling him from the reserves back into active duty. "I don't know why you did it."

"Did what?" she asked, her brow furrowing with confusion.

Jed leaned down, so that his forehead nearly touched hers. "I don't know why you helped frame me for murder. Or was it all your idea?"

From having once interviewed her for a job, he knew her educational background and IQ. She was more than smart enough to have masterminded the embezzlement, murders and frame-up herself. And he wasn't the only man on whom she might have wanted revenge.

She gasped, and her breath was warm against his face. "I didn't. I had nothing to do with those murders."

Jed eased back to study her beautiful face. No wonder she had fooled him into falling for her lies and for her; she was a damn good actress because she nearly had him believing she wasn't involved. And he knew better.

"You had to be in on it," he insisted. "Or you would have come forward when I was arrested. Instead you disappeared."

She shook her head, tumbling her blond hair around her slender shoulders. In a bulky wool sweater, she looked so small and fragile. But he wouldn't let her looks deceive him again.

"I didn't disappear," she protested. "My aunt Eleanor's health was failing, so I came home to take care of her."

"My lawyer couldn't find you." And Jed had told the man that she might have returned to Miller's Valley where she'd grown up with her great aunt.

Her brow furrowed again. "Mr. Leighton definitely found me. I talked to him."

"No…"

Marcus Leighton wouldn't have lied to him. He was more than Jed's defense lawyer; he'd been his fraternity brother, too. And his friend.

"If he found you, he would have made you come forward." And provide the alibi that would have cleared Jed of all the charges against him.

"Mr. Leighton didn't want me to testify," she said, "because my testimony would only make you look guiltier."

Now he knew she was the one lying. He chuckled at her weak attempt to fool him. "I was with you during the murders. Your testimony would prove my innocence. You were my alibi."

Her face flushed bright red, but she shook her head again in denial. "I can't testify to what I can't remember."

"What the hell…? You're claiming amnesia?" There was no way Marcus would have believed that, and if he'd put her on the stand, the jury would have realized she was lying, too. Why hadn't Marcus put her on the stand if he'd actually found her?

"I was drugged," she said. "And I have the test results to prove it. I don't remember that night."

No matter how hard he'd tried over the past three years, he hadn't been able to forget that night. Or her…

How could she claim to remember none of it?

"So if using me was part of your plan, it didn't work," she said, anger replacing the fear in her eyes as she glared up at him. "I can't alibi you."

"You're lying." She had to be, otherwise he had lost his one hope of proving his innocence.

"Why would I lie?" she asked.

That was the question that had nagged at him.

*Why?*

A board creaked behind him, alerting him to someone else's presence. Had he been set up again?

He grabbed Erica, wrapping one arm around her waist and his other around her neck, so he could threaten to snap it if her backup had a weapon. Then he whirled toward the intruder.

And pain clutched his heart with all the force of a gunshot. But he hadn't been shot; he'd just been shocked by the appearance of the child who stumbled down the hall, wiping sleep from her dark eyes.

"Don't hurt her," Erica pleaded in an urgent whisper. "She's just a baby."

The child was actually two—probably almost three years old. She blinked and stared blearily up at him and Erica.

"Mommy?"

"Sweetheart, you need to go back to bed," Erica said, her voice tremulous despite her obvious efforts to sound calm and reassuring.

The little girl's lips pursed into a pout. "I wanna a drink," she stubbornly insisted.

Suddenly aware of how tightly he held her, Jed dropped his arms from around Erica's delicate frame. "You can get her the drink." He pitched his voice lower, so only she could hear him. "I won't hurt her."

Erica glanced from him to her daughter and back, obviously reluctant to leave him alone with her child.

But this kid was his, too. She was the spitting image of his sister, Macy.

Erica must have taken him at his word because she left the little girl standing in front of him. But the refrigerator was only steps away, through an open archway. Erica watched him carefully as she backed into the kitchen.

He dropped to his knees in front of the little girl and asked, "How old are you?"

Her chocolate-brown eyes widened as she studied him. She was as fearful as her mother had seemed of him. But his size had even intimidated violent criminals enough that during his three years in one of the most dangerous prisons in the United States, not very many inmates had been brave enough to try to mess with him. So of course he was going to scare a small child.

But she lifted her pointy little chin, as if forcing herself to be brave, which made her even more like his feisty kid sister. Then she held up two fingers.

"You're two years old?"

"I'll be thrwee soon," she replied with a slight lisp, like the one his sister had had until the speech therapist their parents hired had corrected it.

His parents had constantly been hiring specialists to *fix* Macy, so that she could be as *perfect* as they had considered their firstborn: him. But he had only been perfect until he had been charged with double homicide; then they had stopped considering him their son entirely. They'd forgotten all about him just as Erica had apparently tried to forget him.

"What's your name?" he asked the child.

"Isobel," she replied. "What's yours?"

*Dad. I'm your father.*

Sure, Erica had been engaged before that night she'd spent with him—the night she claimed not to remember. But Isobel was not Brandon Henderson's daughter, or she would have been blue-eyed and blond-haired like both her parents.

Instead she shared his coloring and looked exactly like his sister. She even sounded like Macy had at her age. Jed didn't need a DNA test; he was certain. But before he could open his mouth to utter anything, Erica interrupted.

"Here's your water, sweetheart!" She pressed a sippy cup into her daughter's small hand and lifted the child into her arms. "Now let me tuck you back into bed."

Jed could have vaulted to his feet and stopped her from carrying the child off down the hall. His reflexes were quick or he wouldn't have survived three years at Blackwoods, not to mention his tour in Afghanistan.

But he let them go.

Then he slowly drew in deep breaths, steadying his racing pulse. The apartment was small, so he overheard their conversation, no matter how softly they spoke.

"Who is that man?" the little girl asked her mother. "What's his name?"

"Jed," Erica replied.

"But who is he?" The little girl persisted as stubbornly as she had demanded her now-forgotten glass of water. "I never seen him 'fore. And he's so big."

"He's just a friend," Erica murmured. And he was surprised she didn't choke on her lie.

But that proved just how consummate a liar she was. She was obviously lying about not remembering that night, and now he had the proof. No matter what she claimed about her child, he knew the truth.

He had a daughter.

So whoever had framed him, obviously with Erica's help, hadn't just stolen years of Jed's life. He had lost precious years of Isobel's life, as well. He had missed his daughter being born, taking her first steps, uttering her first words...

Somehow, that person would have to pay for what he had taken from Jed.

THE BLACKWOODS COUNTY JAIL offered the same basic amenities that the prison once had—before it had been destroyed during the riot. Former warden Jefferson James had a cot on which to sleep. He went to the cafeteria for meals and a recreational area for entertainment. But what he'd just seen on television hadn't been entertainment, so he'd demanded to return to his cell.

The DEA agent continued to make Jefferson's life difficult. If only Kleyn had killed him, like Jefferson had ordered the inmate...

But instead of killing him, he'd helped the DEA agent escape Blackwoods. Now the DEA agent wanted to return the favor and prove Kleyn innocent of the crimes of which he'd been convicted. He probably was innocent—that was why he'd disobeyed Jefferson's order to kill. But his innocence made him even more dangerous to Jefferson. If proved unjustly convicted, his testimony would carry more significance. That was why he couldn't testify...

A shadow, sliced by the bars, fell across the floor in front of Jefferson. "You wanted to see me?"

*No.* He could barely look at Sheriff Griffin York. The young lawman was everything Jefferson despised—self-righteous, honorable and law-abiding as well as law-enforcing. But he did want to talk to the man.

"Took you damn long enough to get here," Jefferson griped.

"Kind of got my hands full cleaning up the mess from the riot," York bitterly remarked.

"Did you round up all the escapees yet?"

York's gaze hardened with resentment. "It's only been a few days."

"So you haven't apprehended any of them?"

"Some of them," the sheriff claimed and then goaded, "and some of your guards, as well. They're already talking. They have a lot to say about you."

Jefferson's lawyer wasn't worried about the testimony of coconspirators who had benefited from the crimes of which he was being convicted. It was Kleyn he worried about; he was the one who couldn't talk.

"What about the cop killer?" he asked. "He still at large?"

The sheriff's nostrils flared. "You don't need to worry about him."

Hope lifted Jefferson's spirit. "He's dead?"

"No. But his face is all over the news. He will be apprehended soon."

Jefferson didn't want him arrested. He wanted him dead. He had already put into motion the shoot-on-sight order; he just had to trust that someone else out there wanted Jedidiah Kleyn dead as badly as he did.

If the man had been framed, then the real killer would probably want to make sure Kleyn didn't live long enough to discover his identity...

*He's out. How did the son of a bitch break the hell out of prison?*

How had he survived it? How had he survived the year he'd spent in a war zone? Jedidiah Kleyn was some kind of superhero. Or he had been, until his shining armor had been permanently tarnished.

He grinned, his chest swelling with satisfaction in

accomplishing what he had barely considered possible. The perfect murder. Murders.

And the perfect revenge. Jedidiah Kleyn had lost everything.

But his life. Now it was time to take that, too.

# Chapter Three

"I was wrong," a deep voice murmured. Jed spoke from where he stood in the hall, as if reluctant to step any closer to the child he had helped her conceive.

Erica stared down at her daughter's sleeping face. After a sip of water, the toddler had dropped immediately back into a deep slumber. The stranger hadn't unsettled or scared her like he had Isobel's mother. But that was because Erica knew him, although he wasn't the friend she'd told her daughter he was. If he had actually been a friend, she would have known him better; she would have known better than to trust him, let alone fall for him.

And even though he had been sentenced to spend two lifetimes in prison, Erica had known that this day would eventually come. She had known she would see Jedidiah Kleyn again. She stepped out of Isobel's room and closed the door.

He stared at it, though, as if he could see through the wood. As if he could see his child…

"You were wrong?" She prodded him for an explanation and a diversion. Hoping he would follow her, she led him away from her daughter, down the short hall and back into the living room.

She hadn't wanted to let him near her daughter. But

she hadn't wanted to scare the little girl either by showing her own fear. Some instinct, as well, had assured Erica that no matter what else Jed might have done, he wouldn't hurt a child.

"You're not my alibi," he agreed as he rejoined her in the front room.

Finally he admitted it, banishing the doubts that had plagued her for the past three years. What if his lawyer had been wrong? What if Jedidiah hadn't committed those heinous crimes? But Marcus Leighton had known Jed far longer and better than she had. If his own friend had believed he was guilty...

"Isobel's my alibi."

She gasped in surprise at his bizarre claim.

"She's irrefutable proof that I was with you that night."

Anger surged through her, chasing away her fears. She stepped close to him and stabbed his massive chest with her fingertip. "She's irrefutable proof that I was drugged and raped that night."

His neck snapped back as if she'd slapped him. "You think I raped you?"

"You drugged me—"

"I did not drug you," he insisted with a weary-sounding sigh. From the dark circles beneath his eyes, she doubted he'd had any sleep since his escape. He had probably spent every minute of that time tracking her down. "I don't even believe you were drugged."

"Your lawyer has the lab results," she informed him. "When I told him that my memory of that night was cloudy, he had my blood drawn."

She should have known better than to believe, even for a moment, that Jed might have actually cared about her. Her own parents hadn't. She had been just a few years older than Isobel was now when they'd dropped her off at her great aunt's with the promise that they would come back for her. Despite sending her cards and letters over the years that had reiterated that promise and renewed her hope, they had never come back.

"When was that?" he asked, his dark eyes intense.

She had to refocus on their conversation to realize what he was asking, but she still didn't understand why. "Three years ago, of course."

"No," he impatiently replied. "How many hours or days after we were together?"

Erica shrugged, wondering why he thought it mattered so much how many days or hours had passed. "I don't know. It was after you were arrested."

"So at least two days after that night?" he prodded her.

Would it have mattered how many days or hours? Her pulse quickened as she began to wonder and hope that she might not have been so wrong about him. Cautiously, she replied, "I guess."

He shook his head with disgust, as if he'd caught her in a lie. "If you had been drugged, it wouldn't have been in your system any longer."

"How do you know that?" she asked, her stomach tightening with dread.

She had hoped she was wrong about him; that he hadn't been the one responsible. But he seemed familiar with the drug she'd been slipped, probably in the water he'd given her at the office before she'd left with him that night.

He wouldn't have had to drug her to get her to go home with him. She had been so grateful, and relieved after a year of worrying, that he'd come back from

Afghanistan alive that she would have done anything for him. And to be with him…

"Everyone knows that the drug you're talking about—the one that erases your memory—doesn't stay in your system very long," he said.

Growing up in Miller's Valley with her great aunt, Erica had been sheltered. She knew nothing about drugs. At her high school no one had used anything more dangerous than marijuana.

"I didn't know that," she murmured, embarrassed by her naïveté.

"I know you're lying," he said.

"I really didn't know—"

"You're lying about that night," he clarified. "I was with you. I know you weren't drugged. You were just upset after catching Brandon with another woman."

That hadn't upset her. Brandon Henderson hadn't even been her real fiancé; he had just been too stubborn and too arrogant to accept her no to his proposal. So he had insisted she think about it and wear his ostentatious diamond ring while she did. When Jed had returned from Afghanistan, she had realized why. Brandon had wanted to stick it to the friend he had always envied and resented. That was why she had gone into Brandon's office the night the man had been murdered—to tell him where to go with his ring.

"I was upset," she agreed. But not for the reasons Jed thought. She'd been upset that she had let Brandon use her to hurt him. But then Jed had used her, too, and far worse than Brandon had.

After being a pawn in their sick, deadly game, she had realized that she should have stayed in Miller's Valley. It was much safer for her here. So even if her neighbor hadn't called to warn her about her great aunt's deteriorating health, she would have come home.

But Marcus Leighton had always known where she was. Why had he lied to Jed?

Had he lied to her, too?

If Jed's rage was out of control, as his friend had claimed, wouldn't he have killed her already for not coming forward with the alibi he'd planned? But he had yet to lay a hand on her. Her pulse quickened at the thought of him touching her. Again.

"I took you back to my place," Jed said. "You remember that, don't you?"

"I remember you threatening to kill Brandon for hurting me," she replied.

"His girlfriend remembered me threatening him, too," he said with a sigh. "And she testified to it in court. She also claimed that she left me and Brandon alone together."

Doubts began to niggle. She hadn't heard that testimony. But she hadn't gone to court. Leighton hadn't wanted her there. And she had needed to be with her aunt in Miller's Valley. She had followed news reports, though, but must have missed the day the girlfriend had testified.

"You and I both know she lied," Jed said, "that you and I left *her* alone with him. You could have testified to that even if you really don't remember what else happened."

"I don't remember…" But heat warmed her face at the lie. She didn't remember everything, but images flashed through her mind. Images of the two of them, naked and wrapped tightly in each other's arms.

"You're lying again," he accused her, his voice sharp with frustration.

"I remember that you took me back to your place," she admitted.

"It was close to the office, and I didn't want you driving, as upset as you were."

She remembered that, too, and that she had been mad, so mad that the anger had made her light-headed and unsteady enough that Jed had carried her up the steps of his loft to his bedroom. Then when Marcus Leighton had told her she'd been drugged, she had realized it hadn't been the anger that had affected her like that.

"Just rest," Jed had told her, as he'd leaned down to press a kiss to her forehead.

But she'd grabbed his hand. She'd stopped him from leaving her. And she suspected she would have done that even if she hadn't been drugged.

"You remember more than that," he challenged her, as he studied her face.

It had to be flushed because her skin was hot and tingling.

"You know I didn't rape you," he said, leaning down so that his mouth was mere inches from hers. "You wanted me…"

She swallowed hard, unable to deny her desire. "I was a fool."

"Is that why you didn't come forward?" he asked, his brow furrowing in confusion. "Because you were too embarrassed?"

"I went to your lawyer," she told him again. "Mr. Leighton said—"

"Forget Marcus for now," he said as if he couldn't deal with the possibility that his friend might have betrayed him. "Why didn't you go to the police?" he asked. "I told the investigating detectives about you, but they didn't believe that I really had an alibi. Did they even talk to you?"

She shook her head, and sympathy tugged at her that no one had believed him. But his sister...

The news crews had relentlessly hounded Macy Kleyn, ridiculing her for supporting a cop killer. The young woman had always staunchly defended her brother's innocence.

Had he been innocent?

"Why didn't you go to the police?" He repeated his question.

"I didn't know if my testimony would help you or hurt you," she explained. Because even then, despite what his lawyer had said, she'd had doubts about his guilt. But she'd written those doubts off as pride that she hadn't wanted to have been so wrong about the man for whom she'd fallen. "And Marcus was adamant that it would hurt you."

"How?"

"It would have shown premeditation. The prosecutor would have said that you drugged me to provide yourself with an alibi." He had used her, just as his friend had in their rivalry against each other. But, as Marcus Leighton had said, Jed had taken their sick rivalry too far. "Once I passed out, you left me and returned to the office and killed Brandon. With as close as your apartment was to the office, you had plenty of time."

"Plenty of time to bludgeon him to death, carry him down to the parking garage, put his body into his car and set it ablaze?" Jed fired the questions at her as if he was the lawyer, and she was the one on trial. "Oh, and kill the police officer who caught me burning the dead body?"

"It's possible..." *Wasn't it?*

He shook his head. "I made love to you all night." His voice dropped even lower so that it was just a rough whisper as he added, "Over and over again."

Those images flitted through her mind again— their naked bodies intimately entwined, their mouths fused together. Their hearts beating in the same frantic rhythm. So many images had haunted her over the past few years, staying as vivid as if they'd just made love hours—not years—ago.

Would he have had time to commit those horrific crimes and make love to her so thoroughly?

"*I* never left you," he insisted. "You left me."

"I left you that morning," she admitted. When she had awakened in his bed, in his arms, she'd slipped out of his loose grasp and hurriedly dressed. She hadn't been able to believe what she'd done—how she'd given in to her desires to spite her pride. After he'd dumped her before leaving for Afghanistan, she never should have trusted him with her body or her heart. "But you'd left me first—more than a year before."

"I got deployed."

"You left me before you got deployed," she reminded him. "You didn't want me waiting for you." And, haunted by all the years she'd spent waiting for someone she loved to come back for her, she had readily agreed to end their budding relationship even though— or maybe because—she had already fallen for him.

"We'd only gone out a few times before I got called back to active duty," he reminded her. "I couldn't ask you to wait for me."

"Yes, you could have." Then, even if she hadn't been able to agree to wait, she would have at least known that he cared about her, too. "But you told me that you didn't see us working out anyway. That we weren't really compatible."

And she had believed him...until she'd seen his face when he had returned and found her in Brandon's office, wearing his ring. She had been trying to give it back that day, too. She'd only gone out with his business partner a few times over the year Jed had been gone, and mostly just so she could ask about Jed. So she had been using Brandon as a connection to the man she really wanted. That was why she had let him talk her into wearing that ring to think about his proposal—because she'd felt guilty.

"I was lying then," Jed said.

"I didn't know that. I believed that you really didn't see any future for us," she said. And that was why she had felt like a fool when she'd awakened in his arms. What if he'd only been jealous of his friend and hadn't really cared about her at all? Because if he had, how had he dropped her so easily?

Just as easily as her parents had dropped her at Aunt Eleanor's and never returned despite all their promises...

"Is that why you didn't come forward to offer me an alibi?" he asked. "Because you wanted revenge over my dumping you before I left for Afghanistan?"

She sucked in a breath. Apparently he didn't think very highly of her at all. When he'd told her that he saw no future for them, he must have been telling the truth then. And he was lying now, to try to make her feel guilty enough to help him.

"I have told you," she said, "again and again that I did come forward. I talked to your lawyer."

Jed shook his head, once again rejecting her claim. "Marcus swore to me that he never found you."

"Then he lied."

And, she thought, if Marcus really had lied to his friend and former fraternity brother, he would have had no qualms about lying to a woman he had barely known. Had Marcus lied about everything? Jed's guilt? His violent temper?

After that first initial jolt of fear at realizing she had let Jed into her apartment, she hadn't remained afraid—if she had, she would have tried to get to the phone or she would have shouted for her neighbor to call the police. Of course she would have had to shout really loud for Mrs. Osborn to hear her, but the elderly lady definitely would have come to her aid.

But instinctively she had known that she was in no real danger from Jed—that he wouldn't physically harm her or their daughter. He may have had reason to harm her, though, had she stupidly believed lies about him…

Jed's brow furrowed. "I don't understand…why would he lie?"

"He thought you were guilty," she divulged. "He said that Afghanistan changed you—that you came back so angry and violent."

A muscle twitched along his jaw, as if he tightly clenched it—controlling that rage of which his friend had warned her. "Was I violent with you that night?"

"From what I remember…?" She bit her lip and shook her head. He had been anything but violent. He had definitely been passionate but gentle, too.

"So I didn't rape you."

"No, but I was drugged. I don't care if the results came too late. I know that something wasn't right that night. I felt dazed or drunk, and I'd had nothing but that water at the office." At the time, she'd thought it had just been the surrealness of finally making love with the man she had loved for so long and had worried that, because of his deployment, she would never have had the chance to be that close to him.

Jed nodded, almost as if he was beginning to accept that what she told him was the truth.

"My memory of that night is sporadic," she continued. "I can testify that I was with you that night, but I can't swear that you never left me. Your lawyer was right that I wouldn't have been a convincing alibi—that my testimony could have actually hurt you more than I could have helped you."

And that was why she hadn't gone to the police, despite the twinges of guilt she'd felt over staying silent. While she believed that a man should be punished for his crimes, she hadn't wanted to help dole out that punishment. Not to Jed—not given what he might have endured in Afghanistan.

According to his lawyer, there had been more than sufficient evidence for his conviction without her muddying the waters. But would she have muddied the waters, or had Leighton already done that?

His broad shoulders slumped, and his breath shuddered out in a ragged sigh. "I spent all these years thinking that all I had to do to clear my name was find you."

"Is that really all you want?" To clear his name—not to kill her? If she could have been his alibi but hadn't come forward, she wouldn't blame him for wanting to harm her.

He glanced toward the hall down which was his daughter's room. "That *was* all I wanted."

"To clear your name?"

"I am innocent, Erica," he insisted, his voice and gaze steady with sincerity. "I didn't kill anyone. Not in Afghanistan and damn well not when I returned."

Guilt gripped her heart, making it ache. Had she been wrong? Had she stood by and done nothing while an innocent man rotted in prison? "But there was the witness—the one who actually saw you shoot the cop."

Jed shrugged. "He was a vagrant who hung out in the parking garage. He was usually drunk. His testimony shouldn't have held any weight."

"He didn't look like a vagrant in court. The jury believed him." And so had she.

"You followed the trial?"

Erica nodded. The judge had opened up the courtroom to news crews, which had covered and replayed every salacious detail of the trial. "But your lawyer told me how it would go before it even started. He knew the evidence against you was insurmountable, and that my testifying would only make you look guiltier, that it would help prove premeditation."

"Or your alibi might have given me reasonable doubt…"

Instead she had been the one with the doubts. But then, pretty much everyone she had ever loved had lied to her. Over and over again…

"Your lawyer showed me pictures of the crime scene, too." She shuddered. Because of the graphic nature of the images, the media hadn't been allowed to show crime-scene photos on the news. For years Erica had wished she had never seen them, either.

"Why would Marcus do that?" Jed asked.

"I don't know…" She hadn't understood any of it— the rivalry between men who were supposed to be friends and business partners or the lawyer being so certain that his client was guilty. She'd wondered then if Jed had actually confessed to his friend.

Jed's brow furrowed with lines of confusion. "It's as

if he was trying to convince you of my guilt when he was supposed to be doing everything in his power to prove my innocence."

"He didn't prove your innocence to a jury. He did a much better job of proving your guilt," she said, "at least to me."

Jed shook his head, as if trying to make sense of it all. "I thought he was my friend. He and Brandon and I all belonged to the same fraternity."

"Brandon wasn't really your friend," she pointed out.

Jed must have realized how much his former fraternity brother and business partner had envied and resented him. But then Brandon had been very good at hiding that resentment behind a façade of charm and humor—otherwise she never would have spent any time with him—not even to stay connected to Jed.

"And apparently neither was Marcus," Jed said with a heavy sigh. "So is he the one who framed me?"

Framed? The idea didn't seem all that preposterous anymore. In fact it seemed highly likely, which both relieved and sickened her.

"It would explain why he knew how much evidence there was against you—if he planted it." Just as he had planted the doubts in her muddled mind, so that she had done nothing when Isobel's father had gone to prison for a crime he hadn't committed. She should have at least talked to him, let him tell her his side of that night.

But she had worried that she would fall for his lies again.

What if she'd been wrong about him?

Her head pounded, and her stomach pitched as she realized the full impact of what she'd done...to Jed and their daughter. She had cost them three years together, and, from what she had seen on the news about the corruption at Blackwoods Penitentiary, she had nearly cost Jed his life.

"I CAN'T BELIEVE JED KLEYN got out," Marcus Leighton said, his hand shaking as he poured himself another drink.

"It was your job to make sure he stayed in prison for the rest of his life," the man with Marcus reminded his partner in crime.

But Marcus had never really been a partner, just a greedy ally. Not even so much an ally as a puppet, really. Easily manipulated. Too easily...

Marcus stared up at his companion, his eyes already clouded with confusion and drunkenness. "I'm not responsible for him breaking out of prison."

"He was supposed to die in prison." That had been how the plan—the brilliant plan—was to have concluded.

"He'd only been inside three years." Marcus was sober enough to remember. As if realizing that his brain was fogging, he pushed his glass aside. Alcohol sloshed over the rim and onto the case file lying on his mahogany desk. It was an antique, like most of the furnishings in the elegant office. Marcus enjoyed the finer things in life.

"Three years wasn't long enough." Jed wouldn't have suffered enough. Not yet. If he had lasted just a few more years, an inmate would have been rewarded—just as Marcus's ineptitude had been rewarded—for taking Jedidiah Kleyn's life.

But maybe this was a better and far more satisfying conclusion to his plan. Now he would get to take Jed's life himself—with his own hands. And he would be able to watch Jed's face while he did it.

"He'll be apprehended," Marcus said. "It doesn't matter how many other prisoners escaped during the riot, every cop is out there looking for Jed."

He shook his head. "You heard that DEA agent on the news, didn't you? The guy praises Kleyn for saving his life. He believes his claims of innocence."

Marcus's breath shuddered out. "That's why he asked for copies of all my records. He already got the police files and court transcripts."

His heart pounded a little faster. Marcus was so inept that he might have left something in those records that could lead back to *him*. "When is he coming for them?"

The color left Marcus's face, leaving him even pastier than the long Michigan winter had. "He's coming by tomorrow."

He had time. "Then we'll have to destroy them tonight."

Marcus nodded eagerly, and his shoulders slumped with relief. "Of course. Yes, we will."

The man really was an idiot, which made him a liability. "We'll have to get rid of any evidence leading back to me."

"To us."

"No, to me." He lifted his gun from beneath the edge of Marcus's desk. "Just like the evidence, you're going to get destroyed tonight, my friend."

It wouldn't matter who had begun to believe Jedidiah Kleyn's claims of innocence. He wouldn't be able to prove it. He wouldn't die a hero; he would die a killer.

And like Marcus Leighton, he would die soon. But first he would suffer so much that he would be almost grateful for death…

# *Chapter Four*

Jed stood in the open doorway, casting a dark shadow over his sleeping daughter.

*His daughter.*

He had a child—one he would have never learned about had he not broken out of prison. Knowing *about* Isobel and now wanting to get to *know* Isobel made him even more determined to prove his innocence. But most of all he couldn't have her growing up with the stigma of everyone thinking her father was a killer. Or worse yet, with *her* thinking her father was a killer.

Because he wasn't.

*Yet.*

His skin prickled on the nape of his neck, and the muscles between his shoulder blades twitched. He was no longer alone with his daughter. After three years in one of the most dangerous prisons in the world and, before his incarceration, a year in Afghanistan, his instincts were finely honed. So honed that he didn't need to turn around to know that Erica had joined him. He could smell her—that sweet vanilla scent that reminded him of baking cookies and pies. And he could feel her as his skin tingled with the heat of awareness.

"I couldn't find the business card Marcus Leighton gave me," she said.

Regret tightened his guts. He didn't have any time to waste tracking down the Judas who'd betrayed him. Not only had Marcus not put Erica on the stand, but he'd convinced her that Jed was guilty.

Why?

Unlike Brandon, Marcus had always been a true friend to Jed. He hadn't been competitive with him; he'd actually seemed to be in awe of him—more fan than friend.

"But I looked him up online," Erica said, "and I found his address."

For the past few years he'd thought she had sold him out. But like him, she had been a victim, too. Along with the jury of twelve of his peers, she had believed the evidence that had been manufactured to prove his guilt.

Had Marcus manufactured that evidence? But he had no motive to frame Jed…unless he had been hiding his own guilt. Brandon Henderson and Marcus Leighton had not been friends. Brandon had bullied and harassed Marcus, as he had bullied and harassed everyone but Jed.

Jed had thought he only needed to find his alibi and make her come forward to prove his innocence. But Erica had raised valid points about her testimony. With the holes in her memory, she wouldn't be able to convince an appeals court that he hadn't left her alone in his bed that night, gone back to the office and committed the double murder.

No, the only way to prove his innocence beyond a shadow of anyone's doubt—the appeals court, Erica's and their daughter's—was to find the real killer. "Where is he?"

"I'm not going to tell you," she said.

Finally able to drag his gaze away from Isobel, he turned to Erica. She stood in the light from the hall, still looking like an angel, but from the firm set of her jaw and the hard gleam in her eyes, she intended to be as stubborn as the devil to keep the information he wanted from him.

Over the past few years, he had dealt with people far more stubborn than she could ever be. Like the warden of Blackwoods, who had been the very devil himself. Now Warden James was behind bars for all his criminal activities.

And Jed was out.

A bitter chuckle at the irony slipped through his lips, and he glanced back at Isobel, worried that he had awakened her.

"She sleeps like a rock," Erica assured him. "She doesn't hear anything when she's out."

"That's good," Jed said. "Then she won't hear me take your computer from you to look up Marcus's address."

He was *not* going back to prison to serve out his two life sentences; he had already served enough time for crimes he hadn't committed. Realistically, he would probably have to serve time for breaking out of prison, but he could accept the punishment for a crime he had committed.

"You don't need to look up his address," she said. "I'll drive you to his office."

"His office will be closed now." He gestured toward the darkness beyond Isobel's bedroom window. "And you're not driving me anywhere."

"He lives above his office," she explained, "in Grand Rapids. You'll need a ride there."

"I got here and buses don't run to Miller's Valley," he

reminded her. He didn't need a ride. And he definitely
didn't want Erica with him when he questioned Marcus.

"So you stole a car, too?"

In addition to what? Murder? Did she still have her
doubts? Was she not able to completely trust him? But
wouldn't that make her more anxious to get rid of him
than to want to go along with him?

"You can't leave Isobel here alone." And he wasn't
about to take his daughter anywhere near a possible
killer.

"My neighbor from across the hall is coming over to
watch her," she said. "I told Mrs. Osborn that I have an
emergency in Grand Rapids."

"You don't have anything in Grand Rapids," he said.
"I do." Hopefully his vindication. "Stay here with our
daughter."

She shook her head, which swirled her golden hair
around her slender shoulders.

He swallowed a groan, fighting his attraction to
her. It didn't matter how damn beautiful she was; he
couldn't trust her. He only really had her word that
Marcus had lied to her. His friend deserved to give his
side of the story before Jed entirely condemned him. Jed
had known Marcus far longer and, he'd thought, better
than he'd ever known Erica Towsley.

"I have questions only Marcus can answer," she said.
"I want to hear, from his mouth, why he lied to me. And
I want to know why he lied about you."

And, obviously, she didn't trust Jed enough to bring
those answers back to her. But then she had spent the
past few years convinced that he was guilty of murder.
He was lucky she hadn't called the police instead of her
neighbor.

A knock rattled the front door, and Jed's heart rattled

his rib cage with a sudden jolt of fear. What if she had called the police? What if she had only been playing him when she'd acted as if she was beginning to believe in his innocence?

"Open Isobel's window and go out the fire escape," Erica said, her soft voice pitched low with urgency.

"What— Why?"

"You can't let Mrs. Osborn see you," she explained. "She obsessively watches the news. She might recognize you from all the media coverage of the prison breakout."

The door rattled again.

"Go down the fire escape," she ordered him. "My car's the blue minivan parked below it in the alley. It's unlocked." Her blue eyes gleamed as she added, "I have the keys, though."

"I don't need your van," he reminded her.

He had one of his own parked in the very same alley. The black panel van had belonged to a guard, like the clothes that Jed had found packed in a suitcase in the back of it. The guard, one of the warden's henchmen, had obviously planned to flee before charges could be filed against him. But he hadn't made it out of the riot. Like a few others, he had died behind bars because of the crimes he'd carried out for the warden. He had tortured and killed the prison doctor who'd helped the DEA agent escape.

The death of the doctor, who so many of the inmates had loved, was what had inspired the riot. When he'd ordered Doc's murder, the warden had gone too far. He'd ordered Jed's death, too, but the riot had protected and eventually freed Jed. But even without Rowe's warning, he would have known that he was probably in more danger outside of prison than he'd ever really been in it.

At least he didn't need to worry about Warden James anymore...

"But you need Marcus Leighton's address," she reminded him.

"Fine. I'll wait for you," he assured her. He also waited before going out the window. Hiding in the dark shadows of Isobel's bedroom, he watched Erica walk down the hall toward the door.

Her hips, fuller than he remembered, swayed in her jeans. His guts tightened with desire. It wasn't fair that she was so damn beautiful...

"Thank you for coming," Erica said as she opened the door. "I'm sorry I woke you up."

"It's okay, honey," a female voice, gruff with sleep and possibly age, assured her. "I know that you would never do that unless you had an emergency. I hate the thought of you going out after dark, though—what with those escaped convicts on the loose. They're all armed and dangerous, you know."

"I'm sure the media is exaggerating that," Erica said, keys rattling as she grabbed her purse.

"No, honey, they're bad men—every last one of them. But that cop killer—he's the worst. I hope they catch him soon." A board creaked, as if the woman had moved down the hall.

Toward Isobel's bedroom.

If Jed didn't leave now, he might get caught. He pushed up the window and stepped onto the wrought iron of the fire escape. The wind rustled Isobel's curtains, so he pulled the window closed. Hopefully Erica would come back and lock it.

He hated the thought of leaving Isobel alone. The old woman sitting with her was no protection for the vulnerable child—not with a killer on the loose who had already tried to ruin Jed's life once. Harming his daughter would hurt Jed more than spending the rest of his life locked up.

But, hopefully, no one else knew about Isobel. While Erica claimed that his lawyer had always known her whereabouts, Marcus might not have realized she was pregnant. He had certainly never given Jed any hint that he had become a father.

But then he couldn't trust anything his lawyer had ever told him because he'd apparently kept much more from him than Jed had realized. Like the documents that might have helped Jed in his defense, if he'd been able to track down the funds that had been embezzled from his clients' accounts. If Marcus had lied about Erica, he might have lied about the warden denying Jed access to those documents.

Or was it Erica that he shouldn't trust? Maybe she had been working with Marcus. Maybe she was still working with the lawyer.

Maybe instead of driving Jed to Grand Rapids, she intended to drive him right to a police station…

COULD SHE TRUST JED? Erica studied his face in the glow of the dashboard lights. He had insisted on driving, his hands clamped tight around the steering wheel. His square jaw, shadowed with dark stubble, was also clamped tight—as if he fought to hold in his rage.

How much had that rage built up during three years in prison for crimes he hadn't committed? If he hadn't committed them…

Had she been a fool to so easily accept his claims of innocence? While she now remembered more of that night, of their making love again and again, she couldn't

remember every minute of it. She couldn't swear that
he had never left her...

"I didn't do it," he said, as if he had read her mind.

She jumped and knocked her knee against the dash,
pain radiating up her leg. She had the passenger's seat
pulled up close to it because the child booster seat was
behind it and Isobel always kicked the back of it. "How
did you know what I was thinking?"

She had never been able to truly tell what Jed had
been thinking or feeling. So it wasn't fair if he could
read her that easily...

"I figured you would start doubting my innocence
again," Jed said. "After all, it would be easier for you if
I was guilty."

"Easier?" Then she had willingly gone off alone with
a killer. At least she had drawn him away from Isobel,
though. At least she had kept her daughter safe...

But she remembered the look on Jed's face as he had
stared down at their sleeping daughter. His jaw hadn't
been rigid then. His dark eyes hadn't been hard. They
had been soft and warm with awe and affection. He
would never hurt Isobel.

"If I was really the killer, your conscience would be
clear," he replied. "You wouldn't feel guilty for doing
nothing while I was sent to prison."

"I explained why I did nothing." Except for the reasons she'd kept to herself, except for her personal bag-
gage. She had never admitted to him that her parents
had abandoned her with her great aunt. He had probably
assumed she'd been an orphan—not unwanted.

A muscle twitched along his cheek. "Because of Marcus's lies."

He turned the van onto a cobblestone street and
parked at the curb. At this hour there was no fight to

get a meter. Every one of the metal meters stood guard over an empty parking spot.

"Are you sure this is the place?" he asked as he gazed up at the brick building, which was sandwiched between a restaurant and a bookstore.

"Yes," she confirmed, as she located the address on the building. The numbers on the brass plate matched the address she had found online.

A couple of lights glowed in the two stories above the ground-floor office. But lights glowed in the office windows, as well. At three o'clock in the morning, it was the only building with more illumination than just security lights.

"He was even written up in the Grand Rapids magazine about his renovation of this historic building," she said, remembering the article she had found online when looking for his address.

"He must have been more successful with other cases than he was mine," Jed murmured, "because it seems that since my incarceration, he certainly moved up in the world."

Erica hadn't found much else online about Marcus Leighton except his address and articles about his representing the cop killer, Jedidiah Kleyn. "I don't think he had any other high-profile cases, or they would have come up when I searched for his name on Google."

"If losing my case or, hell, just representing me, hurt his career, he didn't pay for this place with what I paid him." That look was back on Jed's handsome face, the intense rage that he was barely managing to control with a clenched jaw and flared nostrils.

Afghanistan may not have made him a violent man, but surely surviving three years in a prison as dangerous as Blackwoods Penitentiary had. If she hadn't insisted on coming along with him, she could not imagine what Jed might have done to Marcus Leighton to get the answers he wanted.

Erica wanted those answers, too. She reached for the door handle, but he leaned over and covered her hand with his. His skin was rough and warm against hers. Since it was spring, she had already packed away her gloves and winter gear. She wished she was wearing gloves now, not because of the unseasonable cold but because of how Jed's touch affected her. It brought all those images—of the two of them making love—rushing back to her.

"You should stay in the van," he said, leaning closer to her—so close that only inches separated his head from hers.

"No," she said. "I didn't come with you to just sit in the van."

She wasn't sure she would mind if he stayed in it with her, sitting so close that she could feel the heat of his heavily muscled body. But he didn't intend to stay with her; he was going to leave to go after his lawyer. She wasn't certain what his intentions were when confronting Marcus Leighton. And that was why she had insisted on coming along, to stop him from really becoming a killer.

"If he set me up for the reason I think he did, it's too dangerous for you to go in there with me." He glanced at the building. "I have a bad feeling about this."

"Because of the lights?" She wondered herself why so many of them were burning.

"Yeah, what's he doing up at this hour?" Jed asked, his eyes narrowed in suspicion as he stared up at the building. "It's almost like he knew I was coming. We could be walking into a trap."

She sucked in a breath as fear squeezed her lungs. But maybe he was just trying to scare her…

Jed turned back to her, his face still close as he leaned across her, his hand covering hers on the door handle. His eyes were so dark that she couldn't read the emotions swirling in them. But she almost believed one of them could be genuine concern for her safety.

Then she remembered where they were. "We're only a couple of blocks from the police department. Surely, no one would be bold enough to set up a trap here— where they could so easily be caught."

Or where Jed could so easily be caught. Maybe it was a trap.

"Erica…" He lifted his hand from hers to cup her cheek.

His touch had her skin tingling and nerves jangling. She had to get away from him and from all those feelings his touch brought back, so she pushed open the door and jumped out of the minivan. Before he could get around the front of the van, she was at the door to the office. It stood open, as if Marcus really had been expecting them.

Jed cursed beneath his breath as he joined her at the open door. "I don't have a weapon," he said, as he reached into his pocket. Instead of a gun, he drew out gloves and pulled them on, stretching the leather taut over his big hands. The gloves obviously weren't his any more than the wool jacket, which was too tight in the shoulders, was. "So I can't protect you."

She doubted that Jed really needed a weapon to protect himself or her. All he needed was his size and his muscle. But then that wouldn't be very effective against bullets.

"You have to stay out here," he insisted.

Maybe he was right. She had no protection against bullets, either. And she trusted that he wouldn't let her get hurt. If he had wanted her dead, he could have killed her at any point in the past few hours. If she went inside with him, though, and he lost control of the rage that boiled within him, she wanted to calm him and prevent the lawyer from getting hurt.

There was no telling what he might do if she let him go inside alone.

And if something had already happened inside, wouldn't the lights be off? Would a killer wait for them with all the lights burning?

She shook her head, unwilling to be left behind. "Jed—"

But he had his own argument for her to stay outside, one she couldn't fight. "Our daughter needs her mother."

She shivered as snow began to whirl around them, a cold wind whipping up the powder that already lay on the ground, and tossing around the falling flakes. She nodded, as if she intended to wait.

But he was inside for only a minute or two when she slipped through that open door and down the hall to where the lights burned on the first floor. She passed through a dark reception area to the open door to what must have been Leighton's office.

She followed him because their daughter needed her father, too. The little girl had already been denied him too long.

But it wasn't just for Isobel that Erica had gone after Jed. Like Jed, Erica wanted to know why he had been framed. Actually, she wanted to know if he had been framed. But she didn't intend to use violence to find the answers to all her questions and doubts.

Her muscles paralyzed with horror, she froze in the doorway—unable to move, unable to believe what she was seeing. She hadn't seen anything as gruesome since the lawyer had showed her those crime-scene photos.

Marcus Leighton was already dead. He was slumped in his chair, his shirt red with his own blood—his eyes open in shock.

ONE MAN DEAD. ONE TO GO.

He had no illusions that Jedidiah Kleyn would be as easy to kill as Marcus Leighton had been. If Kleyn was that vulnerable, he would have already been dead. He wouldn't have survived Afghanistan.

And he damn well wouldn't have survived Black-woods Penitentiary. But he was in more danger out here, especially if he showed up at Leighton's office and stepped into the trap left for him.

While he had left the door open, he had reengaged the alarm. Once someone crossed the threshold, a call would be placed to the local police department.

As close as the office was to the police station, there was no way Jed would escape if he were the one to trip the alarm. Once police officers discovered the escaped convict standing over a dead body, they would assume the worst, and they would react accordingly—with bullets.

But if Jed hadn't yet figured out Marcus's betrayal and someone else set off the alarm, a contingency plan was already in place—thanks to what he'd discovered in Marcus's files.

He actually hoped that Jed didn't spring the trap he

had set at Marcus's office. Because the contingency plan would be a much more painful end to Jedidiah Kleyn than going out in a blaze of gunfire.

# Chapter Five

A gasp had Jed's muscles tightening in apprehension. That breath hadn't come from the body; Marcus Leighton was dead. Jed had checked his pulse to confirm death. The man's skin was already cold. And so was Jed's blood—cold with dread.

He turned toward the door and found Erica watching him—her eyes as wide with shock and horror as Marcus's. She obviously thought Jed had killed his lawyer. He shook his head in denial of the question she hadn't even bothered to ask. She had just assumed his guilt, not even looking around as he had, for the real killer.

No one else was inside the building; it was just the two of them. And the dead man.

"He was shot." Jed pointed to the hole in Leighton's chest, burned through his blood-soaked shirt. He lifted his palms. "I don't have a gun."

With a trembling hand, Erica pointed to the one sitting across the desk from the body. Leighton must have been visiting with someone who'd pulled the Glock 9 mm gun on him, shot him and then left it on the desk next to the half-empty glass of liquor. So whoever had shot the lawyer was someone he had known well enough to drink around. Back in the frat house, Marcus had discovered that he was a cheap and sloppy drunk, and so he'd learned to only imbibe around people he could trust.

"You think Marcus handed me the gun to shoot him with?" He snorted at her suspicion. "Touch him. He's already cold. I did not kill him."

But the fact that she automatically thought he had shot Marcus told him what he needed to know: Erica would never trust that he wasn't a killer. Maybe not even after he found the real killer…

It wasn't Marcus.

He hadn't sold out Jed to hide his own guilt. He'd just sold him out for money.

Jed gazed around the office with its mahogany paneled walls. Filing cabinets had been built right into the walls, beneath rows of shelves. Jed reached for one of the handles, grateful that he wore gloves—ones he'd found in the guard's vehicle. He closed his fingers around a brass handle, pulling open a drawer to search for his records.

He pulled open drawer after drawer until he found the *K* section—or where the *K* section should have been. All the records under *K* were gone. Before he could search elsewhere in the office, a noise caught his attention.

His muscles tightened at the distant wail of a police car. Just like the last murder, this one was probably also a setup.

If the killer had called the police to report his crime, he hadn't left any evidence for Jed to find. Undoubtedly there was nothing in the office that would lead back to the real culprit. Like last time, it would probably all lead to Jed.

He hurried toward the door where Erica had stayed

in fear, probably of him more than the corpse. "We have to get out of here."

Her hand still trembling, she gestured toward the body this time.

"He's dead. He's been dead for a while," he reminded her. "We can't help him."

"But we can't just leave him here like that," she said, her voice cracking. "We can't just leave. We need to call the police."

"Someone's already done that for us," he pointed out as the sirens grew louder. And his heart pounded faster with fear and dread.

"If the cops catch us here, I'll be a dead man, too," he said. And he couldn't promise that Erica wouldn't get caught in the crossfire. "There's a shoot-on-sight order out on me."

*Shoot on sight...*

The words echoed in Erica's head. The police would kill Jed rather than try to apprehend him? They considered him that dangerous a criminal?

"Did you touch anything?" he asked, his hand gripping her arm as he pulled her through the reception area toward the front door.

She had left it open behind her, just as she had found it. "I didn't touch anything..."

Because she'd had a bad feeling over all those lights being on at three in the morning. How long had Marcus been dead? Hours? Minutes?

She hadn't checked the body to see if it was as cold as he had told her it was. She glanced back toward Marcus Leighton's office, but it was too far away and Jed's hand too tight around her arm for her to escape him and go back to check now.

Then he ushered her through the front door and into the passenger's side of the van. He turned his head back and forth, his gaze scanning the street before he hurried around to the driver's side. He opened the door and jammed the key in the ignition just as he settled onto the seat. "They're getting close."

Erica glanced back and noticed lights flickering in their rear window. Her neck snapped as Jed pressed hard on the accelerator and swerved around a corner. "You're sure we shouldn't have stayed, that we shouldn't have explained what happened…"

He emitted a bitter chuckle. "I told you—shoot-on-sight. That doesn't give a person any time for explanations."

"But I could—"

"Either get shot with me," he said, as he maneuvered the van around the tight curve of the freeway on-ramp, "or go to jail for aiding and abetting a fugitive."

"Aiding and abetting?" The words chilled Erica's blood, so that she was probably as cold as Marcus Leighton. And of course he would have been cold since his door had been left open, probably when his killer had fled.

"You aided and abetted because you didn't call the police the minute I showed up at your apartment," Jed explained.

With a shudder, she relived that first flash of terror and panic she'd had when she'd realized she had opened her door to Jedidiah Kleyn. "Like you would have let me reach for the phone…"

"It wasn't as if I bound and gagged you," he said. "You had access to your phone. You called your neighbor."

"But you had convinced me of your innocence by

then." And it hadn't even occurred to her to call the police when he had been standing over their daughter's bed, watching her sleep. He had looked like a devoted father, not a dangerous escaped convict.

"You're not so convinced anymore," he said, and the bitter expression on his handsome face turned to one of hurt and disappointment.

Regret clutched at her. "Jed…"

"It's my fault. I shouldn't have brought you along," he said, his voice gruff now with self-condemnation even though she hadn't given him a choice.

But he could have driven off without her when he had gone out the fire escape. His van had been parked in the alley behind her house. Instead, he had waited for her and maybe not just for the lawyer's address. Maybe he had wanted her to be there when Marcus Leighton took back all those things he'd told her that had convinced Erica of Jed's guilt.

A dead man couldn't take back his lies…

"But if I hadn't brought you along," Jed said, "and you heard about his murder, you would have been certain I'd done it." He sighed. "So now you only have suspicions…"

She shook her head, finally pushing aside those initial knee-jerk doubts to make room for common sense. "I know you didn't do it. I was only outside a few minutes before I followed you in, and I didn't hear a shot."

"The gun could have had a silencer," he said, almost as if he wanted to keep her suspicious and fearful of him.

She didn't have any more experience with guns than she did drugs. "Did it?"

"No," he replied. "But I don't think it matters much to you what I say. You can't quite bring yourself to trust me."

"Jed, I spent all these years thinking you were guilty of horrible crimes." The murders had been the worst, but she had felt like a victim, too. She had loved him and believed he'd only used her to provide him with a false alibi.

"You spent all these years thinking that only because Marcus convinced you of my guilt," he said, his voice so gruff with anger that she wondered, if Marcus hadn't already been dead, would Jed have killed him?

She shuddered at the thought. "And now he's dead and we're fleeing the scene of the crime."

He glanced in the rearview mirror. "I don't think the police saw us pulling away. At least they're not following us now."

She turned toward the back window and checked for herself. There were no lights flashing behind them. At this hour, there weren't any other vehicles on the highway. She expelled a breath of relief.

"Or they did see us and noted the plate number and they'll be waiting for us when we go back to your place," he warned her, stealing away her brief moment of relief. "Maybe we should go someplace else until we know for certain."

Erica shuddered again at the thought of armed policemen waiting outside her building or, worse yet, inside her home. "I don't care. I have to go home—to Isobel."

She rarely left her daughter at all and only ever with Mrs. Osborn. If she didn't return, her little girl might feel like Erica had as a child…abandoned and unwanted. Panic clutched at her lungs, stealing away her breath. "I—I have to see my daughter."

*Now.*

"If they catch us together, you'll lose her," he said.

"You'll go to jail for aiding and abetting me, and she'll go to whoever you appointed her guardian—"

"There's no one…"

She had no idea where her parents were now or even if they were still alive. Until she'd had her daughter, the only real family she'd ever had was Aunt Eleanor. But the elderly woman had died just a few months after Isobel had been born, and she'd left Erica the modest estate in Miller's Valley.

"Then child protective services will take Isobel and place her in a foster home," he said, a muscle twitching in his cheek as he clenched his jaw—as if he battled his own concerns for a daughter he hadn't even known he had.

Erica trembled with nerves, realizing her stubbornness could have cost her little girl the chance at any relationship with her father, as well as the relationship Isobel already had with her mother. Panic gripped her, and she fumbled inside her purse for her cell phone. She should have called the police right away.

Maybe if she called them now, they wouldn't press charges against her. Maybe she wouldn't lose her little girl.

But if she called them and gave up his whereabouts, would they do as Jed had claimed—would they shoot on sight?

SHERIFF GRIFFIN YORK STARED through the bars at him with suspicion hardening eyes that were already shadowed with fatigue. "I don't like that you got a call from your lawyer at this hour," he said as he tested the cell door, as if to make certain that Jefferson James was really locked up.

"Breuker is working hard to represent me," Jefferson replied with satisfaction. Of course, with what he was paying the man, Rick Breuker damn well better be working his ass off. But his attorney might not be the only person Jefferson needed to pay.

Sheriff York wouldn't accept his money, but there were some other officers who weren't as honorable as he was.

"You're not going to get away with all the crimes you committed," York advised him.

He chuckled at the man's naïveté. He'd been surprised and disappointed that a man this young had won the election for sheriff of Blackwoods County. But York wouldn't last in politics, since he had no idea what the real world was like. "You might be surprised…"

James was surprised. His lawyer, Rick Breuker, had called him with the news that the police had been dispatched to Kleyn's lawyer's office. And a dead body had been discovered.

Breuker, who had connections in law enforcement, believed the body belonged to the lawyer, Marcus Leighton. And Kleyn was the number-one suspect, proving wrong the DEA agent's claims of the inmate's innocence, as well as confirming how dangerous Kleyn was to anyone who crossed his path.

That shoot-on-sight order was certain to be carried out now. Kleyn wouldn't be apprehended; he would be dead.

Soon.

Jefferson James had offered an *unofficial* reward for Kleyn's demise to ensure the convict's fate. And once the number-one witness for the prosecution was dead, the case against Jefferson was certain to fall apart. He wouldn't be behind these bars much longer before

York would be opening the door for James, not to take a phone call but to go home.

To his daughter…

Emily had yet to come visit him, but with the reporters hounding her, maybe she just didn't dare leave the house. When Jefferson was freed, he would explain to her that it had all been a horrible misunderstanding. That the only thing he was really guilty of was loving her and wanting to provide for her…

The sheriff studied him through narrowed eyes. "You're up to something…"

Maybe the guy wasn't as naïve as Jefferson had thought. But it wouldn't matter. By the time he figured out the plan, it would be too late for the sheriff to step in and play hero.

Nobody would be able to save Jedidiah Kleyn this time.

*THE CONTINGENCY PLAN…*

He had intended to destroy the files relating to Kleyn's murder case, just as he had destroyed the lawyer who had ineffectually defended Jedidiah Kleyn so that he had been sentenced to prison for two lifetimes.

Because Marcus Leighton had been so incompetent, he hadn't thought there would actually be anything of value in that file. He hadn't thought that the man had had the balls to hold out on *him*. But Marcus had been keeping a secret, maybe out of guilt or maybe out of misplaced loyalty to Jed.

So he was glad that he'd been thorough, that he'd gone through every paper and scribbled note in the folder before torching it. He had found information in those case files that he could use to finally bring Jedidiah Kleyn to his knees.

War hadn't hurt the man. Neither had prison. But now he knew what would.

Hurting his daughter. Losing her, before he'd ever gotten a chance to spend any time with her, would finally push Jedidiah Kleyn over the edge.

Then, at last, he would prove that the man everyone else had always treated like a superhero was really just a mere mortal.

And mortals died, like Jed would eventually die after he'd finally and sufficiently suffered.

# Chapter Six

*Betrayal.*

It struck him again like a shiv in the chest. And the same woman was betraying him all over again. He closed his hand around hers, snapping her cell phone shut before she could punch in the last *one* of nine-one-one.

"What the hell are you doing?" he demanded. Hadn't she listened to a single warning he'd given her?

"Calling the cops, which is what I should have done the first moment I had the chance," she said, her voice hoarse with self-disgust and fear.

"So much for not doubting me…"

"It doesn't matter what I believe about your guilt or innocence of those murders," she replied. "You were convicted. You were sentenced. And you escaped. You're a fugitive."

"And you're going to turn me over to authorities," he said, bitterness welling up inside him. He never should have started to trust her again.

"I have to," she said, her voice cracking now with emotion and regret. "I can't risk losing Isobel. Not even for you…"

His pulse leapt at the torment apparent in her pale blue eyes. "Not even for me?"

"I should have come forward," she explained, "no matter what your lawyer said. I should have talked to the police then and told them about that night."

"Yes, you should have," he agreed. But now, knowing what she would have told them, he doubted it would have helped. He still would have spent the past three years in prison.

She held tight to her phone and tried to tug free of his grasp. "I need to talk to the police now."

The van swerved slightly as he gripped the wheel with only one hand. But he didn't let go, even though he glanced to the rearview to make sure no one followed them and had noticed the erratic driving. He didn't need to get pulled over now, so close to Miller's Valley and their daughter. "They're not going to believe your story."

His stomach lurched, along with the van across the snow-slick road, when he realized that. He regained control of the vehicle, but that was all he could control of this situation. No matter what she said, it was too late for her to salvage another error in her judgment.

As he had warned her, she would get in trouble for helping him now. Erica would go to jail, and their daughter would go into protective custody with strangers.

Unless…

"Give me the phone," he ordered her in the tone of voice that had always had fellow inmates cowering in fear of him.

Erica didn't cower; she glared at him instead. But she released the phone, tugging her hand free of his, as if unable to bear his touch. She hadn't felt that way that night…

But had she been drugged, as she'd claimed? If she hadn't been drugged, would she have really wanted him at all? She had easily accepted his breaking up with her before he'd left for Afghanistan. She'd never had the feelings for him that he'd had for her—or she never would have doubted his innocence no matter what lies Marcus might have told her.

Because she had no feelings for him but suspicion, he couldn't trust her. Driving with just the one hand on the wheel yet, he punched numbers into her phone.

"Who are you calling?" she asked, her beautiful blue eyes narrowed with suspicion.

Listening to the phone ring, he murmured, "The only lawman I can trust…"

"Agent Cusack," Rowe answered.

"It's me."

"You stubborn son of a…" His future brother-in-law cursed him—obviously not pleased that Jed had terminated their call earlier. "You need to tell me where you are, so I can bring you in. And if you hang up on me again, I will track you down and shoot you myself."

Jed chuckled at the threat. "It's nice to hear your voice, too."

"Your sister can't sleep with worrying over you. She's going crazy." So the DEA agent was more concerned about Macy than Jed.

That was good. Rowe Cusack was the right man for Jed's little sister. The DEA agent loved her like Macy had always deserved to be loved—completely, devotedly and unconditionally. Now if only Jed could find a love like that for himself…

He swallowed a snort of laughter at that thought. Given his luck, there was no way he would ever find a love like his sister had. He'd be lucky to stay alive and alone.

"Tell her not to worry," Jed said. "She'll see me soon."

From the passenger's seat, Erica shot him a glance—obviously wondering about the *she* he talked about and how he expected to see her soon.

Rowe sucked in an audible breath. "You're coming here?"

Jed maneuvered the van onto the slick off-ramp to Miller's Valley. Each mile closer to Isobel brought him farther from Rowe and his sister. "Not yet."

"Damn it, Jed—"

"You will see me soon," he promised, earning another inquisitive glance from Erica. "But you need to get some information for me first."

"I'm already picking up the case files from your lawyer's office tomorrow."

For years Jed had wanted to get his hands on those files, specifically on the ledgers that had provided the motive for killing his business partner. Embezzlement. But he hadn't taken his clients' money. And if he'd been able to go over those ledgers, he might have figured out who had.

"You're too late," Jed informed him. "The files are gone."

Rowe groaned. "Please tell me that you didn't break into his office and take them…"

"I didn't have to break in," Jed replied. "His killer left the door open—"

Rowe cursed now—fervently. "And you walked right into a trap."

"If it was intended as that, I didn't get caught." Or so he hoped; he would find out for certain when they returned to Erica's apartment. "Whoever killed Leighton must have also taken my file from his office."

And just what the hell had Marcus detailed in his file? Erica's address? The fact that she'd been pregnant during the trial?

Leighton had told Jed that he'd never tracked her down, but he hadn't told Jed the truth about anything. Why would he have admitted to knowing her location? He wouldn't have wanted Jed to send someone else to talk to her and learn what Jed had tonight, that Marcus had actually convinced her not to testify.

Despite the heat blowing out of the vents, she wrapped her arms around herself as if she was cold. Or scared.

"This is really bad, Jed," Rowe said, his raspy voice pitched low, probably so that Macy wouldn't overhear him. "You're going to be the number-one suspect for his murder."

He sighed. "I know."

He had been set up. Again.

"Did you…?"

"Hell, no." But he couldn't swear that he wouldn't have killed his lawyer if he had been right about Marcus framing him for murders that his old fraternity brother had actually committed himself.

"I'm sorry, man, that I had to ask and I'm sorry that it happened," Rowe said. "This is a tough break."

"Maybe not," Jed replied. "Although I didn't get to talk to Marcus before he died and find out who paid him to help frame me—"

"What!" The phone cracked with Rowe's exclamation. He'd obviously forgotten to be quiet.

Erica startled as if she'd heard his shout, too.

"Leighton helped set me up," Jed said. His death was proof enough for Jed of his involvement. Marcus's duplicity also explained how Jed had been convicted on just circumstantial evidence and eyewitness testimony that should have been easily discredited. "His partner must have killed him tonight."

Rowe's mind followed the path Jed's had taken. "The killer was worried that Leighton would give him up."

Or *her*.

He glanced at Erica now. Of course she had had no more opportunity to kill Marcus than he had. But another woman could have been involved—Brandon's girlfriend who'd lied in her testimony. Had she been covering up her own guilt? She had really been the last one to see Brandon alive.

She wouldn't have had access to his clients' funds, but Brandon had. He could have embezzled it, and then she killed him to keep the money all to herself. Except for what she'd paid his lawyer.

Then she'd killed him.

Regret tugged at Jed that Marcus was gone now. "He would have told me who'd betrayed me," Jed insisted. He would have either coerced or guilted a confession out of his old friend.

And the killer must have known that, too.

How well did the killer know Marcus? And Jed? Was this about revenge or had he just been a convenient patsy to take the murder rap?

Rowe sighed. "So this is literally a dead end then, man."

"Marcus was paid off."

He never would have been able to afford that historic building if he hadn't been—not with the limited case load he'd had. There hadn't been many files in those drawers, and Jed doubted the killer had taken anyone else's.

"Probably with the money that was embezzled

from my old accounting firm. Track down that money, Rowe."

Jed had wanted to go through those records himself, but Marcus had claimed that he couldn't get permission to bring them in to Blackwoods. Given how corrupt the warden had been, Jed hadn't questioned him. But he should have because Marcus had probably lied about that, too. He just hadn't wanted Jed to track that money down himself because it would have led to Marcus's own wallet.

"During your trial, court-appointed accountants went through those ledgers and bank statements," Rowe said, sharing what he'd learned from the transcripts. "No one was able to figure out where the money had gone. They figured you had secret accounts."

"I didn't." He had never seen any of that money. "But the killer must have. Try to track down the payments that were made to Leighton for throwing my trial."

"What about Erica Towsley?" Rowe asked, seemingly out of the blue. "Who is she?"

Jed chuckled. Rowe had kept interrupting him to keep Jed on the phone long enough to trace the call this time. "Check that angle, too."

"For the money?"

"Follow the money." Jed pulled the van into the alley behind Erica's building.

He doubted it would lead back to her, though. Her vehicle was a piece of junk that looked as if it had more knocks and rattles than a demolition-derby car. And the building where she lived was old, as had been all the furnishings inside her drafty apartment. If she'd been paid off, her payments hadn't been as generous as Leighton's.

"What angle?" Erica whispered.

He shook his head. "And if you can't figure it out, I'll go over the ledgers and statements when I meet up with you."

"If court-appointed accountants couldn't figure it out, I doubt I will be able to," Rowe said.

"Then concentrate on the witnesses," Jed said. "I bet you'll find they were paid off just like Leighton was. Track them down. And I'll track down the money."

"I'll bring the ledgers to you," Rowe offered. "I know where to find you."

Even though the DEA agent couldn't see him, Jed grinned at the man's persistence. "Don't waste your time. I would be gone by the time you got here."

"I could send the police ahead to detain you," Rowe warned him.

"You wouldn't risk it," Jed said with absolute certainty. "You wouldn't risk my life."

Or Macy would probably take Rowe's—no matter how much she loved him. He didn't trust that Erica wouldn't risk his life, though, since she had already almost reported him.

He caught her as she reached for the door handle. "You're not going anywhere."

"Damn it, Jed—"

He clicked off the cell without explaining to Rowe that he hadn't been talking to him.

"Let me go," Erica demanded, her voice rising with panic as she tugged at her arm.

"No. I can't let you go…"

HIS WORDS, SPOKEN SO matter-of-factly, chilled Erica's skin so that goose bumps lifted beneath her heavy clothes.

"I'll scream," she threatened.

"Then I'll have to shut you up." He leaned closer.

Erica closed her eyes, flinching even before he struck her. But he didn't hit her. Instead his gloved fingers slid along her jaw, tipping up her chin. Then his mouth covered hers.

She expected cruelty—for his mouth to punish. But instead his lips slid lightly across hers, brushing gently back and forth. Her breath caught and then escaped in a gasp.

And he deepened the kiss, pressing his mouth tighter against hers until her lips parted. Not for breath.

She didn't need to breathe anymore. She just needed him—needed the passion that warmed her blood and quickened her heart rate. No man had ever affected her like this one.

But those effects hadn't always been good. He had broken her heart when he'd dumped her before his deployment. It hadn't mattered that they'd been broken up, though. She'd spent a year worrying about him and yearning for him.

And loving him.

So it was no wonder she had fallen into his arms and his bed almost literally the minute he had returned home. But he hadn't professed his love then. He had only used her—maybe not for an alibi. But he'd used her all the same.

And broken her heart again.

She lifted her hands between them and pushed against his chest. He had always been muscular, but now his chest was like a concrete wall—hard and immovable. But Erica didn't have to struggle or scream.

He pulled back, his nostrils flaring as he drew in a deep breath.

"I didn't want to do that now," he said.

Finally she breathed, drawing in a sharp breath as his admission stung her pride.

And her heart.

"I wanted to do that the minute you opened the door to me," he continued, "even when I thought you had betrayed me and left me to rot in prison."

"Jed, I didn't—"

"I realize now that you didn't betray me three years ago, but you were about to do it now," he reminded her. "You can't call the police, Erica."

"I can't," she agreed, "because you took my phone." But even if he hadn't, she doubted she would have been able to punch in that last digit. She was almost grateful that he had taken the phone from her.

Who had he called to help him? Who was the lawman he trusted? A guard from the prison? It had sounded like they were all corrupt. Or the DEA agent whose badge he had used to trick her into opening the door for him?

"You have a landline in your apartment," he said. "So you're not going inside without me."

"But if Mrs. Osborn sees you, she will call the police for certain." Taking the impossible decision out of Erica's hands but putting custody of her daughter and Erica's own freedom at risk.

Jed shrugged off her concern. "I doubt she'll recognize me. I don't look like the photo they keep showing of me on the news."

No. He looked even more dangerous than the mug shot taken before his trial. After three years in Blackwoods Penitentiary, he was undoubtedly more dangerous.

"I'm not worried about *her* calling the police on me." He narrowed his eyes, which were dark with suspicion as he stared at her.

He was worried about Erica. Even though she had explained why she hadn't come forward at his trial, he didn't trust her, and now that he was dead, Marcus Leighton couldn't confirm that he was the reason she hadn't provided Jed with an alibi. In addition to that, she had almost reported him to authorities, so she couldn't blame him for not trusting her.

"I won't call the police," she promised. "I'm not sure I believe you completely about that shoot-on-sight order. But I can't risk it."

His gaze widened slightly, but then he shook his head. "Somehow I don't think I'm the one you're worried about losing."

She had already lost him twice. First to Afghanistan and then to prison. But then, he had never really been hers to lose.

"I can't risk Isobel's safety," she said as she pushed open the passenger door.

He didn't stop her this time, and she felt a moment's flash of disappointment as she stepped onto the snow-covered pavement.

"I can't risk her getting shot in the crossfire," she said. "That's why you need to get into whatever vehicle you brought here—" she gestured at a car and a van parked in the alley "—and drive as far away from us as you can get."

"You're right," he agreed—almost too easily as he slammed shut the driver's door after joining her in the alley. "I never would have come to you if I hadn't thought you alibi-ing me would be the fastest way to get my conviction overturned."

"I'm sorry…"

"And I never should have let you come with me to

see Leighton," he said, his voice gruff with guilt and frustration.

"I didn't give you a choice," she reminded him as she headed toward the back door of her building. "I didn't tell you his address."

"But I could have gotten it out of you…"

He could have—had he kissed her like he just had. So she didn't argue with him, just closed her eyes and relived those few brief moments when his lips had covered hers.

"I'm not giving you a choice now," he said as he slid his arm around her.

She opened her eyes, both anticipating and fearing another kiss. But he wasn't even looking at her.

He had only reached around her for the door knob. "I'm going up to your apartment with you," he said. "I'm going to make sure you and Isobel are safe before I leave."

She shook her head. "Mrs. Osborn—"

"Will never get a good look at my face," he said as he opened the door. "No one has recognized me since the prison break. No one will."

The collar was up on his dark-colored wool coat, but it didn't hide much of his face. Dark stubble did that, as did his expression, which was so intimidating that nobody was likely to stare at him long enough to recognize him.

Erica drew in a shaky breath and inhaled the scent that had always been Jed's alone—rain fresh but musky male. "You'll leave once you see Isobel?"

He nodded.

"Okay." She followed him inside and up the back stairs to her apartment. "Let me go in first and distract Mrs. Osborn."

Jed was already reaching for her door, too, but he didn't have to turn the knob. It stood ajar, the apartment so dark inside that only shadows spilled out into the dimly lit hallway. Something clattered to the hardwood floor inside, and Jed shoved open the door and bolted into the living room.

"Stop," she called after him in a loud whisper. When she was watching Isobel, Mrs. Osborn usually left the doors open between her apartment and Erica's. And the older woman often dropped things.

But Jed didn't stop.

So Erica rushed inside after him. He wasn't alone. But it wasn't Mrs. Osborn he grappled with in the dark living room. The black-clothed figure was nearly as big as he was. But not big enough to overpower Jed, even though the man swung a punch at him. While it connected, it didn't even faze Jed.

Then Jed swung back, knocking the man to the ground. He reached for the intruder and dragged him to his feet, but the man broke free of Jed's grasp.

He turned toward the open door. Erica stood there, blocking the exit. Her heart slammed against her ribs, and her muscles froze so that she couldn't move out of the way.

But he didn't charge at her. He didn't even look at her. He kept his head down, as Jed had demonstrated he did so that he wasn't recognized. Then the man turned again and ran down the hall toward Isobel's room.

Despite his size, Jed's reflexes were quick and his stride fast as he pursued the intruder. Erica's muscles recovered as fear and determination pulsed through her, and she chased after them.

Her primary concern was protecting her daughter.

She wouldn't let anyone hurt her little girl. Size and muscle was no match for a mother's protective instinct.

Jed's primary concern was obviously catching the intruder, since he didn't spare so much as a glance toward the little twin bed as they ran past it. The men did not even stop inside the small bedroom. The intruder vaulted through the open window, and, with a hard thump on the metal, Jed followed him out onto the fire escape.

The curtains fluttered in the breeze blowing through the open window, whipping the hot-pink satin against the walls. It was freezing in the room, but it wasn't nearly as cold as the blood pumping hard and fast with fear through Erica's veins.

She stopped next to her daughter's bed, but she didn't even need to look down at the tangled blankets to know that it was empty.

Her baby was gone.

# *Chapter Seven*

"It'll be too late. By the time you get there, he'll be well on his way somewhere else," Macy warned her husband-to-be.

Rowe cursed and dropped his car keys back onto the desk before dropping his body onto the chair behind his desk. "I know. But…"

"But what?" she asked. "You've been keeping something from me, and we promised we'd never do that."

"I want to protect you," he said.

"But I'm not in danger."

"Not anymore," he agreed, his deep voice vibrating with the torment of remorse for what she had recently endured. He blamed himself.

She blamed Warden Jefferson James.

"But Jed is," she said.

"Macy…" The torment hadn't left his voice.

Her pulse quickened. "How much danger?" she demanded to know.

"You know everyone considers him a cop killer…"

"That's why you went on the news," she said, suddenly realizing. "You wanted to put doubts in the minds of the officers looking for him. You wanted to make it so that they won't shoot first and ask questions later."

A muscle twitched along his tightly clenched jaw, and

he nodded. "Someone put out a shoot-on-sight order on him."

"Someone?" She snorted. "It's Warden James. He doesn't want Jed able to testify against him." And the unscrupulous man had already proven he had no problem with killing. Of course, he always had preferred that others get the blood on their hands instead of him getting it on his.

Rowe nodded again, sending a lock of blond hair over his furrowed brow. "Someone even put out an unofficial reward…"

"For my brother's murder?" She sucked in a breath as pain jabbed her heart. "Does he know this?"

"I warned him about the shoot-on-sight order. I didn't know about the reward until another officer told me what he'd heard."

"So Jed knows he's in danger out there, but he won't come in?"

Rowe shook his head. "I promised I'd protect him."

Her brother had always been stubborn…but she understood what he was thinking. "He won't turn himself in until he proves his innocence."

"His lawyer was murdered—"

"Marcus?" She wouldn't have chosen the man to represent her brother for a parking ticket, much less murder. But Jed had always been loyal to his friends. She suspected they couldn't say the same.

"It looks like he was paid off to throw the trial," Rowe said. "I was already beginning to think that from going over the court transcripts."

Macy had been premed, not prelaw, but she'd thought so, too. "He never objected to anything."

"And he didn't really challenge the eyewitness testimony," Rowe said. "Your brother asked me to find the witnesses."

She met her fiancé's gaze. "Jed didn't kill his lawyer."

"I had to ask him…" He groaned. "If someone had helped set me up to spend the rest of my life in a hell-hole like Blackwoods…"

"I know." She crossed the room and dropped onto his lap, looping her arm around his neck. "I understand why you would have doubted him. But he's not a killer. He won't hurt the witnesses."

Rowe pressed a kiss to her lips, the stubble on his jaw erotically scraping her skin. "You even wondered if he might not want revenge more than justice."

"We have to make sure that we help him choose justice. Find the witnesses."

Rowe sighed. "I'd rather find Jed. Bringing him in is the only way to make sure he stays safe."

He wouldn't be safe in custody, either. They both knew it. "The only way to make sure my brother stays safe is to prove his innocence."

"We have to find the real killer," Rowe agreed.

Before Jed found him…

THE FIRE ESCAPE VIBRATED beneath Jed's feet as he chased the dark shadow down into the alley he had left just moments ago with Erica. His borrowed van was parked alongside hers. If he had done as she'd asked and gotten into it and left…

She would have walked into her apartment alone—and at the mercy of a brute of a man who'd immediately attacked Jed. If the guy had attacked Erica…

His fist stung from the one blow he'd connected, which had knocked the guy back on his feet and loose from his grasp. Jed hadn't been able to catch him since.

The guy had been just enough faster than he was that Jed hadn't been able to outrun him in the hall. And he'd lost him on the fire escape.

He dropped off the last rung of the metal ladder and connected with the asphalt, his ankles stinging at the impact. Jed focused on the snowfall, trying to discern footprints. But the wind had whipped up, swirling around the light dusting of snow, so that he couldn't track him. But the guy had to be around here somewhere. The short hairs lifting on his nape, Jed could feel him close. Maybe crouched behind one of the vans?

Jed moved silently, as he had learned to move during his deployment. He crept closer to the van and peered through the windows, trying to spy a shadow on the other side. Then he held still—perfectly still—and waited. As he'd learned in his National Guard training, he could hold his breath and slow his heart rate.

Could the man he'd chased from Erica's apartment do the same? Eventually the guy would have to breathe, and Jed would hear him as he listened intently.

But he didn't hear a breath. He heard a scream. Erica's scream. It rent the eerie, predawn silence.

His heart lurched, shifting in his chest. "God, no…"

Instead of wasting time to go back through the building, Jed jumped for the last rung of the fire escape and pulled himself up. As he vaulted up the steps, his heart pounded hard with fear and dread.

Had he followed out a staged distraction while the guy's accomplice had stayed behind for Erica and Isobel? Had that accomplice already hurt them?

He stopped outside the window and peered into the room to assess the situation before rushing in blind. Erica stood alone by Isobel's bed, her hands clasped against her mouth as if she fought to hold back more screams. He scanned the corners of the room, checking for a man holding a gun on her. Because if this was an ambush, it would be for him. And Jed wouldn't be able to protect her and their daughter if he was dead.

But seeing Erica in such fear and pain was killing him. He stepped through the window and joined her inside the room. "You screamed—"

She whirled toward him. "She's gone! He took her, Jed! He took our daughter!"

He cupped her shoulders and then her face in his slightly shaking palms. "No. He wasn't carrying anything down the fire escape. He didn't take her."

He damn well wouldn't have let the bastard grab their child. If he had seen the man even reach toward the bed, he would have finally become that murderer everyone already thought he was.

Erica's voice cracked with hysteria. "She's gone…"

He pulled her into his arms, clutching her trembling body close to his chest. "He didn't take her…"

But Jed must have been right about the accomplice. Instead of staying behind, though, he had gone ahead—with Isobel. And the other man had provided the distraction so that he could get away with the child.

Jed had only known about Isobel for a few hours, but he'd already lost her. He clutched Erica closer, but instead of offering comfort, he was seeking it. He didn't deserve it, though; this was his fault.

Isobel had been taken because of him. Whoever had framed him for murder had found an even more effective way to hurt him than sending him to prison.

No matter how close Jed held her, Erica felt no comfort. His heart raced at the same frantic pace as hers. He was scared, too. Maybe even more scared than she was because he had seen more horrors in his life than she had in her relatively sheltered one.

Even though she watched the news, those things happened to other people—not her. In her safe little world here in Miller's Valley, her child could never be taken. Her child would not be harmed. But Jed had shaken her safe world. He'd brought danger and murder to her life, making all horrible things possible. Even to her sweet angel baby...

Sobs broke free of her control, shaking her—making her so sick with fear that she nearly gagged. Big hands patted her back, trying again to offer comfort. But his touch chilled her, making her shudder.

"Erica, we'll find her," he promised. "We'll get her back."

"No, I want you out of here!" she yelled, wedging her hands between them so that she could shove him away from her—out of her safe, little world. "I want you to leave! This is your fault. This is all your fault!"

He flinched. He was so big and muscular that he probably couldn't be physically hurt. But she had emotionally hurt him. Even though he had only just discovered he had a daughter, he cared about Isobel. He was as scared as she was.

A twinge of guilt penetrated her fear and hysteria. But anger pushed that guilt away. "It's your fault that my baby is gone!"

Jed's breath caught, and his eyes widened.

But she didn't care anymore that he was hurting, too. She stepped back again. She didn't care if he got hurt, either. She was going to call the police this time. She couldn't waste another moment worrying about Jedidiah Kleyn.

But before she could turn away from him, a small hand slipped into hers and tugged on her fingers.

"Mommy, I'm not gone," a soft voice informed her. "I'm right here."

Erica whirled around and dropped to her knees to wrap up Isobel in her arms. "Oh, sweetheart…" Tears streaked down her face.

"Mommy, why are you crying?"

She couldn't tell the child about the man who had broken into their home. But she couldn't lie to her, either. "I was scared, honey, when I found your bed empty."

"I was at Mrs. Osborn's," the little girl explained. "I woked up and she tooked me over there."

Erica glanced up, her nerves returning as she discovered her neighbor standing in the bedroom doorway. The older woman's gaze was focused on Jed's face, her faded blue eyes narrowed with suspicion.

"Mrs. Osborn—" Erica jumped up and headed toward her, trying to block her view of Jed. But he was so much taller than she was—until he crouched down in front of their daughter.

"What's going on here?" Mrs. Osborn demanded to know with equal parts anger and fear.

With a pointed glance at Isobel to indicate that she didn't want to talk in front of the child, Erica guided the woman back down the hall toward the front door. "Nothing's wrong…"

Not now that her baby was back.

"I heard screaming and nearly called the authorities." Mrs. Osborn stared down the hall toward the dark shadow enveloping the little girl. "Looks like I should have called."

"No. I just overreacted to finding Isobel's bed

empty," Erica explained with a self-deprecating chuckle. "It's late and I'm tired."

"And you're not alone," Mrs. Osborn said. "Who is that man? I've never seen him around before…"

She had never seen any man around Erica unless he was a client of her accounting business. After Jed, she hadn't dared trust another man—especially when she had Isobel's safety to worry about even more than her own.

Her stomach pitched again with the horror over what could have happened to her baby had Isobel been in the apartment when that man had broken in…

The old woman's wrinkled brow furrowed into deeper lines of confusion. "Actually I think that I might have seen him before…"

"He's an old friend of mine," Erica said. "You've probably seen him in some pictures I've had around here." She opened the door to the hall before the woman could ask to see those photos.

But Mrs. Osborn was already peering into the living room and, with a trembling hand gesturing toward it, noted a lamp lying on the floor.

Erica forced a smile. "He—he couldn't find the lights in the dark."

Mrs. Osborn leaned closer and clasped her hand. "If he's threatening you, I'll go back to my apartment and call the police. I'll get you help."

"I don't need help," Erica lied.

She desperately needed help. She had stumbled into a murder scene, had had her apartment broken into and, for long, horrific moments, had believed that her daughter had been abducted.

"Everything's fine." She glanced back at Jed and forced a smile. "He really is a friend."

"Oh." Mrs. Osborn nodded in sudden understanding. "He's an old *boy*friend."

"Yes." She hadn't had to lie this time.

For a short while before his deployment, Jed had been her boyfriend. Their connection had been so instant and deep that she had believed it could have lasted forever.

But, like everyone else who had mattered in her life, he hadn't given her the chance.

Now she couldn't give him one. She had to get rid of him this time—had to make sure that he took his danger out of her previously safe world.

She clasped Mrs. Osborn's hand tighter—ready to give her the message the older woman had already suspected Erica wanted to give her.

*Call the police...*

JEDIDIAH KLEYN HAD CHANGED. That was the first thing he'd noticed before he'd punched the man. With his buzz cut and bulky muscles, Jed didn't look all that physically different from the war hero who had returned from his tour in Afghanistan with a Purple Heart.

But he was very different—mentally and emotionally.

He was harder. Tougher. Ruthless in a way that he had never been. Jed would undoubtedly kill to protect the woman and her child.

Before Jed and Erica had walked in on him, he'd had time to look at all the *family* photos inside the apartment. But the kid hadn't been in her bed. Not that Jed would have given him time to grab the little girl. He had been too focused on catching him.

And killing him?

He rubbed his jaw, which had swollen from the blow Jed had dealt him. He snorted in derision at his quick flash of anger. He had no right to be mad about it. He'd had that one coming. Hell, he had a lot more than one coming to him.

But Jed wouldn't land another punch. Jed had already won too much in his life.

It was *his* turn to win.

And Jedidiah Kleyn's turn to die.

## Chapter Eight

Trying not to imagine who she had entertained here, Jed ignored the red walls and white lace curtains of Erica's bedroom. His attention was focused on the tiny female tucked under the red-and-white quilt. She slept deeply. Peacefully. He would probably never sleep again.

But then it was already morning. Sunshine radiated through those lace curtains, warming the hardwood floor and enveloping the bed and the sleeping child in a circle of ethereal light.

Voices emanated from the living room. The old woman had left a while ago. Who the hell…

He spared one last glance at his sleeping daughter, assuring himself that she was safe in Erica's room. There was no fire escape so that someone could break the window and quickly grab her without being noticed. Isobel was much safer in her mother's room.

But what about her mother?

He didn't hear her voice. As he crept down the hall toward the living room, he realized the voices came from the television set. Erica stood before it, the remote clasped in her slightly trembling hand.

"Isn't that too loud?" he asked, then remembered that their daughter was a sound sleeper.

Erica didn't bother reminding him. She just gestured at the screen. "They're running your story again."

He didn't even glance at the TV. "That's not *my* story."

Someone else had concocted the story that had sent him to prison for crimes he hadn't committed.

"The part about breaking out of prison and being an escaped convict is your story," she said. "And that's what Mrs. Osborn will see when she watches this. She'll recognize you. You have to leave before she calls the police."

She tossed the remote onto the couch and moved toward the door, as if to see him out. But he didn't follow her. Instead he headed to where he'd brawled with the intruder. She had righted the lamp that had fallen to the floor, but the shade was dented from where it had struck the hardwood.

He would have had Rowe check it for prints, but the man had worn gloves. What had he been looking for? The lamp sat atop a bureau crowded with picture frames. Isobel's face, so much like his sister Macy's, smiled out of most of them from infancy to her current age. The drawers were shut, no papers disturbed.

Jed doubted the man had been looking for files like those taken from Marcus Leighton's office. Jed was afraid that what he'd been looking for had been across the hall with Mrs. Osborn...

"I'm sure your neighbor is asleep in her bed after her late night," Jed assured her. The woman was very old, her eyes foggy as if she had cataracts. He doubted she had been able to see much more than his shadowy outline, let alone enough of his features to recognize his face.

Instead of worrying about her neighbor, Erica should

be in her bed with their daughter. Dark circles rimmed her pale blue eyes. But she trembled with anxiety.

"You need to leave," she insisted. "Now. Before it's too late."

"You really think I should leave?" he asked. "After what happened last night?"

Her breath shuddered out as her mind followed a different path into the past. "A man died."

"I didn't kill Marcus." He'd thought he had convinced her of that, but obviously she still had her doubts about him.

"I know." She pointed toward the TV again. "But the authorities won't. They'll think you're even more dangerous than they already do."

They were already going to shoot him on sight; now maybe they wouldn't even wait to make sure it was him before they started firing. Would sticking close to Erica and Isobel keep them safe or put them in more danger?

"If I leave, that man might come back," he warned her.

"And if you stay, and Mrs. Osborn recognizes you, he won't be the only one breaking into my home." She glanced toward her door, her eyes widening as if she could imagine a battering ram breaking apart the wood and a SWAT team bursting into her living room.

He could imagine the same thing, but he could also imagine that man coming back…for her and Isobel. And his gut told him that man would prove much more dangerous than any lawman with a shoot-on-sight order. "I can't just leave you…"

"Why not?" she asked. "You didn't come here to protect me. You came here to force me to provide you with an alibi and clear your name. I can't do that. I can't perjure myself and swear that you never left me that night."

"I didn't want you to perjure yourself," he said. "I wanted you to tell the truth."

"I have," she said.

He wished he could be certain that she told the truth. But after learning that yet another friend had betrayed him, he dared not trust a woman he really hadn't known very well at all. She hadn't just kept his possible alibi from the police; she'd kept his daughter from him, too.

"So why are you still here?" Erica asked with such intensity that the question must have been nagging at her for a while.

He gestured toward her bedroom, to where their daughter lay sleeping. He couldn't put into words what he already felt for his child—the protectiveness, the affection, the devotion…

"Until a few hours ago, you didn't even know Isobel existed," Erica reminded him.

"Whose fault was that?" he asked, the question slipping out with his bitterness. She could have gone to his trial or visited him in prison to at least let him know that he had become a father.

Her delicately featured face flushed, but she shook her head in rejection of any culpability. "It was Marcus Leighton's fault for convincing me of your guilt. If there was any chance that you were the killer your own lawyer thought you were, I didn't want you to have anything to do with my baby."

Jed couldn't fault her for that. She was a good mother. Instead he cursed the man whom he'd once considered a friend.

Macy had wanted to get him a better lawyer, one with more experience with criminal cases, but he had been loyal. Why hadn't Marcus? The man had promised that no one else would work as hard at proving Jed's innocence than he would, and Jed had trusted him.

Now he knew better than to ever trust again.

"Go," Erica urged him. "Find out who bribed him to betray you. Find out who wanted you to spend the rest of your life in prison."

"I intend to," he said. That hadn't changed, but it was no longer his first priority. "Proving my innocence was my whole reason for leaving during the riot at Blackwoods."

"So go," she urged him again—almost desperately. She had been afraid of him earlier—when he'd tricked her into opening the door. But this fear, haunting her blue eyes, was even greater. She wasn't afraid of him anymore, but she was afraid of the danger he'd brought into her life.

"I can't leave without you and Isobel," he said. Chances were good her intruder would return. Soon.

She shook her head. "We can't go with you. We can't live on the run. You can't ask that of us…"

"I don't want you living on the run," he said. "I just want you living. I want you safe."

But he wanted more than that. He wanted *her* in every way. He stepped closer to her, and she must have seen desire in his eyes because her breath audibly caught.

And maybe she wanted him, too, because she leaned toward him. He lowered his head to hers. She gasped at his nearness, and her breath warmed his lips. Then he covered her mouth with his.

A man on the run from authorities and a killer, he had no time for kisses. But, in this moment, there was nothing he would rather be doing than kissing Erica Towsley.

ERICA LIFTED HER HANDS, pressing her palms against his chest. She needed to push him away—to push him out of the door and out of her and Isobel's lives.

But instead, her fingers curled into his shirt, and she clutched him closer. Rising up on tiptoe, she pressed her mouth tighter to his. He parted her lips, deepening the kiss.

His tongue touched hers and ignited a fire within her. Her legs trembled as desire rushed through her. Her nipples tightened, and heat filled her stomach. And all those disjointed memories from that night—the night they conceived their daughter—flitted through her mind.

As if he felt her trembling, he swung her up in his arms—clasping her tight to his chest. And he kissed her more deeply, his tongue sliding in and out of her mouth until she moaned.

She ran her hands up the back of his neck to clasp his head, and his closely cropped hair tickled her palms. She tingled all over as passion pulsed inside her.

He groaned and moved, carrying her over to the couch. He lowered her to the cushions and followed her down, covering her body with his.

He was so big. So muscular. So heavy, even though he balanced most of his weight on his bulging arms. She wrapped her arms around him and pulled him closer. Then she wrapped her legs around his waist and arched into him—wanting, *needing,* more.

He lifted his mouth from hers and stared into her eyes; his were dark and hot with desire. "Erica…?"

How could she have ever thought that he had drugged and taken her choice away from her? Even though he'd been locked up for three years, he was giving her a choice now—instead of just taking what she was freely willing to give.

Why was she so willing? Maybe she had been locked up, too, for the past few years—afraid to trust because of what she had considered such a betrayal of her love. But Jed hadn't betrayed her.

If anyone had betrayed anyone, she had betrayed him when she had let Marcus Leighton make her doubt him. She'd already apologized, but she had to say it again. "I'm sorry…"

With a shudder, he rose up—pulling away as if she'd rejected him. "No, I'm sorry," he said. "This is crazy. We can't do this—"

"We shouldn't," she said.

For so many reasons. The most pressing was that he couldn't stay. He was a man on the run who had already brought her nothing but heartbreak and danger.

"But we can," she continued. It wouldn't make up to him the three years of his life that he'd lost, but it might help them regain some of the closeness and promise they'd had before he had gone off to Afghanistan and broken off their relationship.

"And I want to." She grasped his shirt in both fists and tugged him down toward her.

His hands covered hers, and he stared at her, his gaze dark with a breath-stealing intensity. Then he pulled her fingers from his shirt.

At least one of them had the sense to realize this was neither the time nor the place for making love. But still she had to blink back tears of disappointment. Then she was blinking to clear her eyes as he pulled off his shirt and tossed it onto the floor next to the couch. All rippling, sinewy muscle, he was so damn sexy.

Her breath caught as desire overwhelmed her. She

touched him, sliding her fingertips across the hair-dusted silky skin. Then she lifted up to press her lips to his chest. His heart thudded against her mouth.

"Erica…"

He lowered his head and kissed her—deeply. And she kissed him back with all the passion she felt for him. It pulsed low in her body, winding a pressure tight inside her. It filled her ears with the sound of her own blood rushing through her veins.

But a rapid beep, beep, beep broke the grip of desire, clearing her head, so that she heard the broadcast announcement:

"Early this morning the governor has issued a special press release. In order to apprehend the convicts who escaped during the prison riot at Blackwoods Penitentiary in northern Michigan, he has put a bounty on the head of each of the prisoners. These bounties will be paid either to the person who actually apprehends these escapees or to the person who provides information leading to their apprehension."

His voice quavering with excitement, the reporter stated the amount on each convict. "But the highest bounty will be paid for the apprehension of cop killer Jedidiah Kleyn."

A pithy curse escaped Jed's lips with a hiss of breath. "That's not a bounty," he murmured. "It's a death warrant…"

He hadn't been lying about the shoot-on-sight order. In light of the bounty, he'd probably actually downplayed how much danger he was really in.

"You have to leave," she urged him as panic gripped her.

Mrs. Osborn might have believed that Jed was Erica's friend, but that wouldn't matter if she recognized his photo and thought she could collect that kind of money for reporting his location.

And she would recognize the photo that filled the television screen. It wasn't his mug shot, with his full head of dark hair and clean-shaven square jaw, that they had previously shown. This was his prison ID that must have finally been retrieved from the ruins that was all that was left of Blackwoods Penitentiary. In this picture, there was more stubble on his jaw than his shaved head. And he looked hard and dangerous—like he did now.

He swore again. Then he grabbed up his shirt from the floor and dragged it over his head. "Erica—"

"Go," she said, the panic stealing away her breath as it pressed heavily on her lungs. "You have to get out of here before it's too late."

But then a noise penetrated the thin window panes of her home. Sirens.

It was already too late.

The authorities were coming for him with orders to shoot on sight.

"You MANIPULATIVE MONSTER," Drake Ketchum shouted through the bars of the Blackwoods County jail.

A smile tugged at Jefferson's lips. "Are you supposed to be talking to me without my lawyer present?" he goaded the ambitious, young Blackwoods County district attorney.

"I'm going to trace this back to you and add it to the other charges you're going down for," Ketchum threatened.

"Trace what back to me?"

"You're behind the bounty," Ketchum said. "You talked the governor into it!"

Jefferson chuckled. "You give me entirely too much

credit. Do you really think I'd still be in here if the governor was taking my calls?"

Ketchum was the real master of manipulation; at the arraignment, he'd talked the judge into denying bail for Jefferson.

"Then you put your sleazy attorney up to it."

Jefferson shrugged. "Prove it," he challenged the man. "You won't be able to do that any easier than you'll be able to prove I ordered the murder of an undercover DEA agent, since your star witness is dead."

Sheriff York stood beside Ketchum—two young men who were stupid and idealistic enough to believe they ruled this county. Jefferson nearly laughed again, but it was York who chuckled this time.

"Kleyn isn't dead," the sheriff said.

He shrugged again—unconcerned because they were entirely too concerned. "You have him in protective custody then?"

"Not yet," York admitted.

"Then you better get him there soon," he spoke to Ketchum, "or you're going to lose that star witness for sure—what with every law-enforcement officer and bounty hunter in this state and probably most of the surrounding ones gunning for him."

Ketchum's gaze slid from his to the sheriff. "He's right. You better find him first."

Jefferson was enjoying this visit immensely. It was good for these young fools to know who really had all the power. "And, since you don't know where he is, I feel compelled to point out that you don't know for certain if he's still alive."

"Thanks to that bounty we know," Ketchum replied. "If he was dead, someone would have tried to claim it."

Jefferson nodded. "True. Unless the person Kleyn's

in the most danger from has no use for the bounty. If that convict is actually as innocent as he claims and the DEA agent believes he is, then there's someone who wants him dead even more…"

"Than you do?"

He chuckled at Ketchum's weak attempt to trap him. "You're going to have to do better than that," he warned the man. Then he turned to the sheriff. "And so are you if you want to bring that escapee back alive."

"You should have figured out by now that the man isn't easy to kill," York reminded him. "Your fellow guards have already told us that you ordered his murder after the prison doctor's. But then the riot broke out."

And everything had gone to hell. Because of Jedidiah Kleyn. Now it was his turn to go to hell.

# Chapter Nine

In tight fists, Jed gripped the steering wheel of Erica's van. He had to stay in control. For so many reasons...

The most important one slept in her car seat in the back. He glanced into the rearview mirror at the reflection of her peaceful face. Since he'd met her, he had spent a lot of time watching Isobel sleep.

Then he turned toward the woman who sat in the passenger seat beside him. She had not slept at all the previous night, and from the tension gripping her body and beautiful face, she would not sleep anytime soon.

She was another reason for him to stay in control. The other was the authorities they had barely escaped, passing the patrol cars minutes before they would have pulled up to her building.

He had to stay calm and keep his wits about him because not only would the police be after him now, but so would every bounty hunter and civilian who wanted to collect the reward for his head.

Just being with him was putting Erica and Isobel in danger, too. He drew in a deep breath, bracing himself for the answer to the question he had to ask her. "Why did you agree to leave with me?"

Erica turned toward the backseat and their sleeping daughter. "Mrs. Osborn will tell the police that I called you a friend. Then they'll believe that I'm aiding and abetting you. They would arrest me and take Isobel off to child protective services—just like you warned me."

"I'm sorry…" That he had been right, and he was also sorry for letting her go along with him to confront Marcus. The minute he'd realized she had been duped just like the jury of his peers, he should have left her and Isobel. But he hadn't entirely believed that she was telling the truth. He couldn't trust her.

He shouldn't trust anyone. But to protect her and their daughter, he had no choice.

"Now we're forced to live like you—" her voice cracked on a sob, but she forced it down with a deep breath "—on the run."

"I'm sorry…" He glanced into the rearview mirror again but not to watch their daughter sleep. Instead he tracked the vehicle that was closing the careful distance at which the driver had been following them from Miller's Valley.

He'd taken her van and had left his in the alley because authorities had probably figured out by now that the guard's van was missing. They would have issued an APB on that license plate. But maybe one had already been issued on Erica's, too.

Living on the run might be the least of her concerns because it looked as though they were about to get caught. The only question was, who was doing the catching…

ERICA'S BACK PRESSED AGAINST the seat as the van accelerated. She followed Jed's gaze to the rearview mirror. "Is someone following us?"

"I think so," he tersely admitted.

"Is it a police officer?" She turned around to check again for flashing lights.

He shook his head. "It's not a patrol car, and it doesn't look like an unmarked police car, either."

"You think it's him—the intruder," she said, as he accelerated some more.

"It could be a bounty hunter." His mouth curved into a cynical half smile, as he added, "Hell, it could even be your neighbor Mrs. Osborn determined to collect that reward."

An image of the old woman chasing them down with her battered Bonneville elicited a giggle from Erica. "The doctor took away her license until she gets her cataracts removed."

"So it's not Mrs. Osborn," he surmised, his half smile slipping into a full grin for just a minute before it disappeared.

"No, it's not."

How much had he had to grin about over the past three years? Nothing, she would bet.

"It might not be anyone," he said. "It could just be someone who's coincidentally traveling the same road we are."

"Toward your friend's house?"

When they had heard the sirens in the distance, he had urged her to come with him. He promised that he knew someone, probably the one lawman he had faith in, who would be able to protect her and Isobel. And in the heat and panic of the moment, she had believed her instincts were right and trusted him.

She hoped like hell she wouldn't regret giving that trust because it wasn't just her heart at risk this time—it was her daughter's life.

Jed shrugged, but his nonchalant gesture didn't fool her since he focused on the mirror again.

"You don't think it's a coincidence," she said. "And if it is that person who broke into my house, then he's going to know where you're bringing us."

"I'll lose him." And he accelerated again. But her van was old, and the engine shuddered instead of shifting. He cursed beneath his breath.

"You're not going to lose him in this." The mechanic had warned her that she needed a new transmission. However, she didn't often have to drive anywhere in Miller's Valley, so she had been waiting until she needed to travel somewhere. She hadn't imagined that the van would have to make two long-distance trips within a few hours.

And that it would have to outrun a faster vehicle. The rev of a powerful engine echoed as the car behind them accelerated.

They should have taken his vehicle, but he'd explained that the police might have already been looking for it. Now she wished they'd taken their chances with the police...

She repeated the fear that was causing that fluttery panic in her chest again. "He's going to follow to wherever you're bringing us."

She really should have asked where he was bringing them; she shouldn't have given her trust so blindly. But after how she'd given him her mistrust in the past, she'd felt as if she'd owed him.

But she couldn't worry about Jed anymore; she had to worry about her daughter. "Isobel will still be in danger."

"Not with Rowe Cusack."

"The DEA agent?" she asked. The one whose badge Jed had flashed to fool her. "He's been helping you?"

A muscle twitched along his jaw as he glanced into the rearview mirror. And he didn't reply.

"Jed?" she prodded him, her stomach clenching with apprehension. "Does he know you're coming? Is he *really* helping you?"

"He will."

But the DEA agent wouldn't be able to help them if they couldn't get to him. The car had gained on them, coming up so fast and close that it struck the rear bumper of the van.

Isobel woke up with a scream that echoed Erica's.

Erica fought back her own panic and forced a smile as she leaned over her seat to face her daughter. "It's okay, sweetheart. No reason to be afraid."

The car connected with their rear bumper again. Even though she saw it coming, a scream bubbled back up in Erica's throat. She choked it down and offered Isobel another shaky smile. "See, it's just like playing bumper cars at the fair."

Isobel's eyes widened. "But this isn't a bumpa car, Mommy."

"We're just pretending it is," Erica explained. But the other car wasn't just pretending; it really was hitting them, and very hard.

The tires skidded as they tried to grip the snow-covered pavement. She needed new tires, too. But that was another thing she had thought she would be able to put off purchasing for a while. The van spun around, nearly sliding off the road into one of the ditches on the side. Because the ditches were so deep and usually filled with water, people drowned if their vehicles went off into them.

Isobel screamed, but with no fear this time. She had bought Erica's story of make-believe. So when the car struck them again, the little girl squealed with excitement and joy.

Erica blinked against the sting of tears and hung onto her fake smile even as she turned toward Jed. He wasn't smiling. He was so focused on driving that he might not have even heard the lie that she had told their daughter. He'd heard the story she'd given Mrs. Osborn, too—first about her emergency in Grand Rapids and then about Jed being her friend. He probably thought she lied very easily and very often. He would never trust her now, and she didn't blame him.

His knuckles turned from dark red to white as he gripped the steering wheel. And a muscle twitched in his cheek, above his rigidly held jaw. He was determined to protect them. But it was obvious that he wasn't convinced that he could.

Neither was Erica.

A CRASH REVERBERATED inside Macy's head, jerking her awake. Her neck ached from how she'd fallen asleep leaning over the armrest of a chair near Rowe's desk.

Strong fingers brushed hair back from her face. "Go back to sleep," a deep voice urged her. "Go lay down in the bed this time, though."

She squinted against the sunlight pouring through a window high in the wall of the apartment that had been carved out of a corner of an abandoned airport hangar. "I can't sleep."

"You've been out for a couple of hours," he pointed out, his sexy mouth sliding into a crooked grin.

"I can't sleep now," she said with a shiver. "I have a really bad feeling."

Rowe came to her, lifting her from the chair only to settle back into it with her wrapped in his arms. "Sweetheart…"

Tears stung her eyes. "He's in too much danger—even more than he was in at Blackwoods. I'm afraid I'm never going to see my brother again."

Rowe said nothing, just tightened his strong arms around her and pressed a kiss to her forehead. She regretted now making him promise not to keep anything from her. She wished he could offer her some pretty lies that Jed was perfectly safe—that he would be fine and proven innocent soon.

She had spent the entire trial believing the fantasy that an innocent man wouldn't go to prison. Then she'd spent three years believing that his innocence would be revealed. She had wasted too much of her life believing that justice would win out. Now she knew better than anyone—but Jed—how unjust life could be.

But nothing would be more unjust than Jed dying a convicted killer. However, the sick feeling in her stomach worried her—that it was already too late for Jed to find the real killer. That eerie sense of foreboding that had jerked her awake had her convinced that the real killer had found Jed first.

FOR THREE YEARS, Jed had been locked into a six-by-six cage. He had been allowed out to eat in the cafeteria and to exercise in the prison yard. He hadn't been allowed to drive. But before his arrest, he'd been driving Humvees in Afghanistan.

The instincts that had aided him in avoiding ambushes and roadside bombs and had earned him that Purple Heart kicked in again. The minivan was no Humvee, but Jed—full of determination to protect his family as he had protected his men during their missions—steered it like it was one. He wrenched the wheel, driving into the skid across the slippery spring snow.

He avoided the deep ditches on the sides of the road, but metal crunched, bumpers connecting. The van slid again, still Jed held tight to the wheel and accelerated. This time the engine responded, kicking into a higher gear. But even with a working transmission, it couldn't outrun the more powerful car.

It drew alongside them, on the wrong side of the yellow line. Jed hoped like hell that someone came upon them from the other direction and sent that son of a bitch hurtling into the ditch.

Despite the fact that the sun had finally risen, it was too early for much traffic. Unfortunately, these were the only two vehicles on the road.

The black sedan was longer and heavier than the van, and its windows were tinted nearly as black as the rest of it. So, despite the morning sun that illuminated the inside of the van and Erica's beautiful face so pale with fear, Jed could not see inside the car.

He had no idea who was after them. The intruder from the apartment? An overly ambitious bounty hunter? Or the devil himself…

But then the passenger window of the car, which was on Jed's side, lowered. And he caught a glimpse of the driver.

His heart slammed into his ribs, and his hands shook so badly he nearly lost his grip on the steering wheel.

It couldn't be…

*No, it's not possible.*

He had gone too many days without sleep, so his mind was just playing tricks on him.

That had to be it…

But before Jed could determine whether or not he was hallucinating, the window rose back up.

And the car crashed into the side of the van, sending it spinning out of control…like Jed's imagination.

## Chapter Ten

They weren't dead. Thanks to Jed. Erica didn't know how he had managed to keep the van from being totally submerged in the deep ditches on the side of the road. But he had avoided them as well as losing the car that had tried to run them off the road.

There had been no sight of the black vehicle behind them as they had traveled the rest of the way to Rowe Cusack's secret hideaway—an airplane hangar at an old private airstrip on the outskirts of Detroit.

At first she hadn't thought it was a meeting place. It seemed more like a means to escape to another country with no extradition. But no matter how much Jed trusted him, Rowe Cusack was still a lawman—who had vowed to uphold and not break the law. And there probably weren't many laws more severe to break than aiding a fugitive.

But she would learn the legalities for certain once she was caught. She had no illusions now that she wouldn't be. The prison van had been left in the alley behind her building, and Jed's fingerprints were all over her home.

And her body…

She tingled in remembrance of how they'd been touching each other before that news bulletin had interrupted them and they'd heard the sirens in the distance. They'd barely gotten out of Miller's Valley to avoid arrest. Heck, they'd barely gotten out of Miller's Valley alive, thanks to that black car.

She would love to go to that other country with no extradition. But no fueled plane awaited them as Jed pulled the van inside the nearly empty hangar. He stepped out of the van and came around, opening her door before sliding open the back door. A noise made him tense and turn toward the shadows inside the hangar.

Erica reached for their daughter, unbuckling her car seat to pull her into her arms. She clasped the child tight, willing to die to protect her.

"It's Rowe," Jed assured her.

A tall blond-haired man stepped out of the shadows where he must have been waiting to meet them, but he hadn't come alone. Instead of armed officers, only a dark-haired woman stood inside the hangar with the DEA agent.

The woman could have been an agent, too, but instead of drawing a weapon on Jed, she ran toward him with her arms outstretched. Jed met the woman, catching her up in his arms for a big hug.

Erica's chest felt tight, her heart compressed, as she watched their joyful reunion. This was the "she" that he'd promised would see him soon. The woman couldn't have met him while he was in prison, so she must have known him before and well enough to wait for him. And long enough that they would have already been involved before he'd slept with Erica the night their child had been conceived.

Erica clasped her arms more tightly around her daughter, who had somehow managed to fall asleep again after the excitement of their bumper car make-believe.

"Macy!" Jed exclaimed, his deep voice vibrating with joy and affection.

And Erica remembered him talking about this woman before, his voice vibrating then with love and pride. The tightness in her chest eased as she realized this was his sister.

Even though Erica had never met her, she should have recognized her. Not from the old picture Jed had shown her when they'd been going out before his deployment, or even from all the media coverage of her during the trial. Macy had given up her plans for medical school to aid her brother's appeal and release from prison. Erica should have recognized her because Isobel was a miniature replica of the young woman.

No wonder Jed had instinctively known, with nary a doubt nor demand for a DNA test, that Isobel was his daughter. It was very obvious that the little girl was this woman's niece.

Over her brother's massively broad shoulder, Macy caught sight of Erica and the unwieldy bundle in her arms. "Jed, who did you bring with you? Who is this?"

She pulled away from her brother and walked toward Erica. As her gaze focused on the sleeping child, her breath audibly caught.

"Is she my…?" Macy asked Erica, not her brother the question—more with her wide dark eyes than her words, which emotion had choked off.

Erica nodded, and the gesture must have shifted the little girl so that she awakened with a sleepy murmur of protest. "This is your niece, Isobel. Isobel, this pretty lady is your Aunt Macy."

"She is pretty," Isobel whispered in shy agreement.

"You're the pretty one," Macy said. "I am so happy to meet you." She held out her arms.

The little girl hesitated for just a moment before leaning toward her newly introduced aunt. Macy pulled her close, hugging her as tightly as she had her brother. Tears glistened in her eyes. "I was so worried I'd never see you again. But here you are and you're not alone…"

Jed approached, either to comfort his sister or explain. But the DEA agent intercepted him and led him off into another section of the hangar.

As if she had silently communicated with the blond man, Macy carried Isobel off toward an open door and stepped inside a room. Unwilling to be separated from her daughter again, Erica followed closely.

She gasped at the room in which they stood; it wasn't an office, as she would have expected. It was a studio apartment complete with kitchenette, skylights, queen-size bed and wall-unit furnace. "This is so nice."

"Not what you expected?" Macy asked.

"Nothing has been," Erica replied, "since Jed showed up at my door."

So many questions widened Macy's dark eyes, but she only remarked, "I can relate." She settled the little girl onto her hip as she reached into a cupboard and pulled down a box of crackers. "Are you hungry, sweetheart? What about you…?"

"Erica."

Macy's breath caught again. "Erica Towsley?"

"You know who I am?"

"I know Jed wanted Marcus to find you for the trial," she replied. "He never really told me why, though."

"He was with me the night of the murders," Erica admitted. "That was actually the night your niece was conceived."

Macy let out a whoop of excitement that had Isobel giggling. "That's it—the evidence we need to overturn his conviction."

Erica shook her head and, with regret, replied, "No. My memories of that night aren't very clear. They wouldn't hold up in court."

"But Isobel…"

"Is not proof that he never left—that he didn't do what he was convicted of."

Isobel hadn't asked about her daddy yet. Maybe she was too young and too sheltered in Miller's Valley to even realize that she didn't have one. But she actually did have one, and when she was old enough to ask about him—how ever would Erica explain why he hadn't been part of her life?

He couldn't go back to prison; he couldn't lose any more time with his daughter. The little girl deserved a father.

But, regrettably, Erica knew that life wasn't fair. And a child didn't always get what she deserved.

"He was framed," Macy maintained, as she resolutely had throughout his trial. "There has to be some way to prove that."

"Find out who framed him," Rowe said as he stepped inside the room with Jed.

Erica suspected Jed already knew. He had evaded that car that had been so determined to run them off the road. He had driven with the skill and composure that had had him surviving Afghanistan and probably prison, too.

But for just one moment he had lost it—when the car window had lowered. His broad shoulders and body had blocked her view, so Erica hadn't caught a glimpse of the driver. But Jed had.

She hadn't been able to question him about it yet, not with Isobel in the van with them. But confident Macy would care for her newly discovered niece, Erica stormed over to Jed and pulled him out into the hangar with her.

"You already know," she accused him. "You saw who was driving that car and you recognized him!"

He shook his head in denial, but he didn't meet her gaze.

She grasped his arm, and his muscles bunched beneath her fingers. She couldn't shake the truth out of him; he was too big. She could only demand he tell her. "Who was it? That monster tried to kill my daughter. I have a right to know who he is!"

Jed's dark eyes filled with torment and regret. "Erica…"

"Mommy?" The little girl must have wriggled free of her aunt, who stood in the doorway behind her, as Isobel ran to them. She squeezed between her father and mother and clung to Erica's legs. "I'm scared…"

Regret had nausea rising in Erica's throat as she realized that her daughter must have overheard her outburst. "You're safe, honey."

Jed's big hand cupped the back of their daughter's head. "You're safe, sweetheart," he assured the child. "I will protect you."

Because he knew what the threat was. Because he knew who it was…

JED HOPED HE HADN'T just made a promise he wouldn't be able to keep. He had seen the skepticism on Erica's lovely face. She didn't believe him. She didn't trust him. He didn't blame her. He stared after her as she carried their daughter back inside the studio apartment with his sister.

Rowe stayed behind, standing at Jed's side. Probably ready to slap the cuffs on him.

If he tried…

Well, Jed already knew he could take the Drug Enforcement Administration agent. Even though he didn't want to fight a man he now considered a friend, he would in order to keep his promise to Isobel. To protect her…and her mother.

"She seems to know you well," Rowe remarked, almost idly.

"If she knew me well, she wouldn't have spent the past three years thinking I'm a killer," Jed said, wondering if he would ever get over his bitterness and mistrust.

"But she was right that you did recognize the driver."

Jed shook his head, unable to believe what he'd seen hadn't been just his exhausted mind playing tricks on him. If he shared his suspicion with anyone, they'd lock him up for certain—in a sanatorium, though, instead of a prison. "No, she's wrong. I haven't slept in days. I could barely see the road, let alone his face."

Rowe uttered a heavy sigh of frustration and weariness. Dark circles rimmed the DEA agent's eyes. He had already tried talking to Jed once.

But he'd evaded Rowe's questions and insisted on checking on Erica and Isobel instead. After the harrowing trip away from Miller's Valley, he had wanted to make certain they were really all right.

He hadn't been convinced that Erica had allayed their daughter's fears despite her valiant attempts. She was an amazing mother. But Isobel was an intuitive child and had figured out that more was going on than a pretend game of bumper cars.

"Jedidiah," Rowe said, commanding his attention again, "I can't help you unless you tell me everything that you know."

"There's nothing to tell." Yet. "What about you? You got anything to tell me?"

"About the money?" Rowe asked. "I checked all her financial records. Erica Towsley doesn't have it."

Jed released a breath of relief. For three years he had believed she had betrayed him, and he'd hated her for it. And he'd hated himself for being a fool for her. It was good to know that he had been wrong about that. About her…

"A couple of years ago she inherited some money," Rowe continued, "a building and a bookkeeping business in a trust from an aunt, but there's no other money. She barely has enough to cover her expenses."

He had seen the building and the bookkeeping business on the main floor of it. It was nothing like the building Marcus Leighton had owned. As dilapidated as it was, she hadn't inherited much—more a money pit than a source of income.

"What about Leighton? Did you check his financials, too?"

"He got a chunk of change before your trial began and some mysterious deposits over the past three years," Rowe said, confirming his suspicions, "but not the amount that was embezzled from your clients and your firm before the murders."

"That money had to go somewhere…"

"I can't find it," Rowe said, frustration making his voice even raspier. "I've brought the records along with me, so you can go over them. That's your area of expertise, not mine."

"You track down drug money all the time, following it up the ladder to whoever's in charge." That was partially how the man had busted the warden of Blackwoods Penitentiary. The other part involved the hit the warden had put out on the DEA agent, ordering Jed to carry out that murder.

Rowe nodded in acceptance, not arrogance. "But this person's skills exceed mine. By far. Whoever hid those embezzled funds knows how to hide money where it won't ever be found."

Oh, God, it had to be…even though it made no sense, even though it wasn't possible…

"She's right and you're a damn liar," Rowe accused him, his eyes narrowed as he studied Jed's face. "You definitely know who the hell set you—"

Sirens saved Jed from uttering another lie. They echoed inside the hangar, bouncing off the tin walls and ceiling. Then the thump, thump, thump of helicopter blades drowned out the sirens.

Had Jed been a fool to trust this lawman? Had he been set up? And now, even before a voice announced it, he was surrounded with no means of escape.

JED PROBABLY THOUGHT he'd lost him. He ignored the quick sting to his pride. It didn't matter what Jed believed. It didn't even matter if he believed what he'd seen…

Nobody else would believe him if he shared his suspicions. It sounded crazy and would make Jed sound crazy. And the escaped convict would have no way of proving his suspicions.

*He* would make certain of that. He twisted a silencer

onto the end of his gun. All he had to do was wait for the perfect moment.

It would all be over soon.

No one else would know who was really responsible for Jedidiah Kleyn's tragic fall from hero to desperate convict but *him*.

And Jed...

# Chapter Eleven

Was this how prison had felt for Jed?

Enclosed?

Tight?

Airless?

Erica had never realized she had issues with claustrophobia…until now. Thank God Isobel was safe with her aunt, and even though Erica had just met Macy, she knew the woman would protect her niece. While Erica worried about her child, she wouldn't have wanted her with her mother.

Erica was trapped beneath a grate in the cement floor, in a shallow drainage tunnel through which oil, gas and water ran from overhauled planes into holding tanks under the hangar.

But was it the small space in which she was confined or was it the man with whom she was confined that had her feeling panicked and overwhelmed?

Jed lay half-sprawled across her, as if shielding her with his body in case someone opened fire on them. But no one knew they were here…

"I know he's here," a deep male voice declared with absolute certainty.

"Sheriff York, you wasted your time coming all the way here from Blackwoods County," Rowe Cusack told the man. "And you wasted the time of all of these local officers you brought in as backup."

Fortunately the sheriff had already dismissed those officers after they had thoroughly searched the hangar. Or maybe not so thoroughly...

York pitched his voice lower when he replied, "I'm out of my jurisdiction, so I had to notify the local authorities that they potentially had one of the escaped convicts in their area."

"You should have let me handle this," a woman remarked with little respect for the sheriff's efforts. "Since I wouldn't have had to notify anyone. They overreacted and scared off the escapee before I had a chance to apprehend him."

"Ms. Franklin is a bounty hunter," Sheriff York explained to Rowe, his voice gruff with disdain. "She is the one that used some questionable measures to determine that you're helping Kleyn."

Rowe snorted loudly. "And you believed *a bounty hunter?*"

"On national television and to me personally, you admitted yourself that you think he's innocent," York said.

Erica had seen the DEA agent's interview replayed that morning when Jed had been in her room, watching their daughter sleep. Until then she hadn't seen the whole interview, just a few terse responses from the DEA agent to the reporters' incessant questions. He had been much more loquacious during his interview and had shared his opinion of Jed with the reporters.

"I do believe he's innocent," Rowe told the sheriff and the bounty hunter. "And I intend to prove his innocence so that his conviction gets overturned and he's released from prison."

"But first he has to go back to prison in order to be released," the sheriff pointed out, "so tell us where he is."

"Why do you think that Jedidiah Kleyn would come to me?" Rowe asked.

"Because you're dating his sister," the bounty hunter answered. Apparently it was no lie that she had some sources.

"I'm engaged to his sister," Rowe corrected her with obvious pride in his fiancée. "But I'm still a lawman. If Jed comes to me, I will bring him in to authorities myself."

Ms. Franklin snorted now as loudly—and unlady-like—as Rowe had. "Like your *fiancée* is going to allow that."

"My fiancée respects the law," Rowe replied, his voice deepening with the implication that the bounty hunter did not.

"Who's the kid she's hanging on to?" Ms. Franklin asked, prying for even more information. "I pulled up some information on Kleyn's sister and nothing ever mentioned her having a baby."

Over Jed's shoulder and through the thin slats of the grate, Erica discerned the shadow of the woman's arm pointing toward the room where Macy had stayed with Isobel while Mommy and her friend Jed "played hide-and-seek" with the police officers.

"But she looks just like your fiancée," the woman continued, "so she must be a relative."

Erica opened her lips, but before so much as even a gasp of fear could slip out, a big hand closed over her mouth. And Jed's face blocked her view of the grate, his eyes staring down into hers. With no words, he was

asking her to trust him—that somehow, he would protect their daughter.

"She's proof that Jed's not here," Rowe said. "No one
would want a child anywhere near a wanted man with
a shoot-on-sight order out on him."

"That's not true," the sheriff said, quick to deny the
claim.

"It may not be official, but it's true," Rowe insisted.
"The governor put out the bounty on his head and someone else put out the shoot-on-sight order with a substan-
tial reward offered for his death."

The sheriff sucked in a breath as if in acknowledg-
ment of what the DEA agent claimed.

"He's right," the bounty hunter agreed. "There actually is a shoot-on-sight order out on this escaped convict. He killed a cop, man—"

"He didn't kill anyone." Rowe defended him, his
voice rising in anger.

"He was convicted," Ms. Franklin stubbornly maintained, "so in everyone else's mind, that makes him
guilty."

Jed's stare intensified, as if he was looking in Erica's
eyes to see if she also found him guilty. While she had
completely accepted his innocence of the crimes for
which he'd been convicted, she couldn't trust that he
hadn't changed in prison. That being sent there despite
his innocence hadn't so embittered him that he wasn't
an entirely different man from the one she'd fallen in
love with so long ago.

"And a lot of people don't think that two lifetimes
was a sufficient sentence for what he'd done," the
bounty hunter said. "They think he deserved death."

"Michigan doesn't have the death penalty," Rowe reminded her.

She snorted again—even louder than before. "That's too bad."

Erica shivered at the woman's coldness. No doubt she would comply with the shoot-on-sight order if she actually caught sight of Jed. If Erica were stronger, she would have shifted them around, so that she was on top. But she wasn't big enough to hide Jed. She could only hope that the bounty hunter didn't look into the grate and discover them.

"Cusack's also right about not wanting the kid around," Ms. Franklin continued. "Kleyn might be monster enough to use a child as a shield…"

Jed's body had already been tense as he lay atop Erica, but now his muscles tightened more, as if he were struggling for control.

Was that why he had insisted that she and Isobel come along with him? Not to protect them but to protect himself?

*To use his daughter as a shield…*

A muscle twitched along his jaw, as if his control was slipping. Or as if he had read her reaction and knew that her doubts were back.

She had been a fool to trust him, though. A fool to come along with him. While it might not have been a good idea for her to wait for the police to show up at her apartment, especially given the way they had stormed the hangar, she could have taken Isobel someplace else. She had enough money in her account to hole up in hotels for a few nights.

The woman continued, "But I doubt Cusack here would do the same. Until this mess at Blackwoods, his record was exemplary."

"Still is," Rowe said. "Sheriff, you wasted your time and the officers' time in coming here."

"I don't think so," the sheriff replied. "I think you know a lot more than you're willing to admit."

"Yes," the bounty hunter agreed. "But he's not going to tell us anything."

"No." Rowe confirmed her accusation. "I'm not…"

"If you're aiding and abetting him, you're going to lose your job," the sheriff threatened, "and your freedom. Again."

According to what he had shared on the news broadcast, the DEA agent had been undercover at Blackwoods Penitentiary when his cover had been blown and someone had nearly killed him. So he knew what it was like to be locked up like Jed had been locked up the past three years.

"Don't worry about me," Rowe said. "Worry about catching all those escaped convicts. Kleyn isn't the only one, you know."

Several prisoners had broken out of Blackwoods Penitentiary during the riot—not just Jed, but Jed was the one everyone had focused on apprehending.

Or killing.

MACY COULDN'T STOP STARING at her brother's child—her niece. The little girl was so adorable. And smart. She'd said nothing when the officers had stormed the hangar. But her little chubby fingers had tightly gripped Macy's hand—as they did now while they waited to see if Mommy and her friend were discovered in their hiding place.

*Her friend?*

She didn't know Jed was her father. But then how would Erica Towsley have explained to the child why she couldn't see her daddy—because he was in prison for two murders.

Macy wanted Erica to explain some things to her, though, like why she hadn't come forward at Jed's trial. And why she had never let Jed know that he was a father. He couldn't have known before he'd broken out of prison, or he would have asked Macy to check on the little girl and her mother and make sure they were doing okay.

They weren't doing okay now. Just by being with Jed, they were in danger. Those local officers had all had their guns drawn until Sheriff York had ordered them holstered. If he hadn't been present, she was certain shots might have been fired.

And if Jed was discovered hiding in that grate, she suspected that shots might still be fired.

Macy lifted the child in her arms and turned away from the window that looked onto the rest of the hangar. She couldn't protect her brother now—not if the sheriff and the bounty hunter found him.

But she would protect his daughter. She didn't want the little girl to witness the executions of her parents...

EVEN AFTER THE HANGAR DOOR slid closed again, Jed held his breath. Rowe might not have really convinced the sheriff and the bounty hunter to leave. They might have only pretended to accept his claims and could be waiting for Jed to step out of his hiding place.

If he had been alone, waiting them out would have been no problem. He'd waited three years for the opportunity to prove his innocence. And those three years had been spent in a hole far worse than this hiding place.

The reason it was so hard to wait was Erica. She lay under him, her body soft and warm beneath his. Her face was so close to his that all he had to do was turn his head slightly to skim his lips across hers. But he wanted more than her kiss.

More even than her body.

He wanted her trust, too. And those damn doubts were back in her eyes, as clear as the sky-blue color that had haunted him the past three years. Everything about Erica Towsley had haunted him the past three years. Maybe she had been duped into doubting him once. But if she had really cared about him, she would not have been so easily fooled…

"I think they're gone," she whispered, her warm breath feathering across his cheek. And then she squirmed, her hips arching against his.

He swallowed a groan, as his body reacted—hardening and demanding release. Desire hammered at him, pulsing in his veins and tightening all his muscles. They had nearly made love earlier, at her apartment, until the breaking-news bulletin had returned them to their senses. Now the sound of shoes scraping across the cement floor above them drew Jed back to reality.

He couldn't make love to Erica here. He couldn't make *love* to Erica anywhere because he could never love a woman who did not believe in him. Having everyone but Macy turn on him and look at him with fear and disgust had destroyed something inside him—his self-respect and maybe his own ability to trust.

And to love.

As he had earlier, he covered her mouth with his hand—holding back any gasps or words she might have inadvertently uttered. Anyone could have stepped back inside the hangar.

Her breath warmed his palm and had a tingling sensation shooting up his arm—straight to his heart. The damn woman affected him as no other ever had. If only she could have loved him…

But she hadn't had enough faith in him to have had any real feelings for him.

"They're really gone," Rowe said. He knelt beside the drainage tunnel and pulled up the grate. "I waited and watched to make certain that they drove away."

"And knowing you, you probably threw out a few threats and a couple more lies," Jed said. He tried to get up, but he didn't want to put any more of his weight on Erica

Rowe reached down and offered him a hand up. As Jed grabbed it and hauled himself to his feet, Rowe said, "I wasn't lying to the sheriff."

He had to force it, but Jed grinned at the DEA agent's semantics. "You didn't tell him that I was here."

"That was an omission," Rowe clarified.

To pretty much everybody else and most especially Jed, a lie of omission was still a lie. Erica not coming forward to alibi him was a lie of omission he might never be able to forgive.

"I was telling the truth about bringing you in, though," Rowe warned him.

Jed nodded. "Of course you will—once I go through the financial records from my and Brandon's accounting firm, and I have the evidence I need to prove my innocence. Then you'll bring me in until my conviction can be overturned."

That didn't guarantee his immediate release, though. He would have to do jail time for breaking out of prison. But until he had found out about Isobel, he hadn't cared that he would have to go back…because he'd known it was for a crime he had actually committed. And then everyone would know the truth—that he wasn't a killer.

Jed turned back to Erica, reaching one hand down to help her from the tunnel. But the hole was shallow so she was already hauling herself up the cement side.

Cold metal encircled his wrist and then snapped tight around it. The sensation was horribly familiar.

Rowe dragged his other hand behind his back and manacled it, too. "No, Jed, I have to bring you in *now*. I have to arrest you for breaking out of prison. I have to bring you back."

"Back to Blackwoods?"

Back to Hell?

"There isn't much left of Blackwoods," Rowe reminded him. "It'll take them years to rebuild that prison. Your name will be clear for a long time before the construction is done on Blackwoods Penitentiary. You'll never have to go back there."

"I won't have the chance," Jed said. "Once you take me in, I'm a dead man. And I'm going to die a guilty man, convicted of crimes I never committed."

And worse than that, he finally had an idea who was really responsible for those crimes. But until he could prove it, nobody would believe him. However, he wouldn't be able to prove anything if he was behind bars or dead. "Don't do this, Rowe…"

"I have no choice," he replied, all DEA agent now instead of friend and future brother-in-law. "I'm putting you under arrest…"

"You're putting me six feet under…"

He was definitely a dead man.

# Chapter Twelve

"He's arresting him," Erica whispered, as she stared through the window that looked onto the hangar. Her stomach clenching with dread and fear, she was as horrified now as she had been when Rowe Cusack had first slapped the cuffs on Jed.

But before he could drag him off, Macy had rushed out and joined them. Instead of staying there to support Jed, Erica had hurried toward her daughter. She hadn't wanted Isobel to see any more than she already had. So she'd caught the child up in her arms and carried her back inside the apartment.

"You played hide 'n' seek real good, Mommy," Isobel praised her. "Nobody found you."

Too bad Rowe had known where they were…

Not that she had wanted to stay inside that tunnel with Jed forever. The confinement had been overwhelming or maybe that had just been her feelings—her desire—for the man that had overwhelmed her. Being too close to Jed made her lose her objectivity and her common sense. Maybe it wouldn't be bad if Rowe took him back to jail as long as he could keep him safe.

But she doubted anyone could guarantee Jed's safety now. Too many people wanted him dead.

"Is it my turn to play hide 'n' seek now?" Isobel

asked. "I want Jed to be my partner." The little girl followed Erica's gaze out the window and wrinkled her
nose in confusion. "Is he playing a game with that other
man now?"

She wished it was just a game. Apparently so did
Macy as she yelled at her fiancé. They were too far
away for Erica to hear the words she shouted, but her
argument must have been effective because he removed
the handcuffs.

When Erica had been out there with them, she had
heard his words and knew the DEA agent had spoken
them with grim determination. He didn't like this part
of his job, but he wasn't able to ignore his duty to uphold
the law. Rowe Cusack was definitely going to bring Jed
back to prison.

"I guess they are playing a game." One neither man
really wanted to play, though.

The little girl yawned. "I'm kind of sleepy now. I can
hide 'n' seek with Jed later."

The child hadn't really had much sleep—at least un-
interrupted sleep—since Jed had shown up at their door.

Erica hugged her daughter, holding her close and
rocking her back and forth in her arms. She was already
comforting her because, if Jed went back to prison, the
child wasn't going to be able to seek out her father for
a while.

Maybe never.

"Damn him!" Macy said, as she stepped back inside
and slammed the door shut. Horror and regret widened
her eyes, and she lowered her voice. "I'm so sorry. I
forgot all about…"

Her niece.

But then, she had just become aware of the child's existence. "It's okay," Erica assured her. "Isobel can sleep through anything."

"I've heard kids are resilient," Macy remarked with obvious envy. She crossed the room to the brass bed near the fireplace and dragged back the blankets. "You can lay her down here."

Erica followed Macy to the bed, but she hesitated before releasing her daughter. If the police had discovered Jed and her hiding beneath that grate, she could have lost her child forever.

Macy reached out and squeezed Erica's shoulder. "She's safe here. I would never let anything happen to her," she promised. "I would never let anyone take her or hurt her."

Had Jed told her about the man in her apartment? If Isobel hadn't awakened and gone with Mrs. Osborn to her place, that man might have taken Isobel.

"I'm her mother. I'm supposed to be the one to protect her," Erica said, feeling as though she'd failed miserably.

"She's a happy, healthy little girl, so you obviously have protected her all of her life," Macy said. "But I want to help you now."

"Why?" Erica asked, confused that a virtual stranger could be so generous. "You don't even know us."

Macy moved her hand from Erica's shoulder to Isobel's cheek. "She's my niece. My brother's daughter..." Her voice cracked as emotion overwhelmed her. "When I was growing up, Jed was always there for me—giving me the love and support our parents couldn't give me. I failed Jed when it mattered most. I wasn't able to save him from prison. Three years ago—" she glanced out the window and bit her lip "—or now."

"You got Rowe to take off the handcuffs," Erica

pointed out. And the DEA agent hadn't put them back on yet.

"I talked him out of arresting Jed in front of his daughter," Macy said.

When Erica finally settled Isobel onto the bed, Macy's breath caught as if she feared that her fiancé had been waiting for just that moment before he hauled her brother off to prison again.

"Rowe can't take him in," Erica said. All those claims the bounty hunter had made rushed back to her, bringing fear and panic. "He'll die in custody."

Because every law-enforcement officer wanted him dead out of vengeance over the death of the young cop. Apparently officers never forgot a fallen comrade.

Macy shook her head, unwilling or unable to consider how much danger her brother was in. "Jed survived three years in the most dangerous prison in Michigan."

"And maybe that's how he survived," Erica pointed out. "Maybe his label of cop killer actually protected him inside the corrupt jail. But now…"

Macy's breath shuddered out in a shaky sigh. "Now he'll be sent somewhere else until we can find the real killer and clear his name."

"Jed knows who the killer is." Even though he wouldn't admit it. And why wouldn't he admit it? Was he actually protecting the real guilty person? Or was he protecting everyone else he cared about? Everyone else but himself…

"DAMN IT, ROWE, YOU CAN'T bring me in now." Not when he was so close to proving his innocence. All he had to do was prove his sanity—to himself—first.

Rowe glanced toward the window leading to that

little apartment inside the hangar. "I know it has to be damn hard, just finding out you have a kid and having to leave her again. But, Jed, I can't have you out here— at the mercy of every bounty hunter and cop with a grudge."

"I'll be even more at their mercy when I'm locked up," Jed argued. "You were in there—you know what it's like."

"That was Blackwoods and Blackwoods is gone. And Warden James will probably be locked up for the rest of his life."

Jed snorted in derision.

"The D.A. made sure his bail was denied," Rowe said, "he's not getting out."

"Not now but anything could happen at his trial." No one knew that better than him. He had been so convinced that he wouldn't be convicted of crimes he hadn't committed. He'd been so naïve. "Plenty of guilty people have gotten off." Especially if Jed wasn't alive to testify against him.

Rowe shook his head, unwilling to believe it. "Not James. He's guilty as hell."

"And I was innocent. You can't trust that the justice system is going to work." There were times a man needed to take justice into his own hands. And if Jed was right about who had set him up, he would mete out his own justice to the bastard who had stolen three years of his life.

Rowe must have misunderstood what justice system Jed was talking about because he asked, "You really think you'll be in danger in jail?"

"You were the first one who warned me about the shoot-on-sight order out on me," Jed reminded him. "And now the governor put a big bounty on my head.

Do you really think I will ever make it out to see my daughter again?"

"Jed…" Rowe narrowed his eyes with suspicion, as if he thought Jed was deliberately playing on his emotions.

Maybe he was. "I can't go back inside until I find the evidence that'll clear me."

"I'll find it," Rowe assured him.

"*You* don't know where to look." He wasn't sure that he did, either.

How did one go about tracking down a ghost?

"So Erica's right." Rowe cursed him. "You did recognize the person who tried to force you off the road on your way here."

He shrugged. "It's probably the same person who broke into her apartment. If Isobel hadn't been across the hall at the neighbor's who was watching her, she might not be here with us."

"You don't have to be out of prison to be able to protect her," Rowe said. "I will protect her for you. I'll make sure no one threatens or hurts that little girl."

Some of the weight on his shoulders eased. "I'm counting on that."

"You have my promise."

Jed nodded in acceptance. He knew the DEA agent didn't give his promise lightly and that once he did, he kept it. Or Macy wouldn't be here yet. Rowe had promised to protect Jed's little sister, and that was a vow he had nearly died to keep. "Thank you."

Rowe drew in an audibly ragged breath. "So I'll take you in now. And I'll make sure that nothing happens to you in custody."

"I'm not going in," Jed argued, desperation clawing

at him. "I have to dig up more information to prove my innocence."

"Tell me, and I'll get it for you," Rowe offered.

"Did you find the witnesses from my trial? Brandon's girlfriend?" She was the key.

"The last person you believe really saw your business partner alive," Rowe replied, almost as if stalling for time before divulging, "She's dead."

*Damn it all...*

"She was murdered." Like Marcus Leighton, she'd been a loose end that needed tying up.

"Her death was ruled a suicide," Rowe said. "She hung herself shortly after the trial. Maybe the guilt over lying on the stand..."

Jed shook his head. That woman had felt no guilt; in fact she'd almost been gleeful when she'd testified, as if she'd been privy to a big joke that no one else had known. "I'd like you to look into it more. I think she was murdered, like my lawyer."

Rowe studied him for a moment before nodding in agreement. "Okay. I'll have the investigation reopened. I'll take a look at the autopsy report myself. If she was murdered, we'll find out."

"What about the other witness—the man who testified to my killing the cop?" Jed asked. "Is he dead, too?"

Rowe shook his head. "No."

Not yet. But Jed had a bad feeling that if they didn't get to him soon—it would be too late. "Do you know where he is?"

Rowe nodded. "I intend to go see him as soon as I guarantee that you'll be safe in jail."

Jed shook his head. "That's a guarantee you'll never

get until I'm proved innocent. Let me prove my innocence, Rowe."

"How?" the lawman asked. "By threatening the witness? That'll just get you in more trouble."

"I can't get in more trouble than I already am," Jed pointed out.

"You can get dead just like Marcus Leighton and that female witness," Rowe warned him. "The real killer is out there and determined to cover his tracks, Jed. You're in danger from him, too."

"If this guy wanted me dead, he wouldn't have gone to the trouble of framing me for crimes I didn't commit," Jed reasoned. "He would have just killed *me*." That would have been far more merciful than ruining his reputation and then his life.

"*Whoever* this guy is—" Rowe rolled his eyes "—and I'm with Erica that you know his identity or at least strongly suspect, he really hates you or he wouldn't have wanted you sent away to prison for life."

"Two lifetimes," Jed reminded him of his sentence. That sick psycho had given him two lives; now maybe he would try to take two lives. He glanced toward the hangar apartment but could only see Macy inside. Maybe Erica had been so exhausted from her sleepless night that she'd lain down with their daughter. "You have to protect Erica and Isobel."

"They are in danger," Rowe agreed. "We all are for helping you. If anyone can prove that we have…"

He swallowed hard. Mrs. Osborn might testify against Erica, saying that she had claimed him as an old friend. No matter if he proved his innocence of the original charges, he had still broken out of jail and she had still helped him. He would do what he could to protect them. He would claim that he'd forced her to help him, but nobody had believed him when he'd professed his own innocence. Why would they believe him when he professed hers?

"Let me get the hell out of here. Then you can get Isobel and Erica away, too," he suggested. "You need to take them someplace where no one can find them."

As his trial had proven, anyone could get bought off. Lawyers, witnesses…probably police officers could, too. He had learned to trust no one but Macy. And because of Jed's love and devotion to her, the DEA agent was an extension of his sister.

Rowe shook his head as if denying his request. But then he groaned and said, "I'm a damn fool for going along with this."

"Not arresting me will make Macy happy," Jed reminded him.

"Your getting killed will make her hate me." Rowe's throat rippled as he swallowed hard. "Forever."

"That's a good reason for my not going to jail until I can prove I was framed."

"I'm not as worried about that shoot-on-sight order as I am about you confronting a killer all by yourself, Jed. I'll go with you."

"No." He rejected the DEA agent's suggestion. "I need you to take care of them."

Rowe shook his head. "You don't need me to do that. Your sister is pretty formidable."

"I wouldn't put my sister in that kind of danger. She's not formidable enough to handle this guy without getting hurt or killed," Jed warned him. "This man is more devious and more powerful than even Warden James. He has to be stopped."

The thought of his fiancée in danger had Rowe reaching for the tense muscles in the nape of his neck, just below his blond hair. "And you think you're the only one who can stop this monster?"

"I know I am," Jed confirmed.

Rowe shook his head in disbelief—not in what Jed had claimed but apparently over what he had decided. "There's a car in the back of the hangar under a bunch of tarps. The plate and the vehicle identification numbers are untraceable. Use it and get the hell out of here before I change my mind."

Jed didn't say goodbye to anyone but Rowe. He didn't step back inside that apartment to kiss his sister goodbye or take one last look at his daughter. And Erica.

If he had, he might not have left.

And he had to leave to keep them safe.

WARDEN JAMES KEPT HIS EYES closed but his ears opened. He wasn't the only one disgusted with the new sheriff. The jail guards weren't happy with him, either—especially as he kept running off to chase down escaped convicts and came back with precious few.

He wouldn't have to worry about York much longer. The mayor would probably call a special meeting with the town council and have him recalled. And thankfully, he probably wouldn't have to worry about Jedidiah Kleyn much longer, either.

Sure, the sheriff wasn't wrong about Kleyn being hard to kill. But then, probably not even in Afghanistan had the man ever had as many people gunning for him then as he had now.

It was just a matter of time before he turned up. Dead.

And then the case against Jefferson would die, too, when the only witness against him, who hadn't benefited from his crimes, was gone.

Jefferson hoped that eventually it was discovered who really committed the murders for which Kleyn had been convicted. Because he wanted to shake that guy's hand...

THE MORE DISTANCE JED PUT between himself and his family the easier he breathed. The pressure, over his mere presence putting them in danger, eased off his chest.

Just over a week ago, Rowe had promised to protect Macy from the fallout of helping the DEA agent escape from Blackwoods and the hit the warden had put on him. Rowe had kept that promise, but as he'd said, Macy was formidable. She could defend herself.

Could Erica defend herself, if she had to? She had been stubborn with him when she'd insisted on going along to see Leighton. But was she strong enough to fight for her life and their daughter's life if she had to?

He didn't have to worry about her, though. She and Isobel were safe with Rowe and Macy. He expelled a ragged breath of relief and heard an echoing gasp from the backseat.

His muscles tightened in reaction. He wasn't alone. For three years, in the most dangerous prison in Michigan, he hadn't let anyone get a jump on him.

Ever.

Just a few days out of prison and already his reflexes had dimmed. But the car had been covered with all those tarps, so he hadn't thought to check to see if anyone had crawled inside. The windows were all tinted, so he hadn't even been able to see into the backseat. And peering into the rearview mirror revealed nothing.

Had he imagined the sound? His gut told him no. Every nerve taut with awareness, he knew he wasn't alone.

He doubted it was the sheriff. The man would have shown himself before now, before Jed had gotten so many miles away from the hangar.

Unless that was what he'd been waiting for—distance and seclusion so that no one would witness him gun down the escaped convict—the cop killer—in cold blood.

If distance and seclusion was what the *law*man wanted, Jed would make sure he got it. He pulled off the two-lane highway onto what looked like a two-track that probably led to someone's seldom-used cottage or maybe to an abandoned oil well.

At least he hoped the road was seldom used because he didn't want his stowaway calling in reinforcements. Jed wasn't about to go out without a fight…

# *Chapter Thirteen*

It wasn't Jed that had made Erica feel panicky earlier in the confined space. And even though she was wedged in tight behind some seats and covered with a dusky, mildew-smelling tarp, it wasn't the confined space either that had her so scared. It was the fear of being caught.

If only the tarp wasn't so thick, it would have been easier for her breathe. But it was also so foul-smelling that she'd been compelled to hold her breath until she'd had to gasp for more.

Had he heard her?

Was that why he had pulled onto some bumpy road? Or was he just following the directions Rowe had given him to the witness's house? If so, that man hadn't received the payout that Marcus Leighton had. Or maybe he had already drunk or drugged his way through whatever money he had received to perjure himself on the stand.

She bounced against the floorboards as the car hit every rut. Her elbow knocked against the metal bracket that fastened the driver's seat to the floor, and her fingers tingled and went numb. She swallowed a curse at the pain. She had to stay as quiet as possible.

The car stopped, sparing her any more abuse from the bumps. The driver's door opened and slammed closed. Maybe this wasn't the witness's house. Maybe this was actually where the man Jed had recognized driving the car lived.

Anxious to see, she closed her fingers over the edge of the tarp. But before she could pull it away from her face, the back door opened. Through the heavy canvas, big hands grasped her legs and dragged her from the floor. Her head struck the metal opening of the door, then gravel bit into her back as she dropped to the ground.

"It's me," she said, but the heavy canvas muffled her voice.

And what if it wasn't Jed?

What if they hadn't really lost that man in the black sedan and he had returned and run Jed off onto the bumpy road? She reached in her pocket for the weapon Macy had pressed into her hand earlier. She hadn't wanted it; she had been more concerned about hurting herself with it. But now she unsheathed the blade and hacked at the heavy canvas, trying to cut through the tarp to defend herself.

A man cursed, but his voice was muffled, just as hers undoubtedly was to him. She couldn't yell out his name, though, because what if it was the police or maybe that husky-voiced female bounty hunter who had pulled him over? Then they would know she was willingly with him.

She would not willingly go with them. She pushed the scalpel through the canvas again and elicited another curse from the man. It was definitely a man—not the female bounty hunter.

Then the tarp lifted, as he pulled it off her face and body. She rolled with it, coming up on her side with the hand holding the scalpel trapped beneath her body.

The blade nipped through her heavy jeans and nicked her hip.

She gasped at the little stab of pain and tried to roll off the weapon. But a foot was on her other shoulder, shoving her into the ground. She turned her head toward her attacker. And she gasped again. Fear had her heart racing as she stared up at the look of intense rage on his face.

She had thought she would only be in danger if it was someone other than Jed who had dragged her from her hiding place. Now she wasn't so sure. He looked as though he intended to kill her.

He cursed her but lifted his foot from her shoulder. "What the hell are you doing here?"

"What I should have done three years ago," she said. "Help you prove your innocence."

He reached a hand down toward her to bring her upright, and blood dripped from his fingers.

"Oh, my God, I hurt you."

He nodded in agreement, but she suspected he referred to more than the shallow wound on the back of his hand. The canvas must have taken the brunt of the blade. She'd hurt him more with her doubts than she ever could have with the scalpel.

"'Least I don't have to worry about you being able to defend yourself," he remarked as he smeared his blood off on his jeans.

Erica had been worried that she wouldn't be able to use the weapon even if she needed it. So pride overtook the twinge of guilt she felt for hurting him. "Your sister gave it to me."

He nodded. "I figured that out. What I can't figure out is why you're here. Why aren't you with our daughter and Macy and Rowe?"

"She's safe with them." She truly believed that Macy and Rowe would protect her little girl as if Isobel were their own. Or she never would have left her precious baby with them.

"I know that," he agreed. "That's why I asked Rowe to protect her." He stepped closer and pushed her tangled hair back from her face. "I also asked him to protect you. By letting you get into this car, he broke his promise to me."

She shook her head. "Rowe doesn't know I climbed into the back."

"It was my sister's idea?"

"It was mine," she corrected him. "Macy only mentioned the car when it looked as though Rowe wasn't going to arrest you. She'd hoped that he'd brought the car there for you to use as an escape vehicle."

"Yeah, some escape," he said, his voice gruff with irony.

"You wanted to escape from me, too?" she asked. "You tracked *me* down." Something she hadn't thought he would be able to do, or she would have hidden from him the moment she'd learned of the prison break. But then she might have never learned the truth. And she needed that knowledge—for Isobel. So the little girl learned the truth about her father instead of the lies everyone else—including Erica—had believed.

"That was because I thought you could help me," he reminded her.

She flinched that all he had wanted from her was an alibi. But then, what could she expect from him after he had spent the past three years believing she'd betrayed him?

"I can help you." She could stop him from doing something he would live to regret. As she'd snuck out to the car, she had overheard his conversation with Rowe and knew that Jed was on his way to talk to the remaining witness. Or threaten that witness as he had probably intended to threaten Marcus Leighton.

Or was that just what he had told Rowe so that the DEA agent wouldn't suspect that he was on his way to confront the real killer?

Rowe might have been willing to trust Jed to go off alone, but she couldn't. Her silence might have cost him three years of his life; she wasn't going to be silent again while he wound up serving more jail time.

"You can't help me," Jed insisted. "You're just going to get in my way."

As she suspected, he was going after the real killer—not the witness. "Jed, you can't do this alone."

He shook his head. "I can't do this with you."

"I can take care of myself," she reminded him.

"A scalpel isn't going to save you from a bullet," he pointed out. "And no one's going to save you from me."

Erica gasped at his ominous tone. She lifted her gaze to his face. He had that intense look again—the one that had her fearing for her safety. She'd hidden in the vehicle because she had been afraid for Jed. Now she was afraid of him…

HER EYES WIDENED and all the color left her beautiful face; she was scared of him. He should have felt satisfaction since that was what he'd wanted. But regret clutched his heart.

He had so many regrets where Erica Towsley was concerned. And now he was about to have another. He reached for her, dragging her up against his body, which was hard with desire for her.

She was still hanging on to the scalpel; she could

have used it on him. He wouldn't have blamed her since he'd intended to deliberately frighten her.

And maybe he had intended this kiss to scare her, too, because he started out rough. He pressed his mouth tightly against hers, forcing her lips apart for the bold invasion of his tongue.

She gasped for breath and lifted her hands to his shoulders. Instead of pushing him away, she clutched him closely and moaned. Her reaction snapped his control. He didn't care that she was scared of him and that she didn't trust him; all he cared was that she wanted him, too.

He pulled her down to the ground with him, releasing her only long enough to spread the heavy tarp across the dirt path next to the car. Despite the trees that densely lined both sides of the two-track lane, the sun had melted whatever snow had fallen here. That bright sun had also warmed the day so that it felt like spring again—fresh and full of promise.

They had once had that promise before he'd gotten the orders calling him back to active duty and deploying him overseas. Their instant attraction and emotional connection had been so strong.

Maybe it was because he'd been locked up for three years, but that attraction felt even stronger now. He couldn't fight it. And she wasn't fighting him.

Instead she was lying down beside him on the tarp. Her hands ran up his chest, her palm settling against his pounding heart. Maybe she'd wondered if he still had one.

He was actually kind of surprised that he had; he'd thought he had lost it three years ago. He'd thought she'd stolen it and stomped all over it. He wanted her. But he wouldn't give her his heart again. He didn't trust her any more than she trusted him.

"Why?" he asked her.

"Why what?"

"Why aren't you fighting me?" he wondered aloud. "Why aren't you jabbing that scalpel into my chest?"

She shivered. "Should I be fighting you? Are you going to hurt me?"

He had to answer her honestly. "Probably."

IF HE HAD LIED TO HER—if he'd made her promises that they both knew he might not be able to keep—she would have pulled away from him. But his honesty increased her desire for him. And she'd already never wanted anyone—even him—more.

He still scared her, but what she felt for him frightened her more. She couldn't fall for a man she didn't even know anymore…if she'd ever really known him at all. Before she'd gotten the chance to really know him, he had pushed her away and left her for war. Then he'd only been back a short while before he'd left her for prison.

She knew she would never be able to keep him, but she wanted these stolen moments off the beaten track. So she clenched her hands in his shirt and dragged it over his head.

Sunlight shone through the trees and shimmered off his massively muscled chest. Her breath caught in appreciation and desire. But she had barely a moment to enjoy the sight of him before he pushed off her coat and pulled her shirt over her head.

"Are you cold?" he asked, dragging her tight against his naked chest.

Heat flushed her skin, which tingled everywhere she touched him. "No…"

Then he was kissing her again—deeply, his tongue sliding through her lips and over her tongue. She could taste him and feel him. And she wanted him too much to feel anything but desire. She certainly didn't notice the cold.

Her fingers trembled as she reached for the snap of his jeans, pulling it loose. Then his hands replaced hers, and he shucked off his jeans. She fumbled with her own snap, but his hands were there, too, pulling off the rest of her clothes.

Cool air rushed over her, raising goose bumps on her skin. He cursed and rubbed his palms over her arms and then her breasts. "You are cold."

Her nipples peaked, and tension wound tight inside her. She moaned, and he replaced his hands with his lips, tugging at one of her nipples until she whimpered with desire.

Her hands were busy, too, sliding over all his smooth skin. Muscles rippled beneath her touch. She ran her fingertips down his back to his butt.

He groaned against her breast. "Erica…"

"I want you…" She shouldn't. She had so many reasons not to trust him. Not to want him. But she wanted him.

Her admission snapped his control because he pushed her back onto the tarp. And his mouth went crazy, covering every inch of her with kisses that heated her skin. When his mouth slid lower, between her legs, she arched off the tarp. She shuddered with ecstasy and screamed his name.

And then he was there, filling her. She had forgotten how big he was. She stretched and arched, trying to take him deep inside her.

He held most of his weight onto his arms, the muscles flexing and bulging. She slid her hands over them and then over his shoulders to his back. She wrapped her arms and legs around him, holding on to him as tightly as she could for as long as she could.

She had no illusions that it would be long. But she would enjoy it while she could. She kept arching into him, meeting his thrusts.

He sank deeper and deeper into her. And that pressure that had wound so tight inside her finally broke free. She screamed his name as pleasure overwhelmed her.

Then, with a deep guttural groan, he joined her in ecstasy. His big body shuddered, but instead of dropping on top of her, he rolled to his side. Then he pulled her tight against him.

His hand ran up and down her back. "You're cold…"

Sweat beaded on her lip, but the wind was chilling her skin.

He grabbed up their clothes and arranged them over her. Something scratched her hip and she flinched, fearing the scalpel had found her again. But when she tentatively reached out, she realized it was car keys that had fallen out of his pocket.

"Sleep," he urged her. "You were up all night."

"So were you," she said. And she suspected that hadn't been the only night's sleep he'd missed. "Are you going to sleep, too?"

"I haven't really slept since before the riot," he admitted. But from the tension in his big body, she doubted that he would be able to sleep even now.

She was pretty certain that he had a plan. And he

wouldn't sleep until he saw the plan through. She wondered now how much that plan was about clearing his name and how much about vengeance.

She had to stop him from doing something that would put him back in prison for good. But she couldn't stay awake; her eyelids had grown too heavy to keep open. She would close them for just a minute.

Just a minute…

But when she awoke what might have been only moments later, she was alone.

WHERE THE HELL WAS JED? Had prison slowed down the man? From the skirmish in Erica Towsley's apartment, he knew Jed hadn't physically slowed. But maybe prison had dulled his usually quick mind. He should have been here by now. For most of their lives, Jed had been ahead of him—in class, in accolades.

Except for the past three years.

Then Jed had fallen behind. He hadn't been smart enough or fast enough to figure out how he had been framed or who had done it to him.

Now that Jed had seen *him* behind the wheel of the car that had nearly driven his family off the road, Kleyn knew the truth.

But he would never be able to prove it. No one would. No, Jed would die before he would ever be able to prove his innocence.

He would die a guilty man—as soon as he stepped into the trap that had been set for him.

# Chapter Fourteen

Leaving her alone had been so hard. But Jed had wrapped her in her clothes and the tarp to keep her warm. He had also left her the drop cell phone Rowe had given him. He suspected the DEA agent had a GPS on it, so he would find Erica.

Hopefully before it grew dark.

Could he leave her alone?

He had yet to start the car and drive off. He hadn't even shut the driver's door because he hadn't wanted to awaken her. The engine would when he started it, but by then it would be too late for her to catch him.

He drew in a deep breath and reached for the keys. But they didn't dangle from the ignition. He must have taken them with him when he'd jumped out of the car. So he searched his pockets. They were empty.

Where the hell were the keys?

Metal creaked as she pulled open the passenger door and settled onto the seat. She held the keys out between them. "Looking for these?"

Back when they had first met, he had admired her quick brain. She had been applying for a job with his firm, and he'd wanted to hire her. But he had wanted to date her even more. When he'd told her that, she had willingly withdrawn her application. She'd already had a job with her aunt's bookkeeping firm in Miller's Valley, but she had wanted to move to a bigger city. She had wanted more opportunities than Miller's Valley had offered.

She had found another job in Grand Rapids. And he had found her.

"Erica..."

"I can't believe you were going to leave me alone here in the middle of nowhere," she said, glaring at him—her blue eyes icy with fury and hurt.

"I left you Rowe's cell phone," he pointed out. It protruded from the front pocket of her jeans.

She nodded. "I don't have a clue where I am, though."

"He would have found you." He swallowed hard. "He *will* find you."

"You're going to throw me out of the car?"

"I can't bring you with me." He wasn't going to talk to just the witness. There was someone else he was determined to find—unless he was just chasing a ghost.

"Why not?" she asked, but she gave him no chance to answer. "It's not because you're going to talk to the witness. It's because you don't want any witnesses when you settle the score with whoever framed you."

"I don't want you getting hurt." So maybe he shouldn't have made love with her. But he suspected he would be the one who got hurt over that, over letting down his guard enough to get that close to a woman he would never be able to trust. Any more than she trusted him...

She shook her head, rejecting his claim. "You don't think I'll get hurt with you leaving me in the middle of nowhere?"

"Rowe will find you," he insisted, reaching for the keys.

She pulled them back, holding them near the passenger's door. "But will *he* find me first?"

Jed's arms were longer than hers, his grip stronger, so he easily reached across her and took the keys from her. But then he replayed her comment in his head. "What do you mean?"

"That man who broke into my apartment—the man you recognized but won't admit that you did—he could find me before Rowe gets here."

His breath stuck in his lungs for a moment, then escaped in a ragged sigh. "Damn it…"

She was right. If she hadn't stolen the keys from his pocket, he might have left her at the mercy of a maniac. Sure, he'd been watching his rearview mirror and hadn't noticed anyone following him. But then he hadn't noticed her in the backseat, either.

He could have a missed a tail. The sheriff or the bounty hunter or maybe the killer himself if he hadn't already bought off someone else to do his dirty work as he had last time. "I need to talk to the witness."

He needed to learn what the man had really seen that night so that Jed would know if he could trust that what he'd seen hadn't been just a figment of his overexhausted mind.

"You're going to have to take me with you," she stubbornly insisted as she buckled herself into the passenger seat.

She was right. He couldn't leave her here. But he worried that bringing her along might put her in more danger than leaving her behind.

NOT ONLY HAD SHE GRABBED his keys but she'd grabbed up the scalpel again, too. It was sheathed and inside her pocket. The slight weight of it against her hip comforted her. It was the only comfort she had as Jed remained silent and tense behind the steering wheel.

Not many more miles passed from the two-track lane where they had made love before he turned off onto another street, this one lined with houses. He pulled the car up to the curb in front of a modest brick ranch. Tall trees from the thick woods behind it cast the house in shadows despite the brightness of the afternoon sun.

Finally he cleared his throat and deigned to speak. "You're staying in the car."

"No." He was bigger and stronger than she was, but he wasn't going to bully her. She wasn't going to calmly accept the decisions other people made for her anymore. Her parents hadn't consulted her before dumping her on her great aunt. Jed hadn't asked if she'd wait for him before he'd dumped her. And Brandon had insisted she wear his damn ring even though she'd turned down his proposal.

People weren't going to ignore her opinions and wants and needs anymore.

"Erica, think about our daughter," he said, as if her every waking thought wasn't already about her precious baby. "She needs her mother."

"She needs her father, too," she insisted. "That's why I'm here. I have to make sure that Isobel will have the chance to get to know you."

His lips curved into a slight grin. "So you're here to protect me?"

"Yes." From himself.

"I survived three years in prison without you," he pointed out.

She shuddered at the thought of where he'd been. The things the media had reported about Blackwoods had been horrific—a warden who encouraged inmates to murder each other…

"I wouldn't have survived what you have," she admitted.

She hadn't been that strong—until she'd found herself pregnant and alone except for an aunt that had needed her help even though she hadn't been able to remember who Erica was.

She'd had to learn to be strong, so that her daughter would have someone she could count on as Erica had never been able to count on her own parents.

His smile slid away. "I don't know about that." He lifted his hand from the wheel. The blood had dried on his wound. "You're tougher than I realized."

Pride warmed her. "That's why I'm not staying in the car."

He sighed. "I guess it's better if you go inside with me than follow me in later."

As she had at the lawyer's. Then she had doubted Jed's innocence. "Do you think we'll find this man the same way we found Marcus Leighton?"

"Dead?" He nodded. "I think it's a possibility. Hopefully Rowe tracked down the man's address before the killer did." He cursed beneath his breath and muttered, "I should have come right here."

But instead he'd made love to her.

Or had he only been trying to distract her so that he could leave her behind? Neither one of them had declared any feelings for the other. But why would he fall for her now, after blaming her for his going to prison, when he hadn't fallen for her before then?

He would never love her. But maybe he would forgive her for not talking to the police when she should have. The police might have figured out what Marcus had been up to—deliberately throwing Jed's defense.

And maybe, if Erica helped prove his innocence, Isobel would forgive her, too, when one day she learned the truth about her parents. When she learned how her father had been in prison for the first few years of her life while her mother had done nothing to help him. Then.

"I'm sorry," she murmured.

"This is a bad idea," he said. "Macy shouldn't have let you stow away with me."

"Macy understood my need to help you." The young woman had acted as if Erica was in love with her brother. But Erica didn't love Jed any more than he loved her.

She had given up on love long ago—receiving it and giving it. To anyone but Isobel. Her daughter was the only one Erica would trust with her heart.

It beat faster just over Erica thinking about her. The little girl was safe with her aunt and uncle-to-be. But Jed was right that Erica wasn't safe. If she stepped inside that house with Jed, would she ever see her daughter again?

"You don't have to do this," he said. "I can drive you into town and drop you off in a well-populated area where you'll be safe until Rowe can pick you up."

"I have to do this," she corrected him.

The witness might not respond to Jed's threats, but maybe he would to her plea to give her daughter back her father. She drew in a deep, bracing breath and reached for the door handle.

Jed met her on the other side of the car. He kept glancing around as they headed toward the front door of the small brick house. "He must not have gotten as much money as Leighton."

How did one set a price for a man's life, though? Because in testifying against Jed and sending him to prison, this man had cost Jed his life.

Jed sighed. "But then he was homeless when he testified against me. This probably seems like a castle to him compared to the parking garage he was living in."

And it probably did because the yard was well kept, all the windows and trim freshly painted. There was pride in ownership. Was there pride in what he'd done to achieve the house?

If so, she would never be able to convince him to do the right thing. This man obviously felt no guilt over sending an innocent man to prison. If he had felt any remorse, he probably would have been back on the streets, lost in the bottle.

She knocked on the front door, anger making her pound so hard that the door opened.

"I don't like this," Jed remarked.

"It's broad daylight." Not like the eerie predawn hours when they had found Marcus Leighton dead in his office.

"Crime happens even during the day," he replied, reminding her how naïve she was.

Growing up in Miller's Valley with her great aunt had been like growing up in a fifty-year-old time warp. There was no crime or criminals in Miller's Valley. Everyone but her aunt had always left their doors unlocked.

That was another reason why, in addition to caring for her aunt, Erica had returned to Miller's Valley. After the fiasco with Jed and Brandon, she had wanted nothing to do with city life anymore. This house was in a smaller town, the witness having chosen to leave the city behind, too.

Jed stepped in front of her and pushed the door open the rest of the way using just his broad shoulder. Then he called out, "Hello?"

"Maybe he's gone," she said. But then she noticed the suitcase by the door.

He had intended to leave, probably after seeing the press coverage of Jed's escape from prison, but he hadn't gotten very far. The house was small and open, so it was easy to locate him without taking more than a couple of steps over the threshold. His body lay facedown by his back door, as if he had tried to make a run for it when the killer had come in his front door.

Jed crossed the living room to the kitchen and knelt beside the man, feeling his neck for a pulse. From the blood pooled on the linoleum beneath the body, Erica doubted he would find one.

He turned toward her and shook his head. "He's already cold."

"We were too late," she said. Her stomach churned with regret that they hadn't been able to save the man and that they hadn't been able to talk to him or Leighton. Or that woman who had lied about leaving Jed alone with Brandon. Had she really committed suicide, or was it murder as Jed suspected?

From the bullet hole burned through his bloodied shirt, this man had obviously been murdered. He could not tell them now who had paid him to lie on the witness stand.

Jed cursed. "We were too damn late again."

"Should we search the place?" she asked. "And try to find something linking him to whoever paid for his testimony against you?"

She was out of her element here, just as she had been from the first moment she had met Jedidiah Kleyn. But she had never been more so than now. She was a small-town bookkeeper, not a trained investigator. She had no idea how to behave at a murder scene, but at least she had managed last time and this time to control her stomach and her hysteria. She would not get sick, and she would not freak out and dissolve into sobs of hysteria.

Jed stood up. The knees of his jeans were stained with the dead man's blood. "No, we should get the hell out of here."

"But what if we miss something that could help clear you…" They couldn't help this man anymore, but maybe they could still find something that would aid Jed in his quest.

"*He* wouldn't have missed anything," Jed said, his voice rough with certainty and bitterness.

He definitely knew who had set him up. While he might not have been sure before, as he'd claimed to Rowe, he was obviously convinced now.

She glanced around, trying to discover what had cemented his conviction. But she saw nothing. "Are you sure?"

He jerked his chin down in a quick nod. "He's too smart and too thorough. The only thing he left here is a trap for me to get caught." He grabbed her hand and pulled her toward the front door.

But as he stepped toward the open doorway, shots rang out. The jamb, inches from his head, splintered. "Damnation…"

He slammed the door shut, but shots pinged against the steel and shattered the small rectangle of glass near Jed's head. Her hand still clasped in his, he pulled her along with him toward the back door. She stumbled over the body, slipping in the blood.

Jed half lifted her across the corpse and pulled open the back door. "We have to run for it," he told her as the front door creaked open, propelled either by the bullets or someone's foot.

Her heart pounded so hard, she could barely hear him. "Where do we run?"

"We can't get to the car," he said. "We'll have to run out back, into the woods."

He stepped out first onto the driveway at the side of the house, and then he pulled her out just as shots were fired inside.

Something whizzed past her head. If not for him pushing her toward the woods, she might have frozen, her muscles paralyzed with fear. But he kept her moving even as more gunfire erupted.

The backyard was wide-open with no trees or structures to deflect the bullets. He stayed between her and the house, shielding her with his body as if muscle and flesh could deflect metal.

She ran faster, her legs burning with the effort. She did not want him to take a bullet for her. And she suddenly remembered the game at the carnival where the contestant shoots the air rifle at the row of ducks.

But she wasn't the contestant with the air rifle; she was one of the ducks—waddling back and forth until the gun knocked her down.

And just a couple of yards from the woods line, she fell. She sprawled across the weeds at the edge of the lawn, her body too numb with fear for her to tell where she had been hit.

JED SPRAWLED ON TOP OF ERICA, protecting her with his body as more shots rang out behind them. More than one gun fired at them. He turned his head and peered over his shoulder.

In black uniforms with the sun glinting off the shiny badges on their chests, police officers fanned out from the house, coming toward them. But instead of identifying themselves or telling Jed and her to stop, they just kept firing.

Hoping Erica wasn't hit, Jed clutched her close. Then he rolled with her down the back slope of the lawn and into the trees. Without giving her a moment to catch her breath or for him to catch his, he dragged her up and, half carrying her, ran deeper into the woods. Briars and branches caught at his clothes and scratched his head and face.

Erica gasped and panted for breath, but she didn't slow down—just pressed close to his side as he wrapped his arm tight around her. She kept pace with him as they ran deeper and deeper into the woods. But then the crack of a shot echoed within the forest, sending birds rising up from tree branches and flying off in a frenzy. This gunshot came from ahead—not behind them.

Erica stopped short against him, realizing as he had that they were surrounded.

Trapped.

The police officers had been like deer hunters flushing out their prey to the hunter who would make the kill shot.

The killer.

Jed couldn't see him; he wasn't showing himself again—maybe because he intended to let Erica live. Or maybe because he had been in hiding for so long that he wasn't used to being out in the open.

Or he didn't want the police officers to see him. But hell, they had probably already seen him when he had paid them to help him set this trap. Maybe they didn't act out of a sense of vigilante justice but out of greed. Had they been promised more money if Jed didn't come out of these woods alive?

The officers were getting closer. Twigs and branches snapped behind him as Jed pulled Erica down into some thick brush.

She pressed her hand to her mouth, as if trying to hold back a scream or maybe just the sound of her panting breaths. She had kept pace with him through the woods, running faster than he'd thought she would be able—especially if she'd been hit when she'd first dropped to the ground at the edge of the lawn.

But then fear had probably made her oblivious to her pain and given her speed. She stared up at him, her eyes wide with questions he couldn't answer.

He didn't know how to save them. He had no gun— no weapon besides the little scalpel Macy had given Erica. Rowe wouldn't give him a gun—only the use of the vehicle and the burner cell phone.

He could call Rowe, but talking would reveal their hiding place. And Rowe would never get to them in time to save them.

Then there was no time at all for him to do anything as the cold barrel of a gun pressed into the nape of his neck.

"I'm sorry," he mouthed the words to Erica.

He would never get to know his daughter now, and he had cost the child her mother, as well. After witnessing his murder, she wouldn't be allowed to live, either.

# *Chapter Fifteen*

"I want my mommy!" the little girl whined from her car seat in the back of the vehicle her daddy had given Macy when she'd graduated high school.

Macy glanced at the rearview mirror, but instead of checking for vehicles following them as she had constantly been doing, she met her niece's frightened gaze. Tears welled in the child's big, chocolate-brown eyes.

"I know, sweetheart," Macy commiserated with the toddler. She'd once wanted her mother, too, but Beatrice Kleyn had never been a mommy. She'd never been as loving and warm as Erica was with her daughter.

The woman had done a great job of raising her baby alone. It was obvious how much she loved Isobel. So Macy was moved that Erica had trusted her to keep the child safe. And Macy would protect her niece from all physical harm. But could she protect her from the emotional harm of losing her mommy?

Rowe had been right to get angry over her allowing Erica to stow away with Jed. She would have given up the blonde woman's whereabouts before her brother had driven off if she hadn't identified so well with the woman's need to help the man she loved.

And no matter that she hadn't been at his trial, Erica Towsley loved Jed. She'd claimed she wanted to help prove his innocence for Isobel's sake, so that her daughter would grow up knowing her father.

But Macy had seen the way Erica looked at Jed—the same way Macy looked at Rowe—like he was the only man in the world. Maybe Erica had doubted him before, and maybe she feared what he might do if he'd gone off alone to confront witnesses and track down evidence to clear himself, but she loved him.

Hopefully that love wouldn't cost Erica Towsley her life and little Isobel both her parents…

"DON'T MOVE," A DEEP raspy voice warned.

Erica couldn't have moved had she wanted to. Jed was wrapped tightly around her, once again using his own body to shield her.

But then some of the tension eased from him, and he whispered, "Rowe?"

"Shh…"

The DEA agent crouched down in the brush with them, keeping low while branches and twigs snapped around them. The taller trees blocked the late afternoon sun, casting them in shadows.

Erica held her breath but her heart pounded so hard that the sound of it echoed inside her head. Could the gunmen hear it, too? Would she be the one who gave away their location? Who cost them all their lives?

Several long moments of silence passed before Rowe's hoarse whisper advised them, "Let's go…"

Jed caught his arm and stopped him from moving from their hiding place. "The police weren't the only ones firing at us."

"You saw that guy again?"

He shook his head. "No. But he's here."

A furrow creased Rowe's brow. Then he reached beneath his jacket in the back and pulled out another gun. "I didn't want to do this…"

Arm an escaped felon?

Jed hesitated before reaching for the weapon, and then he closed his big hand around it. "Thank you."

Rowe didn't accept the gratitude, just shook his head as if disgusted with himself. "Let's get the hell out of here."

They backtracked through the woods. But instead of coming up to the yard that was swarming with police officers and crime-scene techs, they snuck through another yard several houses over that was thick with weeds and overgrown trees, offering them cover.

The men kept her in the middle, both of them shielding her. But she caught the glint of metal as someone raised a gun behind them. "Down!" she yelled as she crouched low.

Bullets whizzed over their heads. But the men didn't drop to the ground. Rowe took the lead, running toward the street. He clicked a button on a key chain and a sliding door opened on the side of a van parked near the curb.

Jed lifted her into the back and jumped in behind her as Rowe slid behind the wheel. Before either door shut completely, he was tearing away from the curb. Rubber squealed as he careened around a corner and onto another street.

Erica's heart raced, and she trembled with nerves and fear.

"Are you hurt?" Jed asked her. "Were you hit?"

She shook her head, realizing now that she'd only fallen earlier because Jed had knocked her down and knocked the breath from her lungs. She was alive, but she was mad as hell and not just about getting shot at.

She reached into the front seat and smacked Rowe's shoulder. She didn't really care that he had rescued her and Jed. She cared only about one thing—his promise to protect her daughter. "Why did you leave her?"

"Who?" Rowe asked, sparing her only a quick glance in the rearview mirror as he continued steering the van around tight curves at high speeds.

Hysteria rose, pressing on her lungs and stealing away her breath more than the mad dash through the woods had. "Isobel! Where's Isobel?"

Jed grabbed her shoulders, as if trying to calm her down. She shook off his grasp, though, refusing to be comforted.

She had trusted Macy and Rowe to keep her daughter safe. Why, after everything she had been through in her life, had she been stupid enough to believe she could trust anyone?

"She's fine," Rowe assured her. "Don't worry about her."

"She's right to worry," Jed said, and his words offered more support than his touch. "You promised that *you* would stay with her. But you used this damn phone—" he pulled it from the pocket of her jeans; she was surprised that she hadn't lost it in the woods "—to track us."

"Macy insisted that I keep an eye on the two of you," Rowe said. "She took Isobel to safety and made me follow you to keep you safe."

"How do you know they made it to safety?" Erica asked, her panic increasing.

"Yeah, how the hell do you know?" Jed echoed her question. He apparently didn't care any more than she did that Rowe had saved his life; he cared more about their daughter's and his sister's lives.

She felt closer to him now than she had even when they had made love.

"Take us to her," she pleaded. "I have to see her." She had to hold her baby close and never let her go again.

"You can't see her now," Rowe said.

"Where did Macy take her?"

"I'm not going to tell you," he said. "It's better for her if you don't know…"

She sucked in a breath of pain. Was that what child protective services would say when they took Isobel away while the police eventually took Erica off to jail for aiding and abetting a fugitive?

"You can't go anywhere near her right now," Rowe explained, "because you would only put her in danger."

Erica posed a threat to her own daughter? Because the police were after her now or because the killer was?

"Be good for Aunt Macy." Erica spoke into Rowe's cell phone, her voice shaky but forced into sounding bright and happy, too.

Jed already knew that she would do anything for their daughter; she was a great mother. To give Isobel her father was the reason that Erica had put her own life in jeopardy.

It was a miracle that she hadn't been hit with all the shots that had been fired at them. He shuddered now, thinking of how much danger she'd been in…because of him. Love hadn't motivated her into tagging along, though—at least not love for him. But love for their daughter…

And guilt.

"I'm glad I didn't give *her* the gun," Rowe told Jed. With an uneasy chuckle, he added, "She might have shot me back there."

"You're lucky I didn't shoot you," Jed admitted. In the heat of the moment, he hadn't realized what Erica had—that Rowe had left their daughter unprotected.

"Your sister has proven again and again that she's formidable," Rowe reminded him, with obvious pride in, and awe of, the woman he loved. "She won't let anything happen to her niece."

Jed nodded in agreement. Macy was tough—far tougher than he had ever realized. So was Erica. She had survived finding dead bodies and getting shot at, and her only worry and concern was for their child. She was another formidable woman.

"Isobel is in no danger," Rowe assured him. "She and Macy are in a safe house that only I know about, like this one."

*This* was a log cabin on a hill overlooking Lake Michigan. The setting sun streaked across the water and through the windows that overlooked the rocky hill that was washing away into the lake. It was a wild, beautiful, remote area just north of Muskegon.

"How the hell do you find these places?" Jed wondered. "And vehicles?" The van he'd picked them up with had been like the car, with untraceable plate and vehicle identification numbers.

"It's all seized property," the Drug Enforcement Administration agent briefly explained.

"But no one else knows about them?"

Rowe shook his head. "Not anymore. The only other agent that knew about this one and the one Macy's at is gone now."

His handler agent had recently been killed, as Rowe nearly had been in Blackwoods. While Jed regretted the agent's death, he breathed a sigh of relief. "So Macy and Isobel are really safe?"

Rowe nodded his assurance. "Yes. You and Erica aren't, though."

A headache of frustration gnawed at Jed's temples, which he rubbed. "But you said no one else living knows about this place…"

"We could have been tailed from the crime scene," Rowe said. "I don't think we were, but…"

"But this guy always seems one step ahead." At least one step. Maybe more.

"And the authorities are right behind you," Rowe needlessly reminded him.

"They never identified themselves," Jed said. "They never even tried to apprehend us. They just started shooting."

Rowe gave a grim nod. "I know. I'd like to believe that not everyone would do that, that they were convinced that you'd just killed a man and that you were armed and dangerous…"

"But you know that's not the case." They'd wanted him dead, and it had had nothing to do with protecting themselves from a dangerous suspect. It may not have had anything to do with his being convicted of killing a cop, either.

"You weren't armed," Rowe acknowledged. "Then…"

The gun was cold and heavy against the small of Jed's back. "Thanks for the weapon."

"I would rather you *not* use it."

"You and me both." But he couldn't promise that he wouldn't be forced to.

He glanced over to where Erica stood in the kitchen, leaning against the soapstone counter while she clutched the cellular in both hands, as if she was holding her daughter instead of a phone. "I need something else from you," Jed said, pitching his voice lower.

Rowe expelled a weary sigh. "I'm almost afraid to ask…"

Jed was aware and sorry that the DEA agent had had to compromise his principles and his career in order to help him. But because he had, the man deserved the truth—no matter how crazy it sounded.

"I don't think you're the only one who's faked his death," he said.

Rowe's brow furrowed with confusion. "No one thinks you're dead. You'd be a hell of a lot better off if they did, though."

"*Dead* won't clear my name," Jed pointed out, "only finding the real killer will."

"So you do know who it is…"

Jed nodded, not even caring that he might sound crazy. "He's a dead man."

"You said you weren't going to use that gun unless you had to," Rowe reminded him, with a nervous twitch of the muscle along his jaw.

"No. He's *already* a dead man," Jed clarified.

"That wasn't a dead man shooting at us," Rowe pointed out.

"He's been dead for three years," Jed explained. "At least that's what everyone believes…"

The furrows in Rowe's brow deepened as his confusion deepened. "Who the hell are you talking about?"

"Brandon Henderson, my former partner," Jed said. "The man whose murder I was sentenced to serve life in prison for."

Rowe still looked skeptical.

"Think about it," Jed said. "It all makes sense." And that was why he was disgusted with himself for not figuring it out sooner. "He embezzled the money from our clients just before I left for Afghanistan." Because Rowe had been too distracted to realize what he'd been doing. "Then he staged his murder because he knew that when I came back I would figure it out and find the money."

"I brought the books," Rowe said. "They are beyond my area of expertise."

It was Jed's area of expertise. But he hadn't thought he would have time to go over the old records, what with trying to stay ahead of the authorities determined to either put him back in prison or kill him.

"I'll go through them," Jed said. "But I can use your expertise in another area. DNA. I need you to rerun everything from the crime scene. That wasn't Brandon's body that burned up in that car."

Rowe studied his face, as if trying to gauge his sanity.

Jed waited for all the comments he had already anticipated. That he was grasping at straws. That he was crazy. Those comments and his own doubts were why he hadn't shared his suspicion with the DEA agent right away.

"You saw him?" Rowe asked.

"Not clearly," Jed admitted. "And his hair is a different color and he's wearing a beard. But my gut tells me it's him." Even though his head had kept telling him he was crazy.

After another long moment Rowe nodded. "It makes sense."

Jed should have known that if anyone would believe him, it would be the man who had already staged his own murder. In that play, Jed had also been cast as the killer.

BRANDON LIFTED HIS GUN and fired it, sending bullet after bullet into the target. He pushed a button and brought the target close to the booth at the deserted shooting range.

Jed's mug shot covered the head of the cutout. Two bullet holes pierced each of his eyes, while another single shot penetrated his forehead.

He breathed a sigh, relieved that he could have killed Jed—had he wanted. But it had been more satisfying to have the man trapped in the brush like a rabbit—too stupid and helpless to save himself or the woman he loved.

The officers Brandon paid had come through for him, shooting *at* but not hitting Jed. Just as they had been instructed. He hadn't even had to pay them much since they thought Jed a cop killer and Brandon a relative of the deceased officer who wanted justice. They had been more than happy to help him.

He had thought that, given his convictions, Jed would have had no one to help him. But someone had come to his rescue, getting him out of the woods and into a getaway vehicle before Brandon could kill him. First he would have killed Erica Towsley, though.

The stupid prude hadn't given him the time of day, but she had given Jed everything. Her heart. Her soul. Even a child.

When he killed the woman and the little girl, he would take all those things away from Jed. Then—and only then, when the man had absolutely nothing—would Brandon take his *best* friend's life.

He didn't even have to try to track down Jed again. Brandon knew him too well. Jed would find *him* this time. And when Jed did, Brandon would be waiting… and ready.

He lifted his gun and fired again.

And again.

Brandon pushed the button and brought his target back to the booth. The face of the outline had been covered with a picture he had taken from the collection of family photos in Erica Towsley's apartment. It was the gorgeous blonde, smiling brightly, as she held her daughter tight in her arms.

A bullet hole pierced the paper between her beautiful blue eyes. A matching hole pierced the paper between the big, dark eyes of the child.

He would definitely be ready next time to, once and for all, win this rivalry with Jedidiah Kleyn.

## *Chapter Sixteen*

A fire burned inside the hearth, the flames casting light and warmth on Erica. She stood in front of it, but she couldn't stop shivering.

It was the conversation she had overheard before the DEA had left, not the cold, that had chilled her to the bone. The outside door creaked open, so she reached into her pocket and closed her fingers around the sheathed scalpel. Jed had gone outside to say goodbye to his friend and future brother-in-law, but that didn't mean he was the one coming back inside. She'd heard an engine a while ago and had just assumed it was from the car Rowe had had stashed in the garage. But what if it had been that other car, the one that had nearly forced them off the road leading away from Miller's Valley? What if they had been followed from the house of the dead witness?

Something crashed, and she withdrew her weapon and whirled around. Jed stood next to the box he had dropped onto the rough-hewn wood coffee table.

"Sorry," he said. "I didn't mean to scare you."

A laugh, more from hysteria than mirth, bubbled out of her. "Not this time," she conceded. "But you've wanted to scare me other times. Like when you first showed up at my door."

"I wanted to scare you into doing the right thing then," he said.

"Coming forward as your alibi."

"Instead I scared you into doing the wrong thing," Jed remarked with a weary-sounding sigh. He dropped onto the floor next to the coffee table and lifted the lid from the banker's box.

"Wrong thing?" she questioned. What had she done wrong besides trusting her daughter to a relative stranger? Besides nearly losing her life? Apparently she'd done everything wrong.

"I made you feel guilty, and now you've risked your life to help me prove my innocence," he said, his eyes dark with regret and torment. "I never wanted that. I never wanted to put you in any danger."

She laughed again with more dark humor than hysteria now. "I imagine, since you believed I helped set you up, you spent the past three years wanting to kill me yourself."

His mouth curved into a slight grin. "Maybe," he conceded.

"I don't blame you," she said. "I can't imagine being locked up for crimes I didn't commit."

"You believe that now?" he asked. "Because I still see doubts in your eyes." But he wasn't looking at her. He was focused on the contents of the box instead.

She nodded and admitted, "I have doubts." About the kind of man he had become, about what he was capable of. And now she had something else to doubt. "I overheard what you told Rowe."

His broad shoulders tensed, but he didn't look up from the files he'd pulled from the box. "You did?"

She shuddered. "It's not possible. Brandon Henderson can't be alive."

"It's possible to fake your own death," Jed said. "Rowe did it when his cover was blown in Blackwoods, and we had a lot less time to plan his escape than Brandon had to plan his."

"Escape?" she repeated. "What would Brandon need to escape from?" The man had loved his life and lived it to the fullest, going to the nicest restaurants, owning the fastest cars and wearing the most expensive tailored suits.

"Embezzlement charges," Jed replied. "When I was deployed for that year, he must have started embezzling from our clients."

She nodded with sudden understanding of Brandon's motive. "And he would know that you would figure out what he had done when you returned. And that you would turn him in."

Jedidiah Kleyn had been the kind of man who would always do the right thing. Was he still that kind of man?

"I think he was counting on me not coming back," Jed said.

She gasped. "He didn't think you would make it home from Afghanistan?"

She hadn't been the only one to think that he was never coming back. But then, in her experience, people didn't come back for her once they'd left her…

Jed nodded. "That was probably when he decided to start siphoning money from my clients' accounts."

"Because he had a scapegoat for the embezzlement charges that would eventually be filed when the clients discovered their money missing," she said, following how Brandon's twisted mind would have worked. "But how could he frame you when you were gone…"

She joined him at the table, stepping away from the

fire; it wasn't warming her. "How could he make it look like you were responsible?"

"Because he started when I got my orders—when I was still home but distracted." He glanced up at her, as if she were to blame for his being distracted. But he had broken up with her.

He hadn't even given her the chance to find the courage to wait for him. If he'd given her any indication that he'd shared her feelings, she might have become brave...

He returned his attention to one of the files. "And he was tapping my clients, the accounts that I thought I was the only one who could access."

"Are you sure it was him?" she asked.

"You think it was me again?" he asked, his voice gruff with frustration. "You think I embezzled that money but hired Marcus as my lawyer? I knew he wasn't the most competent representation, but he was a friend. He was also all I could afford."

In the end, Marcus Leighton had cost him much more than money, though. He had cost Jed his reputation and three years of his life and maybe more if they couldn't find any evidence to clear him.

She knelt on the floor beside him and reached for the files. "Can I help?"

"You've already done more than you should have," Jed said. "I shouldn't involve you anymore."

"It's too late." She had been too involved even before he'd broken out of prison and shown up at her door flashing a DEA badge.

As she knelt beside him, he reached out and grabbed her hand. "I'm sorry. I'll do everything I can so no charges are pressed against you for aiding and abetting. I don't know if anyone will believe me, but I'll swear that I coerced you, that I threatened you."

"It's my own fault," she admitted although she was touched that he would try to take the blame and risk more charges against him. "I shouldn't have insisted on going along with you to Leighton's. I shouldn't have stowed away in the car at the hangar."

"Why did you?"

"For Isobel," she assured him, so that he didn't worry that she was falling for him. It was enough that she worry. "She deserves to have a father."

"I'm not sure how this will all turn out," he cautioned her. "Even if I'm cleared of the murder charges, I will face other charges for breaking out of prison."

"So, no matter what, you're going to have to go back?" She should have realized as much, but she'd just been focused on learning the truth of what had happened three years ago. She hadn't thought about current charges. So no matter what, Isobel would be denied a relationship with her father.

Disappointment overwhelmed Erica, and she realized she wasn't upset just for her daughter. But she didn't want a relationship with Jed, though.

He had already broken her heart more than once; she knew better than to ever risk it on him again. Especially now, knowing that he wouldn't truly be free even if he was cleared of the murder charges.

"I don't know how long they'll give me for breaking out," he said. "It won't be as long as a murder sentence. I will get out again."

"That'll only happen if you're still alive," she said. And if Brandon was alive, if he stayed alive and Jed didn't kill him when he caught up with him. Or Jed would wind up serving time for murder. Even if he didn't kill Brandon, he might be charged with killing his lawyer and the other witness. It didn't matter that he was innocent; a case could still be made against him, just as it had in the murders of Brandon and the police officer.

"I survived three years in Blackwoods—"

"Back at the witness's house those cops were all shooting at you." And her. But she couldn't remember that or she would start trembling in reaction. She had held it together during their ordeal, but exhaustion undermined the strength she hadn't known she had.

"That's because they think I'm a cop killer," he said. "That's why I need to prove it wasn't me."

"It was Brandon?"

"You don't think he's alive?" he asked, studying her face again as if trying to gauge if she thought he was crazy for even considering it.

She shrugged. "I don't know what to believe about anything anymore." She had spent the past three years believing an innocent man guilty. She could have also spent three years believing a live man dead.

"Help me find proof then," he said, and he passed her a file folder.

After going through that one, she grabbed another and another. Reading through printed ledgers and bank statements, her eyelids drooped, growing almost too heavy to keep open. Maybe if she closed them for just a moment…

She jerked awake, disoriented from a sense of weightlessness and moving, almost as if she were flying, through a dark room. She opened her lips to utter the scream choking her.

"It's okay," Jed assured her. "I'm bringing you to bed."

Her pulse quickened and then raced.

"You're exhausted," he said.

"But I didn't find anything to help you. I need to keep looking over the statements," she protested, struggling in his arms.

He lowered her to a soft mattress. "You're not going to find anything. The son of a bitch covered his tracks very well. The transfers from my client accounts all went into my account."

"But the money isn't there anymore."

"It sure as hell isn't," he replied with a bitter chuckle. "There was a transfer to an untraceable, offshore account."

Purpose reinvigorated her, chasing away her drowsiness. "We need to find that bank and get proof that the account belongs to Brandon."

Jed shook his head. "Those banks constantly change their routing and transit numbers to hide their assets as well as their clients' assets. We're not going to track them down."

"And we're not going to track down Brandon." She shivered. "He's going to track down us."

Rowe's safe house wouldn't stay safe long—not if Brandon was really still alive and hell-bent on protecting himself. He had already fired at them in the woods. What would he do to them here?

"I won't let him hurt you," Jed promised. "I'll protect you." He stepped back, but before he could turn toward the door, she reached for him.

She clutched his hand. "Who will protect me from you?" she asked because Erica was afraid that she was going to fall for him again, and he had already broken her heart too many times.

He shook his head. "I'm sorry about earlier—about taking advantage of you…"

"I'm not," she admitted. "And you didn't take advantage of me."

He had given her the chance to change her mind, but she'd wanted him too much. Then. And now.

She tugged him down onto the bed with her.

"Erica, this is a bad idea," he warned her. "I told you that I'll have to go back to jail. We have no future."

"I know," she assured him. And maybe that was why she wanted to make love with him so badly—because she didn't know if she would ever be this close to him again. She didn't have to worry about her heart; she didn't have to worry if she should trust him.

She only had to worry about holding on to her heart tonight.

"You deserve more," he said.

"I have more," she assured him. "I have Isobel." Their daughter was all she needed in her life.

The little girl was safe; Macy had assured her of that earlier. And she had believed it when she'd talked to Isobel. While the little girl had missed her mommy, she had also been thrilled to be getting to know her fun, new aunt.

If only Isobel would be able to get to know her father, too…

But Jed was right; there hadn't been any clues left in those ledgers and bank statements. Nothing to clear his name, nothing to point to Brandon's guilt or his present whereabouts if he really wasn't six feet under.

Jed expelled a ragged breath. "You are so beautiful," he murmured, "whenever you talk about our daughter, you glow…like an angel…"

She didn't feel like an angel tonight. She reached for the bottom of her sweater and dragged it up and over her head. She tossed it onto the floor, and then she un-clasped her bra.

Jed groaned now. "Damn, woman…"

He followed her lead but shucked off all his clothes and then dragged her jeans down her legs. He kissed her everywhere, taking his time first with her mouth. He pressed hot kisses to her lips and then parted them for his tongue. He kissed her deeply.

She arched against him and moaned, wanting all of him. Pressure built inside her, making her ache for him. But he was pulling back to kiss her shoulders, the inside of her elbow, the curve of her hip. He dipped his tongue inside her navel and then moved it lower. She lifted off the bed. "Jed!"

He made love to her thoroughly until tears streaked from her eyes as the pressure wound tighter, then re-leased in a rush of pleasure. "Jed!"

He parted her legs and thrust inside, joining their bodies as their hearts would never be joined. Except that, as she clutched him close, she felt his heart beat-ing in perfect, frantic rhythm with hers. It was as if they shared one heart, one body.

He kissed her passionately, as he thrust deep inside her. She arched and clutched at him, digging her nails into his back and then lower, into his butt.

He groaned. "I can't—" His control snapped and he came, filling her.

And she joined him, her scream of ecstasy echoing his shout. She didn't let go, didn't let him go, but fell asleep holding him close…until she wouldn't be able to hold him anymore…

A RINGING NOISE JERKED Jed awake. He hadn't heard a phone ring in three years, but he recognized the sound and fumbled for the phone that lay atop his jeans beside the bed. He glanced at the woman lying beside him. Maybe she slept as soundly as their daughter because she didn't so much as shift or murmur over the noise or his moving beside her.

He had to pull his arm out from under her. It tingled, asleep even from her slight weight. He slipped out of bed and took the phone with him out to the living room. Studying the high-tech screen on the cellular, he pushed a button but didn't say anything.

"Jed?"

He grunted as he recognized Rowe's voice. "Yeah…"

"Sounds like I woke you up," the DEA agent mused. "I didn't think you would be able to sleep."

If not for making love with Erica, he wouldn't have been able to close his eyes…not without the fear of seeing Brandon's face.

"I haven't slept since I broke out," he admitted. "Actually not since the riot started."

"Guess you haven't had a safe place to sleep until tonight," Rowe remarked.

"I have to wonder how safe any place is," Jed said. "It's him, isn't it?"

"Yes!" Rowe said with triumph. "I had an FBI tech rush the DNA report from the old crime-scene evidence. We got what we need to get a new trial, Jed!"

"I don't want a new trial," he said. "I want justice. He's not dead?" Yet.

"It wasn't Brandon Henderson in the burned-out vehicle," Rowe confirmed. "The dental records used at the trial were obviously fakes."

"Why wasn't DNA used then?" Jed wondered.

"It was ordered but the results weren't back before the trial," Rowe said. "And your lawyer agreed with the

D.A. that the dental records were confirmation enough of the dead body's identity."

Jed cursed Marcus and himself for so blindly trusting him. Hell, he'd trusted Brandon, too—not much but enough to go into business with the man. Brandon Henderson had been smart and ambitious; Jed had had no doubt that theirs would be a successful firm.

He just hadn't realized exactly how smart and ambitious Brandon was.

And how criminal…

"You could have had a new trial at any time," Rowe said, the triumph replaced with the hard edge of anger, "if anyone had bothered to follow up about the DNA."

"I don't want a new trial," Jed repeated.

"But just because Brandon wasn't in the car doesn't make him the killer."

"Bullshit," Jed replied, his frustration growing. "If he wasn't the killer, why hasn't he come forward before now?"

"He came forward in the woods today," Rowe said. "There were shells found from a gun that wasn't police issue."

"So shouldn't that help clear me or at least get the shoot-on-sight order rescinded?"

Rowe cursed now. "Those unidentified shells prove to the police that you're armed and dangerous because they think that gun was yours. I have to bring you in, Jed. Or you'll get shot for sure. But until we can get that new trial, the DNA evidence will be enough to cast doubt on your convictions. You'll be safer now."

"No." He wouldn't be safe until Brandon was six feet under for real. The man had gone to a lot of trouble to take away from Jed everything that had mattered to him—his reputation, his freedom.

Erica...

He glanced toward the bedroom and jumped when he noticed her leaning against the doorjamb. She was wearing his shirt with only half the buttons done up, displaying her slender legs and the hollow between her full breasts. His body hardened again, wanting her.

Rowe was still talking. "I'm not giving you a choice, man. I'm going to be back there in a couple of hours, and I'm bringing you in."

"No," Jed repeated. Instead of arguing with him, he just clicked off the cell. He wouldn't be there by the time Rowe arrived.

"No?" Erica asked. "It wasn't him?"

"It wasn't him in the car," Jed confirmed.

She sucked in a sharp breath of air and fear. "So Brandon's still alive?"

He nodded. *For now.*

"Do you know where he is?" she asked.

He forced a shrug. But he knew. Brandon was waiting for him. Just like Jed, he would have realized that it was time for them to end this. Their rivalry had begun in elementary school and had lasted too damn long. Jed had always considered it a healthy, competitive rivalry that had made them both stronger and more successful.

That hadn't been the case. It hadn't been healthy for either of them, or for anyone who had come into contact with them. Erica had been hurt. Marcus Leighton and the witnesses were all dead...

"You know where he is," Erica said, with that insight into him that no one but Macy had ever had. "And you intend to kill him."

He had to kill Brandon before the man killed him. Or worse yet—her and Isobel.

DESPITE THE LATE HOUR, the jail was alive—excitement dancing in the air and in Jefferson's lawyer's eyes. Something had happened.

Hopefully something good for him.

"Looks like the DEA agent may have been right about Kleyn," Breuker remarked. He drummed his fingers against his briefcase. "A source informed me that the agent rushed DNA from the old crime scene."

"It wasn't Kleyn's?"

"It wasn't the man he was accused of killing—his business partner."

He choked out a laugh at the irony. "He faked his death…" Like Kleyn had talked an undercover agent into faking his to save his life.

But this wasn't good news for Jefferson. Having an innocent man testify against him would be so much worse than having a convicted killer…

"This is bad news," he pointed out, wondering at his lawyer's excitement. Maybe the man wasn't as brilliant as his reputation claimed, just as Jed Kleyn hadn't been as ruthless as his.

"York and Ketchum are having a big powwow right now," Breuker shared. "Something's going down…"

"A showdown," Jefferson mused.

Kleyn might have been an innocent man when he'd been sentenced to Blackwoods, but three years there had stolen away that innocence and his humanity.

"He's going to want revenge."

"And his partner's going to want to protect himself…"

Jefferson laughed again as the lawyer's excitement

tingled in his veins. "Sounds like they might wind up killing each other…"

And that would be very good news for Jefferson James.

## Chapter Seventeen

Erica shivered at the coldness on Jed's handsome face. He hadn't denied her accusation. He fully intended to kill Brandon Henderson.

She had been right not to give him her heart. He wasn't the man she had once known and loved. Maybe Afghanistan hadn't changed him, but Brandon's betrayal and Blackwoods Penitentiary had.

"How can you just kill a man in cold blood?" she asked, horrified.

He laughed. "You think it'll be in cold blood? I think it'll be in self-defense."

Erica shook her head, denying his claim. "No. You know where he is. You don't have to go there to meet him. Call Rowe back. Tell him where he can find Brandon. He'll bring him in alive."

"He won't know if it's Brandon or not. The guy's changed his appearance," Jed reminded her. "Rowe won't recognize him from some old photograph."

He was probably right; Brandon was too smart to waltz back into the country looking like his old, *dead* self. "Then go with Rowe. Point Brandon out, but stay out of it."

"Brandon took away three years of my life. He broke into your house, probably to abduct our daughter, and then he shot at us," he said, listing the man's recent crimes. "I'm not giving him the chance to take anything else away from me."

She laughed now, just as he had, with irony and bitterness. "If you kill him, he'll take away your humanity and your honor."

"He took that away when I got locked up in hell three years ago."

Yes. Blackwoods had changed him.

"I'm going with you," she insisted, turning for the bedroom to grab her clothes.

Jed followed her in and grabbed up his clothes, too. He pulled on his jeans and shirt and then lifted the gun from the floor.

God, why had Rowe given him a gun?

"You're not going with me," he said. He didn't point the gun at her, but there was something threatening about just the way he held it, staring down at the trigger as if he could pull it with his gaze since his finger was nowhere near it.

"You're not going to shoot me," she said, calling his unspoken bluff.

"Why not?" he asked. "According to you, I'm a cold-blooded killer." He stared at her now instead of at the gun, but his dark eyes weren't cold. They were full of emotion—anger and hurt.

"Not yet," she said. "But if you confront Brandon alone, you're going to become one."

"You're not coming along," he insisted. "I don't want you anywhere near Brandon ever again."

The man had tried to use her before to hurt Jed; he would undoubtedly have no qualms about using her again. "I don't want to be anywhere near him," she admitted. "And I don't want you near him, either. I want you to wait for Rowe."

He shook his head. "I can't. I've waited three years for justice, Erica. I can't wait any longer." He shoved the gun into the waistband of his jeans at his back as he turned for the door.

She reached for his arm, trying to hold him back. Muscles bulged and rippled beneath her grasp, and he gently shook her off. But he stopped in the doorway and faced her again.

Maybe she'd gotten through to him. Maybe he'd changed his mind about meeting Brandon alone. She breathed a slight sigh of relief.

Then he stole her breath with a kiss. It was deep and full of passion and promise. She closed her eyes and smiled, grateful that he had changed his mind.

For her?

Did he want to be the man she had once fallen for, the man she had once loved?

He lifted his mouth from hers and stepped back because she couldn't feel the heat of his body anymore.

"Jed…" She opened her eyes. But she didn't see his face. She only saw wood as the door snapped shut between them. She reached for the knob, grabbing it, but it wouldn't budge.

He was either holding it, or he must have shoved something beneath it, because moments later an engine revved.

Tears stung her eyes. "Damn you, Jed…"

He might have had to go back to prison because of the escape. But he wouldn't have had to serve much time—not what he would have to serve for murder.

Isobel would never get to know her father. And Erica would be left with only a few memories of her passionate lover. He would never be anything more to her, never be part of her future—only a bittersweet part of her past.

No. They all deserved more than that; they all deserved a future. He might have jammed the door, but he hadn't had time to lock the window. She crossed the room to it and lifted the sash. The ground dropped off below, moonlight shimmering on the rocky hillside. If she tried going out that way, Brandon Henderson might not be the only one who died tonight...

*SOMEONE WAS GOING to die tonight.*

Unlike Erica, Jed wasn't as convinced that he could pull the trigger and take a life. He had the reasons and the rage to want to. It wouldn't be in cold blood, as Erica had said, that he would kill. It would be in hot blood.

Anger heated his body, so that he didn't notice the cold wind blowing around as he walked down the ramp leading to the basement of the parking garage. This was where he would find Brandon and where he should kill him—since this was the crime scene where he had already been convicted of killing him.

No attendant sat inside the booth. The gates stayed down, so Jed skirted around them. The security lights had been broken out; glass crunched beneath his feet as he strode through the darkness. But moonlight crept over the concrete walls, casting an eerie glow on the cement and shifting the shadows of the few cars parked inside the garage.

"You took your time," a deep voice remarked. "And you're already a man on borrowed time."

His gut tightened with dread. He didn't need to see Brandon's half-assed disguised face. His voice was unmistakable—not just the tone and the timbre of it but the arrogance in it. Nobody else was that damn cocky.

It used to amuse Jed; now it infuriated him…because Brandon was entitled to that arrogance. He had fooled everyone.

Even Jed.

"I've got all the time in the world," he said with a bitter laugh. "You saw to that."

"Two lifetimes." Brandon's perfectly capped teeth flashed brightly in the shadows. "But you're taking a little break right now. It won't last, you know, not with all those cops out looking for you." He laughed. "If they find you, you won't last long at all."

Jed yawned as if bored with Brandon. The man had always prided himself on being everything but boring. "That's old news now. I'm old news. The hot new story is how you faked your own death."

"Good luck proving that."

"DNA came back." Probably years ago. "It proves that yours wasn't the body in the car."

Brandon snorted, dismissing the evidence. "That doesn't prove that I'm alive and well."

"Oh, you're not well at all," Jed agreed. "You're bat-shit crazy, my old friend."

Brandon laughed again but with genuine humor this time. "I have missed you, my old friend," he said, turning Jed's words back on him. "You always entertained me."

"I always annoyed the hell out of you," Jed corrected him, "because you could never be better than me."

Brandon's voice rose with patronization as he replied, "I think we both know that's not the case anymore."

The son of a bitch was choosing his words carefully,

as he always had. He had always managed just enough charm to hide the fact that he was actually a psychopath.

"You ruined my life," Jed admitted. "But I'm thinking you ruined your own life, too."

"How's that?"

"You're not *you* anymore," he scoffed. He wasn't talking about the blond dye or the colored contacts and the unkempt goatee, although those were all things macho Brandon Henderson would have mocked.

"Fishing for my new name?" Brandon laughed at his attempt. "Fish away…"

"Your name meant something to you," Jed reminded him, striking out at the only place Brandon felt anything—his pride. "You wanted everyone to know it. But no one remembers the first murder victim from my trial. They remember the officer who died too young in the line of duty."

Brandon snorted. "Line of duty or wrong place at the wrong time?"

"I guess only the young officer himself would know that, and of course, the man who really killed him would know…"

"I guess," Brandon conceded without really conceding anything at all.

"But the thing people remember most from my trial is *me*. It's *my* name everyone remembers," Jed taunted him. "It's *me* everyone talks about." And he'd hated that so much. But Brandon wouldn't understand that; he'd never cared about what people said about him as long as he was all they talked about…

Brandon's wide shoulders moved in the shadows in a jerky shrug—his nonchalance totally feigned. His pride was stinging as well as that resentment of Jed that he'd never quite been able to hide or control. He struck back at Jed with, "That must drive you crazy—that everyone talks about how the hero became a villain."

"At least they're talking about *me*. You're entirely forgotten, my friend. I think even you have forgotten who you are." He tsked his tongue against the roof of his mouth, pouring on the pity.

"I know who I am," Brandon insisted. "You're the one who's lost himself. You've totally changed."

"Yes. I have," Jed conceded. "I wasn't a killer when you framed me for your murder and that young officer's murder."

Brandon snorted again. "But you are a killer now?"

Jed lifted his gun. "I will be."

"You want a third life sentence?"

"I can't be convicted of your murder again," Jed reminded him. "That would be double jeopardy." He moved his finger to the trigger and prepared to squeeze.

"No!" a female voice screamed. Panting for breath, Erica ran into the parking garage as if she'd run all the way from the lake. "Don't do it, Jed. Don't kill him."

"Damn it! Get out of here!" he yelled at her. His heart hammered against his ribs. Even knowing what a monster Brandon really was, he hadn't been afraid for himself.

But Erica...

Before she could run back the way she'd run in, Brandon grabbed her. He locked his arm around her torso, trapping her arms against her sides, and then he pressed a gun to her temple.

Erica's eyes widened with fear. She hadn't thought her action through—hadn't realized the danger she was putting herself in...

Jed had known the man would be armed and ready and that he would be waiting for just this opportunity.

Brandon wanted to kill Jed but not before he made him suffer more.

"Don't hurt her," he pleaded.

"You're the one who keeps hurting her," Brandon said. "You dumped her before you left for Afghanistan."

"I didn't want to do that," Jed said. "But I didn't want her waiting for me."

"Yeah, you were being self-sacrificing and heroic," Brandon said with heavy disgust.

"I was scared," Jed admitted. "I didn't think I was coming home."

Brandon sighed. "Yes, I thought you were going to die over there, too."

"That's why you started embezzling from my accounts." He wasn't just trying to get him talking now; he was trying to figure out how to distract him so that he could get Erica out of danger.

Brandon glanced around the parking garage, as if looking for witnesses. Maybe the police officer would have still been alive if Brandon had done that the last time he'd been in this garage.

"Come on," Jed said. "You're going to kill her. I'm going to kill you. Before you go down, you may get a shot off that eventually kills me. Don't you think I deserve to know the truth before I die?"

Brandon chuckled. "That must have been the worst thing about your three years in prison—not knowing who put you there or why."

"Was it because of me?" Erica asked, her voice trembling with fear. "Did you want to put Jed away because you wanted me?"

Brandon laughed heartily now. "You think I was in love with you?"

The man was a narcissist; he loved no one but himself. That was why his former girlfriend and witness for the prosecution was dead; he hadn't needed her. He hadn't ever needed anyone. If only Jed had realized that before he'd agreed to become the man's business partner…

"I was just using you to get to him," Brandon admitted.

"Like now," Jed said.

"But I wouldn't marry you. I only went out with you to feel close to Jed," she said, "so we could talk about him."

Brandon groaned. "I know. Everything's always been about Jed. All my life. My parents were so damn impressed with him. Our teachers. Our clients. Everything was about brilliant, honorable Jedidiah Kleyn."

"So you weren't in love with me," she said, "you were in hate with Jed."

"To frame me for murder—your murder—and send me to prison, you really have to hate me," Jed said.

"Hate is too mild a word for what I feel for you, my old friend," Brandon admitted, the words surging forth as his control finally snapped. "I thought it would be enough to destroy your reputation, to send you to prison, but it's not…"

"What about the money?" Jed asked. "Hasn't that made you happy? You embezzled nearly a million dollars from my clients."

Brandon shrugged, his grip loosening slightly around Erica. Instead of taking advantage, though, and struggling, she stood perfectly still, as if hoping the man would forget all about her. Maybe, with his focus so completely on Jed, he would.

"It was more than a million," Brandon boasted. "And I've doubled that since. I'm a very wealthy man."

"Isn't that enough?" Jed asked. "I'm in prison and you're rich."

"You weren't supposed to last in prison," Brandon said, "just like you weren't supposed to last in Afghanistan."

"You wanted me dead so that I wouldn't eventually figure it out," Jed realized.

"I wanted you dead so I didn't have to keep hearing about you," Brandon said, nearly gagging on the admission as if just the thought of Jed made him physically sick.

"You stayed around here?" Jed asked.

"No, but I stayed in touch with Marcus, making sure that no new evidence came up that would get you off on an appeal."

"That had to be expensive," Jed mused. "Marcus was always very nervous. You would have had to keep paying him to keep him quiet. Is that why you finally killed him?"

"I should have killed him years ago," Brandon admitted.

"Like you killed the woman?"

His bright teeth flashed again. "That was a suicide."

"It was murder. And if you'd killed Leighton, the authorities might have figured out it was strange that everyone from my trial was dying."

"Especially while you were prison," Brandon agreed.

"So you would have had no one to blame for Marcus's murder. Or the other witness's."

Brandon's teeth flashed in another grin. "You breaking out of prison really helped me tie up the loose ends I had to leave after the last murders."

"And what about me and Erica now?" Jed asked. "What are we?"

Brandon shrugged. "Just more loose ends…"

Jed had never hated the man more than he did right now. How could he dismiss Erica Towsley—who was a loving, devoted mother—as nothing more than a loose end?

If only Jed could get the shot…

But even though Brandon had loosened his grip around Erica, he still held the gun pressed against her temple with his finger right on the trigger. If Jed took the shot and missed, she was dead. If Jed took the shot and hit him, she might still be dead; Brandon could pull the trigger as a reflex before he died.

JED WAS DYING TO KILL HIM. Brandon could see the hatred in his eyes as he studied his options, trying to determine if he dared to take a shot.

He wasn't the man Brandon was. He wouldn't dare. He cared too much about the woman to risk her life. So, soon Jed would just be dying.

All these years of anticipation and it might be over this quick? Brandon wanted to savor the moment, wanted to taunt him a little bit more. He leaned forward and pressed his face into the woman's hair.

Erica shuddered as if in revulsion.

"Oh, come on, honey," he said. "Don't act like you don't like it when I touch you. You went out with me after this guy dumped you. You wanted to see what a real man was all about."

Jed's darkly stubbled jaw tensed, a muscle twitching in his cheek.

"If only I had time to show you now," Brandon teased. "You would forget all about this guy—just like you did before. But I don't have time."

He had a private plane to catch, to bring him back to

the island with no extradition treaty where he had spent most of the past three years. He hadn't trusted Marcus or the witness not to eventually give him up.

But when he'd heard about Jed's escape, he'd had to return. The opportunity had been too good to pass up.

Brandon figured either Jed or the woman had some kind of recorder, taping his confession. That was why Jed had kept him talking instead of just killing him the minute he had stepped into the parking garage.

If Jed had stolen three years of his life, his money and his reputation, Brandon would have killed him the minute he'd seen him. Jed cared more about honor than revenge. His very integrity would be what finally destroyed him completely, though.

Brandon would just kill them both and check them for recording devices, probably Jed was using the voice recorder on his cell phone. Brandon would destroy that and then no one would ever know the truth.

"I really appreciate you making this easy for me," he told them. "Your showing up here, Erica, makes it all so easy to stage another double murder. Or should I say murder, suicide."

He grinned as his new plan took shape and taunted them with the details. "Jed here is going to kill himself before going back to prison, and because he doesn't want any other man to have you, he's going to kill you, Erica, before he takes his own life…in the very same spot where he committed those murders three years ago."

"Who was he?" Jed asked.

He snapped at the inane interruption. "Who?"

"The man you passed off as yourself," Jed reminded him. "The man you murdered and then burned his body to pass off as yours."

Brandon sighed. "Enough with the questions. It doesn't matter anymore. You're not going to prove your innocence. And you're not going to stall me until help arrives." He laughed at his own joke. "Help? You have no one who can help you."

He must have just imagined that Jed'd had help to escape the woods because if he'd had someone there, the guy would have been here already. He wouldn't have let him walk into the parking garage alone, and he certainly wouldn't have let Erica run between two armed men—especially if it was the DEA agent, the only person besides Jed's sister who had expressed belief in his innocence.

"Everybody hates you now," he reminded Jed. "Your parents, your clients—everyone who thought you were such a hero has forsaken you. Even you…" He pressed a kiss to Erica's temple where he didn't hold the gun. "You doubted him. You believed he was a killer."

"I didn't… I wouldn't have…" she stammered, "but Marcus convinced me."

He snorted in derision. "Marcus never made a compelling argument in his life. You doubted Jed because you didn't trust him then. And you don't trust him now or you wouldn't have shown up here. So I guess you really have no one, Jed, not even the woman you love…"

He cocked the gun. It was time to pull the trigger—time to end all this nonsense and get back to paradise.

# Chapter Eighteen

"You've been so brave," Macy praised her niece, keeping her voice bright and happy.

Over the phone, Erica had calmed her daughter's fears but for just a short while. The little girl must have felt the same awful sense of foreboding that gripped Macy. Something bad was going to happen.

Lives were going to be lost—futures destroyed.

And Macy was helpless to do anything to prevent the pending tragedy. She had accepted her role in this horrible play when she'd promised Erica to keep the little girl safe. As she pulled her car up outside the parking garage, she realized that Erica probably wouldn't consider this the best way to protect the child.

She wasn't bringing her into the line of fire. But they would be able to hear shots from here. They'd be able to know when it was over…just not whose lives were over…

CHOKING ON FEAR, ERICA HELD her breath. It wasn't supposed to go like this, but then nothing had gone according to her plan since she had first met Jedidiah Kleyn. She'd been applying for a job and wound up with a boyfriend. But she hadn't kept him.

She had already known that she wouldn't be able to

keep him now. But she hadn't suspected that she was the one who might wind up dead. Of course it should have occurred to her, since she'd run out between two men holding guns on each other.

But still…it wasn't supposed to go like this.

The look on Jed's face would haunt her…for however long she lived. Fear and horror darkened his eyes even more, so that they looked more black than brown.

"I'm sorry." She mouthed the words to him as he'd once mouthed them to her. And she flinched, waiting for the bullet to strike. That little scalpel she carried wouldn't protect her now. Before she could unsheathe it and stab Brandon, she would be dead.

"You're wrong," Jed told Brandon.

The guy laughed. "This should be good. What am I wrong about? Are you going to try to save her? Going to try to hit me? Your bullet won't be able to hit me before mine tears her brain apart."

Erica shivered at the coldness of Brandon's voice. She had once been taken in by his charm. Not enough to fall for him but enough to go out with him even though she had already been in love with another man.

"You're wrong that I have no friends," Jed informed him. "That I have no one to help me."

Brandon lifted the gun slightly away from her head and glanced around. "I don't see anyone else here. It's just the three of us. For the moment."

"You're not looking hard enough," Jed advised him. "Look harder…"

"We're right here," a raspy voice added, and Rowe stepped from the shadows behind Brandon, his gun trained on the madman's head.

"And if Kleyn and Cusack aren't able to get off a shot

fast enough to save Ms. Towsley, I sure as hell will," added another male voice.

Erica glanced up to where Sheriff York stood on the parking level above them, a sniper rifle trained on Brandon's forehead. And if he doubted the man, he would only have to look in a mirror to see the red laser mark between his eyes.

Brandon sucked in a breath of shock and fear.

"It's over," Jed informed him. "They heard everything."

"And we had the D.A.'s approval to record it," the sheriff added. "In fact he's been listening in the entire time…"

Brandon's breath escaped in a gasp and a curse. "Son of a bitch…"

Erica didn't relax. It might be over according to Jed and the lawmen. But Brandon was used to calling the shots. He was used to having things go his way. He wasn't likely to go out how these men wanted him—in handcuffs—but in a blaze of glory. And he would take her with him, caught in the crossfire.

She saw that same fear in Jed's eyes as he waited, his gun still trained on Brandon.

They might all die yet.

But then Brandon lowered his weapon and stepped back. Obviously he hadn't wanted to die for real. "Goddamn you, Jed. I thought I'd taken you down. Finally. I'd thought you lost."

"If it makes you feel any better," Jed told him as Rowe slapped cuffs around the man's wrists, "you took away three years of my life that I'll never get back. Three years of time I could have spent with my daughter."

Three years of time he could have spent with her.

Erica wanted to tell him that, but he wasn't looking at her. Until Rowe led Brandon away, reading him his rights. Then Jed walked up and grabbed her, shaking her gently.

"What the hell were you thinking, woman?" he asked, his voice cracking with rage and residual fear for her safety. "You almost got yourself killed."

"She was never in any danger," the sheriff assured Jed as he dismantled his weapon and returned it to the case in which he'd carried it. "From the way he was answering your questions, it was clear Henderson suspected it was a setup. He wasn't saying anything that the D.A. could use against him in court."

"But Brandon would never believe that I would let you be part of the trap to catch him." Jed clenched his hands on her shoulders. "And he was right to believe that. I never would have gone back for you if I thought you would put yourself in danger."

He had gone back for her, though. But not just her— he had waited for Rowe, who had brought in the sheriff of Blackwoods County. Together, with guidance from the Blackwoods district attorney, they had concocted their plan to bring Brandon to the justice he had eluded for far too long.

She had never been part of that plan until the sheriff and Rowe had realized Brandon was never going to implicate himself until he was certain Jed wasn't trapping him. Both men had assured her of her safety before she'd run into the garage.

And she had felt safe in the bulletproof vest she wore beneath her jacket—until Brandon had pressed the gun to her head. Then she'd felt stupid and reckless. "You're right," she agreed. "I shouldn't have gotten involved."

"Remember, it got us what we need to overturn your

murder convictions," the sheriff said as he came down from the higher level of the parking garage.

"But nothing Brandon said will get rid of the charges against me for breaking out of prison," Jed said. With a heavy sigh, he turned around—presenting the sheriff with his back, his wrists linked behind him for the cuffs.

A squeal of "Mommy" drew Erica's attention to the entrance to the parking garage. The little girl, still clad in her pajamas and bare feet, ran across the concrete.

Macy followed closely behind her. Rowe must have told her about their plan. "She got away from me. She really wanted to see you."

Erica caught the little girl up in her arms, holding her close. Her daughter had almost lost her mother. And she would lose her father. Not for life but for however long a judge sentenced him for the prison break.

"And I wanted to see you," Macy said, as she reached for her brother.

Jed hugged his sister tightly. But he stared over her head at Isobel, his eyes full of longing. He glanced back at the sheriff. "Is it okay if I spend a little time with my daughter before you take me back to Blackwoods County?"

He'd broken out of prison there, so no doubt he needed to return to the local jail in the county where he'd broken the law.

The sheriff nodded. "Your friend will be turned in to the police department here since this is where he committed his crimes."

His murders. Several innocent people had lost their lives over one man's greed and envy. Jed tensed, as if the same thought had occurred to him, but instead of blaming Brandon, he seemed to be blaming himself.

"He was never Jed's friend," Macy said.

"No," Jed agreed. "I've trusted people I shouldn't have." He glanced at Erica now.

Her stomach clenched with regret. She hadn't betrayed him as he had believed for the past three years. But her believing the worst about him was a betrayal, too. And she had done that more than once.

She wanted to apologize again, but she worried that it was too late for that. That it was already too late for them.

"I'm trusting you to come out to where the cars are parked in the alley," Sheriff York told Jed.

"I'm done running," Jed said. "I'll be out in just a few minutes."

"I'm going back to talk to my fiancé," Macy said. "I'll see if he can do something about the charges for escaping prison. Maybe he can talk to someone…" She hurried out after the sheriff.

Erica faced her sleepy-eyed daughter. "Honey, this is your father."

The little girl blinked thick lashes at her, totally confused.

"This man." She couldn't look at him when she confessed all to her daughter. "My friend Jed—he is your father. Your daddy."

Isobel turned to him for confirmation, her chocolate-brown eyes wide with shock and awe. "You're my daddy?"

Jed's throat muscles rippled as he swallowed, as if choked with emotion. "Yes, honey, I am your daddy." He held out his arms for her.

But she hung back a moment, no doubt overwhelmed with the new information. "I—I have a daddy?"

"Yes," Erica assured the little girl, sick with guilt that she had never told the child about her father.

She continued, "And he wants to spend some time with you, honey."

Before he had to go back to jail...

Erica handed Isobel over to Jed's outstretched arms and turned to leave the garage.

"Wait," he said. "Stay with us."

Either he was nervous alone with the little girl or he was concerned that the little girl would be nervous alone with him. Either reason had Erica's heart warm with love for him. Watching him with their child made her see what kind of man he really was, the man he had always been: gentle, honest and affectionate.

She had to say it—this time aloud. "I'm sorry."

"I know it wasn't your idea to interrupt my meeting with Brandon," Jed replied, absolving her of any care-lessness and stupidity. "I know you thought you were perfectly safe."

She shook her head. "No. I'm sorry about..." She glanced at their daughter, who had affectionately snuggled her head into the crook of Jed's shoulder and neck. "I'm sorry that I didn't believe in you like I should have."

"Why should you have?" he asked.

Because she loved him. But she couldn't tell him that now when her mistrust had already ruined any promise they had once had for a future together.

"I should have known better," she said. And now that he and Isobel seemed so comfortable together, she had no reason to stay. She started toward the entrance to the garage.

"I never gave you the chance," he said, again absolving her.

"What?"

"To get to know me," he explained. "I never gave you the chance."

Now, for as many years as he would be locked up, she wouldn't get that chance.

HE HAD NO RIGHT TO STOP HER, so Jed just watched her walk away. Just as he hadn't when he got deployed, he didn't want her waiting for him. His returning from prison was about as likely as his return from Afghanistan had been.

"No." Erica stopped herself with the word and turned back toward him and their daughter.

"No what, Mommy?" the little girl asked, confused about what she might have done wrong.

"No. I'm not going to do this again," she said.

Macy started down the slope of the parking garage toward them. "Jed—"

"I need a minute with your brother," Erica interrupted the young woman. "Isobel, go play with your aunt for a little while. I need to talk to your daddy alone."

The little girl wriggled down from his arms and whispered, "You're in trouble now. That's Mommy's mad face."

A smile tugged at his lips...until he was alone with Erica. The little girl was right; this was her mommy's mad face. Anger tightened Erica's silky lips and hardened the pale blue of her beautiful eyes.

"What's wrong?" he asked.

"I'm not going anywhere."

"No," he agreed. "The sheriff already talked to the D.A. about making sure charges were not pressed against you for aiding and abetting me. Rowe vouched for you. You won't have to worry about yourself or Isobel."

"I'm worried about you."

"I'll be okay," he said. "No place else could ever be as bad as Blackwoods was. I'll survive my time—however long they give me." He didn't dare hope that they'd commute his sentence for the time he had already served for the crimes he hadn't committed. She walked up closer to him and lifted her hands to his shoulders, which she clasped as she pressed her body against his.

"You will survive," she said. "And I'm going to be waiting for you."

"Good," he said, breathing a sigh of relief that she wasn't going to try to deny him time with his daughter once he was done serving his time. "I want to be part of Isobel's life."

"No," she said. "*I* will be waiting for you. I'm not letting you push me away like you did before. I'm going to wait for you to be free."

Even though his heart leapt with the hope she offered him, he shook his head in rejection of her offer. "Erica, I can't ask you to do that."

"Can't or don't want to?" she asked. "Will you ever be able to forgive me for doubting you?"

"It's not so much forgiving as trusting that you won't doubt me again," he admitted.

"I should have talked to you," she said. "I should have gone to the jail where you were being held before your trial and talked to you."

"But Marcus had told you not to," he said. He completely accepted that his lawyer had manipulated her.

"I shouldn't have trusted him over you."

"I trusted him, too," he said with a weary sigh. He hadn't thought Marcus was smart enough to lie, but then he had had Brandon, the master manipulator, coaching him. "We both made mistakes."

"Then don't make another one," she warned him. "Don't push me away if you really want me."

He couldn't have her putting her life on hold any more now than he had been able to years ago. She was a mother; she and her daughter needed more than he could offer them. So he gripped her shoulders and gently pushed her back. "Go…"

She blinked, as if fighting back tears. "I hope you're pushing me away because you can't forgive me and not because you think you're doing what's best for me. Thinking that you hate me or that you don't want me—" her voice cracked with emotion "—that isn't what's best for me. That hurts me."

And hurting her hurt him; pain clutched his heart. He loved her. He had always loved her. That was why he wanted more for her than him.

"I can't…" he murmured, unable to say more.

"Can't forgive me?" She nodded in response to her own question before he could even form a reply. "I don't blame you. I can't forgive myself."

As she turned for the entrance again, where his sister and daughter waited just beyond hearing, he reached out. Grabbing her arm, he whirled her back to him and pulled her into his arms. "I can't let you go again."

Her breath escaped in a shaky gasp of surprise. "Jed…"

"I love you, Erica," he said, finally declaring the feelings he had denied for far too long, "so I should be unselfish. I shouldn't ask you to wait for me, but…"

"I would anyway," she said. "I waited when you went to Afghanistan, and without even knowing it, I waited while you were in prison. There has never been anyone else for me but you."

He lowered his mouth and took hers in a deep, possessive kiss. Her lips parted as if she breathed him in, as if she needed him for air. As if she needed him as he needed her.

"I love you, Jed," she said. "And that's why I never should have doubted you."

"Maybe that's why you did," he said. "Because your love made you vulnerable and scared." He held her closely. "You never need to be again. I will come home to you and Isobel. I will come back."

"You never have to go away," Macy said, her face flushing with embarrassment at getting caught eavesdropping.

Jed flashed back to all the times, while they were growing up, that his pesky little sister had barged in on him with a girlfriend. She had jealously wanted all his attention back then because their parents had given her none of theirs. But she seemed very willing to share him with Erica. As smart as she was, she would have realized before he had how much he loved and needed to be with Erica.

"The district attorney, Drake Ketchum, waived all the charges against you," Macy said, her voice shaking with excitement.

"Why?" Jed asked, too cynical now to believe it was possible.

"You served three years for crimes you hadn't committed," Erica said. "You shouldn't have to serve any more time."

Jed stared at his sister. "Did Rowe have something to do with this?"

"No," she said. "The D.A. is using you as his star witness against the warden."

Jed chuckled. He'd been right to be cynical. Nobody was selfless except for the woman in his arms, who had willingly put her life at risk for his. "I take it that he doesn't want me showing up in court to testify in an orange jumpsuit."

"Who cares what his motive is?" Erica asked. "You're a free man, Jedidiah Kleyn."

"I don't want to be a free man," he said with sudden realization.

"But, Jed," she said, her eyes wide with shock, "you served three years already—"

"No." He dropped to one knee on the cold concrete. "I don't want to be a free man. I want to be your man, Erica. I don't just want to be Isobel's father. I want to be your husband…if you'll have me. If you can trust me…"

For the first time since he had pulled her into the nightmare that had been his life, she cried, tears streaming down her face. "I trust you, Jed. I trust that you'll be a gentle, loving father and a loyal, protective husband." She wrapped her arms around his shoulders and hugged him tightly. "I will marry you."

Her acceptance meant more to him than finally clearing his name. That had been all about his past. She and their daughter were his future. "Now I'm the luckiest man in the world."

Finally the promise of their first meeting and that instant connection was fulfilled. That promise had been tested and strained and had nearly broken over the past three years. But now it was a promise that they would keep for the rest of their lives.

# *Epilogue*

"You better get used to that side of the bars," Drake Ketchum taunted him. "You're never getting out now."

Jefferson had already heard the news. The district attorney definitely had a star witness in Jedidiah Kleyn. No one would doubt his testimony now.

"And you're not getting to Kleyn before the trial. There's no bounty—no amount of reward you can offer for someone to risk hurting him. He's well protected."

And damn near impossible to kill, Jefferson had already discovered. But with all his time alone behind these damn bars, he had figured out who wasn't protected—who was so damn cocky that he thought he couldn't lose.

But it wasn't just the trial Ketchum was going to lose. It was his life.

\* \* \* \* \*

*A sneaky peek at next month...*

# INTRIGUE...

**BREATHTAKING ROMANTIC SUSPENSE**

*My wish list for next month's titles...*

In stores from 17th August 2012:

❑ Mercenary's Perfect Mission – Carla Cassidy

& Cowboy Conspiracy – Joanna Wayne

❑ Soldier's Pregnancy Protocol – Beth Cornelison

& In the Enemy's Arms – Marilyn Pappano

❑ The Widow's Protector – Rachel Lee

& Death of a Beauty Queen – Mallory Kane

❑ Cowboy Under Siege – Gail Barrett

In stores from 7th September 2012:

❑ Trace of Fever – Lori Foster

**Available at WHSmith, Tesco, Asda, Eason, Amazon and Apple**

*Just can't wait?*

# Special Offers

Every month we put together collections and longer reads written by your favourite authors.

Here are some of next month's highlights — and don't miss our fabulous discount online!

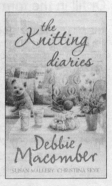

On sale 17th August     On sale 7th September     On sale 7th September

**Save 20%**
*on all Special Releases*

Find out more at
**www.millsandboon.co.uk/specialreleases**

*Visit us Online*

0912/ST/MB384

## MILLS & BOON® Book Club
### 2 Free Books!

### Get your free books now at
### www.millsandboon.co.uk/freebookoffer

---

## Or fill in the form below and post it back to us

**THE MILLS & BOON® BOOK CLUB™—HERE'S HOW IT WORKS:** Accepting your free books places you under no obligation to buy anything. You may keep the books and return the despatch note marked 'Cancel'. If we do not hear from you, about a month later we'll send you 5 brand-new stories from the Intrigue series, including two 2-in-1 books priced at £5.49 each and a single book priced at £3.49*. There is no extra charge for post and packaging. You may cancel at any time, otherwise we will send you 5 stories a month which you may purchase or return to us—the choice is yours. *Terms and prices subject to change without notice. Offer valid in UK only. Applicants must be 18 or over. Offer expires 31st Janaury 2013. **For full terms and conditions, please go to www.millsandboon.co.uk/freebookoffer**

Mrs/Miss/Ms/Mr (please circle)

First Name

Surname

Address

Postcode

E-mail

**Send this completed page to: Mills & Boon Book Club, Free Book Offer, FREEPOST NAT 10298, Richmond, Surrey, TW9 1BR**

Find out more at
**www.millsandboon.co.uk/freebookoffer**

*Visit us Online*

0712/I2YEA

*Mills & Boon® Online*

Discover more romance at
**www.millsandboon.co.uk**

 **FREE** online reads

 **Books** up to one
month before shops

 **Browse our books**
before you buy

*...and much more!*

---

**For exclusive competitions and instant updates:**

Like us on **facebook.com/romancehq**

Follow us on **twitter.com/millsandboonuk**

Join us on **community.millsandboon.co.uk**

*Visit us Online* | Sign up for our FREE eNewsletter at **www.millsandboon.co.uk**

# Have Your Say

*You've just finished your book.*
*So what did you think?*

We'd love to hear your thoughts on our
'Have your say' online panel
**www.millsandboon.co.uk/haveyoursay**

- ❧ Easy to use
- ❧ Short questionnaire
- ❧ Chance to win Mills & Boon® goodies

*Visit us Online*

Tell us what you thought of this book now at
**www.millsandboon.co.uk/haveyoursay**

YOUR_SAY